D1615770

The Last Californian

Felix Arthur

April 8, 1987

The
Last
Californian

AN HISTORICAL NOVEL
of
THE RANCHERIA MASSACRE

by

Feliz Guthrie

Illustrated with Drawings by the Author

QUINTESSENCE PUBLICATIONS

First Edition

Quintessence Publications
356 Bunker Hill Mine Road
Amador City, California 95601
U. S. A.

I. S. B. N.: 0 - 918466 - 13 - X.
Library of Congress Catalogue Number: 86 - 62388

Dedicated to
Dad and Licho

With special thanks to

Mary Welch

AUTHOR'S NOTE:

This book was based in part on *The History of Amador County, California*, Thompson and West, Oakland, 1881,—especially Chapter XIX, "Rancheria Murders." Certain historical details have been altered to facilitate the tale's telling.

The Last Californian

Table of Contents

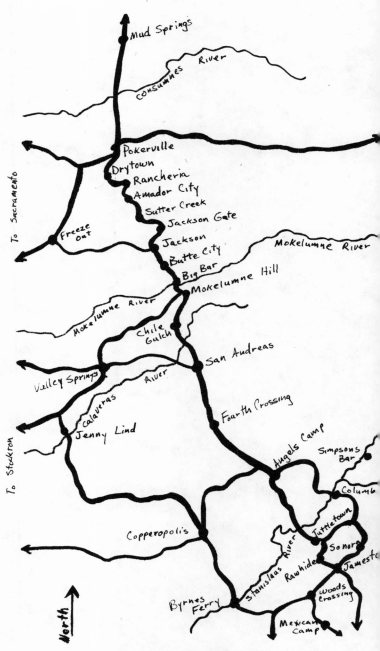

Main Roads of the Mother Lode of Northern California.

The Last Californian

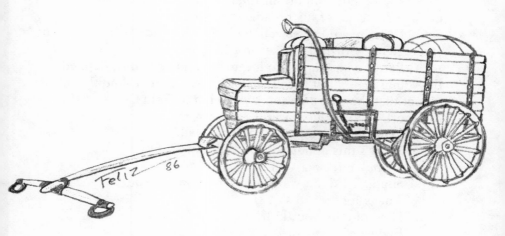

CHAPTER ONE:

THE SIMPSON BROTHERS

On Saturday, July 28, 1855, Matthew Hindshaw looked up from his desk in the Drytown Freight Office to see a young man standing respectfully before him.

"What do you want, kid?" Hindshaw demanded gruffly.

"I'm looking for work, sir. I have a letter of reference." The boy held out a folded sheet.

Hindshaw took it, opened it, and scowled at its script, musing meanwhile that here was a priceless opportunity to get back at the freight driver, Boston Williston, who had declared only the day before that he would no longer work for less than five dollars a trip. But though Hindshaw determined between one moment and the next that he would hire this young man in Boston's place, it was not in his nature to let the applicant know it immediately. Instead, he scrutinized the boy's threadbare shirt and twice-patched pants as if his clothes were more important than the honest look in his eyes or the square set of his broadening shoulders.

"If you're so danged reliable, son," he said, "why didn't you stay on with Jack Parker in Mud Springs?"

"Because I'm hoping to locate my uncle's family," replied the young man. "But I really don't know where to find them, except that they must be somewhere in the Gold Country. If I can work as a freight driver, I can earn my way between the diggings while I look for them. That's all."

"What's this about your kid brother?"

"Sydney hires on with me."

"Suppose I don't want more than one of you?"

"That's for you to say, sir."

"How old are you, kid?"

"Eighteen."

"You don't look it. How old is Sydney?"

"Fifteen and a half."

"Yeah? What's he good for?"

"He's a crack shot with a rifle. And he can skin a mule as well as I can."

"Is that sayin' a lot for him or not much for you?"

"Mr. Parker was satisfied with our work." The young man gestured at the paper Hindshaw held. "He offered us a permanent job if we wanted it."

"Where is this brother of yours? I'd better have a look at him."

"He's waiting outside. If you'll excuse me, I'll call him."

"You do that." Hindshaw tossed the letter of introduction to the desk top and began flipping through a stack of receipt slips as if the interview were concluded and the applicant in front of him had vanished.

The boy returned to the door with an even stride and leaned out of it. "Syd!" he called. "Come here!"

"You get the job, See Saw?" asked a younger voice.

"I don't know, yet. Mr. Hindshaw wants to look you over. Come on in."

The freight clerk glanced up as the young man returned with his brother at his side. The boy in question was slight of build and wary of manner in contrast to his sibling who already stood over six feet in height and whose calm brown eyes had met Hindshaw's so frankly. That the two boys were related, however, could not be doubted. Their broad brows and snub noses, their tapering of chin, and the curly reddish-brown hair that showed under their hats were remarkably like. But the younger one was more lavishly freckled. And he looked as if he would never grow any bigger. His hands and feet were small. His out-sized, ragged clothes were gathered to his waist under a cartridge belt that wrapped twice round. A rifle was slung by a strap from his shoulder.

Hindshaw scowled at him, unimpressed. "You're Sydney, hey?"

The scowl was cordially returned. "Yep," said Sydney.

"Your brother says you can hit what you shoot at."

"Sometimes."

"Well, you want to look out how you go braggin' round about it, kid. Somebody might ask you to prove it." The freight clerk turned back to the older boy. "I got a wagon loaded with supplies for the National Hotel in Jackson. I need a driver that can be ready to leave right off. But I ain't goin' to hire Sydney, see? If he pays his way, he can ride along with you as a passenger. Or I can take the cost of it out of your salary."

The brothers exchanged a look. "How much for the passenger fee?" the older one asked.

"Ten dollars," replied Hindshaw. "Or half an ounce of gold dust."

"And what would be my salary?"

"Ten dollars," said the freight clerk.

Syndey took a step forward. "You'll have to pay him in advance then. We don't have that much between us."

4

"You've got your wages from Parker, ain't you?"

"He only paid us in grub and blankets."

Hindshaw thought the matter over. "All right. I guess it don't matter. I can pay you nothin' at this end as easy as they can in Jackson." He pulled out a fresh sheet of paper and wrote up a statement of contract, dated it and shoved it at the older of the two boys.

The young man studied it carefully while his brother read it over his elbow. "Have him pay you, first, See Saw," Sydney advised.

"No," said the older boy. "That wouldn't be right. I'm sure Mr. Hindshaw will honor his contract." Putting the paper on the desk in front of him, he bent to sign his name. He wrote easily, with a practiced flourish. "You can pay me the ten dollars now, sir."

Hindshaw opened his desk again and took out a ten dollar gold piece. He held it up between his thumb and forefinger and then would have returned it to the drawer, but the young man reached out his hand to receive it. Hindshaw shrugged and gave him the coin. The boy laid down the paper and put the gold piece in his pocket. Then, he turned to go.

"Hey!" Hindshaw half rose.

"Yes, sir?"

"You got to pay the fee for your passenger, or he can't go."

"Oh, Sydney has a horse. So, he'll just ride alongside. I guess the road is free for anybody to use if he wants to, isn't it?"

Astounded, the clerk dropped back into his chair. "You two ain't so wet behind the ears as I figured! Here! Take this inventory list. The wagon's waitin' around back. And every box and bundle of what's in it had better get to the hotel in Jackson! By the way," he added, "what's the name of this uncle you're lookin' for?"

"Peter Simpson."

"Simpson?" Hindshaw referred to the contract for the

boy's signature as if he doubted it less than the young man's spoken word. " 'Cecil Simpson'," he read. "You boys heard tell of Simpson's Bar?"

"No. Where's that?"

"It's a diggin's way the hell up the road. Jackson is on the way. If I was you, I sure wouldn't miss askin' for my Uncle Pete at Simpson's Bar. Good luck," he added, then regretted having thawed enough to say it. "I don't guess those two will run into much trouble they can't handle," he muttered as the boys left the freight office together. And Hindshaw returned to his much thumbed pile of receipt slips.

On the porch, Cecil Simpson paused to look over the inventory list, again holding the paper where his brother could see it. Then he put it in his pants' pocket and nodded for Sydney to mount the spotted Indian pony that stood hitched to the rail in front of the freight office. "Bring Red Dog around back, Syd. Might be the mules will follow him better than I can drive them alone."

"Sure, See Saw. You s'pose we can put our pack in the freight wagon?"

"Yes. Mr. Hindshaw didn't say not to. And I'm not going back in there to ask him. Come on." And Cecil stepped down off the porch to the sun-baked road.

His brother unwrapped the pony's checked leather reins, threw their knotted loop over the animal's head and leaped easily astride. There was no saddle. The brothers had been forced to trade it for a square meal in Mud Springs a week before. But a blanket roll stuffed with their meager supplies was tied across the little horse's withers. Sydney nudged the pony after Cecil to the rear of the freight office. Awaiting them there was a long, heavy wagon to which two men were harnessing five pairs of sleek mules.

"Well!" said the nearest man, turning from the buckles he had been adjusting. "And what can we do for you boys?"

Cecil pushed back his weather-stained hat and appraised the rig with a practiced eye. "I'm your driver," he said. "Mr. Hindshaw hired me to take this wagon to the

National Hotel in Jackson."

At this, the second man straightened and traded a look of surprise with the first. "Oh, he has! We was expectin' somebody else. A man name of Boston. He takes care of most of the drivin' from Drytown to Jackson."

"That," said Cecil, "is between Mr. Hindshaw and Boston. Sydney, tumble off and help me check the harness, will you?"

"Hey, we just finished with this hitch!" said the first man. "Do you think we don't know our business, kid?"

"Mister," said Cecil, "I don't expect to find a single tug twisted nor a single buckle loose. But I make it my policy to double check a rig before I start, even if I did the harnessing myself."

Sydney untied the pack from the pony and slung it onto the driver's box before he followed his brother down the line, looking for weak places in the harness that even Cecil's careful eye might have missed. He found a repair where a strap had been broken and spliced with rawhide lacing. But judging it durable, he moved on.

When Cecil was satisfied that the hitch was sound and properly in place, he dismissed his brother to the head of the teams and climbed onto the box. "Anything either of you gentlemen might want to tell me about these mules?" he inquired of the men who still stood by.

"Well," said the first, "they all got four legs and a tail."

"They're wild as mustangs," said the other. "They've taken Boston himself on a ride or two. When you get over the second hill and start down toward Rancheria Creek, you want to watch they don't spook. 'Cause once they get to runnin', it will take more than your strength to stop them."

"Nevermind the mules," said the first man. "What you boys want to look out for is Mexican bandits. They're thicker through these hills than fleas on an Injun blanket."

"Much obliged," said Cecil, unwinding the heavy reins from the brake handle. "We'll be sure to keep our eyes peeled." He picked up a long whip that was coiled at his feet.

"Headin' out, Syd!" he called to his brother and swung the whip to crack it over the backs of the teams. Sydney brought his quirt down on the rump of one of the lead mules. The wagon jolted forward.

Drytown's collection of tents, adobe huts, and brick and wooden buildings was erected on the banks of Dry Creek whose waning, seasonal flow trickled from pool to pool over its naked bed. The road that ran through it dipped sharply down into the town and rose still more sharply out of it. All ten mules must throw their shoulders into their collars to haul the loaded wagon up the grade.

The road mounted in a wide curve, hiding the town from view before it leveled out onto a short bench and then continued butting its way skyward. Riding on ahead, Sydney was soon out of sight of the wagon. He dismounted when he reached the hilltop to wait for his brother to catch up. Hitching his rifle over his shoulder, he stood looking as far on along the road as its twists and turns allowed.

A long curve led down the shoulder of the hill into a wooded gulch. In the wet season, there would be a rushing stream at the heart of that stand of scrub oak and digger pine. But now, in the heat of summer, it was sure to be dry.

To the right of the trail, the ground fell steeply into a narrow valley where Dry Creek and several of its slender tributaries met at the feet of the brush-covered hills. It was a pleasant scene, and the boy was not unaffected by it. But his reverie was interrupted by the sound of a gunshot at a distance.

Startled, Sydney jerked his gaze back to the wooded gulch, fully prepared to see some of the bandits they had been warned about. He was not disappointed.

On the road below, a rider burst from the opening between the trees. He was bent low over his horse's neck and held a pistol at ready to snap a shot behind him when he saw his opportunity. It came an instant later. Five mounted men pounded out of the gulch after him. They returned his shot with a volley of bullets, none of which found its mark. And then the man's horse struck a large, loose stone and was thrown off balance. The animal lunged and floundered to keep its feet, and though its rider stuck to his saddle, he could not shoot again, and his flight was disastrously slowed.

The horse plunged across the road but was stopped by the steep fall of ground. The next shot from behind hit the rider. His hat flew over the edge. His horse reared. And he fell to the side of the trail.

Sydney had not had time to do much more than witness these events, but now, he muscled a shell into his rifle, cocked it, and dropped to one knee to steady his aim.

Across the tip of his barrel, he saw the bandits descend on their victim. They felt him all over for valuables and came away with various prizes. They were stripping him of his jacket when Sydney pulled the trigger. The robber standing with his back squarely to the road clapped a hand to his left ear and looked wildly around.

Sydney put in another shell and raised the rifle again. In the time it took him to do it, the bandits remounted, leaving the robbed man where he lay. Sydney's second shot missed. He had no chance for a third. The four horsemen dashed for the woody gulch, the fifth trailing them by a few horse lengths and leading the riderless animal alongside. In a moment, they had entered the trees and were out of sight.

Sydney rose slowly to his feet, uncocked his rifle and stared down at the road. It looked just as it had before except for the body that lay at the edge of the precipice, hatless, coatless, and apparently, lifeless.

CHAPTER TWO:

SIMON RUIZ

Cecil stood on the driver's box, anxiously watching the road above him. "Syd!" he called, relief in his voice as he saw his brother coming back down the slope to meet him. "What happened?"

"Bandits, See Saw! Chasing somebody! I scared them off, but I think it was too late for the man they were after. They shot him, and he's lying there on the roadside. I came back to tell you so you'd know I'm all right."

"Bandits! I thought those men behind the freight office were only trying to scare us. Were they Mexicans?"

"Yep. All of them. Even the man they shot down and robbed."

"Are you sure?"

"Well, their clothes looked like it. And their faces were dark."

"Wait, Syd!" said Cecil as the younger boy turned his pony. "Wait for me at the top of the hill. Don't go on by yourself. The bandits might come back."

Sydney frowned rebelliously, but he nodded before he put Red Dog up the slope again. By the time he reached the top, the little horse was breathing hard. He rubbed his head on one knee while Sydney stared down at the road. The bandits' victim lay just as before.

Sydney glanced back. Cecil was not in sight, yet. Impatiently, the boy kicked his mount and galloped down the hill and around the curve to the side of the fallen man. Here, he threw himself from his pony's back and knelt down cautiously.

The man was not dead. He was breathing. But one side of his face was covered with blood. He looked young, not more than twenty-five or thirty. He was certainly Mexican. Or Spanish Californian. Sydney had heard there was a difference, though what it might be was not apparent. In any case, he was a man of some wealth. His trousers were of fine leather on the inner leg and were sewn with gold braid on the outer. They were laced with velvet cord from waist to knee and split below that around tooled leather leggings. Assuming his jacket were a match for the pants, Sydney could understand why the bandits had taken it.

Untying his own neck scarf, the boy used it to clean the blood from the man's cheek. There was no wound under it.

The boy tried higher, sponging up the bright flow which slipped down again almost as fast as he could wipe it away. Its source proved to be a cut at the hairline where the bullet had burned by, laying open the skin but no worse. That the man was still unconscious must be due to his having struck his head when he fell. Sydney pressed the scarf tightly over the cut and was casting about for something to bind it in place when the man sighed and drew up one knee, scratching the rowel of his spur deeply through the dirt. Then, he opened his eyes. They were black as coal.

"¡Eh! ¡Ladrón!" He caught Sydney's arm with a grip that hurt. But, "No," he added, more to himself than to the boy. "No. Imposible. Who are you, pecoso?"

"Nobody much," said Syndey. "One of those bandits creased you. I shot at them and they ran. But they'd robbed you already, and they took your horse."

"**You** shoot at them?" Pushing off the boy's touch, the Spaniard held the cloth to his head himself. "Where you are coming from?" he asked.

Sydney jerked his thumb at the hilltop.

"You are not alone? Who is with you?"

"My brother. He's driving a freight wagon."

The Californian sat up and took the scarf away to look at it. A fresh tendril of scarlet slipped instantly to his eyebrow and dripped onto his knee. Clapping the bloody wad back over the cut, he wiped his forehead with his sleeve and stared at the garish stain it made on the fine white linen. He looked from it into Sydney's eyes. "I am Simón Ruiz Silvestre," he said and waited for an appropriate response. But the boy only returned his gaze. "Who are you?" he insisted. "What is the name?"

The answer came from the top of the hill. "Sydney! Sydney!" The mule team snaked over the crest. Cecil had both hands full of the reins. Sydney got up and waved before he offered to help the Spaniard rise. But the man motioned him aside. Yet he staggered as he stood and must catch the boy's shoulder to steady himself. Yielding further to necessity, he leaned on him heavily while the freight wagon came rattling and creaking down the hill.

"See Saw," Sydney greeted his brother as Cecil hauled the mules to a stop beside them, "this is Sea Moan Reese Silvesper."

"Hello, Señor," said the older Simpson. "My brother told me he thought you were dead. I'm glad to see he was wrong. Are you badly hurt?"

"No. No es nada," the other professed, letting go of his brow to gesture the insignificance of his wound but immediately recovering it as the blood fell again.

"You'd better get into the wagon," judged Cecil. "You look pretty wobbly. Syd, why didn't you **tie** that rag on his head so he didn't have to hold it? Here," he added, pulling at his own neck scarf. "Use this."

Sydney would have accepted it, but Ruiz was taller and retrieved it over his head, yet he swayed without his support and surrendered the scarf so that he could lean again on the boy's shoulder.

"I can't reach," said Syndey, looking up. "If you want me to do it, you'll have to be lower."

Slowly, Ruiz let himself down on one knee. But as his hand slid from the boy's shoulder to his waist, it felt a broad bandage wrapped tightly round his upper midriff. "¡Cómo! You are hurt, too! You break a costilla? A rib? I am too heavy for you to hold up with the broken costilla!"

Sydney reddened as he answered: "It doesn't hurt much now." He folded his brother's scarf to a narrow strip and laid it across the Spaniard's brow, tied its ends at the nape of his neck while the Californian studied the boy's sober face and his voluminous shirt, which would have fit Cecil far better than him, and the twice-wrapped cartridge belt at his waist.

"Don't you have a hat, Señor?" asked Cecil. "You'll soon be feeling the need of one in this hot sun."

"It flew over the bank," Sydney explained.

"Climb into the wagon, Señor," said Cecil. "Syd, see if his hat's within reach. If it's not, he's welcome to mine."

The Californian got back to his feet, still using Sydney as a crutch, and accepted Cecil's hand to help haul himself onto the driver's box. He leaned gratefully against the low back of the wooden seat. "Where you are going?" he asked.

"As far as Jackson with this wagon. After that, we'll see. You were headed the other way, yourself?"

"Sí. They tell me talk to the judge name Cortés who live in Drytown. I have business to propose him. Not far, eh? Over this hill?"

"That's right," said Cecil. "But we don't know any judge. And we can't take you back there. The road's too narrow to turn the mules around. Maybe at the next town, we can find somebody to oblige you. It's only a couple of miles, isn't it?"

"It make no difference," declared Ruiz. "I have other business, now. Is to catch the cholos that rob me! So I don't go to Drytown, anymore. I go with you to Yackson."

While his brother and the Californian were talking, Sydney crouched at the edge of the bank and peered over it. He saw Ruiz' hat at once. It had caught in a bush just out of reach, perhaps six feet below the road. He got up and came back to stand beside the wagon.

"You find it?" concluded Cecil. "Can you get to it?"

Sydney nodded. "With a rope. Or the whip's probably long enough. You want to hold it for me, See Saw?"

"I'd better have a look." Cecil wrapped the reins around the brake handle and jumped to the ground, went to the bank and looked over. "All right," he agreed. "If you'll tie the end of the whip to your belt."

It was soon done. Cecil set the heels of his worn boots in the outer rut of the road while Sydney dropped over the edge as lightly as a cat, holding to the whip's braided leather line with one hand. He returned with the Californian's dark hat jammed on top of his own so that he had both hands free to climb back up. Cecil took the hat, removing Sydney's with it inadvertently. Separating them, he replanted his brother's on the boy's reddish curls while Sydney untied the whip from his cartridge belt and rerolled the lash.

"You show me much kindness," the Spaniard said when Cecil gave him his hat. He ran his fingers around the inside of its crown before he put it on. "What do you call yourselves?" he asked. "What is the name?"

"I'm Cecil Simpson. And that's Sydney. We're newcomers from Indiana. What was your name again?"

"I am Simón Ruiz Silvestre," the Spaniard announced for the second time. "I am nephew of don Diego Silvestre. He is ranchero in the Valle. Allá," he added, motioning westward. "Raise the cattle, grain. I come here to sell some. That is the business I tell you. On my way back, I take orders for more. Your name you also say again?"

"Cecil Simpson."

"Sssss . . .! I call you César. You come alone together from that place call Indiana? That is far?"

"Yes, it's far enough. It took us four months. We came with others, but we got separated from them during a storm in the mountains. We're still hoping to find the rest of our party. Have you ever heard of Simpson's Bar?"

Ruiz thought a moment. "Sí. Mining camp to the south from here. More beyond Angel Camp." Again he made a graceful gesture that seemed to leap the hills and the tangled road across the long miles of Mother Lode. "Is the place you are going?"

"Maybe. How far is it?"

"No, pues . . . it takes you only two days steady travel on a good horse. But in wagon like this? Sabrá Dios."

Sydney had caught and mounted Red Dog by this time. But Cecil beckoned him back. "Tie your pony to the tailgate, Syd, and climb up here with us. I don't want you to ride scout anymore."

The rebellious frown returned to the younger boy's face. He said nothing nor moved to obey.

"Syd," warned Cecil, "do what I tell you."

"Why?" demanded Sydney darkly.

"You know why. We could meet those bandits again at any time. And I don't want you to meet them, first."

"If I ride in the wagon, you'll owe Mr. Hindshaw ten dollars."

"Don't argue," said Cecil.

Sydney reined around. Tying his pony to the back of the wagon, he swung up to traverse the load, lightly treading the bundles and barrels and boxes and vaulting the back of the driver's bench. He sat down on its outer corner and turned a shoulder to his companions. Cecil started up the mules, and the wagon rumbled on toward the woody gulch.

"I doubt the bandidos, they stay around here," said Ruiz in defense of the younger boy.

Cecil made no reply.

"They expect the whole posse be after them soon. They know that a man with a rifle see them red-handed. He report in the towns. No, the bandidos, they don't stay around here."

Sydney half turned to look at the Californian. The black eyes that met his were warm and approving. The boy's gaze fell to the gold braid on the borders of the man's trouser-leg and the fine white linen that showed under the velvet lacing.

"You like?"

Sydney looked up in surprise.

"You want to have a pantalón like this one? I remember. I give you."

"Don't spoil him, Señor," said Cecil.

"I don't forget you, pecoso," continued Ruiz. "You and César, you can work for me if you don't find those you look for. I bring cattle from the Valle. You like to help to drive them? You like to be my vaquero?"

Sydney darted hopeful looks at his brother's stoic profile.

"That's kind of you, Señor," said Cecil. "But we wouldn't be able to search for our relatives while we worked for you. And I'm confident we'll find them, sooner or later."

The light in Sydney's eyes went out and he turned away again to stare at the passing trees, for they had entered the woody gulch.

CHAPTER THREE:

BOSTON

"You tell me about the relatives?" inquired Ruiz. "Maybe I hear of them or can help you some way to find them. Who they are?"

"Our uncle is a man named Peter Simpson," replied Cecil. "He and our Aunt Agnes and their sons, Tim and Jacob, and their apprentice—a boy my age named Paul McCormick—came west with one wagon. Our father, Eli Simpson, had the other. We were traveling together, all of us. Before we reached the mountains, we had a skirmish with some Indians. We lost our wagon, and our father was badly wounded. So, of course he had to ride in Uncle Peter's wagon after that. Then in the Sierra Nevada, we hit a big storm, and Syd and I were cut off from the rest."

The Californian listened seriously to this. "So, you do not know if the father, he lives?"

Cecil shook his head.

"You do not speak of the mother."

"She died when Sydney was three."

Ruiz turned to the younger boy. "But you remember her, eh, pecoso?"

"Not well," Cecil replied for him.

Sydney flashed his brother a loaded glance. "I remember her as well as you do," he said.

"So! Is much tragedia for you!" concluded Ruiz. "You must find your tío and hope that the father still lives." He drew a deep breath and passed his hand across his brow beneath the brim of his hat.

"Are you all right, Sea-Moan?" asked Sydney.

Surprised at finding himself on a first name basis with the younger Simpson, Ruiz dropped a look into his brown eyes. "I am all right, Cindy," he said.

The boy blushed crimson. "Sydney!" he corrected.

"That is not what I say?"

"No. Sydney. Syd-ney."

"Cindy. Cin-dy," repeated Ruiz.

"No," the boy insisted. "You're putting the 'd' on the wrong side of the 'n'."

"It makes some difference?"

"Cindy is a girl's name," explained Cecil.

"¡Ah, ya!" exclaimed the Spaniard in comprehension. "Seed-nee!" he essayed, displaying a row of even white teeth beneath his black mustache in an effort to master the proper order of the consonants. "Like that?"

The boy shrugged and nodded.

But then Ruiz leaned forward and let his head drop between his shoulders, cradling his brow with one hand. "¡Por Dios!" he sighed.

Sydney was instantly on his knees on the bench beside him, touching his arm solicitously. "You feel dizzy?"

Ruiz made no answer.

The boy brushed off the dirt that was clinging to the Spaniard's back from his having lain in the road.

"¡Agua!" muttered Ruiz. "You have water?"

Sydney turned to the supply pack he had thrown into the wagon earlier and retrieved a waterskin that was bound to it. He uncorked it with a strong tug and proffered it. But Ruiz did not see it. His head was sinking farther toward his knees. Sydney braced a hand under the Spaniard's hunching shoulder. "See Saw!" he cried. "He's going under!"

"No!" said Ruiz with an effort, flinging himself upright against the seat back. "I am all right." But his face was grey, and his head was so heavy, he couldn't hold it up for long. He let it loll onto his shoulders.

Distressed by such involuntary weakness in a man who was evidently both strong and vigorous, Sydney slid a supporting arm behind the Californian's head.

"He'll be all right, Syd," said Cecil, watching warily. "Just leave him alone for a little."

Sydney pressed the leather bottle against the hand Ruiz half raised. His fingers closed on it, and the boy helped him guide it higher to jet water into his mouth. But the jolting of the wagon made their combined aim uncertain even at close range. Some of it shot across the Spaniard's face.

Finding this refreshing, Ruiz squirted himself with a full stream. Then he drank long. "¡Mejor!" he declared. "Enough. Gracias."

"I guess you lost a lot of blood."

"No, is more the blow of my head to the rocks, I think. It is passing. Already, I am better. What I need is a taste of aguardiente to set the spinning of the world in straight. In next town, Ranchería, I get some."

"You mean whiskey?" asked Sydney.

"Weeskey," agreed Ruiz.

"There's whiskey in this wagon. Lots of it!"

"Syd!" came Cecil's warning voice. "I signed a contract to deliver our freight intact to the National Hotel in Jackson."

"So? You told Hindshaw that I'd ride Red Dog, too." The boy pulled his arm from across Ruiz' shoulders and would have climbed back over the seat to plunder the cargo immediately, but the Spaniard caught his elbow.

"¡Espérese! Your brother, he is right. The load of the

wagon is in your trust. I don't die till we get to Ranchería. Siéntese. You sit here and talk to me. That keeps me from . . . how you say? 'Go under'."

The boy settled back, and Ruiz let go, rubbing his eyes to clear his vision.

Ahead of them, the road was rising out of the trees into another long, steep-climbing slope. Cecil swung his whip and whistled. The mules threw their shoulders into their collars, and the heavy wagon rumbled up the grade.

Then from behind them, out of the brush-grown gulch, came three American men on horseback. The foremost rider shouted as he saw them: "Hey! Stop that wagon!"

Cecil looked around, but he didn't slow the mules. Sydney unslung his rifle from his back to rest it across his knees. Ruiz groped at his right boot top but did not find the knife that usually rode there. The bandits had taken it. His hand moved to Sydney's gun and closed on its barrel. Yet upon meeting the boy's offended look, he let go. "You haff a knife, Cindy?" he asked under his breath.

The younger Simpson felt in one of his pockets for a claspknife and slipped it into the Spaniard's hand as the three riders came up beside the wagon.

"You hear me tell you to stop?" demanded the leader. He was a big man, so broad chested that his shirt strained at its buttons. In his right fist, he held an iron crowbar.

Cecil looked at him coolly. "I'm not stopping this wagon till the top of the hill, mister. If you want to tell me your business, you can do it while you ride alongside."

"Who's that Greaser?" the other asked, jabbing his bar at Ruiz.

"Who wants to know?" countered Cecil.

"Jimmy, you ride to the head of the mules and stop them," the man told one of his two companions. Then reining closer, swung from his saddle into the wagon. He strode heavily among the crates and bundles and whacked at a box with his crowbar.

"Here!" cried Cecil, starting to his feet, his grip tightening on the whip. Ruiz rose to one knee on the driver's bench, catching the back of it to steady himself. Sydney's knife was completely hidden inside his other hand. The boy himself broke his gun to be sure it was loaded, then cocking it, looked back.

Cecil whirled his whip at the man with the crowbar just as the third rider jumped to the driver's seat to grapple with him. Meanwhile, the first continued to wade through the cargo, bashing crates and ripping open bundles. That Ruiz should launch himself against him apparently unarmed surprised the man so much that he paused to face him, raising his crowbar threateningly.

But Ruiz dodged under it and caught the ruffian by the belt to pull himself up against him, and at intimate range, showed him the blade of the clasp-knife. "Drop the hierro!" he advised.

The man blanched and let fall his crowbar. "On the knees!" said Ruiz. "Cindy! Some rope!"

Sydney had not been idle, either. Leveling his rifle at the one called Jimmy, who had been sent to stop the mules, he waited until the man leaned to reach for the reins of the leading team. Then he fired. The bullet whizzed across Jimmy's back and lifted a strand of his horse's mane. The animal bolted in fear, unseating its rider, who sprawled on his nose in the dirt. The horse galloped on over the hilltop, head and tail held high. Jimmy scrambled to his feet and galloped after it, his head held low.

Sydney was force-feeding his old single-shot again when Ruiz called to him. The boy looked around. "Some rope, Pecoso!" the Spaniard repeated.

Yet it was Cecil rather than Sydney who obliged Ruiz. The older boy's defense had been at once more vigorous and more skillful than his attacker was prepared to meet. And when the man took a misstep off the edge of the driver's bench, Cecil hurled him to the road. Then coiling his whip, he tossed it to Ruiz in lieu of a rope.

While the Californian bound the hands and feet of his man with the slender end of the lash, and Cecil gathered up the lines, Sydney dropped out of the wagon. Untying his pony, he leaped to Red Dog's back and kicked him to a run.

"Sydney!" shouted Cecil, but Sydney pretended not to hear. He crossed the crest of the hill just as the lead mules reached it. Excited by the gunshot, the teams were lunging against the traces in spite of Cecil's hauling on the reins. And once they had started down the far slope, the animals broke into a full run.

Jimmy's riderless mount was plunging on ahead of them toward the creek at the bottom of the grade. The man himself was nowhere in sight. Unable to catch his horse, he had taken to the brush that grew thickly along one side of the trail.

Halfway down the hill, Sydney looked back to see the mules charging after him. He saw his brother lying back on the lines. He saw Ruiz on the driver's bench beside him, bracing his weight against the long brake lever. The sickle-shaped brake shoes squealed and smoked against the rear wheels, but the wagon came on.

Sydney fired into the air the shell he had been saving for Jimmy. The noise served to slow the mules' dead run to a stiff-legged gallop. But it was the creek itself that stopped them. The off mule of the lead team refused to ford it. Sitting back in the harness, he pulled his partner to a halt. The teams behind piled into them, forcing the balky animal into the water. As the wagon straddled the creek, they came to a complete stop. They stood snorting and dripping sweat.

Cecil unwound the reins from his hands and rubbed his aching arms. Simón slumped onto the seat. Their passenger, tied hand and foot with the whip, lay cursing quietly among the bundles in the wagon bed.

Sydney came to the near wheel. "This must be Rancheria Creek," he said.

"Yes. I'm sure it is," said Cecil. "And so far, those tips the men behind the freight office gave us have all been right on target. I don't know if I'm glad or sorry they didn't tell us more." He swung a leg over the back of the driver's bench.

"I'll have a look at the damage done to the cargo."

Sydney dismounted onto the wagon wheel and climbed to the seat. "You all right, Sea-Moan?" he asked.

The Californian showed a white smile that turned into a soft chuckle. "This day, I don't forget him soon," he said.

Together, they watched Cecil poking among the rent bundles and the cracked crates. Their prisoner watched him, too. But Cecil ignored the man. One wooden box he found stained with dampness around its splintered break. Catching up the ruffian's crowbar, Cecil pried off the lid and looked in. "You still want a taste of whiskey, Señor?" he asked Ruiz.

"¡Por Dios!" exclaimed the Spaniard. "By now I need more than a taste! You offer me?"

"If you don't mind drinking from a broken bottle." Cecil produced a headless flask, two-thirds full, and another half full. "I'm afraid this one has glass in it," he said and emptied it over the side of the wagon. The other he handed to Sydney who had come after it.

Cecil peered into the crate again. "I'm surprised the damage isn't a lot worse," he said. Then he leaned on the box and directed a full stare at the man lying fettered beside him. "Do you have anything to say for yourself, mister? What's your name?"

"Williston," the man growled.

"Are you and your pals from around here?"

A grunted affirmative.

"Do you know a Judge Cortez?"

"Cortez? You mean Curtis," the man sneered.

"Well, does Judge Curtis know you waylay freight wagons between Drytown and Rancheria?"

"This is my wagon!" Williston declared, testing the knots in the lash. They held.

"What do you mean, it's yours?"

"I drive the freight between Drytown and Jackson is what I mean! And I ain't goin' to be robbed of my job by a couple of cocky kids and a goddam Mexican!"

"You must be Boston! You know, mister, if it had been you driving this wagon, the bandits would probably have helped themselves to your freight. And maybe killed you, besides. You owe us quite a lot. At the next town, we'll give you a chance to make good. Because you're going to pay for the damage you did to our load. And it might be Judge Curtis would be willing to help us collect."

Cecil straightened and returned to the driver's bench. "Señor Ruiz? How much farther to the town of Rancheria?"

The Californian was comfortably propped against the seat, sipping whiskey from the tin cup Sydney had given him from his supply pack. "Less than one mile from here, now," he replied, nodding at the road which led up the creek into a narrowing canyon.

"Good," said Cecil. "Let's hope nothing else happens before we can get there. "Sydney, get back on Red Dog, and help me start these ornery mules, will you?"

"Sure, See Saw," the boy said.

CHAPTER FOUR:

FRANCE'S STORE

The two most imposing buildings in the town of Rancheria were Dynan's Hotel and France's Store. These two places of business faced each other across the hard-baked road. And it was between these two establishments that Cecil Simpson brought the freight wagon to a halt.

It was quickly surrounded by curious citizens of the town. John Dynan and Albert France appeared in opposite doorways. Both men greeted Ruiz.

"Don Simón!" exclaimed Dynan. "Tell us what has happened!"

"We heard gunshots!" said France.

Meanwhile, the men who had gathered round the wagon peered in at Williston in surprise and derision. For he still lay among the bundles, bound hand and foot with the lash. "What are you doin' trussed up like that, Boston? Did you get tangled in your whip? Or are you goin' to Jackson as a part of the cargo, this time?"

Williston made no reply, but his face was nearly purple with shame and wrath.

"Gently-men," said Ruiz, laying a hand on Cecil's shoulder, "I present my two good friends: name Seensome. To these two friends, I now owe my life."

He was immediately urged to give the particulars. His missing jacket and the bloodstain on his white sleeve were remarked. He was asked about his horse and then about his saddlebags. But before it was quiet enough for his answer to be heard, John Dynan came down the steps of his hotel.

He was a portly man with an air of self importance made tolerable by his prominent role in the Anglo part of the community. "Señor Ruiz," he said, "you appear to have been wounded. There is no need for you to remain sitting in the hot sun and the dust of the street. Allow me to offer you the comforts of my house while someone alerts Constable Cross or Sheriff Phoenix. You should tell your story to the proper authority.

"Albert," Dynan added, speaking across the wagon to the storekeeper on the other side, "wasn't Doctor Shields with you during the past half hour? Is he there, still? Do you know where he is? Don Simón may have need of his attentions."

But Ruiz interposed. "No! Not to bother the médico. I am all right. Gracias, Señor Dino, es muy amable. No, I don't come in. But al Cheriff Finits, him I talk to, yes! Some one you men go find him! This brusco that we have here, he is for the cheriff. He lose the job to los Seensome, and he is not enough a man to let them drive the wagon they are hire to do! He has two helpers. One name Yeemy. You ask him. Bastón," the Spaniard added to Williston himself, "you tell the truth, or I show you my knife again. ¿Comprende?"

Then Ruiz turned toward Albert France. "Señor! We come into your tienda?"

The shopkeeper bowed a welcome. Nor was he above cocking a triumphant eye at Dynan across the road. "Don Simón, I would be honored."

"You come with me, César," the Spaniard said to Cecil. "The wagon is safe here. El señor Dino watch him."

Yielding to Ruiz' benevolent authority, the elder Simpson anchored his reins and dismounted from the wagon. Sydney slid from Red Dog's back without waiting to be told.

France's Store was larger and better stocked than most in the Mother Lode. Its proprietor catered to whim as well as to necessity. And it was primarily on that account he had become a rich man in less than three years. Miners who came into his store for something they had to have as often went out with something they couldn't resist. Nor did France ignore the Latin passion for silver conchos and gold braid and inlaid spurs. And it was said that his was the only store east of the Valley where one could buy real Spanish lace.

Simón Ruiz strode to the counter and looked into the glass-fronted display case which was France's pride and joy, imported from the coast at great expense. On its first velvet lined shelf lay a brace of pistols, beautifully engraved and inlaid. They had been there for six months. Their price put them out of reach of all but France's most wealthy customers.

"Las pistolas, esas," said Ruiz, gesturing at them through the glass.

"Ah!" sighed the shopkeeper in appreciation of his customer's superior taste. "They are the finest to be had anywhere, Señor!"

"Preste. I look them closer. ¡Oiga!" Ruiz added to an older man who appeared in a curtained doorway behind the counter. "You are empleado? I want two good shirts that fit for my amigos." He tilted his head at the Simpson brothers. The boys stood looking round them, Cecil furtively and Sydney openly, in wonder. "And for the Pecoso, a pantalón like mine," Ruiz went on, snapping the backs of his fingers against his thigh indicatively.

But here, Cecil intervened. "No, Señor. Sydney and I don't need anything. Don't spend what remains of your money on us."

Ruiz picked up one of the expensive revolvers which Albert France had laid reverently on the counter top. He tried it for heft and balance, aimed it at a corner and looked down its dark barrel before turning his eyes upon the elder Simpson. "You don't deny me the pleasure to give you something," he said. "I owe you my life."

"We did no more for you than we'd have done for anyone," Cecil argued. "We want no reward."

"I know that, César. I don't reward you. I give as a friend. You accept as a friend. Are we not friends? If I have no money and need a shirt, do you not buy for me?"

"But I have a shirt!" said Cecil, reddening.

Ruiz looked him up and down, still holding the beautiful gun in one hand. "You need the trouser, too," he judged. "And boots. Suelas must have holes in her. Your toes, they about to come through to the air almost."

Cecil looked down at himself and then glanced at Sydney. The younger boy's face was not red. It was pale. "Señor," said Cecil, "you are very good. But we can't accept these things."

Ruiz studied Cecil's guarded expression a moment, and then he, too, glanced at Sydney. As the younger Simpson met the Spaniard's eyes, all the color that had been lacking from his face before washed over it and left it scarlet. And then his gaze dropped to the floor.

"You refuse me!" exclaimed Ruiz regretfully, turning back to Cecil. "You are too proud, amigo. Don't put them back, viejo!" he called to France's clerk. "I buy them! For my nephews in the Valle," he explained, meeting Cecil's eye again. He put down the gun he had examined and picked up the other one. "You have balas for these?" he asked the shop-keeper.

In response, France bent to retrieve a small wooden box from a lower shelf. He put it on the counter and slid back the lid. A clean row of bullets grinned up at Ruiz. The Spaniard took out half a handful and began to load the pistol he held. "If the gun, she misfire, you take her back?"

"It won't misfire," said the shopkeeper firmly.

"No? We try and see."

France reached across the counter to seize the weapon by its barrel. "One moment, Señor. You must pay for them, first."

"¿Ah, sí? You think then perhaps they do misfire."

"No, I don't think they'll misfire. But I don't want them used until they're paid for."

"You don't trust me to pay you," interpreted Ruiz, neither relinquishing his hold upon the gun nor attempting to pull it out of France's grasp.

Slowly, the shopkeeper relaxed his grip. "It's not the way I do business," he explained. "If you try the guns and decide afterwards you don't want them, you'll only have spoiled them for another man who may like them."

"But if I don't want them," said Ruiz, fitting another bullet into the pistol's revolving cylinder, "is only because they misfire or don't shoot straight. And then no other man wants them. Pistolas, they are meant to shoot, not only to look at them."

At this, there was a stir of amusement in the shop's open doorway where a group of spectators stood. Still others watched through the open windows. Their general consensus seemed to be that Ruiz had scored a point.

The shopkeeper frowned.

Ruiz calmly finished loading the first gun, then began on the second. Behind him, Sydney moved closer to Cecil and looked up at his brother anxiously. The older boy shook his head at him.

Then new activity outside distracted the group in the door and turned the others away from the windows. "It's the sheriff!" someone said. Albert France visibly relaxed.

It was some time before the lawman entered the store, however. He had first to hear a second-hand report from John Dynan and then what little Boston would say. Williston had been untied and allowed to sit on the porch of the hotel, but he had no particular friends among those that guarded him. The sheriff brought him along across the street.

Ruiz had finished loading both pistols and had given France's clerk further orders for items of apparel, including a pair of fine linen drawers for his little nephew in the Valley to wear under the embroidered pantalón of leather and wool. Two pairs of boots also sat on the counter. They had been measured against those of the Simpsons for size. Ruiz claimed his nephews wore the same.

But the Spaniard showed no interest in buying a new jacket for himself nor even in replacing his shirt, in spite of its bloodstain and its smudges of dirt from the road. "I need no chaqueta," he told France's clerk, dismissing the old man's solicitous suggestions. "I get my own one back."

It was at this point the sheriff came into the shop with Williston slouching along at his side. "Señor Ruiz?" said the lawman.

Simón thrust one of the pistols through the gold sash at his waist and turned round. "Para servirle," he professed.

"I'm Sheriff Phoenix. Mr. Dynan says you want to talk to me about this man." He nodded at Boston.

"Is my two amigos who will talk of him," said Simón. "César, tell the cheriff what has happen to you."

"Son?" said Phoenix, directing a straight look at Cecil. The elder Simpson took off his hat and ran a hand through his red-brown, curly hair. "Sir," he said, "I'm Cecil Simpson. I was hired by Mr. Hindshaw in Drytown to drive a wagon loaded with supplies for the National Hotel in Jackson. I was told by some men I met behind the freight office that a man named Boston usually drove this route. I was halfway between Drytown and Rancheria when Mr. Williston and a couple of his friends caught up with me. But before that," continued Cecil, glancing at Ruiz, "my brother Sydney . . ."

"No, César," the Spaniard interrupted him. "What happen to me is my business. We don't bother the cheriff with that. He doesn't waste his time looking for the cholos. I find them, myself." And Ruiz lifted the second gun from the counter.

Cecil hesitated, uncertain.

"Go ahead, son," said Phoenix. "Tell me what happened."

"My brother and I found Señor Ruiz unconscious by the side of the road," said Cecil. He draped one arm protectively around Sydney's shoulders, and the younger boy made no protest. "When he came to himself, we helped him into the wagon. We were starting up the hill this side of the woody gulch when Mr. Williston and his friends tried to stop us. The three of us fought them off, but Williston's friends got away. In any case, it was Williston who actually did the damage to the freight. And he seemed to be the leader. The others only did what he told them."

Phoenix looked at his prisoner. "You have anything further to say, Boston?"

Williston glowered at Cecil. "It's my job to drive the freight to Jackson," he maintained. "And Hindshaw knows it. But Old Matthew don't pay enough. I told him he'd be lucky to find another man willing to do it for two dollars a trip. And then he goes and hires these two freckle-face foundlings for ten dollars in gold! I told him what I thought of that. But I couldn't get no satisfaction from Hindshaw, so I figured I'd go after my wagon myself. This pair of ragpickers got no right to drive it. And if they'd asked anybody in Drytown, they'd have knowed I wouldn't stand for it."

"The Simpson brothers had no obligation to ask permission from you or anyone else," said Phoenix. "Hindshaw hired them. That's his right. And they took the job. That's theirs. And no amount of ramming around with a crowbar will make it any different. Did either of you two boys get hurt in the scuffle?" the sheriff asked Cecil.

"No, sir."

"Good. In that case, I suggest you get back into your wagon and drive it on to Jackson. Have the hotel estimate the cost of the damage done to the cargo and send the bill to me. Mr. Williston will pay it. In the meantime, I'll make sure he doesn't follow you, and we'll look through the brush for his sidekicks."

The sheriff turned to the Spaniard. "Señor Ruiz? Would you care to give your side of this story?"

"No, Señor."

"Why not?"

"Is my business."

"Well, but I want to know why you were lying unconscious at the side of the road when these boys came across you. And why is there blood on your sleeve?"

"I don't answer you, Señor. You don't concern yourself for Simón Ruiz. You take care of the gringos like Bastón. Let the californianos take care of mexicanos. We are compatriotas."

"It was Mexicans that robbed you?"

"¡Pchss! Have I say I am rob? Do I complain?"

"Where is your horse?"

"No horse, Cheriff Finits. I travel to Jackson in the wagon. I am passenger. I pay them ten dollar to take me."

Phoenix glanced at Cecil. "Is that true, son?"

"He doesn't have to pay us," said Cecil. "He's welcome to ride with us as far as he likes. Without his help, we wouldn't have been able to stand off Williston."

Phoenix turned back to Ruiz. "Now, you listen to me, Señor. There's been a bunch of Mexican bandits robbing and murdering on the roads around here since early last spring. If they had limited themselves to attacking other Mexicans, maybe your argument would be valid. But by far and away, most of their victims are American miners and settlers. And as an officer of the law, it's my duty to bring them to justice if I can. If you know anything about them, who they are or where they are, I think you'd better tell me."

"But I do not know," said Ruiz.

Phoenix frowned and took Boston by the arm. "Come on, Williston. At least we can keep **you** off the roads a while."

"Wait!" said Albert France, jerking a detaining hand across the counter.

The sheriff stopped.

France gestured at Ruiz. But on meeting the Spaniard's challenging look, he held his peace.

"You have something to add, Mr. France?" asked Phoenix. The shopkeeper gestured again. And then, with every eye upon him, Ruiz removed his hat. He ran a finger around its inner band, hooking ten dollar gold pieces out of it into his palm. When he had emptied it, he returned the hat to his head, hiding again the bloodstained cloth tied round his brow. The coins he strew negligently across the counter.

Then catching up the bulky paper parcel containing the gifts for his nephews in the Valley, he put it under one arm. He took up the box of cartridges as well. "You decide if that is gold enough for you, Señor," he said to France. "If not, I pay you more next time I come to Ranchería. If is too much, I trust you to give it back then. Is how I do business." And indicating to the Simpson brothers that they should follow him, Simón Ruiz strode by the sheriff and out the door. The crowd around it hastily made way for him.

CHAPTER FIVE:

GENTE DE RAZON

"Señor Ruiz! I water them!" A child's voice greeted the Californian as he stepped into the sunlight of the road. A ragged boy ran forward from the loosely grouped crowd of onlookers. He had uncut, dusty black hair and a smile as bright and white as his face was dark and dirty. In both hands, he carried a wooden bucket. Behind him, a little girl lugged another, sloshing water on her bare legs. "I give the mulas to drink for you," the boy explained, pointing.

"Niño," said Ruiz, "you do me a service. What is your name?"

"Tomasito!" replied the child, his eyes full of admiration for the man who had condescended to answer him. "And Lupita is my sister," he added as the ragged girl came up beside him.

"¡Don Simón!" exclaimed an equally ragged man who was stumbling after the children. "¡Por Dios, Patrón! I wish to drink your health!" He stopped and surveyed the faces of the onlookers. "Here is a true caballero!" he proclaimed, waving a hand at Ruiz. "Here is one of the gente de razón! He is not like you! He is generous! He is honorable! He does not refuse a poor beggar like Port Wine!"

"Hombre," said Simón, "what is it you want?"

"No, su merced, I only want to drink your health! But I have no money to buy the wine for it."

The crowd's unkind laughter did not dismay the man. Nor did he seem to hear when he was advised to return to his claim and pan out half an ounce of gold dust if he wished to drink the health of an honest man. It was suggested he beg food for his children instead of drink for himself. He was reminded that his wife was patching the patches on her family's clothes. But Port Wine continued to extoll the generosity and goodness of the gente de razón and bewail his lack of means to drink the health of a true gentleman.

Simón looked down at the tattered children with their wooden buckets and their thin, dirt-streaked faces. Their smiles were gone. Tomasito dug his big toe into the dust in shame. "¡Niño!" said Ruiz. "Climb into the wagon and look in the corner of the seat between the boards. Bring me what you find there."

The boy darted instantly to obey. Ruiz turned to the Simpsons who had paused uncertainly behind him and were watching with the rest. Cecil still had his arm around his brother's shoulders. "César, you lend me ten dollar?"

The elder Simpson frowned in surprise. But the Californian's gaze did not waver. It burned deep, full of an unasked question, and of confidence in its answer. Slowly, Cecil felt in the pocket of his threadbare trousers to take out the gold that Hindshaw had given him and put it into Ruiz' hand.

"Gracias, amigo," Ruiz said softly, closing his fingers on the coin. He looked around as Tomasito returned from his errand, holding up the broken whiskey flask he had been sent to find.

"Give it to your father," Ruiz directed. "¡Hombre!" he added to the ragged man who watched his every move with eager eyes. "You drink my health with that. Lupita!" He beckoned the little girl to stand before him. "You earn this coin for water the mules." Ruiz put the gold piece into her palm. "But remember! Half is for your brother. You give to mamita. She keep for you, eh?"

Lupita nodded solemnly.

"Bueno. ¡Corra! Run, take it to her, now."

The little girl dropped her bucket in the road and fled.

Ruiz went on to the wagon and climbed the wheel to the seat, put his bundle and his box of cartridges behind it. Cecil gave Sydney a gentle push in the direction of his pony before he followed the Californian.

But now, the younger Simpson seemed to want to ride in the wagon. He looked back often, twisting around on Red Dog even as he rode the pony to the head of the teams to quirt the balky leader and start the mules on up the road.

The animals were quiet. They had had their run, and they went along steadily. When they had pulled the wagon out of the little canyon of Rancheria Creek, a long stretch of undulating hilltop lay before them, and here, Sydney checked his mount. He let the mules pass by; the wagon, too.

Neither Cecil nor Simón made any comment. They sat silently on the driver's bench together, each busy with his own thoughts and neither wishing to share them.

Sydney tied the pony to the tailgate as before and clambered quickly across the cargo and over the back of the seat. "Simón?" he said, his voice urgent.

"Diga." Ruiz' expression softened as he met the boy's brown eyes.

Sydney hesitated, trying to choose among his many questions for the most appropriate to put first. "Why did you give whiskey to that drunk?" he demanded, then.

"It makes him happy," said Ruiz. "And hurts no one."

"What about his children!" insisted Sydney. "It hurts them to have their father be a drunkard, doesn't it?"

"Pues, sí, Pecoso. It hurts them, yes. But if I do not give the man to drink, does that reform him?"

"But you could have given him Cecil's ten dollars and made him promise to buy food for his family!"

"A borracho does not keep the promise. He has money, he spend it on one thing."

"Simón," the boy went on, hitching a little closer in his earnestness, "why wouldn't you tell the sheriff about the cholos? Think of all the other people they maybe will attack before you can stop them! And won't you need help to go after them? You'll be only one man against five!"

"I get help when I need," said Ruiz. "And I find them faster than the cheriff can. I know them better."

"But you could have told him what you know!"

"Is not what I mean, Pecoso. I don't know the things about them that the cheriff wants to know. I don't know their names nor even what they look like very well. I don't ever see them plainly. But I know who to ask about them, someone who maybe does know who they are and where they go to hide. Those people that I ask don't tell the cheriff anything. But they tell me."

"Why? Are you a Mexican lawman?"

"No, Cindy. But I am gente de razón."

"Sydney," the boy corrected him. "What's 'hentay what-you-said'?"

"For gosh sakes, Syd!" Cecil interrupted. "Señor Ruiz doesn't have to answer to you for everything he says and does."

Sydney glanced at his brother, his rapt face clouding.

"Is all right, César," said Ruiz. "I explain it if he wants me. Gente de razón, Pecoso, are the people that they are responsible for others and for the things they do. Two men quarrel, for instance, they come to my uncle, don Diego. He hears both parts of the argument and says which he thinks is right. Poor man cannot feed his children, my uncle helps him

38

and gives him something useful he can do so is not only charity. One man steals from another, my uncle makes him give it back. Or if he cannot catch the thief, he replace the thing is lost so the other man is satisfy. One man kills another one, is my uncle who is told he did, and my uncle who decides what should be done. You see?"

"Is your uncle some kind of governor or something?"

"No, he is big ranchero in the Valle. Don't I tell you?"

"But why is he so special?"

"Because he is Silvestre. Because he has the land and all the cattle. People have the land, the name, the wealth, they have responsibility go with them. I am my uncle nephew. I am my father son. Is my responsibility, now, too."

"But the bandits aren't on your uncle's land."

"No, and they don't dare to be. Before the gringos come to California, there are not any bandits. Because the people here are happy. Everybody has enough. But the gringos change that, and there is trouble often, now. You hear of Joaquín Murieta, Cindy?"

"Sydney."

"Ah, sí. Perdón. D on other side the N. Saidnay. Eh? Like that?"

"M'hm. What's walking what-you-said?"

"Joaquín Murieta is a man the gringos think they kill two years ago."

"Oh. Why? What did he do?"

"He is rebelde. He make war on the americanos. And there are other men like he was who think that is what we should do. But is not a good idea. Even Joaquín Murieta knows that, now."

"He's not dead?"

"No. The gringos kill another man they think is him. I mention him because even though he is true mexicano and not californiano, he also is the gente de razón like my uncle don Diego. But he did more. He tried to take responsibility for everyone and everything in all of California. Was more than he can do. It doesn't work. But yet it almost does. Es lástima: Too bad."

"Where's Walking, now?"

"I don't know, Pecoso. And if I know, I do not tell you. Los amigos de Joaquín protect him."

"Simón?"

"¿Qué más, preguntón?"

"Should you have spent all your money back there in Rancheria?"

"Sydney!" Cecil interposed again. "Will you let up?"

But Ruiz' white teeth flashed in amusement. "You don't approve my purchases?" He drew one of the pistols from his sash and offered it to Sydney. "You know the guns," he said. "Examine this one. Tell me if I make mistake to buy."

"I didn't mean the guns," said Sydney, automatically accepting the revolver. "If you're going after bandits, I guess you'll need them. But why did you give Mr. France all the gold you had in your hat?"

"Because I do not have enough. Little more than half the price of these pistolas I have put there on the counter. And as you say, I need them. So I have to find the way to make the señor France to let me use them until I can pay the rest."

Sydney digested this implication. "You would have gotten them for nothing if you could have," he concluded. "But you knew that Mr. France wouldn't let you get away with it while the sheriff was there." The boy ran his fingers over the elaborate engraving on the gun's black barrel. "That wasn't exactly honest, was it?"

"Sydney!" exclaimed Cecil, directing a punitive look at his younger brother. "I'm sorry, Señor Ruiz," the elder Simpson added to the Californian. "He doesn't have much notion of . . ."

Simón put out a hand to silence Cecil without turning away from Sydney. "I will pay him his price, Pecoso. I come this way again when I get my money and my horse back from the cholos. If the señor France were español, he would trust me for the payment. He would know the name Ruiz is all collateral he needs. But he is gringo. Is not how he does business. You hear him say so. He trust no one. Not even other gringos."

Sydney was silent for a moment. "You'll really pay him later?" he said, finally.

Ruiz gazed at the younger Simpson. "Is a thing that interest me," he said. "The gringo has idea that to be honest in a man, he never ask another man to trust him. I have to trick the señor France, force him to trust me. But I do not steal the guns. I am not a bandit, Saidnay. I think the price of these pistolas is too much, but I don't complain for that. I am not a pobretón that I must haggle for a dollar difference, nor for fifty dollar, either."

"How much gold did you put on the counter?" wondered Sydney.

Ruiz shrugged. "Perhaps one hundred, fifty dollar."

"A hundred and fifty dollars! How much were these guns?"

"Almost three hundred dollar, I think. I look at them before when I come through Ranchería on my way to Drytown."

The younger Simpson's mouth came open, and he stared down at the pistol he still held.

"And your brother, Saidnay, gets his ten dollar back," Ruiz concluded dryly. "I have a friend in Yackson. My friends trust me. So, he will give me money to pay César. You do not go without the gold you work so hard to have."

Sydney looked up. But he did not recognize the rebuke for what it was. His brown eyes met the Californian's as frankly as before. "See Saw and I will help you catch the bandits," he offered.

On Simón's other side, the elder Simpson groaned: "Sydney!"

"No, Pecoso," Ruiz said firmly. "Find the bandidos is my business. Your business is find the Uncle Seensome."

"We could team up," the younger boy suggested. "We could look for the bandits with you, and you could look for our uncle with us."

At this, Cecil threw up one hand, appealing mutely to the hills.

"Saidnay," said Ruiz, "I know that you are brave. I know that you are generous. And I know you offer this because you are my friend. I am grateful. I don't forget, Pecoso. But I don't let you chase the cholos. In Yackson, I go to my friend I tell you, and he gives me another horse. And then I say adiós. Now, try the pistola for me, eh? Shoot her at that rock. See if her aim is good."

The boy did not immediately comply. His head dropped in disappointment, hiding his face beneath his shapeless hat. He turned the beautiful gun in his hands, looking at it, tracing its inlaid design with a forefinger. But then, he sat up straighter, raised the gun and fired it at the dark shape of the stone jutting from the golden grass off to the right of the road. The gesture of his aim was casual, almost negligent, but there was a practiced surety behind it. The bullet hit the rock with a solid thwack.

"¡Válgame Dios!" muttered Ruiz. And taking the second gun from his waist sash, he snapped a shot at the stone himself. He missed. He tried again. And missed again.

"Want to trade guns?" asked Sydney.

Without answering, Ruiz drew a careful bead on the rock. It was closer, now, at right angles from the wagon. He compensated carefully for the distance and the movement of the vehicle. But just as he fired, the near wheel hit a hole in the road, and his third shot was thrown wildly high. Ruiz sat back and laughed. "You do again," he suggested. "Use up the balas. See how many times you hit him."

Color showed in Sydney's face as he raised the gun and emptied it at the stone. It was impossible, however, to tell if he had hit the target, for the retort of the shots masked any sound the bullets might have made on impact.

"Stop the mules!" said Ruiz. And stepping across Sydney, he dropped lightly out of the wagon. Cecil hauled on the lines, and the two brothers watched the Californian striding toward the rock. "Syd, if I thought it'd do any good, I'd tan your hide!" Cecil said under his breath, taking advantage of the moment's privacy. "You must be crazy, offering to chase outlaws with that man! How long do you think it would be before he found out the truth about you and your broken ribs?"

Sydney shrugged. "Maybe I don't care if he does."

"Maybe you're crazy!" whispered Cecil fiercely. "What about Paul?"

"Paul McCormick," said Sydney, still watching Ruiz, "is not gente de razón."

Cecil's breath exploded in incredulous impatience, and he caught his younger brother by the arm. "I can't believe you!" he said, frowning into Sydney's eyes as the boy whirled to scowl back at him. "Now you listen to me, and you listen well! As soon as we get to Jackson, we're going to say 'adiós' to Simón Ruiz so fast it'll make your head swim. He can go look up his friend that trusts him so much, and you and I will deliver this freight to the National Hotel. And then we'll see if we can find a way to get to Simpson's Bar . . . without any help from him!"

"Tomorrow is Sunday," Sydney reminded his brother. "Nobody is going to hire us to take any freight 'way the hell up the road' to Simpson's Bar on a Sunday. We'll have to hire a room at the hotel with some of that ten dollars you're hoping Simón gives you back." And he jerked against Cecil's hold to free himself.

Ruiz, meanwhile, had reached the stone and was examining it for bullet wounds. He found four holes chipped into the rockface and a long groove scarring its top. Sydney had missed the boulder only once. The Spaniard rose, glancing at the wagon to see the brothers still in the midst of their low-voiced argument. He straightened the brim of his hat and thought soberly about something for several moments while his dark eyes considered the hunching hills beyond Rancheria Canyon. Then he returned to the wagon.

CHAPTER SIX:

MANUEL ESCOBAR

Simón Ruiz and the Simpson Brothers made the rest of their journey in comparative peace. On their way, they passed through three more towns: Amador City, Sutter Creek, and Jackson Gate. But in none of them could they gain any news of either the bandits or Uncle Peter Simpson.

It was suppertime when the freight wagon rolled into Jackson. Along the town's main street, horses and mules stood hitched to rails and porch supports. There was still some traffic both on the road and on the boardwalks, but at this hour, most of the populace was indoors.

Midway along its length, the dusty street humped up and then dipped sharply toward an impressive, three story structure standing broadside at its end: the National Hotel.

At the brink of the rise in the road grew a live oak tree whose main trunk had once formed a heavy cluster like the fingers of a giant hand. But half the tree had been cut down, so that only two of these branchings remained. One writhed its way skyward to present a general impression of the vertical. The other arched high out over the street, casting a pool of shadow nearly to the wall of the building opposite.

In the wagon, Sydney sat as before on the outer edge of the driver's bench beside Ruiz. The boy had said little since the quarrel with his brother. The Californian had remained thoughtful as well. Now, his musing glance fell on the tree and rested there. And because it held his full attention for a moment, he did not see immediately what Sydney saw beneath it, in its shadow.

"Simón!" the boy whispered, nudging him.

"¿Diga?"

"Look! Isn't that your horse?"

Ruiz tensed. "¡Caray, que sí!" he breathed. Catching the boy's arm, he pressed it gratefully. "You go to the hotel," he said. "I come look for you later." And starting swiftly to his feet, he dropped out of the moving wagon.

"Where's **he** going?" wondered Cecil.

"To investigate something," said Sydney. He looked back to watch Ruiz striding up the boardwalk, stepping down to cross a side street, his pace purposeful, his eyes intent upon the steel-grey horse, unmistakably his own, which was tied so impudently to the Hangman's Tree.

As the wagon passed under the oak's arching limb, Sydney caught sight of a motion in a nearby doorway: the batwing doors of the Pioneer Rex Saloon pushed wide, and a man clad in as elaborate a costume as Simón Ruiz himself came out to lay hands upon the reins of the beautiful grey horse.

With an indignant gasp, the younger Simpson jumped from the wagon. "Sydney!" cried Cecil, leaning after him too late. "Come back here!"

But Sydney ran on to confront the horse's new owner. Nor could his brother stop the mules. Already started down the grade and with their final destination now in sight, the tired teams broke into an eager, shambling trot. The wagon rattled after them. And Cecil hauled on the lines in vain.

"Señor! That's not your horse!" Sydney declared, startling the man who was preparing to mount the grey.

He turned a fierce and outraged eye upon the boy. "¿Acaso se atreve?" he demanded. "You dare to say this thing to me?"

"It's the truth," said Sydney, stopping suddenly as he met those fiery eyes but not giving ground against them.

"¡Mentiroso! ¡Pelagatos! ¡Aléjese!" The man gestured Sydney to back off, threatening him with a quirt that he held in one hand. The horse, highly spirited and nervous, shied away from the motion, jerking the man sideways a step on the ends of the reins. "¡Quieto!" he commanded the animal, tugging sharply on the lines. The horse threw up its head and danced in place, rolling its eyes and mouthing the heavy bit. In angry irritation, the man struck at Syndey with his whip. The blow missed narrowly. "¡Váyase, mendigo! Go away!"

And then Simón Ruiz came around behind the snorting grey to intervene. "¡Déjelo!" he said. But in astonished recognition, he added, "Manuel!"

"Simón Ruiz!" the other exclaimed, evidently still more surprised.

"¡Sí, Señor! What has happen here?"

"No, nada, Simón. El gringuito este . . ." He gestured at Sydney with his quirt.

"This gringuito, Manuel, is friend of mine," Ruiz informed him, dropping a protective hand on the younger Simpson's shoulder.

The other blinked. "¡Amigo suyo!" His look raked the boy from weathered hat to worn-out boots before he lifted inquiring, disdainful eyes back to Ruiz. But this time, he noticed the bloodstains on Simón's white shirt and the brace of pistols at his waist. "Pero, ¿qué le han hecho a usted?"

"Speak English," said Ruiz. "You do not wish to show discourtesy to my friend? Saidnay," he added to the boy, "this is Manuel Escobar. I have know him many years. Manolo, I present to you Saidnay Seensome."

Manuel Escobar stared at Ruiz and then exploded: "You present this pelado to me, Simón! He has just accuse me to have steal the horse!"

"He is blunt, I know. But he say that which he thinks is true. He has seen the horse today before. And when he see it then, it is not yours. Who sells this horse to you, Manuel?"

Escobar glanced at the grey and back at Ruiz. He hesitated. "I do not understand," he said. "You know the horse?"

"Yes, I know it well," said Ruiz. "Is mine."

Escobar started a third time in surprise, and again he considered Simón's bloodstained sleeve, the pistols at his waist. Then he burst out in Spanish, speaking quickly, earnestly, motioning with one hand to emphasize his words. Ruiz heard him out, displaying no emotion. But his hand on Sydney's shoulder tightened until the boy squirmed uncomfortably, recalling his attention.

"Saidnay," said Ruiz, "go to the hotel, now. I will have some talk with Manuel Escobar. Your brother is worry about you, I think. And you are tire, both of you. Hotel has rooms for not so much. Ah! Almost I forget! You need the gold. Manuel," he said to Escobar, "you lend me algunas monedas?"

The other put his hand into his pocket and produced half a dozen gold coins which he gave readily to Simón.

"Take these, Pecoso," Ruiz instructed, trying to pass the money on to Sydney.

But the younger Simpson shook his head. "You only owe See Saw ten dollars," he objected.

"Twenty dollar," Simón insisted, counting two of the coins firmly into the boy's hand. "Ten I borrow and ten for pay as passenger. Now, you go. I come see you later."

Sydney ducked his head to hide his face under his hat with the excuse of looking at the money in his hand. Then he glanced back up at Ruiz and from there to Escobar. Both men returned his look; both plainly wished him gone. Reluctantly, the boy turned away.

Ruiz watched his retreat. "Are you staying in this town, Manuel?" he asked Escobar in Spanish.

"¡Sí, sí! With a friend, a portugués named Paulo Gonzalves. He has a residence here. But there is no need to stand talking in the street when you are weary and wounded! Mount your horse, my friend. Ride to the house of Gonzalves. Take that side street across the creek and count three houses down the trail leading westward. Tell don Paulo I sent you. I have some business I want to complete before I join you there. And let me say, Simón, how shocked I am to learn you have been robbed. Did you see plainly the thieves that took your horse?"

"No. Who sold it to you, Manolo?"

Escobar shrugged and shook his head. "Some man I've never seen before. I didn't even ask his name. It's a fine animal. The price was tempting. I asked fewer questions than I should have, perhaps."

"But you would know the man if you saw him again."

"I'm not sure. Perhaps I would. But I was looking at the horse, not at the man."

"Did you buy the animal saddled?"

"Just as you see him, now. It is your saddle, too?"

"Yes. But something is missing. Manuel, I am not in the Gold Country only to gamble and amuse myself. I have been selling stock for my uncle and five cartloads of grain. I had concluded my business and was on my way home. The proceeds were in a pair of saddlebags tied behind the cantle. As you can see, they're gone. And with them, I have lost six thousand dollars which belong to don Diego Silvestre Cisneros. I will not return to the Valley until I have recovered them."

"Six thousand dollars! Simón, I wish I could help you. Perhaps if I ask around, I will learn something that will be of use to you. And in the meantime, you must rest before you go looking any further for the thieves. Take your horse! I give him back to you. And it is a true test of my friendship that I do so, for I have not ridden a finer animal. He was bred on your uncle's ranch, of course?"

"Of course," agreed Simón. "My uncle knows the horse. He gave it to me this spring."

"Your uncle is a generous man. But I will not keep you longer, now. Get on! Get on! I will meet you again this evening at the house of Paulo Gonzalves." And Escobar pressed the braided reins into Ruiz' hand.

Simón slipped them over the grey's head and swung lightly into the saddle. Steadying the nervous animal with a light pressure on the bit, he looked back down at Escobar. "Next time, Manolo, ask more questions," he advised. "Nos vemos," he added and wheeled the grey to ride for the side street Escobar had indicated.

But Ruiz did not go in search of the house of Gonzalves. When he had crossed the creek, he turned left and cantered along beside the stream to where it bent sharply around behind the National Hotel. On the rise of the far bank, he halted close beside a building to be able to watch unobserved the unloading of the freight wagon and the reuniting of the Simpson brothers, now in progress. Once satisfied that both were going smoothly, Ruiz spurred on.

His destination was half a mile up the creek's south fork. Here he drew rein before a snug adobe. There were chickens scratching through the sparse, dry grass in front of it. A red and green rooster flapped its wings and crowed to announce the visitor's arrival. In the open doorway appeared the master of the house. He was a small man past his prime, but wiry and well set up. His black hair was greying, and the cheerful expression he had worn all his life was permanently etched upon his face with myriad lines and creases. "Don Simón!" he greeted Ruiz in great surprise.

"Fidel," said Ruiz, dismounting, "I return to you for help."

"For help! How can I help you? You have only to say, and it will be done. Federico! Joselito! Come take the horse of don Simón!" he called. But the two youngsters were already running by him to oblige Ruiz. "You have ridden him hard," Fidel observed. "He has lost flesh. Come in. Come in! My house is yours. ¡Ay! Is this blood on your shirt?"

"Yes," said Ruiz, meeting the hand that Fidel held out to him. "But my wound is not serious. And it is not on my arm. Señora de Buenrostro," he greeted the much younger wife of his host who had come to the doorway behind Fidel. And Ruiz removed his hat, displaying the bloody bandage on his brow.

Amid exclamations of concern, he was drawn into the house where he was made to sit down, and his wound was uncovered and examined. Sydney's scarf had stuck to it and dried, and so fresh blood ran when it came off. A clean bandage was applied while Ruiz told as much of his story as he judged appropriate.

And then he was given water to wash with and fresh clothing to put on until his own could be cleaned. And although Fidel Buenrostro was smaller than his guest, the fit of the clothes was adjustable enough that it made little difference. Simón sat down to the family's supper looking much refreshed if rather less elegant than before.

When the meal was eaten, the two men removed themselves to the evening shadows on the porch. "Who is Paulo Gonzalves?" asked Ruiz.

"You've heard of him? He arrived here recently from some place to the south," replied Buenrostro.

"What else do you know about him? He is Portuguese, of course?"

"Well . . . Brazilian, I think. A criollo."

"And what are his opinions concerning his American neighbors?"

"You have already guessed the answer to that. Don Paulo is sometimes seen in the company of Manuel Escobar. The two of them are always making trouble for the gringos. You know the grievances of Escobar."

"Yes," agreed Ruiz. "But I have come to think of them more as excuses. Manuel spends a good deal of money, I suppose?"

"I'm sure he does."

"And where does that money come from? His father is no longer rich. He has lost his lands to the gringo settlers, his cattle to the gringo thieves. He lives in his adobe in the Valley, poorer than the Indians that used to beg for alms from him. If it were not for his neighbors who remember him as a gentleman of wealth and pride, he might well die of starvation. Manuel seldom visits him. Why should he? There is nothing to be gained. The old man sits in his doorway and sighs for the past. And so, his son has been forced to take up gambling as a means of livelihood. Or so he says. But can Manuel win enough at cards and betting on the bulls and bears and cockfights to be able to afford the life he leads? And if not . . .?"

Buenrostro frowned. "It is not my place to question him, Patrón."

"But it is my place!" said Ruiz. "And I intend to find the evidence to prove that Manuel Escobar is assuaging his grievances by plundering the gringos. And I want to learn besides who are the men that serve him. For I am certain that he knows what has become of the six thousand dollars in coin and gold dust that I was taking to the Valley and my uncle."

"You accuse Escobar of robbing you!" exclaimed Fidel, shocked by his own words.

"Not in person," said Ruiz. "But I do accuse him of harboring the thieves, of aiding them, of directing them, of sharing their gains with them. And I accuse Gonzalves of being his comrade in duplicity. Fidel, have you a horse that you might lend me for a day or two? I wish to stay in town, and I do not wish Manuel Escobar to know it immediately. May I leave my horse with you?"

"Don Simón, I would be honored."

Half an hour later, Ruiz returned to Jackson on a fat sorrel mare. He dismounted at the rear of the National Hotel.

CHAPTER SEVEN:

FANCY PANTS

Ruiz entered the hotel by a side door which opened on the kitchen corridor. Bangings of pots and pans greeted him from one direction and a murmur of mingled voices from the other. He turned toward the latter sound and made his way past a gaming room, up a flight of narrow stairs and so came into the hotel's main lobby and saloon from the rear. Here he paused to look carefully among the idlers for any familiar face. He saw none. He went across to the clerk's cage at the far end of the bar. "You tell me, Señor?" he asked the visored clerk. "I am friend of César Seensome. He stays here. Which one is his room?"

The man surveyed Simón suspiciously. "Scissor Who?"

"Seensome. Tall boy, red curly hair. Drive the wagon."

"Oh! Simpson! Sure. But the kid's not in. He's on the town."

"Small brother with him?"

"Don't know. Likely is."

"These boys, they expect me. I wait for them. What room?"

"Third floor. Room Seventy-Six."

"Gracias, Señor." Ruiz turned toward the stairs. He started up slowly, but halfway to the landing, a new idea took him, and he quickened his pace.

Room Seventy-Six was at the end of a narrow hallway at the back of the building. Ruiz stood aside for a pair of American miners who pushed by rudely, seeming not to see him. Another time, he would not have tolerated it, but now he let it pass. Reaching the door marked Seventy-Six, he struck three businesslike raps on it with the backs of his knuckles.

He heard a muffled exclamation and the thud of boot heels on the floor within. The bolt was shot back and the door jerked open. "What's the matter, See Saw? You lose your key? Oh!"

Ruiz had a only the briefest glimpse of Sydney standing before him, and then the door was flung shut. But he had already advanced, intending to enter, so it rebounded off his toe. He caught the door's inner edge with one hand and would have pushed it further back, but there was something stopping it. "Saidnay? You don't let me to come in? Is Simón!"

"No! You can't."

"Why? What has happen?"

"See Saw's not here."

"Where he is, then?"

"He went to see if he could find out anything about Uncle Peter."

"But why you don't let me to come in?"

"See Saw told me not to."

"And now, de pronto, you do what your brother says? Pecoso! I don't stay long. César never knows that I am here." Ruiz put his shoulder to the door and forced it wider against Sydney's upturned toe which was wedged tightly to its lower crack. When he had opened it far enough to admit himself, he stepped through it suddenly and let Sydney shove it shut behind him. What he saw when he turned around did not actually surprise him.

Sydney was wearing a white linen shirt and elaborately embroidered trousers of leather and wool. Below the hems of the belled, white underdrawers, new boots gleamed.

Simón backed off a few paces to admire the full effect. But there was more than the clothes to admire. The new pants hugged closely the shape that filled them. And the flaring line from waist to hip was all that Ruiz would have needed to see to confirm what he had already expected to find. Yet there was besides a fuller roundness to the seat than the trousers were intended to contain and a smoother tapering of thigh.

Ruiz said nothing. He only stood watching and waiting for more.

Yielding to the inevitable, Sydney slowly turned around. The wide bandage which had supposedly protected broken ribs was washed and draped across two chair backs to dry. And so the new, white linen shirtfront draped softly over a very feminine bosom which was no longer confined by tight bands of cloth nor disguised by the voluminous folds of the outsized garment worn before. The younger Simpson leaned back against the door and stared at the shiny toes of the new boots on her feet.

Stepping forward, Simón took Sydney's burning face between his hands and gently lifted it. Wary brown eyes met his. But the color in her hot cheeks cooled a little as she read in his gaze undiminished approval mingled with his amusement.

And then he bent to kiss her. She did not respond. But neither did she resist. Her lips lay in a quiet line beneath the soft caress. Ruiz drew back to look at her. And while he watched, Sydney slid her upper lip under her lower one and scratched it on her teeth. "Your mustache tickles," she said.

"¿Ah, sí? You want I cut him off?"

She considered, shook her head.

This was invitation enough for Ruiz to try again. He stayed longer, this time, but he didn't get much further. "Pecosa," he whispered, "I teach you a word to say in Spanish. Say, 'Otro.' Say, 'Simón . . . otro.'"

"What's it mean?"

"It means you want the mustache to tickle you some more."

"Simón . . .?" she said promptly. But she followed it with: "Was Manuel Escobar one of the robbers that shot you and took your horse?"

"No, muñeca. Manuel is not bandido. Say, 'otro.' "

"Simón . . .? When did you guess?"

"About you? No, from the very beginning, I suspect. You are too much a woman to wear this disguise. From a distance, maybe, you fool them. But not the man who look close into your eyes. The man who sit beside you in a wagon all day long."

"Simón . . .?" she began again. But he didn't wait for the rest. The last vowel of his name gave shape enough to her lips to serve his purpose. Nor did they retreat to their former passivity beneath his next kiss. And he found their first attempt to cooperate both provocative and sweet.

Ruiz stepped still closer, smoothed a hand down her back to draw her against him. But just as her fine linen shirt-front touched his in two places, Sydney pulled back. With a quick jerk, she took one of the pistols from his waist. And before he could do more than inhale in surprise, she had reached around and stuffed it through his sash at the back. She transplanted the second gun as well. Then she turned up her face under his and closed her eyes. "Simón . . ." she said. "Otro."

With a good teacher and a little inspiration, kissing is an art easily mastered. Sydney was inspired. And she knew no reason to resist. She let him hold her close against him and slid both arms around him in return.

"Pecosa!" said Ruiz, lifting back from the warm nest of her lips. "Do your father and your brother never teach you how to say 'No' to a man that wants you?"

Her eyes came open. She frowned slightly.

"How many years are you, niña?"

"I'm eighteen."

"¡Dieciocho! You tell me the truth?"

She nodded solemnly. "I'm the same age as See Saw. We're twins."

"Ah! Ahora, sí. No wonder he has problems with make you do what he wants you. But why this Pole MaCormie, this aprendiz you tell me, he lets you grow ripe like a peach in his hand, and yet he does nothing about it?"

"What?"

"I come here to say adiós to you, Saidnay. I have my horse back. I have talk to my friend. I follow the trail of the cholos that rob me. And you go on, look for your tío and this stupid boy who call himself Pole."

"You're leaving?"

"Sí, Pecosa. Is the thing I must do. But I don't forget you. And someday, ¿quién sabe? We meet again, perhaps."

"But tomorrow is Sunday! Is it right to chase cholos on Sunday?"

Ruiz stroked her cheek with one finger. "Bandidos, they don't care what is the day of the week, muñeca. Man who wants to catch them musn't, either."

She continued to look up at him for a moment. And then she sighed and took her arms from around him and pushed past him, away from the door. She took two or three steps and stopped. "Goodbye, Simón."

"Goodbye, Saidnay," he replied, dropping his voice to a note of finality. But he did not move. He only stood looking at her, wrestling with his conflicting instincts, unaware of the passing moments until she whirled to confront him with a show of anger.

"Well?" she demanded, gesturing at the door. "Why don't you go?"

He started, nodded, laid hands on the latch. Then he remembered his guns and paused to pull them out of his sash in back and put them in front. Sydney watched him.

"Simón!"

He looked up, one pistol still in his hand. He saw tears on her cheeks. He replaced the gun through his sash in back and took two long strides after her, caught her into his arms again.

But she was not so pliant, now. And her reluctance lanced him with remorse. "Saidnay! I have no choice but to leave you! What more I can do? How I can say to César that I have change my mind and help you look for Uncle Pito? And when he knows I know you are his sister, not his brother, he is twice as much against me. You know is true! And there is my own uncle in the Valle, expecting me to come with all the money that is his. And there are the malditos cholos spending the six thousand dollar and laughing to each other that Simón Ruiz Silvestre does not even dare to look for them. And there is the Cheriff Finits who has hear me say that californianos will take care of mexicanos. Now," he ended, pausing to catch his breath, "what do you have me do?"

"Go," said Sydney. She pushed at him.

"But also, here is a girl who lets me be the first man ever kisses her, telling me with tears in her eyes not to chase cholos on Sunday!"

"Simón . . .?"

"Diga."

"Will you come again tomorrow?"

"Tomorrow? When, Pecosa?"

"It doesn't matter. We'll be here until See Saw finds a way to get us to the next town up the road. And I don't guess he will before Monday. And as long as we're in Jackson, he wants me to stay in this room out of sight and out of trouble so he doesn't have to worry about me.

"I wish we could just forget about finding Uncle Peter," she went on. "Our daddy was dying, Simón. I know he didn't make it over the mountains alive. And I don't care a thing about Paul McCormick. I used to, in a way," she admitted, moving her fingertips over a small space on Ruiz' shirtfront. "He and See Saw and I pretty much grew up together. So he was more like another brother to me than anything else. But then, just before we started west, all of us, he changed. He wanted to boss me around the way See Saw does. And he said I ought to go live with Uncle Peter's family so Aunt Agnes could teach me how to be a girl before it was too late for me to learn. And he said it was a disgrace the way I went around in trousers. But it was easier for me to put on See Saw's hand-me-downs than to get some proper things. And anyway, I didn't see any point in wearing a dress. It just got in my way all the time. The skirt would catch on sticks and brush and would always be flying around in the wind. And if it got wet in the rain, it weighed like lead and took forever to dry out. So I got See Saw to take my side against Paul and make him leave me alone.

"And Daddy, too, never cared if I wore trousers instead of skirts. He was proud of my being able to shoot a gun so well and ride a horse better than See Saw. And he told me that Paul was just fretting because he was falling in love with me and wanted me to be different because of that. But I don't understand how falling in love with a person would make you want them to be different. Do you?" .

Ruiz shook his head, but more in disbelief than in accord with her question.

"I don't want **you** to be any different," Sydney offered as the clincher to her argument.

"Chito," said Ruiz, laying a finger on her lips to hush her. "Don't say any more to me. Is more than I can think about already. I come again tomorrow, to say goodbye to you and César, too, before we go our different ways. Now, I leave you for tonight. César will come and find me here, and we have more problems than before."

He drew away from her and returned to the door, again changing the pistols from the back of his sash to the front. Nor did he look around until he had the door open and easy escape lay ahead of him.

As she met his parting look, Sydney ran after him. But Ruiz stepped quickly through the door and pulled it shut behind him, held it shut while she tried to open it to follow him, nor let go of the knob until he heard her slam the bolt across defiantly. Then he moved quickly down the hall to the stairs and descended them two at a time.

CHAPTER EIGHT:

PROMISING LEADS

"Sydney! Sydney! Good news!" Cecil fumbled with his key. "Open up, Syd! Let me in! I can't make this goldarn key work. Sydney!"

The door to Room Seventy-Six opened to admit him. Cecil pushed through it, took off his hat and sailed it against the far wall. "Heee-haaa!" he cried, whirling back to face his sister in triumphant joy. "We've found them, Syd! We've . . .!" Cecil stopped, his mouth still open.

Turning around from rebolting the door, Sydney regarded her brother calmly.

Cecil's face had been flushed with excitement before, but now, it reddened still further with anger. "Sydney!" he accused her.

"What," she replied.

"What! You know what!"

"I washed my clothes," she explained, nodding at the various garments hung to dry about the room, including the bandage for her "broken ribs".

"But Señor Ruiz bought those things you have on for his nephew!"

"No, he didn't."

"Well, nevermind for a minute. Listen to me, Syd! I've found Uncle Peter! And Aunt Aggie and Paul! They live near here! Only a couple of miles from this town!"

"Is Daddy alive?"

Cecil's joy dampened again. He shook his head. "The person that told me about them didn't know."

"Who told you?"

"The local minister. Reverend Thomson, his name is. When I found out there was a Presbyterian church here, I asked for directions to the parsonage. The Reverend was really concerned, Syd. He wanted us to stay at his place tonight. But I told him we already had a room at the hotel. He says that Uncle Peter and Aunt Aggie and the boys come into town every Sunday to his church. All we have to do is wait till morning! Syd? What's the matter with you? Why are you looking like that? Don't you hear me say we've found them?"

"Yep," said Sydney, sighing. "I hear you." She went to one of the two narrow beds and cast herself onto it, then raised a knee and propped her other leg across it in order to be able to look at the shiny boot on her foot. She ran her hand lingeringly over the gold braid on her pantleg. "I'm sure Daddy's not alive, See Saw," she said. "Probably, the parson just didn't want to have to tell you. Aunt Aggie would have explained to him about it even if Uncle Peter didn't. Did the Reverend act like he'd heard of you?"

"He certainly did! Sydney, what's the matter?" Cecil repeated, unable to comprehend her dull mood. "Aren't you glad we've found them?"

"Nope," said Sydney. "Not unless Daddy is alive."

Cecil came across to the bed. "Syd," he said gently, "neither one of us really expected Dad to make it, did we?"

"I guess not."

"Crying for him now isn't going to help."

"I'm not crying."

"We'll still have a home. A family. People that care about us, that mean something to us. Don't you know how lucky we are to have found them?"

"I would rather have been a cowboy for Simón."

"Hey! Come on . . ."

Sydney turned her face to the wall.

Her brother stood where he was, looking down at her. "Nobody's seen you in that outfit, have they?" he demanded.

"Who would see me in this room?"

"We're going to have to pay Señor Ruiz for those things. He won't want to take them to his nephew after you've worn them. I don't like to ask Uncle Peter for money right off. But you had to go ahead and try them on, didn't you?"

She looked back at him. "You'd better try on the things he bought for you. You need them. And I don't suppose Uncle Peter has many clothes to spare. Anyway, by the time we see Simón again, you'll probably have enough money saved up to pay him . . . if he'll let you."

Cecil frowned in disapproval, but he was too happy to be really angry. "Too bad Simón didn't buy you a dress while he was at it," he said. "I don't know what you're going to do with that rig you've got on. You can't wear it in public."

"Why can't I?"

"Why . . .! Syd, it's one thing for you to pretend to be a boy. We've avoided all sorts of trouble because of it. But those fancy pants give you dead away. And that shirt . . .!"

Sydney turned back to the wall.

Cecil threw up his hands and left the bedside, unbuttoned his own shirt, jerked its tail free of his belt. "Did you save me any water to wash with?" he asked.

"In the pitcher on the washstand." And closing her eyes, Sydney gave herself up to her memories of Ruiz.

Outside, the summer night fell softly. Light lingered on the shallow, chuckling rapids of the creek. In the streets, the activity increased. A group of Mexican musicians struck up a lively tune.

Saturday night in the Gold Towns was a time to cele-

---

brate the gains made during the week. Or a time to forget that there had been none. It was a time to drink and gamble and squander the gold that had been dug from the banks of the streams and crushed from the rocks. A time to believe again in lucky strikes, in a future as bright as the nuggets that always turned up in the next man's gold pan.

In the little canyon to the west of town, the last blush of evening light touched softly the walls of adobe brick and the curled roof tiles of the third house down the trail. In a brushy thicket some fifty yards distant, Simón Ruiz stopped Buenrostro's fat sorrel mare and dismounted. Tying the reins to a branch, he continued on foot, keeping to the deepest shadows until he had approached the house closely. Then he worked his way around behind it, looking for any irregularity in its rear wall that might be a masked entrance.

He was still studying the cracks between the heavy bricks when there was a rustle in the brush nearby. Ruiz sank to the ground on his heels as from the darkness at the far corner of the house, a man stepped out and glanced around impatiently. He whistled low between his teeth. There was an answer from the brush, and a second man came forward cautiously. The first one beckoned him. "García?" he hissed.

"Aquí, Patrón."

"Where are the others?" the first man asked in Spanish slurred with Portuguese.

"They are watching, Don Paulo."

"That man on the road near Ranchería . . . !"

"What has happened?"

"You told me he was dead!"

"I thought he was."

"Don Manuel is inside the house. He is mad with rage. How much did you take from the man you thought you killed?"

"Two thousand dollars in coin. More than twice that in gold dust and nuggets. Tell that to don Manuel. Perhaps he'll be less angry."

"Fool! Didn't you know who it was?"

"A friend of the gringos. With gringo gold."

"Yes. Gringo gold for the most important Spanish rancher near Sacramento. Even if you had killed him, we would have trouble enough. But he is not dead! And he saw don Manuel with the horse. Escobar directed him here, but he has not come. Would you know the man if you met him on the street?"

"Sí, Patrón. Is he in Jackson?"

"He was this afternoon."

"Are we to look for him?"

"Não. You're to bring the six thousand dollars here to-morrow at dawn. And then you are to ride south. Stay well out of range. Don't come back north of Angels Camp for at least a week."

"We have already split the money."

"Collect it again!"

"Most of it is buried."

"Dig it up!"

"Why do we not simply kill this man? I will do it my-self. And I will make sure he is dead. A dead man cannot complain. Nor can he ask for the horse and the money."

"Não. Do what I have said. It is what don Manuel has told me to tell you. Has he not aided you before? Trust him, García. Bring the gold. Amanhã!"

The bandit shrugged. "I will tell the others. But they may refuse."

"Senhor, I advise you as a friend not to test the patience of Escobar. He has little to spare. Do you wish to live to count through the purse of another gringo? Or do you prefer to swing from the limb of the Tree on Main Street?"

"Perhaps it is that don Manuel wants the six thousand dollars for himself alone."

"Idiota! Do as I tell you! Or you will not live to be sorry."

"I am Mariano García," the other man boasted. "Who threatens Mariano García may not live to be sorry."

The Brazilian gestured impatience. But as he would have spoken again, Ruiz' borrowed mare whickered a friendly greeting to the concealed mount of the bandit. Gonzalves froze. "Go!" he breathed. "Or better yet, find the rider. Kill him. Quickly!"

Holding his breath, Ruiz stayed where he was, his hand on the butt of his pistol. He saw García slide like a shadow back into the brush. Ruiz waited until Gonzalves had disappeared behind the corner of the silent house. Then he crept toward the side wall, moving as quietly as he could. Behind him, he heard the restless stamp of a horse. Again the fat mare nickered.

Ruiz followed the wall to its corner and looked out into the road. Before the house a saddled horse stood tied. Simón ran across the open space, jerked loose the reins and leaped into the saddle, spurred the horse to a gallop toward the town.

"Stop him!" shouted the voice of Manuel Escobar from the doorway of the adobe.

Mariano García had reached the mare in the thicket. He flung himself on her back and beat her out of the brush to the road. More shouts from the house raised a group of five or six mounted men who had been hiding farther down the canyon. But by the time they thundered past the adobe, Ruiz was well on his way back to Jackson.

The horse he rode was lean and hard. It easily outstripped Buenrostro's fat mare. García had time to snap only one shot after him before Simón was out of range, riding low on the animal's neck and urging it still faster.

At the edge of town, he leaped the creek and turned north to gallop alongside it half the length of Jackson before he turned up a narrow alley. At its intersection with Main Street, Ruiz leaned to catch the corner support of the covered boardwalk and let himself be swept from the saddle. Swinging around the post, he landed on his feet and darted for the nearest doorway. His riderless horse plunged on up the road into a heavier flow of traffic than there had been at any time that day. When García reached the corner, the loose animal had already been caught, but its rider was nowhere to be found.

The building in which Ruiz sought refuge could not have been better suited to his purpose. It was a dance hall, crowded from wall to wall with cavorting couples, ninety per cent of them male. That there were not female partners enough was no pall on the mood of the dancers. Tying a kerchief around an upper arm, half of them served as partners for the other half, occasionally trading off. What few women actually worked for the hall were kept constantly occupied.

Ruiz pushed among the merry miners, buffeted from side to side and obliged to lock elbows with more than one man to "swing-your-partner" on his way toward a promising doorway at the far end of the hall. It was hung with a curtain. Ruiz stumbled out of the main whirl on the floor and fought his way clear. Pausing to catch his breath, he looked back over the heads of the crowd to the entrance.

"¡Buenas noches, Señor!" said a feminine voice at his elbow.

He turned to confront the proprietress of the Eureka Dance Hall who had only just emerged from the curtained doorway behind him. "You have not been here before," she said in Spanish. Her dark eyes slid over his person and back to his face with piquant curiosity.

Ruiz returned the look with more show of interest than he felt. "Señorita," he replied, "it is only because I did not know you were here."

Snapping open a black lace fan, she smiled from behind it, then struck it lightly to his heart, closing it again. "¡Lisonjero!" she accused him. "If you are looking for don Manuel, he has not come yet tonight."

"No? And can he be so sure of his welcome as to neglect the fairest rose in Jackson?"

"Oh!" she said, tossing her head and shrugging up her shoulders. "He thinks I have nothing better to do than wait on his pleasure. But what I do with my time is my own business."

"To hear you say so makes me hope for a reprieve from

my dark thoughts and cruel solitude," declared Ruiz.

The closed black fan grazed his chin in another coquettish rebuke. Simón caught it, kissed its stiff-cornered folds. "Señorita, tell me your name that I may whisper it tonight as I lie alone with my sorrow."

"I am not flattered by your ignorance of it," she said disdainfully.

"Indeed, my ignorance shames me," agreed Ruiz, glancing again toward the door. Half a dozen Mexicans had pushed through it to stare around in angry bafflement. "Will you not forgive me?" urged Ruiz. "For to be near you and yet not be alone with you is more punishment than I can bear. Will you show me no mercy?"

Then the Rose of Jackson caught sight of the new arrivals. "Oh! There is García!" she said. "I cannot abide the sight of him. Come! Stay with me until he's gone." She drew Ruiz toward the curtained doorway.

Simón followed her closely. "My joy, Señorita, is too great to express."

CHAPTER NINE:

ENCOUNTER

Ding dong! Ding a-dong! Church bells woke Sydney, announcing the end of her life on the trail. There would be no more riding scout with her old single shot slung from her shoulder and the warm, steady movement of her pony between her knees, the light of the horizon in her eyes, and the landscape unrolling ahead of her from the faded prairies of a dying winter to the cool heights of green summer in the mountain passes.

The trek west had been hard. And by it she had lost her father who was the person dearest to her on earth. But of the journey itself, Sydney had no complaint. It had taught her well the inexorable power of single purpose: Nothing could turn them back. Not the attack by Indians. Not the burning of their father's wagon. Not the shrieking storm in the Sierra Nevada. Uncle Peter's wagon had rolled straight on into it to be swallowed by a wall of pounding hail and sleet, taking Sydney's daddy with it, for he had lain unconscious beneath the whipping canvas, dying of an arrow wound.

"Sydney!" Cecil's voice cut through the fog of her half-sleep. "Listen, Syd! Church bells! Uncle Peter and Aunt Aggie and Paul and the boys must be almost to Jackson by now! Get up, Syd!"

Sydney rolled over, kicking off her blanket. She had slept in the Spanish pantalón and the white linen shirt. She sat up and swung her feet to the floor, stretched herself and yawned, blinked at her brother who was tucking **his** new shirt into the top of **his** new trousers. They were not Spanish trousers (which fact spoke plainly of Ruiz' true intentions for them). "Are you going to wear those things to church?" asked Sydney.

"If I'm ever going to wear them at all, I guess there's no better place to break them in," said Cecil. There was a light in his eyes and a lilt in his voice that had been missing since the Indian attack.

"See Saw," said Sydney, "you'd better go without me. I've got nothing to wear but your old hand-me-downs. And this. I'll wait here."

"Aw, Sydney!"

"It's all right. I don't mind."

"I can put my old stuff back on so we'll match."

"No," Sydney insisted, getting to her feet. "You haven't looked that good since Aunt Aggie gave you a whole new suit of clothes for Christmas two years ago. You go without me. I'll change back to my old things meanwhile and re-roll our blankets so everything will be ready when you come back."

"Syd, I can't go to church without you."

"Yes, you can. Just tell Aunt Aggie I didn't have a dress to wear. She'll understand."

Cecil considered doubtfully, wondering if his relatives would blame him more for leaving Sydney at the hotel or for his staying away from the church service himself in deference to her want of appropriate attire.

"Go on," said Sydney. "You don't want to miss the sermon. It'll probably be about us."

"Syd, I don't feel right about this."

She put his hat into his hand and pushed him toward the door. "I feel right about it. Go ahead."

Reluctantly, Cecil went. Sydney watched him down the hall, waved him on when he looked back. Then she shut the door quietly, bolted it, and leaned against it, letting her eyes close in relief. She pretended for a moment that when she opened them again, the room would not be empty. But it was. She moved across it to gather her old clothes into a pile on the bed. She did not change into them immediately. But the minutes slid by until she knew must not delay any longer. And then, slowly, she removed the richly embroidered pantalón, pulled on the faded, twice patched trousers she had worn across the plains and mountains; replaced the fine linen shirt with the old one that had once been See Saw's. But she did not bind herself with the bandage, first.

Slowly, lingeringly, she folded the things Ruiz had bought for her in Rancheria and hid them all inside the blanket roll. All but the boots. Those she would wear from now on. Cecil's discarded clothes she wadded up and tucked through one of the outer folds of the pack. She had only just finished this when there was a knock on the door. She jumped, whirled to look at it. Then, she ran to throw back the bolt and jerk the door wide, her heart thumping as if she had run half a mile to get there.

But it was only Aunt Aggie who came in and caught Sydney in her arms to hug her hard. A tall, spare woman, Agnes Simpson was as strong and stringy as whang leather. "Sydney, honey!" she cried. "Thank the Lord you're safe! We had given up. When I saw Cecil, I cried like a baby. And then when I didn't see you..!" She stood back to look at her niece.

Sydney's freckled face was red, her eyes downcast. "And Daddy . . .?" she inquired, faint hope in her voice.

Aunt Aggie's answer was only to hug her again.

"Where did you bury him?" asked Sydney dully, looking past her aunt to the other woman who waited in tactful silence, watching their reunion with some emotion.

"Right there on the mountain, honey. That next day.

And we stayed for almost a week, hoping you and Cecil would be able to find us. But the storm had wiped out the trail. Paul and your Uncle Peter backtracked to a rock slide. They couldn't get across it. It had taken most of the hillside with it. And so, finally, we came on without you. It was the hardest thing we ever did in all our lives, leaving you behind like that. It was harder than burying your father. Because we just didn't know. This is Ida Thomson, honey," Aunt Aggie went on, gesturing at the woman who had accompanied her, "the pastor's wife."

Sydney looked at her again. "Miz Thomson . . ." she acknowledged.

"Hello, Sydney," the woman said warmly.

"We brought you a dress," Aunt Aggie announced, reaching to receive a package from Mrs. Thomson. "You can get out of those old rags of Cecil's. Here." She put it into Sydney's hands. "It's not brand new, but it will be all right, I think. When we get some time and a little money saved up to buy the cloth, we can make you a better one for Sundays. Sydney? Are you all right, honey?"

"Yep."

"You're not sick, are you?" Aunt Aggie put a hand to Sydney's brow and then her cheek.

"Nope."

"Do you want us to stay here with you while you change, or wait for you downstairs?"

"You can go if you want."

"All right. Don't be too long. We'll be in the lobby. Do you want us to take something down for you?" Sydney's aunt glanced doubtfully at the blanket roll and the rifle that leaned against the bed.

"Nope. I can bring it."

"All right," Aunt Agnes said again, and she drew Mrs. Thomson out of the room behind her. "She's been grieving her father all this time," Sydney heard her say softly to the pastor's wife. "It wrings my heart. Poor child."

Sydney stood where she was until their footsteps had retreated down the hall. Then she let the package she was holding drop to the floor. Running back to the bed, she threw herself down on it and punched the pillow till its stuffing threatened to burst through the seams. Then, she got up again, fetched the package and unwrapped it.

It was as if she were unwrapping her future life in the California Gold Country. She stared unhappily at the plain, brown dress and the grey-patterned apron that she laid out. But she did not look at them long. Swiftly, she changed into them, buttoned up the drab dress. It was loose in the waist and tight through the chest. But when she had tied the bibbed apron on over it, the poor fit was not so apparent.

Again, she undid the blanket roll to lay Cecil's hand-me-downs next to the beautiful Spanish clothes. By the time she was securing the pack once more, tears were falling on the backs of her hands. She dried them on her skirt. Seizing her cartridge belt, she wrapped it twice round her waist and buckled it. She jammed on her weathered hat and slung the heavy blanket roll over her shoulder. Finally, she caught up her rifle and crossed to the door. There, she stopped to look back and bid a last goodbye to the dreams she had dared to dream in this room. And then, she went out.

Aunt Aggie and the parson's wife were waiting in the lobby, surrounded by a group of respectful men. The women were relating the wonderful story of the Simpson Twins' deliverance from what had seemed certain death. But as spellbinding as was this narrative, Sydney's appearance at the top of the last flight of stairs instantly distracted the listeners, and they scrambled to receive her at the bottom. She paused defensively.

"Dan," Mrs. Thomson said to one of them, "will you help Miss Simpson with her things?"

With great alacrity, the privileged one bounded up to meet her, hat in hand.

"That's Daniel Perrin, Sydney," Aunt Aggie called to her reassuringly. "It's all right. You can let him have your pack."

Sydney looked down at her aunt and back at the young man before her. He had a clean, handsome face and a shock of straight brown hair. His eyes were clear and blue. His shoulders were wide and his hips were narrow. But Sydney had a new standard by which she now measured musculine beauty. Daniel Perrin did not have a black mustache, and his strength, though vigorous, lacked a certain native grace and elegance which Sydney had recently come to equate with male desirability. Nor was Perrin likely to call her "Pecosa". "Miss Simpson," he said instead, "if you'll allow me!"

With great reluctance, Sydney surrendered her blanket roll. "Give him the gun, too, honey," Aunt Aggie prompted from the lobby. "You won't need it anymore. There aren't any wild Indians in Jackson."

This brought a laugh from the men at the bottom of the stairs and a quick grin from Daniel Perrin. But Sydney only gripped her rifle tighter. "Then, he doesn't need it any more than I do," she said.

How the men roared! But Perrin's handsome face sobered. "Miss," he said earnestly, "if you'll let me carry the fire-iron for you, I promise I'll give it right back, first Redskin we meet between here and the church." He held out his hand to receive the rifle, confident of her acquiescence.

But Sydney's jaw had set. Deliberately, she slung the gun over her shoulder by its old strap. "Thanks just the same," she said and pushed by him.

The departure of the three women from the hotel emptied the lobby entirely. Had the astounded clerk with the visor been at liberty to quit his post, he would have gone, too. For there had not been such a procession to the Presbyterian Church since the pastor's eldest daughter had wed George Durham, the county's Foreign Tax Collector.

At the head of the parade strode Sydney Simpson with her brown skirts swishing around her new boot tops and her old single shot bumping on her back. On either side of her, Aunt Agnes and Mrs. Thomson kept pace. Occasionally, the two older women exchanged a look over the girl's faded hat.

Just behind them came Daniel Perrin, toting the blanket roll. He moved with a long, easy stride and kept his eyes on the rhythmic rocking of the cartridge belt wrapped twice round Sydney's narrow waist.

Both abreast of Perrin and behind him came a growing company of men: the curious, the hopeful, and the amused. There would have been still more, but on a Sunday morning, the majority of the male population was not yet on the streets again.

From the road that led into town beyond the hotel, a wiry Mexican checked his nervous red colt to watch the parade go by. "¡Oye!" he called to one of the late-comers at the end of the line. "What is happening, amigo?"

"There's a new unattached female in town!" he was told. "Name of Simpson! She'll be your neighbor, Fidel! Her folks live up the creek near you."

"Vea, pues . . ." muttered Buenrostro.

Feliz 86

CHAPTER TEN:

NO REASON TO STAY

Fidel Buenrostro watched the procession climb Church Hill before he rode his prancing colt on past the hotel and up the rise toward the Hang Tree. He crossed himself as he passed beneath its arching limb. Just beyond it, he halted in the middle of the street to stare at a fat sorrel mare that was tied to the hitching rack in front of the Eureka Dance Hall. The animal was asleep, or nearly so.

Unable to believe his eyes, Buenrostro rubbed them and looked again. And then he nudged his colt forward to turn in beside the mare. The young animal greeted its mother with an eager whicker and was nosed affectionately in return.

Dismounting, Buenrostro walked around to the mare's head. He was still standing there, thinking hard, when a dark-clad Mexican came from the corner of the sidestreet to confront him. "Buenos días, Señor," the man said unpleasantly.

Fidel looked round. "¡Muy buenos! Do you happen to know where the man who last rode this horse is staying?"

"I do not know who last rode it."

"That is too bad," mused Fidel. "Because I would like to talk to him. Do you think he is in there?" he added, gesturing at the dance hall.

"Where else?"

"With la Magdalena?"

The other shrugged. "La Magdalena may entertain whatever man she pleases. But when he comes out, he will answer to me."

"Ah! You are waiting for him! But do you not know who he is?"

"He will be the one who dares to claim this horse," said the dark-garbed man. And shooting a suspicious look at Fidel, he added, "You said you wished to talk with him? You must know who he is!"

"I know no more of him than you," professed Buenrostro. "But this horse is mine. It was stolen from me yesterday. Perhaps I should wait here with you."

"It is yours!"

"Amigo," said Fidel, "you do not accuse me of spending the night with la Magdalena? I am a happily married man!"

"¡Señores!" called a new voice from further up the street. It was Manuel Escobar. He came toward them on foot along the boardwalk.

"Carajo," muttered the dark-garbed man. But aloud, he said, "Good day, Patrón."

"Mariano García! They told me you had left town yesterday. They said you were gone to San Andreas."

"I delayed a day. I am waiting for the man who rode this mare."

"Why? Where is he?" asked Escobar.

García motioned at the closed doors of the dance hall. "I was told he went in there last night. But he has not come out. I have kept a careful watch."

Manuel's color heightened. "You have wasted your time, in that case, Mariano. He cannot have spent the night in there!"

"That is for you to say, Patrón."

"Who told you he went in?"

"Several men on the street. I did not know them. They caught this mare running loose and told me the rider had gone into the hall."

"Señor Buenrostro," Escobar said to Fidel, "are you not going to the mass this morning?"

"I was," said Fidel. "But then I saw this horse that was stolen from me yesterday."

"Stolen? You are lucky to find the animal in town. I advise you to take the mare with you now rather than to delay for what little you will learn of the matter here. I am afraid Mariano has spent the night watching an empty net. If he were better acquainted with it, he would know that there are many gaps in its mesh. García," he went on, turning a commanding eye upon the man, "go to San Andreas. Your friends must be impatient for your company."

"Manuel! What news?" This call came from the direction of the Hang Tree. All three men recognized the voice. All three were equally surprised to hear it. They turned as one to watch the approach of Simón Ruiz. He rode his steel-grey horse and wore his pantalón of wool and leather. The white of his shirt was spotless. His new twin pistols were thrust into the front of his gold waist sash.

Ruiz reined his mount to the edge of the boardwalk and returned the looks of the three men with interest. "Manuel," he said, propping himself on his forearm across the silver mounted pommel of his saddle, "who are your companions?" He gestured at García. "Is this Paulo Gonzalves?"

The bandit's black brow knotted into a tighter scowl than before. "I am Mariano García!" he said.

"García?" Ruiz considered him. "Do you work for don Manuel?"

"I work for no one!" declared the bandit. He turned to Escobar. "I take my leave, Patrón. As you have said, my friends await me. Señor," he warned Buenrostro, "if your mare is seen again where she is not expected, the man who rides her will not live to return her to you. Adiós." And touching two fingers to his hatbrim, García glared from face to face before he wheeled and strode off down the sidestreet from which he had first appeared.

"¡Por Dios!" Ruiz exclaimed lightly, watching Escobar. "The extent of your acquaintance astounds me, Manuel. And who is this other caballero? I no longer dare to hazard so much as a guess!"

Escobar glanced at Fidel. "No, he is only a local miner," he said disdainfully. "His horse was stolen yesterday."

"I am sorry to hear it." Ruiz turned to Buenrostro. "The horse thieves in the Gold Country must be numerous. I lost my horse yesterday, also. But I was fortunate enough to find it here in Jackson. Tell me about the missing animal. Perhaps I will be able to learn something about it for you."

"No, Patrón," said Fidel, indicating the fat sorrel mare. "I have already found her."

"This is the one? She was left tied like this on Main Street? I admire the thief's bravado. Have you any idea who he is, Manuel?"

"Of course not!" exclaimed Escobar. "You surely don't imagine that he would still be at liberty if I knew who he was or where to find him!"

"Well, but you do not expect this good man to feel satisfied merely at regaining his lost property. He will naturally want the thief to be identified and punished. And you cannot expect **him** to take up the robber's trail while you stand idly by, uncaring."

"¡Patrón!" Buenrostro hastily put in, addressing himself to Escobar. "I do not complain! I **am** satisfied to have the mare back. I make no demands of you."

Ruiz regarded Fidel in mild surprise. "Señor, can it be you are afraid to ask for justice from the son of don Fernando Escobar? Or that you doubt his willingness to aid you?"

Buenrostro lifted his hands palm out before him. "I have said nothing!" he protested. "I make no such claim! I beg this gentleman not to put into my mouth words that have never entered my head!"

"Manuel," Ruiz said gently to Escobar, "you disappoint me."

Manuel's face was mottling with equal parts of rage and shame, but he dismissed Fidel with a casual gesture. "Señor," he said, "go home to your wife and children with a peaceful heart. I do not blame **you** for the discourtesy of Simón Ruiz. Take your mare with you. And this time, keep her tied up. If you allow her to roam loose as you have so often done, you must not be surprised if some man less honest than yourself is tempted to lead her off."

Buenrostro did not presume to reply. But he looked quickly at Ruiz before he turned away. Simón did not seem to notice.

"You did not come to the house of Gonzalves last night," said Escobar to Ruiz. "Do you take my invitations so lightly, my friend?"

"Ah. Your pardon. I was on my way there when I caught sight of a man I fancied that I recognized. He was acting oddly, and I stopped to watch him."

"Oddly, Simón?"

"Yes. He came out of the rear of this building and looked carefully in all directions before he ran for the corner where he had a horse waiting. Throwing himself into the saddle, he spurred south out of town. I followed him."

"Did you see who he was? Did you catch up to him?"

"No. Unfortunately, my horse was too tired for that. But come! It is rude of me to keep you standing on the boardwalk. You have business to attend to. Otherwise, I would ask you to accompany me for breakfast."

"You have not eaten yet this morning!"

"No. And I am not much acquainted here. Where do you advise me to go?"

"Simón, you must indulge me in a whim. Get down! I'll show you a private breakfast room not many eyes have seen. Dismount. Dismount!"

Ruiz stepped down from the grey and wrapped the braided reins around the hitching rack where the fat mare of Buenrostro had stood as bait for him all night. And he followed Escobar around to the other side of the dance hall to a narrow passage between the outer walls of that building and the next. It ended in a door. At a story's height above it was a small, shuttered window.

Manuel knocked a curious rhythm of taps on the door and stepped back to watch the window. There was no response. He breathed an impatient word and struck the door three smart raps. Then two. Then one. And again he stood back and looked up.

This time, the shutters opened. "¡Ay, Manolito! How many times a morning will you come? Oh!" The fair speaker checked herself as she saw Ruiz. Simón quickly raised a warning finger to his lips, but converted the gesture to smoothing his mustache as Escobar turned round.

"Amigo," said Manuel, "you have said you are surprised at the extent of my acquaintance. I take advantage of it now to present to you la Magdalena, the fairest flower of the town."

"¡Encantado!" said Ruiz, bearing his head. The bandage was gone. The cut on his brow had healed into a deep, dry scratch at his hairline. "I do not doubt I look upon the very Rose of Jackson!" he said.

Magdalena smiled and lifted a hand to her raven hair

hanging loose upon her shoulder. "Who is this caballero, Manolito?" she asked. "And how do you presume to bring him to my private door at such an early hour?"

"This is the friend I told you of, predilecta: don Simón Ruiz Silvestre."

"The gentleman that was robbed!" exclaimed the Rose with some real surprise, for Simón had not confessed his identity to her the night before. And she had tactfully not pressed him. That he was a man of quality, however, she had never doubted for an instant.

"My horse has been returned to me, Señorita," said Ruiz. "But now that I see you, I could wish he were stolen again so to prevent my leaving Jackson in search of the thieves."

"No! Only hear the man! Manuel, you are rash to bring so handsome and courteous a rival with you. But will you come in, Señores?" And condescending another smile on Ruiz, la Magdalena closed the window.

The door below it was opened a few moments later by a pathetically ugly servant girl. Escobar passed by her with the contempt of familiarity. But Ruiz paused. "What is your name, niña?" he asked her.

She stared at him without attempting to answer.

"Can you not speak to tell me?"

She shook her head.

"Then I will call you Violeta. May I call you that?"

She ducked her head in a shy nod. A grotesque smile touched the corners of her twisted lips.

"Do you have a little grandmother, Violeta? Yes? And would you like to buy her a present? Here." He took from his pocket one of the several gold coins Escobar had loaned him the day before. "Buy your grandmother a gift with this. Tell her one of the gente de razón gave it to you, someone who wishes you both well. She will understand you, won't she?"

Another nod.

"Hide it away quickly, Violeta. Let no one but your grandmother know I gave it to you."

The coin promptly disappeared, together with the hand that held it, into an apron pocket.

Ruiz nodded approval and started up the narrow flight of wooden steps before him. Escobar had already gained their head and was impatiently waiting for him.

The breakfast room the two men entered was not large, but it was full of morning light. They were admitted by la Magdalena herself. The proprietress of the Eureka Dance Hall was clad in a crimson dressing gown, belted tightly at the waist. She gave her hand negligently to Escobar, allowing him to kiss it, while her large and luminous eyes were intent on Simón. The moment Manuel released her hand, she extended it to Ruiz.

"Señor," she said, tilting back her head to display a graceful throat framed by silky, midnight tresses, "there must be something special about you that the Flowers of Good Fortune have been so amply strewn before you. Yes, look surprised! What I have to tell you will astonish you. And Manolito, too."

"Magda," Manuel interposed, "I beg you feed my friend before you surprise him. He has had no breakfast this morning, so I bring him to you not only penniless but hungry."

The Rose of Jackson tossed her head. "He shall be neither when he leaves here. Come, Don Simón! Breakfast you can always have. First you must see what I am keeping for you. Trudis," she said to the servant who dodged back from the door as her mistress opened it, "bring breakfast for this gentleman. Run, girl! Don't stand there staring like a silly sheep."

Violeta shied nimbly out of reach and disappeared back down the stairs.

Magdalena drew Simón into the next room off the corridor which proved to be a parlor with lush appointments, including two large mirrors and a velvet loveseat. But it was what lay against the wall next to the door that she had brought him here to see. "There!" she exclaimed triumphantly. "Tell me now, if you dare, that the very angels of

82

heaven do not have you under their special protection!"

Ruiz exclaimed softly and dropped to one knee before his stolen saddlebags whose bulky shape promised well for their contents. But even as he put out a hand to investigate, he whirled and looked up at Escobar. Manuel had followed into the room, and in the first instant of Simón's surprise, he had taken a quick step closer. Now, as Ruiz sprang lightly erect to face him, Manuel retreated, erasing beneath a wondering smile the momentary hostility Simón had glimpsed all too plainly in his eyes.

"Are these packs yours?" asked Escobar. "But it seems a miracle! Magda!" he added, turning on the Rose who stood by watching. "Where did these come from? Who brought them here?"

"My servant's brother," she replied. "He is half witted, Don Simón. He told me he was charged on threat of death to bring them to me. And he begged me to inspect their contents that there might be a witness to his innocence, should there be a single coin too few, a single ounce of gold dust gone when they were given back to you. He left me not an hour ago. Nor could I coax from him any description of the man who had so used him."

"I will not question him myself, then," said Ruiz. "For I do not wish to add to the threat that must hang over him. Indeed, his life may already be forfeit. God grant it be not so. I appeal to you, Manuel. Protect the poor boy. In the name of your father's past pride. In the name of your own heritage. In the name of Ruiz Silvestre. For I promise you, if I hear that he is dead, I will seek you out to learn the reason and the manner of his death."

"¡Por Dios!" replied Escobar, spreading his hands. "You lay a heavy burden on my shoulders. How am I to protect a half wit from his folly?"

Ruiz dropped to his heels and seized the bulky saddlepacks, hoisted them to his shoulder and stood up under their weight without taking his eyes off Escobar. "It is the folly of others you must protect him from, Manuel. Señorita," he added to the Rose, "I will beg you to excuse me from the breakfast you have so generously offered me. I shall do what I can to remove the threat to your servant's brother by removing myself instantly from this town. Perhaps my absence will reassure the thieves that I no longer intend to look for them. Like the honest miner who found his stolen mare this morning, I declare myself satisfied with the recovery of my property alone."

Ruiz turned away, presenting his back to Escobar. But in the doorway, he whirled again to look hard at his peer. "I thank you for your kind attentions, Manolito," he said. "Señorita, forgive me. With your permission . . ." And he went out.

On the narrow stairs, he met the servant coming up them with a loaded breakfast tray. "¡Niña!" he said. "I cannot stay. I am sorry. But you will see me again. Give my greetings to your little grandmother. Hasta luego, Violeta." He left her staring after him and continued swiftly to the lower door.

He did not look around as he strode the length of the passage between the outer walls of the two buildings, so he did not see that the Rose of Jackson opened the window to watch him go. Nor that Escobar joined her there before it closed.

Regaining the boardwalk in front of the dance hall, Ruiz went to his horse, speaking softly to steady the high-strung animal while he tied the heavy saddlebags behind the cantle. "Quieto, potro. Now we go home. We don't even stop at the hotel, first. And the Pecosa will be thinking that Simón Ruiz does not keep his word because he does not care. Because the little gringa is not important to him. That hurts more than it ought to, potro. Quieto. So. So."

Gathering up the reins, he mounted and looked back toward the far end of town. He could see only the upper stories of the hotel jutting above the rise in the street. Yet even as he allowed his thoughts to enter a small, bare room marked Seventy-Six, his attention was commanded instead by the Hangman's Tree at the brink of the road's downslope.

"No," he muttered, checking the grey as it pranced a few steps in the other direction. "It shall, not be. Los californianos take care of their own! ¡Bueno!" he added to his horse. "¡Vámonos!" And releasing the pressure on the lines, he let the grey leap lightly into a rocking canter northwards . . . back the way he had come with the Simpsons in the freight wagon, back toward the little town of Rancheria where he was still owing money for the pair of pistols in his waist sash.

CHAPTER ELEVEN:

UNCLE PETER'S CLAIM

If Simón Ruiz thought with some regret of the room on the third story of the National Hotel, Sydney Simpson's mind was similarly occupied, and her anguish was much the greater. Her vision was of Ruiz' knocking at the door of an empty room, and on finding it unlocked, of his entering in great surprise and more than a little disappointment. She saw him searching through it for the message she had not thought in time to leave behind. She saw him looking from one of the narrow, wooden beds to the other, wondering which one she had slept in. Then, under the edge of hers, she saw him finding the worn-out boots she had discarded. He would pick one up, turn it over to inspect the round gap in its thin sole. She could see his private smile of satisfaction on thinking of the boots that he had bought for her, knowing they were on her feet, instead. He would bend to put the old boot down—he would not drop it—before he returned to the door. There, he would pause as she had, to look back and whisper a final adiós to his Pecosa.

It was upon reaching this point in her daydream that Sydney rubbed her smarting eyes. In silent and mistaken commiseration, Aunt Aggie reached to take her sun-reddened, callused hand and squeeze it comfortingly. Sydney did not return the pressure.

The reunited family was returning to Uncle Peter's Claim after the Sunday service. They rode in the same heavy wagon that had "crossed the wide rivers and crossed the tall peaks and rolled o'er the prairies for weeks upon weeks". Cecil drove. Uncle Peter had insisted that he should. Paul McCormick stood behind him in the empty wagonbed, leaning over the back of the driver's bench. Aunt Aggie sat between Uncle Peter and Sydney, who occupied the outermost edge of the wooden seat. The younger boys, Tim and Jacob, rode double on Red Dog.

Sydney no longer wore her gunbelt. At the church, she had been finally obliged to disarm. But she still had on her old hat, in spite of Mrs. Thomson's kind offer to replace it with something better. The parson's wife would have instantly sent her younger daughter, Amy, to fetch the sunbonnet that hung on a nail at the back door of the rectory, the one that Mrs. Thomson herself wore when she worked in her vegetable garden. It would have been no great sacrifice. Mrs. Thomson had other bonnets. But Sydney wouldn't take it, even though her refusal had embarrassed Cecil, disgusted Paul McCormick, and greatly amused Miss Amy Thomson.

The pastor's daughter was a pretty girl of sixteen, dimpling and plump. She had merry blue eyes and sunny yellow hair. Something about the way her curls bounced caught Cecil Simpson's attention. And Amy was kind enough to give him an encouraging smile upon his being introduced to her. It appeared, however, that this charity did not sit well with Paul McCormick.

Though he was half a head shorter than Cecil, Paul was a year older, and his features could be said to be more handsome. His nose was straight. Cecil's was snub. His jaw was square. Cecil's was narrow. His smile was broad. Cecil's was spare. For the Simpson face was basically sober, both in its masculine and feminine versions. Yet it was precisely this quiet sobriety that lent it charm. The short nose and the red-brown curly hair, the profusion of freckles, made the face clownish even in repose. Its rare smile was whimsical. Amy found she rather fancied it.

The Reverend and his wife had pressed the entire family to stay to Sunday dinner at the parsonage. Had it not been for Aunt Aggie's concern about Sydney, the invitation might have been accepted. Paul, in particular, had looked forward to sharing the minister's dinner table. But he was so glad to see Cecil again that he was not as disappointed as he might have been. Besides, he was just as glad not to have his best friend remain too long before the laughing eyes of Amy Thomson.

"Tell us what happened to you in the storm," he urged Cecil when the wagon had descended the hill and turned up the creek out of the sight of the church and the rectory.

"Well, we were stopped by the landslide," said Cecil. "That's how I lost the mule I was riding. I felt his feet start to go out from under him, and I saw the hillside moving. I jumped off and ran. Sydney was behind me. I waved her to turn around, grabbed her pony by the tail and let him pull me faster than I could run back to solid ground."

"Where did you go after that?" asked Paul.

"We had to ride north for a couple of days before we found a way over the mountains. But we didn't have much trouble. There was lots of game, and Syd had her rifle and plenty of shells. So we always had enough to eat. The worst part of it was worrying over you and Uncle Peter and Aunt Aggie and the boys. And Dad, of course. We thought maybe you had been swept away by the landslide. It was raining so hard, we couldn't see the wagon."

"Well, we're all back together, now," said Aunt Agnes firmly. "And nothing is going to separate this family again."

"Amen," said Uncle Peter.

Sydney glanced the length of the wooden seat at her father's older brother. And she wished ardently that it had been he who had died of the arrow wound and her Daddy who had survived. Uncle Peter looked enough like him to have sent a sharp dart of pain through his niece when she first saw him again at the church. But looks were the limit of the resemblance. Sydney's Daddy hadn't smiled any more than the rest of the Simpsons, but there had always been a twinkling star in his brown eyes and good humor in his quiet face. There had been approval, too, and pride when he looked at his children, especially his daughter. But Uncle Peter's eye was hard and often disapproving. He said little. When he did speak, he was listened to. Even Aunt Aggie heard him with respect. Of course, he usually agreed with her.

Uncle Peter's Claim was on the south fork of Jackson Creek, only three quarters of a mile from town. "I'm surprised no one had heard of you in the places we came through yesterday," said Cecil as he turned the wagon off the road to pull up in front of a tight little cabin made of split rails.

"Well, we haven't struck it rich yet," said Uncle Peter. "And we only go to town on Sundays. Besides, we've not been here very long. Less than a month. And our nearest neighbor is a Mexican."

Sydney turned her head again at this. But she let Cecil ask the questions. "That adobe we just passed?"

"Yes. That's it. The man's name is Ben Rooster. I suspect they call him that for the cocks he must keep."

"Cocks?"

"Fighting cocks. There are cockfights in Jackson every Sunday afternoon. They're popular with all the Mexicans, and with some of the Americans, too, I'm sorry to say. Paul? Aren't you going to help the ladies get down?"

Paul McCormick leaped for the side of the wagon. But when he dropped to the ground, Sydney was already standing in front of him. "I can get out of a wagon without help," she said and turned away.

Paul frowned after her as he reached up to help Aunt Agnes alight. Not but what Aunt Aggie could get out of a wagon without help, and had, several times a day for over four months. But that was no reason to go on doing it, she said, now that they had regained something like civilization.

"Mrs. Simpson," said Paul, as she accepted his guiding hand and climbed down, "something's going to have to be done about Sydney. She made us all the laughing stock in town, today. Poor old Cecil didn't know where to look. I felt really sorry for him when Miss Thomson giggled like that."

"Nevermind, Paul," said Aunt Aggie, patting his hand before she let go of it. "Sydney's had a bad shock, losing her Daddy and all. She doesn't care about anything else, yet. But she will. We just have to be a little patient. She'll soon be thinking about how nice Amy Thomson looked, and she'll want to be like her. You'll see."

"She's got a long way to go," Paul judged.

Sydney was standing in the doorway of the cabin, peering in, reluctant to enter. There was nothing new inside. Every piece of furniture there had come across the continent in Uncle Peter's wagon. The wooden chest, the iron bed, the shelf clock, the rocking chair, the footstool, the bureau and the half cupboard that sat on top of it. There was no table in the cabin. There wasn't room for one. Uncle Peter and Paul McCormick had constructed a trestle table outside. They had made benches to go with it.

"Sure looks like home, doesn't it, Syd?" Cecil said at Sydney's elbow. She glanced up. Her brother stood beside her with their blanket roll over his shoulder. His brown eyes were soft, his voice husky.

"Yep," said Sydney, dropping her own gaze to the ground so that he wouldn't read the lie in her look.

"This is a pretty spot, too, isn't it?" he prompted further, turning to survey the grassy banks of the creek, the little hills folding steeply into each other, the long, swelling slope of the pine-clad mountain.

"Yep," said Sydney.

"I can hardly wait to try my hand at gold panning!"

"Well, the creek's right there. I guess nobody will stop you."

"This is Sunday, you heathen!" Cecil reminded her, punching her shoulder playfully. "Gold panning is work."

"Even if you do it for fun?"

"Take your pack on inside, Cecil," called Aunt Agnes from where she still stood near the wagon with Paul. "Put it on the bed. Sydney and I will take care of it after dinner. Timothy! Jacob! Get off that pony! Give the poor animal some rest!"

"Go ahead, See Saw," said Syndey. "I'm going to look around back." And she left the doorway to circle the house. Behind it, some distance away, stood a grove of willows and beyond them, live oak and scrub. A path led invitingly into this wood, and Sydney was still fighting the impulse to run for it as fast as she could when Paul McCormick's voice recalled her.

"Sydney . . .?"

She turned as he came up to her.

"Sydney, I've not told you yet," he said, forcing out the reluctant words, "how glad I am to see you again. How glad I am that you—and Cecil—got through all right."

"I didn't think you wanted us to die."

"Of course I didn't want you to die!"

"Well, we didn't."

Paul struggled with his impatience for a moment and tried again. "I'm really sorry about your father, Syd."

"Yep."

"I know it makes you feel pretty terrible."

She stared at him suspiciously. "Do you actually have anything to say to me?"

"I just want you to know that I'm sorry."

"I didn't think you were glad."

"Of course I'm not glad!"

"Look, Paul. You can stop trying to be so prissy-nose nice to me. Let Aunt Aggie fire her own bullets. I'm not mooning around for a kind word from you if that's what she thinks. She sent you after me, didn't she? Well, you don't have to try to make me feel better. I'll do fine on my own."

"Oh?" said Paul, stung. He looked her up and down. "I don't know as I'd call what you do on your own so very fine."

"You don't have to like it," she returned. "Just leave me alone."

"That, Miss Simpson, will be my pleasure." And turning on his toe, he stalked back around the corner of the cabin.

The path into the woods was even more compelling, now. But Sydney turned away from it for the moment. She did not want anyone else to come looking for her.

Sunday dinner was not a very gala affair at Uncle Peter's Claim that day. There was food enough to go around, but it was only slightly better than the weekday fare, Aunt Agnes having added an egg custard to the usual beans and bread and bacon. The meal was consumed in silence. Paul McCormick was thinking bitterly of the parson's bountiful table and the parson's beautiful daughter. Cecil's mind made room for Amy Thomson too, among his plans for helping Uncle Peter strike it rich in the creek the next day and his vague worry about his sister.

Sydney was busy with her own plans involving the path through the woods and Cecil's old clothes inside the blanket roll. Her younger cousins, Tim and Jacob, limited themselves to staring at her and poking each other under the table. Aunt Agnes shook her head at them occasionally. Uncle Peter was oblivious to everything but his plate.

"Paul," said Aunt Aggie when the provender had been consumed and there were only empty dishes left, "why don't you and Cecil take the rifles and go hunting? We'll need some meat for tomorrow. I guess I had thought we might stay at the parsonage today, since we didn't know Cecil and Sydney were coming. We're going to be a little short, I'm afraid."

"I'll go with See Saw," Sydney offered quietly.

"No, honey. You can help me clean up here. Then we'll go through your pack and see what washing and mending need to be done."

Sydney opened her mouth to protest but saw the futility of it and closed it again. She turned a mute appeal to her brother.

Cecil glanced away. "Can I use your rifle, Syd?" he asked.

Uncle Peter looked up at this. "That's your rifle, now," he said. "Sydney has no more use for it."

"Can Tim and I go?" Jacob asked his father.

"Nope. You two have your Scripture study to do. Fetch me my Bible, Jacob."

Jacob exchanged a grimace with Timothy and rose slowly from the bench. Cecil and Paul went quickly to the wagon for the guns. Sydney reached across the table for the wooden bowls her cousins had left there and stacked them into her own. Then she rose, also.

Aunt Agnes watched her with a satisfied smile. "Land, but it will be nice to have another woman in this camp!" she said.

Ben Rooster's Rooster

CHAPTER TWELVE:

MRS. BEN ROOSTER

"Tell me about the Mexican that Cecil rescued," said Aunt Aggie when she and Sydney had washed the dishes and put them away in the half cupboard over the bureau. "It was nice of him to buy those clothes. What a shame he couldn't have given **you** something appropriate. Cecil didn't have a chance to tell us much about it at the church. But I gathered that the Mexican thought you were a boy. And so of course what he bought you wasn't right for you to wear."

"Nope," said Sydney.

"Where are those things? In your pack?" Aunt Agnes looked hungrily at the roll of blankets that Cecil had put on the bed. "Perhaps some of them will fit Tim or Jacob." She went to untie them, unrolling them the length of the bed. "These are good blankets," she said. "Where did you get them?"

"Mud Springs," said Sydney.

"Where's that? Oh! Oh, for heaven's sake!" Aunt Aggie ran her hand incredulously over the gold braid on the pantalón of wool and leather which now lay exposed to view. "Will you look at this!" she exclaimed, taking up the garment. But on glancing again at the bed, she saw the fine white linen shirt, and she caught it up, instead. Holding it by the shoulders, she stared at it for a moment. Then she turned toward the door. "Jacob! Jacob! Come here a minute!" She threw an excited glance at Sydney. "I think this will just about fit him!" she confided.

"It's mine," said Sydney. "It fits me."

Aunt Aggie's face blanked. "Sydney!"

"Simón Ruiz bought it for me. As a friend. Not for a reward."

"What are you talking about? You can't wear this, honey! It's a man's shirt. Or a boy's, anyway. And Jacob needs it so badly. The only whole one he has left is his Sunday shirt that he has on now. I've run out of scraps to mend his everyday ones. The last time his elbow went through, I had to cut some off the shirttail in order to patch it."

Aunt Aggie saw the linen underdrawers, next. Without putting down the shirt, she bent over the bed to inspect them. She laid out the fullness of the belled legs to see how much material was gathered up there. "You know," she mused softly, "I think I could almost make a shirt for Tim from these."

"You call me, Ma?" said Jacob from the open doorway.

"Yes. Come here. I want to see if this shirt will fit you."

"What shirt?"

"It's a beautiful, brand new shirt that someone gave Sydney. Turn around. Let's measure it across the shoulders.

There. Bless me! It's just about right. No, it's a little big, isn't it? Well, that doesn't matter. The way you're growing . . ."

"Is it from that Mexican See Saw told about?"

"Cecil," Aunt Aggie corrected him. "Yes."

"Why did he give her that?" Jacob looked over his shoulder at the shirt and then at the bed where the pantalón lay. "Golly Ned! Ma? Can I have those, too?"

"Certainly not! Let me or your father catch you dressing up like a Mexican dandy . . .!"

"It's a Mexican shirt," Jacob reminded her reasonably.

"A white shirt is a white shirt," said Aunt Agnes.

"What are those bloomers? Do Mexican men wear those?"

"Never you mind. Go back to your lessons with Pa. Oh! Wait a minute, Jacob. Sydney, honey, kick off one of your boots, will you? Let him try it for size."

Sydney did not move.

Aunt Agnes looked at her. "Sydney?"

"I don't have another pair," objected Sydney quietly. "Do you want me to go barefoot?"

"Of course not! We're going to get you something else to wear. You won't be tramping around the countryside any-more, so you won't need boots. And Jacob's are coming through in the soles. Tim's are even worse. We just don't have much left after that long trek out here. If it weren't for the kindness of the Reverend and his wife, I don't know what we would have done. Why, we're practically in rags, all of us. Sit down, honey, and pull one off. Just so Jacob can try it."

"No," said Sydney.

Aunt Agnes stared at her niece in shocked silence. Then she turned to her son. "Jacob, go back to your lessons."

But Jacob lingered, looking from his mother to Sydney, almost as startled by his cousin's flat denial as Aunt Agnes had been. "Jacob! Did you hear me?"

"Yes'm!" said Jacob, coming to himself and backing quickly toward the door. But once he was out of his mother's reach, the boy stopped again. He was certain that Sydney was going to be whipped the moment he was gone, and he loitered in part to delay that dreaded punishment for his cousin and in part to witness it, in case his mother's patience ran out before he left.

But Aunt Agnes only returned to the bed. Putting down the shirt, she picked up the embroidered pantalón and folded it into a neat square. Setting the garment aside, she re-rolled the blankets loosely, hiding the shirt and underdrawers and Cecil's old clothes inside them again. When she looked up to see Jacob still in the doorway, the boy dodged out.

Aunt Aggie retrieved her bonnet from a peg on the wall and put it on, tying its strings firmly under her chin. "Get your hat, Sydney, and come with me," she said. Picking up the folded pantalón, she went to the door.

Hesitantly, Sydney followed.

"Pa!" Aunt Agnes called as she stepped outside. "Sydney and I are going to the Roosters'! I want to see about getting her some slippers."

Peter Simpson looked up briefly from his Bible and nodded.

To Sydney's surprise, Aunt Agnes led her around the cabin and straight into the woods along the little path. She set a quick pace. Sydney looked about her with some interest as she walked. Though her aunt's apparent familiarity with the trail had greatly diminished its appeal, still, she was curious to meet their Mexican neighbors. They would not be gente de razón, of course, but they might know someone who was.

The footpath led through the trees for a quarter mile, skirting the bulge of a hill and running roughly parallel to the creek. The brushy woodland opened in several places to allow glimpses of the narrow valley and the road. It ended in a clearing behind the adobe house of Fidel Buenrostro. The crowing of the red and green rooster greeted them, together with the calls of children's voices, both in Spanish and English.

"Misa Agnos! ¡Mamá! ¡Está Misa Agnos! She is here!"
Two little boys, brown as butternuts, and clad only in loose-
fitting trousers, ran around the corner of their house to meet
their mother coming out. She stopped to stroke the two dark
heads that crowded close to her for a moment. Then she said
something that was neither Spanish nor English, and her
sons left her side to run back toward the visitors.

Aunt Agnes checked her stride as they approached her.
"Good afternoon, boys," she said stiffly.

"Gahf-ternoo!" they chorused. They looked past her at
Sydney.

"Mrs. Rooster," said Aunt Aggie, moving on to confront
her neighbor at closer range, "I would like you to meet my
niece, Sydney Simpson. Sydney, this is Mrs. Ben Rooster."

Sydney returned the woman's steady gaze. Mrs. Ben
Rooster was not Spanish at all. She was a Miwok Indian.
"You welcome," she said softly.

"I have something I thought you might be able to use,"
Aunt Agnes announced, smoothing the square bundle she
held. Abruptly, she offered it.

Mrs. Rooster received it calmly, not even looking down
at it. "You come in?" she said.

"Yes, we . . . Yes. Thank you."

Mrs. Rooster led her guests to the front of the adobe.
The cock strutted out of her way, but the hens ran a few
steps after her, clucking and twisting their heads to look up
at her. She moved smoothly, without haste, without wasted
motion. Aunt Agnes seemed all jerks and angles in comparison.

The adobe house was at least twice the size of Uncle
Peter's cabin. Beyond it was a low-roofed stable and a peeled-
pole corral. Tied to a stake in the shade of a tree was a white
goat. The animal lay comfortably on its chest, its knobby
knees folded under it, its lower jaw working with the ease
and regularity of an old gossip's. It watched Mrs. Rooster
with large, liquid brown eyes.

The interior of the residence was dim. There was only

one window, and it was small and placed high. What light there was entered through the wide open door. So did two or three chickens. Aunt Agnes regarded the birds with disapproval, but they did not seem to notice.

"You sit down," said Mrs. Ben Rooster. "I give you soup."

"No, thank you," said Aunt Aggie. "We have only just eaten. We wanted to talk to you about something." She looked around for somewhere to settle and chose a squat, solid chair with a woven-reed bottom. She signed Sydney to another.

Mrs. Rooster sat down on a four legged stool and waited patiently for her visitor to get to the point.

"Will you be able to use those trousers?" Aunt Agnes demanded, motioning at the bundle in the Miwok's lap.

Unhurriedly, Mrs. Rooster unfolded the garment and held it up to look at it. In the meantime, her two sons had sidled in through the door to stand staring at Sydney, touching their faces with their forefingers as if counting freckles on their own clear cheeks and grinning at each other in amusement. But now, they ran to either side of their mother and gazed open-mouthed at the embroidered pantalón. Mrs. Rooster lowered her arms to her lap and looked at Aunt Agnes. "Don't understand," she said.

"Why, I just thought . . . they're Mexican trousers, aren't they? My boys can't wear such things. And these were given to us. Don't you want them?"

"Who give them to you?"

"Sydney? Would you like to tell her the story? Or shall I?"

"Simón Ruiz," Sydney replied simply.

The Indian's eyes opened wide, and she clapped a hand to her mouth. Both her sons mimicked the gesture of astonishment.

"Why, what's the matter?" asked Aunt Agnes. "Do you know the man? You see, when he gave these trousers to Sydney, he thought she was a boy."

Mrs. Rooster's placid face was already displaying all the surprise of which it was capable, but she turned her eyes on Sydney in renewed amazement. Sydney contradicted her aunt with a slight shake of her head in answer.

The Miwok looked at the pants again before she carefully refolded them.

"Can you use them?" Aunt Aggie insisted.

"I keep if you don't want."

"Good." Aunt Aggie breathed a sigh of relief. Then, "Mrs. Rooster," she said, "I was wondering if you might be able to make my niece some slippers like the ones you wear. The boots she has on she is going to give to one of my boys."

This announcement shifted the attention of everyone in the room to Sydney's feet. She tucked them back against the legs of the chair and tried to lengthen the drape of her skirt to hide them.

"I make," agreed Mrs. Rooster. "Want now?"

"Well . . . yes, why not? How long will it take?"

"How good you want them?"

"Oh, just something serviceable. Like the ones you're wearing."

Everyone looked at Mrs. Rooster's feet. They were encased in comfortable moccasins, adorned with a simple star design of beadwork. "Finish one-two hour," she predicted. "You help? Done sooner, then."

"Yes," said Sydney before Aunt Agnes could refuse.

"I get leather," said Mrs. Rooster, rising from her stool.

"Sydney, honey . . ." Aunt Aggie began.

"You don't have to stay," said Sydney. "Here," she added, prying off one of her new boots against her toe. "Take these. See if Jacob can get them on. If his feet are too big, Tim's won't be. And if Tim's are too small, you can always keep them until he grows some more." She picked up the boot and held it out.

Surprised, Aunt Aggie received it, then watched while Sydney loosened the other boot against the chair rung. She rose to stand barefoot on the floor's cool, hard-packed dirt.

"I'll come when my moccasins are ready," she said. "You go ahead." She offered the second boot.

"Well, I don't know, honey," Aunt Agnes demurred. But she took the boot.

"I'll be all right," said Sydney. "I know the way back."

"I'll send Jacob to fetch you later," decided Aunt Aggie, "or Paul."

Sydney said nothing.

Hugging the boots to her bosom, Aunt Agnes took a few steps toward the door. She looked back. Sydney sat down and anchored her heels on the chair rung. Aunt Agnes retreated another few steps. Then turning, she left the house.

Relief washed over Sydney. She leaned back and closed her eyes. But tears rushed into them, crowded out of them. She bent her head to her knees and hid her face in her apron.

"¡Mamá!" one of the little boys said softly. "¡Está llorando!" Sydney felt a small hand patting her elbow. "You hurt, Misa?" She looked up. Warm, dark eyes met hers in mournful sympathy. "I sorry," said the child.

Sydney glanced past him at the empty doorway, afraid that Aunt Aggie might change her mind and would catch her weeping in a stranger's house.

"What you name?" the boy asked.

She looked at him again. "Sydney," she said, sniffing and wiping her nose on the backs of her fingers.

"Cindy?" he repeated.

This brought a new rush of tears, but through them, she smiled a little. She nodded.

"Why you cry, Cindy?"

She shook her head. "What's **your** name?" she asked.

"Federico Alonso Buenrostro," he replied proudly.

"Feather Eek Alone Zoo-what?"

"Buenrostro."

"Oh. What's your brother's name?"

"Joselito."

Sydney looked at the second boy. He was younger than Federico. He gave her a shy smile.

His mother was coming back across the room with a
large basket on her hip. She knelt easily on the floor in front
of Sydney's chair and took off the lid. Sydney leaned to look
into it and saw rolls and scraps of leather and several smaller
baskets. One of these Mrs. Buenrostro handed to Sydney.
The two boys stood close to watch her open it. It proved to
be a collection of tiny shells and assorted beads.

Federico reached in to gather several of the whitest
shells. He turned his hand over with an unconsciously graceful and eloquent motion to offer them to Sydney. She received them into her open palm. Thereupon, both boys made
a serious search of the little basket for more shells to match
the first ones. Their mother, meanwhile, unfolded a strip of
golden leather and spread it on the ground. "Foot here," she
said.

Sydney complied. The Miwok traced it expertly with a
knife blade. Then she turned the leather to a different place.
"Other foot," she said.

When she had the second pattern, she took the strip of
leather to the heavy table where she deftly cut both soles
against the wood. Returning with them, she gave one to each
of her sons. From another little basket, she produced for
them a pair of bone awls rolled carefully in fine leather. The
boys sat down on the floor and began boring a neat row of
holes along the soles' edges while their mother selected softer
pieces of leather to fashion the tops of the moccasins.

Sydney continued to hold the white shells in one hand
and the basket of beads in the other while the boys and their
mother worked busily around her. She saw the red and green
rooster look in at the door with pert jerks of his glistening
head. Then he entered with stately strut, alternately splaying
and folding his long toes and thrusting out his green/gold
chest. No one but Sydney admired this display. There was a
white hen under the table, but it did not so much as look up
from its meticulous search of the earthen floor. A second hen
had fluttered to a chair back and was preening itself like an
animated feather duster. The remaining chicken passed the

cock to potter back outside.

While Sydney sat quietly watching, a deep peace settled on the room around her, enveloping her in its quiet folds. Boots and rifles and shirts and ponies grew less and less important while the antics of the rooster took on a vital interest.

Stealthily, the big bird approached Joselito, apparently stalking the motion of the boy's bone awl. But when it came close enough to strike, Joselito noticed it and waved a hand to shoo it off. The rooster flailed its wings and pranced backward, ruffling its breast and neck feathers and uttering defensive threats.

Joselito laughed and baited the rooster some more. But then from outside came the sound of horses' hoofbeats. Both the boys and their mother got up quickly.

Half alarmed, Sydney rose also. But her fears were soon quieted. It was only the master of the house, Fidel Buenrostro, come home from his morning's adventures in the town.

CHAPTER THIRTEEN:

A LOSING BATTLE

It was after midmorning when Simón Ruiz rode back into Rancheria. Some of the town's citizens were still in church, and some were still sleeping off the effects of Saturday night; but many were now idling in the streets. In the gold towns of the Mother Lode, there was an iron-clad law against working a claim on a Sunday.

On the roads, however, traffic was heavy. Freed from their shovels and picks and pans, the miners spent much of the day visiting each other's towns and camps. By afternoon, the activities and amusements offered in the settlements attracted huge crowds. Horse races, gambling, bull and bear fights, cock fights, dances, and contests of strength and skill were common everywhere.

But at the moment when Ruiz turned his horse in at one of the long hitching racks in front of Dynan's Hotel, such general gaeity had not yet been instigated. The peace of the morning still prevailed.

The hotel's proprietor was comfortably ensconced in a chair on his veranda, enjoying the shade and talking with a grey-whiskered gentleman of genial but dignified appearance who sat there with him. But as he caught sight of Simón Ruiz dismounting at the bottom of the steps, John Dynan's portly figure straightened in astonishment. He started to his feet.

"What is it, John?" asked his companion, gathering himself to rise as well.

"Señor Ruiz!" exclaimed Dynan, half in answer to the other's question and half in greeting to Simón, who came lightly up the stairs.

"Buenos días, Señor Dino," said Ruiz. "I come to ask of you a service."

"But you . . . you have your horse again?" Dynan glanced past the Spaniard at the steel grey tied to the hitching rail. "And your saddlebags!" He took the hand Simón extended to him in greeting, his eyes resting for a moment on the pistols at his waist.

"Sí, Señor," replied Ruiz. "Muy buenos," he added to the other man who had risen politely to receive him.

"Your honor," said Dynan, half turning to his companion, "I present to you a man who was asking for you only yesterday. Judge Curtis, this is don Simón Ruiz Silvestre."

"How do you do?" said the magistrate.

Simón met and returned his firm grip. "Mucho gusto, Señor. I regret I must postpone what I want to talk to you before. I have other things now I must do. But I am honor to meet you."

"My pleasure," said Curtis. The judge had a pleasant countenance and a keen blue eye which generally commanded respect and confidence. "I have been hearing some interesting things about you, Don Simón," he said.

Ruiz bowed, then returned his attention to Dynan. "Señor Dino, I am going to the Valle like before. But I wish to finish with the business that I have with el señor France. Today, he is Sunday, and I know the store is not open for business. But I cannot stay until tomorrow. You direct me to his residence? Perhaps when he knows I come to pay him, he is willing to talk to me."

"More than willing!" put in Judge Curtis with a smile. "I don't doubt he's peering through his shutters and cracking his knuckles this moment! John, if you'll excuse us, I'll accompany Señor Ruiz across the street . . . in case Albert doesn't get the door unlocked before he reaches it." The magistrate motioned Simón to precede him back down the stairs.

"I understand you were waylaid on the road," said Curtis as they paused together at the hitching rack.

Ruiz stepped close to his horse and began to unfasten the saddlebags. "Who tells you this?" he asked.

"The whole town," replied the judge. "Everyone from the county sheriff to the local drunk. It was virtually the only topic discussed here yesterday afternoon. And your own return this morning will furnish the conversation for today, you may be sure. Have you actually found out the robbers so soon as this? And what has become of them?"

"No, Señor. Only the robbers have find out who is Simón Ruiz. And then, my properties are return to me through some persona inocente. I know little more about the bandidos than I did yesterday."

"Little more," repeated the judge. "But something more." Ruiz met the magistrate's sharp blue eyes squarely for a moment. Then he lifted the saddlebags from behind the cantle and threw them across his shoulder. Their weight thudded solidly against his back. "I know they know now who I am," he said. "I know they watch me carefully. I show them I am going home to the Valle and leave them alone."

"But surely you do not expect me to believe you will let this incident rest?"

"I expect of you nothing, Señor."

"Just so," said the judge. "Don Simón, I wonder if you would grant me the pleasure of your company for dinner. Unless you feel you cannot stay in Rancheria for even that amount of time."

Simón again considered the judge's steady gaze again before he answered. "You are most kind. And my horse, he is tire. I let him rest until this afternoon before I can go on. I accept your invitation."

"Excellent," said Curtis. "I am presently staying here in John's establishment. He keeps a decent table. May I expect you to join me when you have concluded your talk with Albert France?"

"Como quiera. As you wish."

The magistrate nodded in satisfaction and accompanied Ruiz across the street to the shuttered door of the General Store.

Albert France had his door open before Ruiz had gained the covered porch. The shopkeeper received his customer with smiles and courtesy. He invited him to come in and pressed him to take some refreshment. This was politely refused. Judge Curtis was urged to remain, also. But the magistrate preferred to return to the hotel. Several passersby pushed in, however, unasked. Albert desired to know how he could be of service to Ruiz.

Simón put his saddlebags down on the counter. "I keep my word to you," he said. "You have count the gold I give you before?"

Albert admitted that he had.

"And do I owe you more? Or do you pay me?"

France rubbed his hands. "I have written up the receipt of the sale," he said. "But you need not pay the balance immediately. If it's not convenient."

"How much?" asked Simón.

"There was the price of the clothing you purchased as well," The shopkeeper insinuated. "And what you paid me yesterday did not cover the cost of the guns alone. I will get the receipt so that you can see the amount for each item."

"¡Hombre! Say at once what I owe you. Here on this counter are six thousand dollar in gold dust and coin. Do you imagine that I come to bargain with you? Your prices, I am sure they are fair. You have the reputation to be reasonable. I have the reputation to pay the fair price. Only tell me what it is."

Albert France glanced around at their several witnesses.

"The balance for the pistols is . . . uh, one hundred twenty-five. Including the box of ammunition. The other things amounted to sixty-eight dollars. The clothing you bought is not made locally. And it is expensive to ship to the Foothills. I must be able to cover that cost and still make some profit in order to stay in business, you understand."

Simón opened one of the flaps of his saddlepack and felt inside the leather pouch. He drew out two buckskin bags which jingled musically as he deposited them on the counter. "These bolsitas have each one hundred dollar in ten dollar coin. You take them. We don't argue the difference, eh?"

"Señor Ruiz!" protested France. "I would not take more than you are actually owing."

Simón untied one of the sacks and turned it upside down on the counter. France helped him trap several bright pieces that would have rolled off the edge. One of these, Ruiz slid toward himself, the rest, he pushed closer to France.

"But this way, you will still owe me three dollars," said the shopkeeper, smiling. "Give me that coin, and I will give you smaller change. Or, if you prefer, you may purchase something else, and we can reach an agreement on the price so that it will come out even."

Impatiently, Ruiz glanced around. A leather lariat behind the counter caught his attention. "How much for la reata?" he inquired.

France followed his glance. "That one there? You have a quick eye for quality. It is the best one I have ever stocked. I was asking fifteen dollars for it. But for you, the price is thirteen."

"Bueno," said Ruiz, tossing up a gesture of indifference. "I buy him." He reached into his saddlepack and produced another buckskin bag. He shook a gold piece from it into his hand and added it, as well as the other, to the loose, shining pile on the counter. Tying shut the sack, he looked absently about him while he waited for Albert France to take down the leather rope.

Hanging against the shelves on the far wall was a beautiful white dress of Spanish style. Its wide skirts were laced with innumerable yards of ribbon and flounced with soft lace. Mentally, Simón tried it on an American girl with red-brown curly hair, then shook his head and smiled at himself in amusement.

But Albert France had turned back toward the counter in time to catch his appraising look. "The gown, Don Simón, would delight any fair señorita in the Valley." He put the coiled lariat on the counter beside Ruiz' saddlepack. "You have a pretty niece, perhaps?"

Simón drew himself up, frowning at the shopkeeper's presumption. But Albert looked back at the gown on the wall, and Ruiz could not help but follow that look. Nor could he keep from seeing Sydney Simpson in the dress, its velvet weskit of emerald green nipping in her narrow waist and its wide, lacy neckline exposing a whole constellation of freckles he had not yet seen, together with part of what the new linen shirt had covered but had not been able to disguise.

Ruiz shook his head again. By the time he could return to Jackson from his uncle's ranch, Sydney would surely be well on her way to Simpson's Bar. Nor would he be at liberty to follow her until he had openly confronted Manuel Escobar and had administered just punishment to his band of rabble thieves. Not that Ruiz had seriously intended even then to look for her. There was no point in his pursuing the acquaintance. Besides, what would Sydney want with such a dress? Where would she wear it? This was nothing but a foolish fancy. Ruiz shook his head a third time.

"There are others," Albert France suggested. "If your niece prefers a different color . . ."

"My niece, Señor, does not expect the tío bring her dresses."

"Of course not," France agreed. "But she does not have to know its source! There are ways in which a man as clever as yourself may give such gifts to one he's fond of, merely for the happiness of seeing the delight of the receiver."

Ruiz' face darkened in hue by several shades as he recognized the man's correct appraisal of his character. Seizing the leather rope, he put an arm through its coil to hang it on his shoulder. But as he laid hands on the saddlebags, he glanced a last time at the dress, and so vividly did he see Sydney decked in all its ribbon and lace, he knew it didn't matter whether she would ever wear it anywhere or not. She could not wear the pantalón he had given her, either. Gifts need not be practical to please. "How much?" he asked.

"Because it is yourself that asks me," replied France, "I will part with it for only seventy-five dollars."

Ruiz darted a sharp look at the shopkeeper's innocent expression. "Señor," he said, "my niece can make a dress with twice the cinta and encajes for half the sum you say."

"I do not doubt it, Don Simón. But it is as I have told you: the price of freight adds double to the cost here in the Mother Lode. And the lace on the gown is imported from Spain. Still, to afford you the satisfaction of seeing that sweet smile of surprise which is tempting your generous nature, I will sacrifice my profit. You can have the gown for fifty dollars."

Ruiz stood a moment longer, staring at the wily merchant, undeceived and undeceiving. "Wrap it in paper," he said and fished in his saddlepack for the buckskin bag he had just returned to it.

CHAPTER FOURTEEN:

THE INTERVIEW

Judge Curtis received his luncheon guest in the privacy of his suite on the hotel's second floor. "Don Simón! Please come in. John has seen to the care of your horse, I trust?" Closing the door behind Ruiz, he directed the Californian through the first room to the second which opened onto the cooling shade of a black oak tree at the corner of the building.

Ruiz laid his saddlebags beside the chair indicated by his host and sat down with a frank sigh of relief. He dropped his hat on top of his pack and ran his hand through his glossy black hair. "Is kind you invite me, Señor Cortés," he said. "I promise I bring a good appetite."

"I shall consider it my duty to fully assuage it, Don Simón." The judge poured his guest a glass of red wine and held it out for him to take.

"Salud," said Ruiz, gesturing a toast before he drank deeply of the fruity beverage.

"I am sorry to have missed meeting you yesterday," said the judge. "John gave me to understand that you were looking for new customers for your uncle's beef. And I am definitely a good prospect for such business."

"Ah, but it is as I tell you before," Ruiz reminded him. "I must excuse myself from the negocio. For I cannot say with certainty when I am able to bring another herd from the Valle. But I do not forget your interest."

"The fact is, I have had some thought of starting my own herd," said Curtis. "I was on the point of approaching Jack Sutherland on the matter. You are acquainted with the Sutherlands, of course?"

"I hear the name. I do not meet the man. Has a ranch near here?"

"Yes," said the judge, sipping his own wine and pausing to appreciate its flavor. "Two of them. One on Dry Creek, near the town of Freeze Out. The other one lies between here and Pokerville. Jack Sutherland is a personal friend of mine. As is William, Jack's son. Will is a young man of about your own years, and of a similar desire to make his mark in the world, if I may presume to say so much."

Ruiz looked at his host over the rim of his glass before he downed another third of its contents. "You flatter me," he said. "I only wish to be of service to my uncle. Things are not the same for the rancheros in the way they were. We see our boundaries acortándose . . . how you say? Coming smaller. We see our neighbors, the americanos, they are helping themselves to what they find around them more and more often. We sell the cattle, Señor Cortés, before they are stolen from us. This way, at least we have something to show for the loss. There has been a time when we give away to a need we see is real. But that time is over. The need will soon be our own."

The magistrate made no reply. He sipped his wine and watched his guest.

Ruiz continued. "This man Sutterlan you say, I do not doubt he does well with his cattle, here. From what I see in the Gold Country, the men that become most rich are those that sell things to the miners. Whether it is cows they sell or a pair of pistolas or a dress with lace for a woman. Not all the bandidos, they are on the roads, Señor."

Judge Curtis smiled. "I fear you are right," he agreed. "Speaking of bandits, did you know that the Sutherlands once entertained the famous bandit chief, Joaquín Murieta, himself?"

Ruiz frowned. "Be careful what you say to me," he warned. "Remember that I am the nephew of don Diego Silvestre Cisneros."

"I did not mean to offend. I offered the hint only because I believe I know Joaquín's story better than do many 'americanos'. And while I cannot say I am precisely one of his admirers, still I believe much of what he did and tried to do was not without justification. I believe he was a man of great talent and some honor. The story of his association with Jack Sutherland and his son, William, is a case in point. May I tell it to you?"

Ruiz threw himself back in his chair and stared at the magistrate without answering.

Curtis sipped his wine. "It seems Joaquín was passing through this region with some of his men, looking for a likely place to spend the night," the judge said evenly. "He did not know of the Sutherlands' new holdings on Dry Creek. But he was acquainted with Jack. He had had some sort of dealings with him earlier . . . all quite above board and amicable, according to Sutherland, though he doesn't talk about it much. Under the circumstances, I suppose that is understandable. At any rate, a feeling of mutual respect had already been established between them.

"On this particular occasion I am telling you about," continued Curtis, swirling the ruby liquid in his glass, "Jack's son, Will, was alone at the new ranch on Dry Creek. His father had left him in charge there while he himself returned to Pokerville on a matter of business.

"Will would have been about eighteen years old then. But his father had trusted him to carry through on an important sale of stock to certain citizens in Freeze Out. The proceeds amounted to several thousand dollars. William had received the money and was counting it out on the table in the ranch house alone when he heard horses coming. A few moments later, he looked up to see in the open doorway not Jack Sutherland but Joaquín Murieta."

Curtis paused here for effect. Simón was watching him as before. The line of his mouth was sour beneath his black mustache.

"Will Sutherland had never seen Murieta, yet he could not help but guess who he was," said Curtis. "However, he pretended that he was entirely ignorant of his visitor's identity. He asked him to come in and begged his pardon for not having gone out to receive him, explaining that he had assumed it was his father returning.

"Joaquín looked at the piles of gold on the table and asked him if he did not feel he was taking a foolish risk by surrounding himself with so much coin when it was rumored that Murieta was in the neighborhood.

"William replied that he was perhaps too trusting, but that he had no fear because Murieta was well known to his father and it was said that Joaquín remembered his friends and respected their property.

"Thereupon, Murieta demanded his father's name. When he learned it was Jack Sutherland's son to whom he was speaking, the outlaw's expression changed, but he still advised Will to put away his gold. Young Sutherland then asked him if he and his men would care to join him for supper. Joaquín accepted. He requested permission to spend the night there as well. Will told him he was entirely welcome.

"In the morning," went on Judge Curtis, "Murieta courteously took his leave and insisted that Will should have payment for his hospitality. Putting down a handful of double eagles on the table, he suggested that it might perhaps be better if Will were not to mention to anyone but his father that he had had guests for the night. You may be sure that William took this hint to heart. The story did not come to light until after Murieta's death."

Judge Curtis paused again to steadily return Ruiz' look. "There have always been rumors, of course, that Joaquín is not dead," he said. "And of late, those rumors are growing. Forgive the question, but I trust your word above so many others to whom I have had access. Don Simón, in your opinion, is there any basis for such speculation?"

"Señor," said Ruiz, "you may ask questions which I do not choose to answer them. But I think you want to know if the bandidos that have rob me and leave me on the road for dead are the men of Joaquín. Or you perhaps wonder if Simón Ruiz himself is Murieta."

Curtis waited calmly, expecting a round denial. But Ruiz only drained his wine glass and leaned forward to set it on a little table within easy reach. Then he sat back again and considered his host.

The magistrate grew a bit uncomfortable under the steady scrutiny of the Spaniard's black eyes. "I assume nothing, Don Simón," he said. "I do not accuse you. But I beg you for a simple answer. Is Murieta dead?"

Simón made no reply, nor so much as twitched a finger.

"You do not trust me," said the judge.

"The bandidos are not Murieta's men," said Ruiz. "And I am only the youngest son of don Sebastián Ruiz Zalamea, a rancher on the southern coast. The holdings of my father are not threatened. Those of my uncle are. I do what I can with honor to assist him. Yesterday, I am returning with the payment from the sales I have make for him when I am rob by some cholos that I don't know who they are. I am rescue by two young americanos and ride back with them to Yackson. There, I find my horse tie to the Hanging Tree. I find my saddlebags in the house of someone who does not know who bring them there. I do meet a man that I suspect, but I must prove him guilty, first, before I can do more. This that I tell you is the truth. And it is more than I have desire to tell you. I have not answer Cheriff Finits, yesterday. I do not answer you, today. I regret that you have press me. I do not wish to show you such discourtesy."

The judge shook his head. "It is I who have presumed upon my role as host," he said. "I beg your pardon, Don Simón. But surely you must understand that the capture of this band of thieves and cutthroats is of vital interest to every community in the area."

"I regret, Señor. I have no proof to offer you."

"But your refusal to discuss your speculations seems suspicious."

"You still think that I am Murieta?"

"I do not."

"But you think that I might be a bandit."

"I think that you might know someone who is a bandit."

"And you think that I go to this man and I say to him, 'Amigo, you have make the small mistake. You have nearly kill me on the road and take my gold. Please to give me back my money and next time, be more careful who you are shooting off the horse.' Eh?"

Judge Curtis smiled slightly. "Is this not exactly what you hope the thieves will think?"

Ruiz started. Then, he made a graceful gesture with one hand. "Señor," he said, "with reason you are the magistrado."

Judge Curtis inclined his head in acknowledgement. "And when you have completed your errand for your uncle, will you return to take up your search for the thieves?"

"I cannot ignore what has happen," Ruiz admitted.

"Surely the leader of the bandits must know that?"

"Perhaps he does. But when a man is corrupt and cowardly himself, he may assume the others are weak as he is. I do not think this man expect me to return alone. Nor does he expect me to come soon. He believe that I must feel as much hatred for americanos as he does himself. And he does not believe I that concern myself in their behalf. He has convince me that I am not attack at his command, that those who allow him to direct them act without his word. He also has convince me that if I return, he will try to kill me. What he has not convince me is to stay away and pretend I do not know he is disgracing his own name."

"He is a man of breeding and education, then," said the judge. "Like yourself."

Ruiz did not reply to this.

"He has robbed you of more than your horse and your gold, in that case," pursued the magistrate. "He has robbed you of your impeccable reputation, merely by association. He has disgraced you as well as himself. So you must avenge your honour by denouncing him. And when you have established this man's guilt beyond his own means to deny it, what then? Will you give him over to the sheriff? Or will you kill him yourself?"

Ruiz' black eyes glittered as he stared at the judge.

"Don Simón," said Curtis, leaning toward him, "I feel it is my duty to remind you that any such action on your part might be construed as premeditated murder in a court of law. I acknowledge that your own social order predates the American one in this state. Yet it is the American one that prevails. And in our society, the power to prosecute and avenge is given only to the Law and to its official representatives. Consider, therefore, whether your private satisfaction will be worth the price."

Still, Ruiz said nothing.

"Will you not give me the name of this man you suspect? Will you not agree to work within the established limits of legal justice so that its powers can aid you? Our goal is identical, Don Simón. Can we not unite in our means to achieve it?"

"Señor Cortés," said the Californian, "forgive me. But I have no faith in your Law and the representantes you call them. Does your Law prosecute the gringos who slaughter and steal the cattle of my uncle? Or those who build their houses on his land and cultivate it as their own before his eyes, to grow rich on stolen harvest? There was agreement the government of your country make with mine: the rights of californianos are to be respect. But where is this respect? Where are its representantes? And yet, when it is mexicanos who are the thieves, you expect me to help you catch them. If those cholos who shoot me shoot only me, if they never fire on a gringo, if they take only my gold, does the Cheriff Finits prosecute them? Señor, I fear that I offend you if I stay longer here. Permit me to leave you." Ruiz reached down for his hat and would have risen from his chair, but Judge Curtis stopped him with a gesture.

"Don Simón! I do not find the truth offensive. Stay! I know you will carefully consider what I have said. And that is all I ask. Come, I have exacted a heavy price for the hospitality I offered you. But no more. Let me refill your glass, and we shall talk of more indifferent matters."

Slowly, Ruiz sat erect. "And what topic would you propose to the man you have suspect to be bandido, have call the asesino to his face?" He put out the flat of his hand to cover the mouth of his glass as the magistrate reached for the wine bottle. "Do we talk of the climate, next? Or the price of cattle on the coast?"

"Tell me what has become of the two young Americans that rescued you," suggested the judge.

"Ah! You imagine, then, that I care little about them. Do you not know I truly owe my life to them?"

"How so? Did they do more than pick you up off the road?"

But now, Ruiz could not sit still. He sprang from his chair and advanced a few steps toward the window. "I do not forget them," he vowed. "And when I have done this thing I must do, I will look for them. If it is not for the Pecosa . . . este, el pecosito, Simón Ruiz is dead. I cannot forget such a debt as that. Can I?" he demanded, whirling to confront the magistrate.

But before Judge Curtis could fit some soothing words into a courteous phrase, the interview was interrupted by the arrival of the promised lunch, graciously borne into the room by Mrs. John Dynan herself. And the presence of the proprietor's lady served to recall Ruiz to all his former cool courtesy. He was prevailed upon to be seated once more. And before he took his leave of the magistrate that day, he had done ample justice to the culinary arts of the chef of John Dynan's Hotel.

CHAPTER FIFTEEN:

COME COURTING

Fidel Buenrostro had declared himself charmed to meet his new neighbor. And when he was told that she was one of the Americans who had rescued Simón Ruiz from the robbers and the roadside, he was all amazement.

"But, Señorita!" he exclaimed. "Don Simón tells me last night they are two **boys** he rides with in the wagon."

"Are **you** the friend he said he had in Jackson?" countered Sydney.

"I have the honor to be his friend, yes."

"Where is he now?"

"Eso sí no sé. I see him in town this morning, talking to another man he knows."

"Was it Manuel Escobar?"

"Yes! But do you know him, also?"

Sydney explained, then, how she had seen Simón's grey horse under the Tree and how she had challenged Escobar for fear he would ride it away before Simón could stop him. And how Simón had introduced her to Manuel.

Buenrostro's surprise deepened into alarm as he listened. Looking around at his family, he saw his own concern mirrored in the eyes of his Indian wife. He saw Sydney's thirst for action reproduced in the eyes of his two young sons. "We go inside to talk more about this," he decided, for they were all still standing in the yard. "Niños, put the yegua and the potro in the corralito. Misa Cindy, you come in again?

"So, don Simón knows that you are my neighbor, but he doesn't tell me," Buenrostro said when they were settled once more on the available chairs. The perching hen had been sent squawking outdoors. The Mexican's wife took up her work on the moccasins as quietly as if it had never been interrupted. But she listened closely to what was passing.

"No. I don't think so," Sydney answered. "Because he thought that See Saw and I were going on to Simpson's Bar. See Saw didn't find out that Uncle Peter had a claim here until after Simón left. Will he come back here today? Simón, I mean?" she added hopefully.

Buenrostro shook his head. "I don't think he does. He has pretend to don Manuel he does not know me. This, so I am not suspect of helping him."

"Simón thinks Manuel is mixed up in it, doesn't he?"

"Don Manuel is not an honorable man," said Fidel. "And he hates the americanos because they have ruin his father. He thinks to make them pay. But he does not do this thing himself. He gets other men to do it for him. Those other men are the bandidos."

"But why did they rob Simón if it's the Americans they're out to get?"

"I don't know. Perhaps is only that the robbers find out he is carrying much gold. And they can't resist to take it. But perhaps is other reason. Perhaps is part because the family of Silvestre and also family of Ruiz is rich. Escobar lose everything. Silvestre has lose little. Don Manuel maybe hates Simón for that. Sabrá Dios. But there is risk for you. Whole town knows there is a señorita, name is Seensome, living here. Whole town knows you come from Drytown in a wagon. And soon, the whole town hears how you have rescue Simón Ruiz. No. I do not like this."

Fidel looked hard at Sydney for a sign of fear. He saw nothing but enthusiasm. "Señorita, I think the best thing we do now is to say nothing, pretend we don't suspect. When I see don Simón again, I ask him what he thinks we ought to do."

"You'll tell him that I'm here? I mean, at Uncle Peter's?"

"Yes, of course, Misa Cindy."

Sydney allowed a sigh of happy satisfaction to escape her. "It'll be all right, then," she predicted. "Miz Ben Rooster?" she added to the Miwok. "Can I help sew those?"

"¡Papá!" said Joselito. The boys were sitting in the doorway, drawing in the dirt with a stick. "Man coming."

"No se levanten," said Fidel, signing his family and Sydney not to rise. "I go see." The Mexican went to the door, stepped over his sons and looked in the direction of the woody path.

"Afternoon to you, Ben Rooster!" came a hearty voice. "I'm sent to bring Miss Simpson home. She's still here, is she?"

"¡Señor Perrino! Sí, cómo no. Pase usted. ¡Pase!" And Fidel gestured his children to move out of the doorway.

A moment later, Daniel Perrin filled it. Hat in hand, he ducked under the low frame and stopped just inside, his blue eyes flashing a circuit of the room before they lit on Sydney.

She looked up from her work on the moccasin, the light in her own glance extinguished, all hint of her recent excitement gone from her serious face. "I can't leave, yet," she said. "I'm still barefoot." She displayed the evidence briefly, artlessly affording Perrin a tantalizing glimpse of her neat ankle and well turned calf as well as her little pink foot.

The Miwok rose. "You sit, Mista Perrino." She indicated her chair to Daniel. "We almost done, now."

Perrin took immediate advantage of this courtesy, and went so far as to position his seat closer to Sydney's in order to inspect her work. "Your folks said I'd find you here, Miss Simpson. I hope you don't mind. I'd have given you more time to get settled-in-like before I came bargin' after you, but tomorrow's Monday, don't you know. I got my claim to work on. And it's a whole week until next Saturday night. I was afraid some other feller might beat me to the punch."

"What punch?" asked Sydney.

"Why, I mean, there's plenty of boys in town that know you've come, Miss Simpson. And a week's a long time to just let well enough alone."

Sydney looked from Daniel Perrin's handsome face to the weathered visage of Buenrostro in search of better explanation. But the Mexican only stood watching, his chin in his hand, his dark eyes thoughtful. Sydney turned to the Mexican's wife. The Miwok was bent over the other new moccasin. And the two little boys had retreated into silence in the presence of the gringo. Sydney returned to her stitching.

"Your folks told me you were mournin' your pa, Miss Simpson," said Perrin. "I was right sorry to hear about it."

"I don't know why you should be. He was nothing to you. You didn't know him."

"But I know you. And you're somethin' to me."

"I am? What?"

"You're the prettiest girl up Jackson Creek."

Sydney stuck her finger with the bone needle. "Heck!" She dropped the moccasin in her lap. "You've been talking to Aunt Aggie, too, haven't you?" She put her finger in her mouth to soothe its sting and stared accusingly at Perrin.

"Miss Simpson, all I talked to your folks about was to ask them where you were and could I come find you." He reached to take her wrist. "Did you stab yourself too deep? Let's see."

She jerked away. "It's all right."

"Señor," said Fidel, coming to Sydney's rescue, "I hear it said in town that there is shooting last night in the canyon to the west. Do you learn more about it?"

Perrin looked around. "Funny **you** should ask **me**," he said. "It's mostly Mexicans live up that way. I'd have thought you'd know all about it."

Buenrostro shook his head.

"Well," said Daniel, shifting his weight to face his host more squarely, "the sheriff and a group of concerned citizens rode over there early this mornin'. They didn't find nothin' much. A few tracks. And near the third house, the brush was some broken. But the place was locked tighter'n a drum. Wasn't nobody there."

"Do you know who lives in it?" asked Sydney, forgetting her work.

Perrin met her brown eyes. "Some Spaniard named Whatchamacallit Gonzales. But I don't know why it should concern you, Miss Simpson. He's nothin' to you, is he?"

Sydney returned to the moccasin in her lap.

"Paulo Gonzalves has leave Yackson?" asked Buenrostro.

But Perrin did not answer. He was watching Sydney. "Hey," he said, leaning to lift her chin on his fingertips, "I was only teasin'."

She withdrew sharply from his touch and hitched her chair farther away.

"You don't really know him, do you?" asked Daniel.

"I never heard of him." Sydney went on with her stitching.

"What's happened to your gunbelt? And your firearm?" Perrin prompted. "You didn't come to visit this Injun squaw here without 'em, did you?

Sydney met his eyes again. He was smiling.

"I hear tell you're a regular sharpshooter, Miss Sydney. The stories about you in town are gettin' taller and taller. Come next Saturday night, you may be asked to prove what you can do with that gun."

Sydney thought about this. A little color crept into her face. But then she shook her head. "Aunt Aggie and Uncle

Peter wouldn't let me," she said. "My gun belongs to See Saw, now."

"Who?"

"See Saw. He's my brother."

"Where'd he get a name like that? Don't he make his mind up too quick?"

"It's just what I've always called him. When I was little, I couldn't say 'Cecil'. And we both got used to the other, I guess."

"What's he call you?"

"Sydney."

"It's a pretty name," said Perrin.

She raised her eyes in amazement. Something in his made her frown again.

"Moccasin done," announced Mrs. Buenrostro. She held it out.

But Perrin intercepted it. Taking it from the Miwok's hand, he dropped onto one knee in front of Sydney's chair. "Here, Cinderella," he said, positioning the leather slipper a few inches above the floor. "See can you fit your dainty foot in this."

Sydney complied hesitantly, sensing a trap, and found that she had indeed put her foot into more than the moccasin. For Daniel Perrin continued to hold it, pressing her heel and pinching her toes, imprisoning her in his warm grasp. "How's that?" he asked.

"Let go," said Sydney.

Perrin released her and got up. But she continued to feel his hands on her foot. And the quality of that touch disturbed her. She was suddenly sure she did not want to walk back to Uncle Peter's alone with this man. Yet she could think of no way out of it. She bent over the remaining moccasin and poked the bone needle through the neat holes in the leather.

"I finish for you," offered the Miwok.

Sydney shook her head. "I'll do it."

"You'd better let her have it, Miss Sydney," said Perrin.

"You're gettin' blood all over it."

He was right. The finger she had jabbed with the needle was bleeding, and the clean leather had soaked up several spots of dark red. Sydney put her finger-end quickly to her mouth once more and sucked on it impatiently. "Heck," she said again.

Perrin took the moccasin from her lap and gave it to Mrs. Buenrostro. Then he hitched his chair after Sydney's and took her wrist firmly. "Let me have a look," he insisted.

She would have pulled away as before, but this time, he wouldn't let go. She must either fight him or yield. And the offense did not seem serious enough to fight. She let him look. Perrin studied the puncture in the tip of her finger with the care of a master surgeon. He watched it bead a scarlet drop, and then he felt in a back pocket for his handkerchief. It was clean. So was his shirt. He had gone to some pains to prepare himself for his second meeting with the prettiest girl up Jackson Creek.

Firmly, he applied the folded pad of the handkerchief to the end of Sydney's finger and accommodated her hand inside his so that he could continue to press the cloth tightly against the tiny wound. "It'll stop in a minute," he assured her.

But a minute was longer than Sydney intended to let him hold her hand. She met his blue eyes with a glare whose power to offend was greatly diminished by the bright color in her face. "You let go of me, mister," she said.

"Daniel," he suggested.

"I don't care **what** your name is!"

"You're even prettier when you're riled." But he let go and sat back, thrusting his thumbs through his belt.

It was time. Fidel Buenrostro had observed his antics with growing disapproval. Only the Mexican's uncertainty as to his own role as mediator between the two Americans had prevented his interference before. Relieved now from having to pit his authority as host against his guest, he leaned back against the table and folded his arms.

The second moccasin was nearly completed. Sydney watched with dread the progress of the Miwok's skillful fingers. She wondered if she ought to tell Buenrostro that her uncle wished to talk to him and ask him to accompany her back to the cabin. She abandoned the lie as too blatant. Besides, she did not trust Uncle Peter to prop up his end of it.

She had still not plotted a workable course of action when the Indian woman tied the last knot in the milkweed fiber thread and rose from her stool to give the moccasin directly into Sydney's hands. "I back go with you," she said. "Misa Agnos need eggs. I take them, now."

"Well, hey! That don't seem necessary!" objected Perrin. "I'm goin' back with Miss Sydney. I can carry the eggs."

"I need talk with Misa Agnos," said the Miwok. "Federico," she added her son, "la canasta."

"I go, too?" asked Joselito as his brother caught up a basket with which to raid the pantry.

"Yes," said his mother. "You bring acorn flour."

It was some minutes before they were ready to go. But once on the trail, they made good time. Sydney took the lead, followed closely by Mrs. Buenrostro who was tagged by her sons in single file. Daniel Perrin served the little troop as rear guard.

a Casa Silvestre

CHAPTER SIXTEEN:

THE HOUSE OF SILVESTRE

Simón Ruiz had ridden far into the night, pushing his tired grey, in order to reach his uncle's ranch before morning. The waxing moon dipped golden in the west as he crossed the lip of the long, shallow swale where a peach grove crowded leafy heads together south of the stately house of don Diego Silvestre.

To the north stood the rings of the tall corrals and the long, low sheds and stables, the barracas for the vaqueros. Huge, whispering willows draped wide bows over the tiled

roofs. A sense of timeless peace pervaded the swale, its buildings and its trees. And the faded gold of the moonlight added
a touch of magic to the whole. Ruiz saw it with a lightening
of heart. Here, surely, the trouble of the outside world could
not penetrate. Here, life could still be lived with grace and
pride. A sense of relief filled him.

At one of the corrals he swung down from his saddle,
tossed the stirrup leather over the seat and began to uncinch.
His horse rubbed its head on the poles of the enclosure and
snorted softly.

"Sí, potro," Simón told the animal. "Here, we can rest.
And for you, there will be no more work for a month. I wish
to be able to look forward to such ease, myself." He pulled
the saddle from the grey's wet back and threw it over a hitching rack before he led the horse into the corral, took off its
bridle and turned it loose. He watched while it pawed at the
dust and lay down to roll, scratching its back and neck on
the ground.

Putting up the bars of the gate, Ruiz went to the hay
stack, seized a wooden fork and gathered up a large, shaggy
clump. The grey scrambled to its feet, shook itself like a dog,
and trotted a few steps forward, whickering eagerly as Simón
thrust the hay between the rails. When he was satisfied that
his horse would be content until morning, Ruiz removed the
bags from his saddle, slung them over his shoulder, and
strode for the house.

The Casa Grande was a handsome structure, two stories high, built as an open square. A covered gallery circled
its second story. And as Ruiz approached the house, he saw a
golden spark of candlelight in a doorway open on that gallery. He saw that someone stood there, leaning on the frame,
looking out at the corrals. It was not his aunt. It was not a
servant.

Mystified, Simón moved quickly on, passed into the
heavy shadows of the wide entrance.

"¡Buenas noches, Patrón!" said a quiet voice from the
darkness of the wall.

"Raúl? Is that you?"

"Sí, Don Simón. Soy yo. I am guardian tonight. What news from the hills? Don Diego was surprised that you did not come back with the vaqueros. But they said you were seeking another market for the cattle. Did you find one?"

"Yes, several. The demand is far greater than the American ranchers can supply. But what has happened here, Raúl? I saw a light upstairs. Is someone ill?"

"It is the viejo, don Fernando, Patrón. He has been here since yesterday."

"Don Fernando! Escobar?"

"El mismo."

"But is it serious, then?"

"They do not expect him to live, Señor."

"There is someone with him of course? I thought I saw someone in the doorway."

"It will have been his daughter, la Amanda."

"Amanda! Was she not staying with her sister in the capital?"

"Yes. And it is most fortunate that she was, Patrón."

"Tell me at once what has happened."

"A group of thieves attacked the house of Escobar yesterday morning. What they could not take, they destroyed. They set fire to the corrals and stables. It was the smoke that alerted don Diego. Mi amo was out with us, checking on a waterhole that we have found twice poisoned. We surprised the thieves and were able to take two of them prisoner. The others escaped. They had beaten don Ferndando. He has not yet regained consciousness."

"¿Y la niña, Amanda?"

"His daughter, Patrón, was in Sacramento, as you said. Don Diego took his two prisoners to the capital in search of justice. He is still there. But he sent me and others back with Amanda so that she might be with her father."

"Her sister did not come?"

"No, Señor."

"The thieves were Americans, of course?"

"Sí, Señor."

"Then, don Diego will find no justice in Sacramento."

"No, Señor."

"I will go up and see how the old man fares. Goodnight to you, Raúl."

"Muy buenas, Don Simón."

Ruiz passed on between the walls and came into a wide, flagged corridor. He turned along it toward a broad stairway leading up to an inner gallery which overlooked the lush garden of the patio. The same hush lay over it as he had sensed at the corrals, but now, the peace seemed ominous.

Quickly, he scaled the stairs. The ringing of his spurs was loud in the silence. Halfway down the upper corridor, a door opened. Yellow candlelight swept across the floor, picked out the banisters of the railing opposite. "Simón?" The call was soft, the voice gentle, its tone at once hesitant and eager.

"Amanda!" he exclaimed in answer. "How is your father?"

"They have told you what happened?"

"Yes."

"There has been no change." She backed into the room as Ruiz came to the doorway. The light touched the saddlebags that hung over his shoulder, winked on the dark, polished handles of the twin pistols at his waist and burnished the braided twist of his hatband. "Simón . . .!" the girl said again. "I'm glad you have come."

Ruiz bent to deposit the bags on the floor inside the doorway. "But do you keep this vigil alone?" He looked past her to the bed across the room. "Where is my aunt?"

"I insisted that she retire for the rest of the night. She was so weary. And I will not be able to sleep until there is some difference in my father's condition." The daughter of don Fernando moved to the bedside.

Ruiz followed. On the bed, lying as still as if death had already entered it, was the broken body of don Fernando Escobar. The skin of his face was almost transparent in its waxy palor. An ugly bruise extended from his temple across his thin cheek to his upper lip. One arm lay motionless on top of the blanket that covered him. It was bound to a splint. The fingers protruding from the bandages were discolored and swollen.

Ruiz looked up from the bed and met the sorrowing eyes of the rancher's daughter. "¡Animales!" he whispered. "Is it not enough that they have ruined him? And my uncle took them to Sacramento! I would not have had so much patience!"

Amanda's eyes widened, reading in his the depth and ferocity of his outrage. Then, suddenly, she was in his arms, her face buried in the dusty linen of his shirt front, her hands clutched into tight little fists against his chest, her whole body trembling with her distress. "He has never harmed anyone!" she cried. "Why have they done this to him?"

"No, niña. There is no reason," agreed Simón, wrapping his embrace around her. "It is only because he was defenseless against them. Because he was an easy target for their violence. They should be killed for the rabid animals they are. My uncle has some influence in the capital. Perhaps he will at least be able to persuade the authorities to put them behind bars. I am sorry, Amanda. I wish there were something I could do."

"He will die," she said, her voice breaking. "He will die! And for what? For sitting quietly on his own doorstep, lost in his memories." She drew a great shaking sigh. Her hands opened, her tenseness relaxed. And she lay against Ruiz, absorbing his strength, trusting in his presence to make the wrong right, the impossible possible, again.

Simón held her another few moments, then gently put her back, looked into her tear-streaked face. "You are tired, Amanda. You must rest. You will make yourself ill. Let me wake my aunt. Or a servant. Your presence does not help your father now. He does not know you are here."

"Oh, but he may waken," she explained. "I must be with him when he wakens. It may be for only a moment.

Can I not bear a single night without sleep for his sake? Has he not spent many such nights watching over me when I was small? Watching over my mother as she lay dying after her last child was born? Let me stay with him, Simón. My weariness is nothing."

Ruiz studied her face, more beautiful in its earnestness and sorrow than he had ever seen it. "Your sister did not come," he said.

"No," she answered softly.

"Her husband would not let her come," he concluded.

"No," she said, still more softly.

"The stubborn fool! And your brother has not yet heard, of course."

She shook her head. "Don Deigo offered to send someone in search of him. But until there is some change in my father, for the better or . . . or worse, I do not want Manuel to know that this has happened."

"But how much longer will you wait? If your brother hears the news from some indifferent source, he will be doubly grieved."

"I know. Only another day! Tomorrow, perhaps, my father will waken. Or . . ." She looked at the bed. Tears filled her eyes. "Surely, he cannot continue much longer like this."

"Amanda," said Ruiz, "whatever happens, I will take the news of it to your brother myself. I intended to go back to the Gold Country as soon as I had spoken with my uncle."

She returned her eyes anxiously to his face. "You have seen Manuel there? You have talked to him?"

"Yes."

"And was he . . . well?"

"Yes. Certainly."

"Did he ask you for news of his family?"

"Our conversation was of a different nature. But I know that thinks of you often."

"Does he?" she whispered.

"Simón, is that you, sobrino?" A new voice spoke from the doorway. "I heard someone talking. I thought perhaps don Fernando . . ."

Both Ruiz and the daughter of Escobar turned quickly to see doña Graciela de Silvestre. Simón stepped to meet his aunt, took her hands and leaned to kiss her. "I have just arrived, Tiíta," he explained. "I have heard this story of the violent crimes committed against our vecino, don Fernando. I am deeply shocked and angered. But my business in the hills is not complete. I was hoping to talk to my uncle before I return there. Yet I find that he is in the capital with the gringos malvados. And how do you fare here? How are my cousins? Yourself?"

Doña Graciela touched her nephew's cheek affectionately. "We are all well, m'hijo. But we are much affected by what has happened. It is a terrible thing. We have done what we could to atone."

"Oh, Señora!" said Amanda, coming to doña Graciela's other side. "You have been more than kind! You have been like family to me."

"But should you have left her alone like this?" asked Ruiz.

"Simón, I beg you again not to blame your aunt. She has had no rest since this morning. I am sorry, Señora, that our voices awakened you. Please return to your bed. And your nephew also must leave me. He has ridden all day, I am certain. He must not spend all night in vigil also when there is so little to be gained by it."

"If my presence will in any way relieve your suffering, then I shall not say little is gained by it," declared Ruiz.

Amanda lifted a grateful look to his eyes. "I will not be so selfish as to allow you to stay. It is enough that you have come. That is all the comfort I could wish for. Please. Leave me alone with my father. Both of you. If anything happens, I will call you. I cannot possibly sleep. Simón," she added, half reaching toward him again, "I will see you tomorrow?"

He took her hand. "I shall hold myself at your command, Amanda," he said. "Goodnight."

"Goodnight, Simón. Goodnight, Señora. Please. Go."

Reluctantly, Ruiz and la señora de Silvestre left the room. Doña Graciela shut the door softly behind them. As it closed, Simón had a last glimpse of the sister of Manuel Escobar, her dark head bowed, her hands clasped in silent supplication to a seemingly indifferent Heaven.

CHAPTER SEVENTEEN:

CONSULTATION

When Ruiz awoke, the morning was well advanced. He lay for a little, reluctant to let his mind take up the unpleasant subjects that had filled it the night before. Seeking distraction, he opened his eyes.

The room was comfortably dim, for the slatted shutters were still closed. Ruiz wadded his pillow under his head to prop himself higher. He refused to think of Amanda upstairs. He refused to think of his uncle in Sacramento. He refused to think of Manuel in Jackson. But he would let himself think about Sydney Simpson.

He pictured her serious face with its comical pattern of powdery freckles. He pictured her red-brown curls under the brim of her weather-stained hat. He pictured her large brown eyes full of urgent questions. And then he saw the even line of her lips rise into a soft oval. "Simón . . .?" he heard her say. "Otro."

Ruiz jerked aside the covers and got out of bed.

The house of Silvestre was still unnaturally quiet. There was activity, now, servants moving to and fro, but voices were hushed in deference to Amanda and her father. The very birds in the garden offered no more than a soft twitter.

Simón washed quickly, dressed himself in fresh garments. Then he went in search of hot water to afford himself a comfortable shave. His aunt was in the kitchen, talking to a servant.

"Buenos días, sobrino," she greeted him. "Are you ready for breakfast?"

"Yes," said Ruiz. "Almost. Why did you not wake me? How is don Fernando this morning?"

"The same."

"My uncle has not returned?"

"Not yet."

"Where are my cousins?"

"Cristina is in the garden. The boys have gone out with the vaqueros."

Ruiz took the steaming kettle off the fire. "Who is with Amanda?" he asked.

"I have just left her, myself. She refuses other company. But I think she would welcome yours."

Ruiz glanced up sharply. "She has not slept at all?"

"She may have drowsed in a chair at her father's bedside. No more than that."

Simón poured the hot water into a crockery jug. "I would like to talk to you about something this morning, Tía. Do you have a few moments to give me?"

"Shall I come to your room?"

"If you will do me the kindness."

Together, aunt and nephew returned along the flagged corridor to one of the two rooms at the end of it. Doña Graciela opened the shutters to let in the light from the garden while Simón set about the process of removing the night's growth of dark stubble from his face.

"My cousin Francisco must be in Sacramento with my uncle," he said. "For otherwise, Amanda would not be so eager for **my** company."

"I do not think it would make much difference, Simón."

"I am surprised that Francisco did not come here with her when the others escorted her from the capital," said Ruiz.

"Amanda has not encouraged Francisco since she met you again last spring."

"That is unfortunate. I think my cousin has been much in love with her."

"Amanda prefers another."

Simón turned to look at his aunt, his razor balanced for its next pass across his chin. "But the preference is slight," he insisted.

"The preference is marked. And ardent, m'hijo."

"You are certain?"

"Can you doubt it yourself, Simón?"

He turned back to the mirror. "I had hoped I was wrong."

"Why? She is a lovely girl. It is not her lack of fortune you object to?"

"Of course not."

"Then?"

"Her family."

"Simón! The name Escobar is as old and honorable as any in California! It is true that her sister has married below her station, but you are not one to be put off by such a thing as that."

Ruiz rinsed his razor and wiped it on the towel. "I would not be brother-in-law to Manuel Escobar though I loved his sister to distraction."

"Manuel? But Simón . . ."

"And when I have finished my business with him, Amanda will feel very differently about me."

"I do not understand you, sobrino."

Ruiz dried his face and inspected it closely in the mirror, felt of his cheeks and chin. "I return to the Gold Country with a grim purpose, Tía. Amanda shall have new cause for grief. I intend to kill Manuel."

Doña Graciela sat down suddenly on a chair.

"I was going to speak only to my uncle about this," said Simón. "But because Amanda is now a guest in your house and has admitted you to her confidence, I cannot leave you in ignorance. Tía, Manuel Escobar has become a bandit and a murderer. His men attacked me on the road and robbed me. And I will not suffer him to live."

"No!" gasped doña Graciela. "Oh, Simón! You must be certain first, before you tell your uncle. Do you know for an absolute fact that Manuel is involved?"

"Yes. But I cannot prove it, yet. I will, before I kill him."

"Kill him!" his aunt whispered in horror, unable to believe it, yet equally unable to believe that her nephew would say a thing he did not mean.

"Do you remember, Tía, how much Manuel was affected by the triumph of Joaquín when Murieta came back from the coast two years ago, after the gringos declared him dead? Manuel volunteered to be a member of the new confederation when Joaquín told us all what he intended. Manuel has never recovered from the shock of Murieta's refusal to accept him as one of his personal cortege. And I suspect he has vowed to be another like him, to take over the role that Joaquín himself so wisely relinquished. But if so, he only parodies the part. Manuel has no great talent for leadership. And he has no great cause to guide him. His men are rabble. He is a little man, making a little nuisance of himself among the gringos. Even if I were to ignore him as beneath my notice, which is the course I might have taken, had his men not tried to murder me, the Americans soon would have discovered him. But I will not ignore him, now. He has dared to challenge me. And I will kill him."

Doña Graciela had not yet found her voice again to make any reply when from upstairs came a rending scream. Ruiz dropped the towel and ran for the door. His aunt followed.

Pushing through the servants who came out into the corridor, Ruiz dashed the length of the passage, bounded up the stairs and on along the upper gallery to the room where don Fernando's daughter had watched throughout the night. He threw open the door.

The daughter of Escobar was on her knees at the bedside, her face buried in the blankets. Don Fernando looked exactly as he had before. "Amanda!" said Ruiz.

She started up. He saw that tears ran down her cheeks. Her eyes were swollen from weariness and weeping. She pointed mutely to her father.

Simón came quickly to the bed, bent over don Fernando, touched his chest, watched his quiet face. Escobar was not breathing. Ruiz felt for a pulse. There was none. He stood up slowly. Reluctantly, he raised his eyes to Amanda's.

She stared at him in anguish.

"Did he waken?" he asked.

She shook her head. "I don't . . . know! I fell asleep! I woke up and found him. Like this! But suppose he did? Suppose he tried to speak to me? I would not have heard him! Suppose . . ."

"Amanda! No." Ruiz opened his arms to her. She flung herself into them and burst into racking sobs.

"Suppose!" she cried. "Suppose he opened his eyes!"

"Chito, niña. Hush. It is not likely that he wakened. He has not moved at all since I saw him myself last night. He is at peace. His pain is ended. His sorrow with it. Be comforted."

"And when you tell Manuel," Amanda went on, almost choking on the words, "he will seek vengeance! And then, they will kill him, too!" She looked up through her tears. "Convince him not to search for them, Simón!"

"Amanda, it is not my . . ."

"Please! He would not hear me though I threw myself on the ground at his feet. But he will listen to you. He respects you. He values your opinion. Tell him that vengeance is a hollow satisfaction. Say that it is better to live and be loved by what remains of his family than to die for honor's sake! Or to live the rest of his life in hiding from the gringos. Promise me, Simón! Promise me you'll speak to him, that you will tell him these things."

"I will tell him, niña."

"Oh!" Amanda turned her face into his shoulder, drew one, great, broken breath, and was quiet.

Simón stood, holding her to him, stroking her hair, staring at the bed.

Doña Graciela came in, followed by several cautious servants who were anxious to help but did not wish to intrude on the grief of Amanda nor on Simón's efforts to comfort her.

Ruiz felt her sagging in his arms, giving way to her weariness. He bent and picked her up off the floor, turned away from the bed. She made no resistance but kept her face hidden in his shoulder. "Tía," he said softly to doña Graciela, "where shall I take her?"

"The room next down the corridor is hers."

Ruiz bore Amanda to the door. The servants stepped aside to let him pass. On the gallery outside stood his fifteen-year-old cousin, Cristina. She was poised to fly from the spectre of Death as if it might emerge from the room in person. But she saw Amanda with a cry of pity and put aside her fear. "Simón! Has she fainted?"

He shook his head. Cristina ran to the door of the next room and opened it for him. Ruiz carried Amanda to the bed there and laid her down upon it. Amanda's eyes were closed beneath a frown of pain. She did not open them, but she clung to Simón's arm as he started to draw away. "Cristina is here with you, Amanda," he said. "You shall not be left alone."

"Simón!" she whispered. "You won't go . . . yet?"

"I will wait for my uncle the rest of this day. But I do not think it wise to delay longer than that. If I am to take word to your brother, it is better that he not hear it from someone else, first. I will ride for Jackson tomorrow."

"Jackson! Manuel is in Jackson? I know of that place.

What is he doing there?"

"He has a friend who lives there. He is staying with him."

"A friend? What is his name?"

"I do not know, Amanda. He did not tell me."

Her eyes came open, looked deep into his. "I will never forget . . . your kindness, Simón."

"Rest, niña. You are in your own house. You are among your own family. We will do everything we can to aid you." He took her hand and lifted it gently away from his arm, stood up and turned aside. "Primita," he said to Cristina. "Stay with her."

"I will, Simón."

Ruiz left the room but only to step to the rail and lean heavily upon it, look down into the garden. Doña Graciela joined him. "Simón!" she said softly. "How can you do this thing you have told me?"

He shook his head, gripping the railing. "I must."

"It will kill Amanda as well."

"I have said the Americans will soon find him out. One way or the other, she will lose him. If she knew fully what he has become, she would have already disavowed him."

"But he is all the family she has left!"

"She has a sister."

"Simón, Amanda loves you. It must not be at your hands that she loses Manuel."

"If the gringos kill him, she will think him a martyr."

"Let her. It will be some comfort to her."

"But he is a pillo!"

"Hush! She will hear you."

"Tía, I know too much to be able to turn my back on it, now. If I do nothing, I implicate myself. I have already been questioned by a sheriff and a judge. I have told them little. But they suspect the rest. And meanwhile, Manuel continues on his crooked course, pillaging, murdering, or sheltering those that do so at his command. I do not doubt that the news of his father's death will push him into more direct association with his band of dirty thieves. And it must be myself who bears that news to him. For I have promised Amanda. Now say if you would rather that your nephew were the means of increasing Manuel's villainy or of administering his merited destruction."

Doña Graciela laid a hand on Ruiz' arm. "At least wait until you have consulted with your uncle," she advised.

"If he comes back today, I will," said Ruiz. "But if not . . . then I will do what I see plainly as my obligation. As my duty to my family. To Amanda."

"Simón. Do you love her?"

Ruiz let go of the railing, stepped back and glanced around as if seeking some way to escape from this most gentle, yet most merciless question. "I cannot answer," he declared. "Besides, it makes no difference. I must do what I must do. Forgive me, Tía. Let me leave you. Has the priest been sent for? Where is he?"

"At the Hacienda de la Rosa. Raúl went early this morning to bring him. He will be here soon."

"Then I will ride out in search of my cousins," said Ruiz.

"But you have had no breakfast, sobrino!"

"I will return in two hours. I will eat, then. I must do something! I cannot stand here. With your permission, Tíita." And wheeling toward the stairs, Ruiz returned to them, descended them. His aunt stood where she was, near the railing, watching him go.

CHAPTER EIGHTEEN:

THE NUGGET

Cecil's first day of panning on the banks of Jackson Creek was not so rewarding as he had hoped. Yet the first time he reduced a shovelful of sand and dirt to a handful of dark grit where several flakes of yellow gold sparked up at him, he forgot about the ache in his arms and shoulders and the hot needle in his lower back. He did two men's work, thereafter.

By Wednesday afternoon, he had "hit his stride", as Uncle Peter said, and had more to show for less effort than Paul McCormick, who was working upstream from him. "You must be dumping it all out, and it's swimming down to me!" he finally called.

"You want me to come help you fish for it?" asked Paul.

Cecil laughed. "I'm not getting quite that much!"

Hearing their exchange on her way back to the cabin with a heavy bucketful of water for washing the noonday dishes, Sydney stopped and watched her brother bending over the small excavation he had dug in the stream bank. She

put down the bucket and went closer. Squatting on her moc-
casined heels, she hugged her skirt around her knees and
watched him swirling the cold water over a quarter panful of
sand and small pebbles. He let some of it escape over the lip
of the pan at every outward motion. "You're getting pretty
good at that, See Saw," she said.

He looked up. "Hello, Syd. Is Aunt Aggie asleep?"

"Nope. She'll be hollering at me in another minute. Can
I try that?"

"It's not as much fun as it looks. Let me finish off this
last bit, here. I'm almost down to paydirt. What are you
supposed to be doing?" he added, returning his attention to
his work.

"Dishes," said Sydney.

"Again?"

"It's only three times a day. Next, I get to chop wood."

"I thought that was Jacob's job."

"He's got a blister."

"He **is** a blister. Sydney, I'm sorry about things, you
know? I guess I didn't realize what you'd be getting into here.
You hate it, don't you?"

"Yep. But I'm almost used to it, now. I can stand it for a
little while longer."

"What do you mean by that?"

"I've been waiting for a chance to tell you. But old Aunt
Agony keeps me squashed under the ball of her thumb till I
haven't been able to talk to you."

"Syd, you shouldn't call her names like that."

"It's better than hitting her with a broom, isn't it?"

"If Uncle Peter finds out . . ."

"Uncle Peter can pickle his peppers. I'm going to run
away."

Cecil unbent his back and stood up in the squelching,
oozy sand. "You're going to what?"

"I've got it all planned. But I'll wait until Simón gets
back from the Valley, first."

"Simón! What are you talking about?"

"I was over at the neighbors again this morning. Ben Rooster knows Simón. He's heard that Simón got his money back, and that he went to take it to his uncle in the Valley. But Fidel thinks . . ."

"Who's Fidel?"

"Ben Rooster."

"Why do you call him Fidel?"

"It's his name."

"Fidel Ben Rooster?"

"Yep. Listen, See Saw. I'm trying to talk to you."

"Go ahead."

"Sydney!" came Aunt Aggie's voice. "Sydney! Where are you?"

"Be right there!" shouted Sydney over her shoulder. She turned back to her brother. "Fidel is sure that Simón will come back to Jackson pretty quick," she said. "He knows he hasn't given up on those cholos, yet. And when he comes, I'm going to . . ." She stopped and pointed down at the gold pan which Cecil had unconsciously allowed to tip farther forward than he meant to. All the water had run out of it. "Is that gold?" she asked.

Cecil looked. The dark quarter moon of grit in his pan was studded with a shining lump. Carefully, incredulously, he dug it out, turned it over on his palm. It was an irregular node the size of a bantam's egg. "Hold this," said Cecil, handing the pan up to his sister with the rest of the sand still in it. Then he bent to plunge his fist into the water and rinse the nugget clean inside it. Straightening, he opened his fingers cautiously, as if he feared he had dissolved the lump he could feel solid in his grasp.

"That's a pretty big one, isn't it?" said Sydney.

Cecil raised his eyes to hers, joy and excitement dawning in his face. Closing his fist on the nugget again, he punched it skyward. "Waaa-hooo!" he shouted.

Upstream, Paul McCormick jerked erect to stare at him. Downstream, Uncle Peter dropped his shovel and came splashing up the bank. Tim was on his heels. In front of the cabin, Aunt Agnes dropped the mending she was doing and galloped for the creek. Jacob momentarily forgot the pain of his blister and followed.

Cecil scrambled out of his hole, still brandishing his fist over his head. "Eureka!" he shouted. "Eureka!"

Sydney poked through the sand in the pan. But the other pebbles were only pebbles. She put the pan carefully on the ground and looked up as her uncle's family converged on her brother.

"Let me see it, son!" said Uncle Peter, reaching out as if he would catch Cecil's waving arm and take the nugget from him by force.

"How big is it?" demanded Paul.

"For pity's sake, show it to us, Cecil!" cried Aunt Agnes, laughing in her excitement.

"What did you do, catch a frog?" asked Tim.

"Dummy! He found a nugget!" Jacob told him.

"I know. You think I don't know? You're the dummy."

"All right, everybody. Gather round," said Cecil, unnecessarily. "Get ready to feast your eyes." And extending his hand, he opened it under their crowding noses.

There was a moment's silence while they stared at it. All but Sydney. She had remained where she was, crouched to the ground, watching them. Now, she rose, glancing toward the cabin as if she might try to take advantage of their distraction. But she hesitated too long. Her family's joy broke loose. Uncle Peter grabbed the nugget and held it high in thanksgiving to heaven. Aunt Agnes grabbed Cecil and hugged him. Jacob hugged Tim, who hit him. And Paul McCormick, for want of other object, seized Sydney in his arms and planted a solid kiss on her cheek.

"Hey," she protested. But Paul didn't notice.

"What do you think it's worth?" was the next question on everyone's lips. They asked each other and speculated on the answer in wilder and wilder terms.

Then Cecil must show them the exact spot where he had delved the shovelful that had produced this treasure. Paul

McCormick clawed through the gritty muck with his fingers, half hoping to turn up another one. Uncle Peter made Cecil finish panning out the left over sand, unwilling to lose even a few flakes in the midst of the family's excitement.

But serious work for the day was over. Aunt Agnes couldn't even be bothered with watching Sydney wash the dishes. Eventually, it was determined that they should take the nugget to the Wells Fargo Office in Jackson that very afternoon.

There was a flurry of preparation. Tim and Jacob must wear their new Sunday shirts. Aunt Agnes put on her best bonnet. Uncle Peter shaved again, nicking his chin in the process. Paul McCormick parted his hair three times and still couldn't get it straight. And Cecil decked himself out in the new clothes Simón had given him. Sydney had nothing new to wear but her moccasins which she wore constantly, anyway. But she combed her hair at her aunt's insistence.

Then, the older boys hitched up the mules to the heavy wagon, and the younger ones caught and bridled the pony. It was Tim's turn to ride in front, since he had sat behind on the way back from church on Sunday. But when he pushed the point, he was told that he could either sit behind Jacob or ride in the wagon or stay at home while the rest went to town. He opted for the wagon, first, but changed his mind and joined his brother on the pony, after all.

Finally, after Uncle Peter had carefully wrapped and unwrapped and rewrapped the nugget in his best handkerchief and stored it in his coat pocket where he could slap its weight occasionally to be sure it was riding all right, the Simpsons set out for Jackson.

By the time they were in sight of the Wells Fargo Building, across the corner from the National Hotel, everyone but Sydney was singing "Oh, Susana!".

But once inside, the rare Simpson boistrousness died to an expectant hush. In tense silence, they watched Uncle Peter produce the lump of gold and put it down on the counter for the assayer to admire. In indignant silence, they watched the man pick it up as casually as if it were a lump of mud. He pried at its crevices and removed a few grains of sand before he weighed it. In anxious silence they awaited his verdict.

"Five troy ounces, ten penneyweight," announced the assayer. "It weighs eighty-five dollars and forty-two cents." He looked up at Uncle Peter. "Were you wanting to sell it?"

When Uncle Peter did not answer, Aunt Agnes blessed herself. "Eighty-five dollars!" she murmured.

"Is that all?" demanded Tim.

"All!" exclaimed Paul McCormick. "It's eighty-five dollars more than we had yesterday!"

Uncle Peter picked up the nugget and looked at it as casually as the assayer had. "I thought it would be worth more than that."

"The going rate is eighteen dollars per troy ounce," said the assayer.

"Well, you'd better give me the money, then," said Uncle Peter.

"Wait!" said Cecil, holding out his hand to his uncle. "Let me see the nugget, again."

"What for?"

"I just want to."

Uncle Peter frowned at his nephew. "Don't be foolish, son." He put it down firmly on the counter. "Give me the money," he told the assayer.

"How do you want it?"

"In coin."

"I don't have that much coin in the till. You'll have to take half of it in dust."

"Very well, then."

The Simpsons watched closely while the amount was counted out in front of them and a small part of it was subtracted for the assayer's fee. Then, richer by one jingling sack of gold coins, which went into Uncle Peter's pocket, and one silent one of gold dust, which was solemnly entrusted to Cecil, the family returned to the street.

There, they took counsel with each other as to their next move. No one wanted to return to the cabin.

"We need so many things, Peter," said Aunt Agnes, brushing her husband's threadbare sleeve. "We'd better stretch the money as thin as we can. Clothes, first, I think. Or dry goods. Sydney and I can probably make them a lot cheaper than we can buy garments ready-made."

"We need to add a room to the cabin," said Uncle Peter.

"But that can wait. Clothes can't. Not much longer."

"I need some boots!" put in Timothy. "Jacob's got new ones."

"I'll bet Mrs. Thomson would be able to advise you about the best buys along those lines," offered Paul McCormick. "Maybe we ought to visit the parsonage, next."

This idea found favor. Accordingly, the family piled back into the wagon while Tim and Jacob scrambled onto Red Dog. Jacob still wouldn't let his younger brother ride in front.

That the Simpsons should come visiting in the middle of the day in the middle of the week was a pleasant surprise for the pastor's wife. She received her unexpected guests with great warmth and courtesy.

"We found a nugget!" Jacob informed her before she could ask.

"A great big one!" added Timothy.

"Ooh! How wonderful!" said Mrs. Thomson.

"A nugget! Can I see it?" Amy came bouncing to the door to peer around her mother. "Hello, Paul. Hello, Cecil."

"We cashed it already," said Timothy.

"Please come in, everyone," said Mrs. Thomson. "I'm afraid the Reverend's not at home. He's out with our son-in-law, George, on his rounds this week. But Susan is here. You've not had a chance to meet her yet, have you? Hello, Agnes. Goodness! Such excitement for you! I'm so glad. You're looking wonderful. Let me take your bonnet. Hello, Sydney. How are you, dear? You remember Amy, don't you? And this is Susan, our eldest. Mrs. Durham, I should say. Your aunt has heard me talk of her ever so often. Good afternoon, Peter. How kind of you to think of us in the midst of your good fortune. Hello, boys. Amy! Run and bring in the chairs from the dining room so there will be a place for everyone to sit."

"I'll help," Paul volunteered.

"Cecil?" prompted Amy, casting a pert look past Paul. "Do you want to come, too?"

Cecil felt a warm something wash over him. "Sure," he agreed.

"Well, come on, then!" Paul said shortly.

After the first flurry of seating the visitors and introducing them to Susan Durham, the Foreign Tax Collector's buxom young wife, Ida Thomson declared herself willing and eager to hear the particulars of the momentous find.

Tim and Jacob simultaneously offered an account but were silenced by their mother so that their father might answer. Uncle Peter's version included the precise location of the find and a fairly accurate description of the piece itself. He did not neglect to point out the Providential intervention so surely indicated by the event. And then, he expressed his opinion of the gold prices in comparison to the uniqueness and perfect quality of the nugget. He only failed to mention who had actually found it.

Cecil didn't mind. He had reward enough in watching Amy and in receiving an occasional bright smile from that quarter. But Sydney was afforded no such distraction. She was at liberty to consider the scene at her leisure. And she was almost ashamed of her brother for his good-natured diffidence, for his unaffected admiration of Amy Thomson, and for the mild way he ignored Paul's repeated attempts to belittle him in the eyes of the parson's daughter.

"I fear Old Freckles here is going to end his days as a hunchback the way he bends over his gold pan," Paul told Amy.

Amy giggled and looked at Cecil.

Cecil's brown eyes did not so much as waver. His quaint smile even stretched the solemn line of his mouth a little farther.

Sydney could bear it no more. "Paul will end **his** days staring at an **empty** gold pan," she said flatly, during the only moment of silence that had fallen on the room since the Simpsons' arrival. "I didn't notice any five troy ounces turning up in his pan."

"Sydney!" cried Aunt Agnes.

"Blessed are the meek," Uncle Peter said sonorously.

Amy stifled another laugh.

"Amy, dear," said Mrs. Thomson, "why don't you take Sydney out to see the vegetable garden. There may be some squash ripe that you can pick for dinner."

"I'll go with you," offered Paul, looking at Amy.

"No, Mama, I'll go with Sydney," said Susan Durham. "Amy doesn't know a ripe squash from a cucumber."

"They do look something alike," mused Paul.

Amy wrinkled her nose at him. "Squashes are yellow," she informed him.

"Except for the green ones," he reminded her.

This witticism sent Amy into another fit of suppressed laughter. And with quick, enticing glances, she invited Cecil to share her amusement until he, too, began to chuckle.

Sydney followed Susan to the back door, glad to escape the entire situation. "What's a foreign tax collector?" she asked as Mrs. Durham led her out onto the kitchen porch.

"Why, it's someone who collects the tax from all the foreigners," explained the pastor's eldest daughter, smiling kindly at her guest's simplicity.

"What foreigners?"

"All of them. The Chinese, the Chileans, the Mexicans . . ."

"Mexicans aren't foreigners," Sydney objected.

Susan led the way on down the steps into the vegetable garden. "They're not Americans," she said.

"But they were here first."

"What a quaint little thing you are," smiled Susan.

"How much is the tax?"

"Twenty dollars a month."

"Twenty . . .! That's more than Uncle Peter can make in two weeks panning gold."

"Your uncle is not a foreigner."

"But we're barely getting by, ourselves. How can the foreigners do it?"

"No one wants them to live here. They can leave if they can't afford it. Besides, it's the law."

"Who made the law?"

"The government, I suppose."

"Our neighbors on the Creek are Mexicans. Do they pay the tax?"

"You mean Ben Rooster? Yes, of course, he does."

"What would happen if he didn't, sometime?"

"Well, he would be told he had to leave. Really, Sydney! You have strong feelings about things, don't you?"

"What would happen to his wife and his little boys?"

"I wouldn't worry about it. Ben Rooster always pays his tax. Oh, look at these nice squash! You and your aunt will have to plant a garden next spring, Sydney. With the creek right there it would be easy to keep it watered. Here, hold up your apron. We should have brought a basket, shouldn't we?"

"If he had a run of bad luck, though," Sydney insisted.

"What, dear?"

"I mean, would they let him miss one month if he promised to pay double the next time?"

"What are you talking about?"

"I suppose he could ask Simón to loan him the money."

"Who?"

"I smell smoke!" Sniffing in sharply, Sydney turned away from Mrs. Durham, still holding the squash in her apron, and scanned the horizon. "Uh oh! Look. That's coming from the creek. Here. Hold these," she added, tumbling her load of squash into Susan's apron which Mrs. Durham lifted just in time. And leaving the tax collector's wife staring after her in amazement, Sydney ran for the kitchen door. "See Saw! Uncle Peter! Fire! Fire on the creek!"

CHAPTER NINETEEN:

THE WARNING

At the sound of hoofbeats from the road, the Miwok looked up from stringing red peppers. "That is not your father," she told her son, Joselito, for the child had jumped up to greet him. "Stay here." Rising, she moved to the open doorway to look out.

She saw her other son standing in the yard, confronting their unexpected visitor. He was a man of wealth, for he wore fine clothing, and he rode a fine horse. But the look on his face was cruel and cold. "How can we serve you, Patrón?" the Miwok asked.

"Where is Buenrostro?" the man demanded in strangely accented Spanish. His eyes swept over the Miwok's person. "Are you alone here, woman?"

Fear soured her mouth. "My husband is in the town, Señor. He will return soon."

"Your husband is a foolish man, chola. He has dared to lie to someone that does not forgive duplicity in underlings."

"My husband does not lie," said the Miwok.

"You dare to answer me! Tell me who is Simón Ruiz."

"He is a rich man from the Valley."

"Yes. Tell me what happened to him."

"He was robbed on the road."

"Tell me who robbed him!"

"That I do not know. Some men. Mexicans."

"You know the name of one of them!"

"I do not."

The horseman took a gun from his belt and aimed it at Federico. "Tell me the name!" he said.

The Miwok's mouth went so dry she could not speak.

The man fired into the dirt at her son's feet. The boy flinched, but he did not give ground. The white goat bleated in fear. The chickens scattered. The cock ran into the house. "Tell me the name!" the visitor repeated. He lifted his aim to Federico's bare chest.

Slowly, the Miwok left the doorway. "I do not know," she said, forcing the words off her stiff tongue. "If I did, I would tell you. Do not kill my son, Patrón."

"Why should I spare the little liar? The boy will grow up to be as false as his father. What are the names of your American neighbors, chola?"

"Everyone in Jackson knows." The Miwok reached Federico's side, slipped a hand over his brown shoulder. "They are called Seensome," she said. "Woman, Misa Agnos. Man, Mista Pito. Boys: Yayco, Teematee, Pole, See So. Girl: Cindy."

"Which of those dared to accuse don Manuel Escobar of riding a stolen horse?"

"I do not know that, Patrón. I have not heard it to be so."

"You are lying, chola."

"I am telling the truth."

There was a motion in the doorway of the adobe. The visitor instantly shifted his aim and fired. The Miwok clapped a hand to her mouth. But it was not Joselito that had ventured into the opening. Only the red and green rooster now lay in a heap of bright feathers on the hard-packed earth of the doorway. "I will visit your neighbors," said the horseman. A wisp of smoke drifted from the muzzle of his pistol.

"They are not home."

"I will find a way to bring them back. And if they ask you afterwards what you know of it, say that I have left them a warning. They must move away from Jackson. For if they are still here when I return, I will kill the boy See So. And I will take the girl, Cindy. And if they tell anyone why they are leaving, I will kill this half-breed bastard of yours."

"Who are you, Patrón? And when will you return?"

"That, neither you nor they need know." The man reined around. But as he passed the white goat, he snapped a shot at the animal. The bullet burned a furrow along its side and shoulder. The goat let out an almost human cry and jumped straight into the air the length of its tether. Its foreleg crumpled beneath it as it landed, and the groove cut by the bullet filled with blood. The man spurred on to the road and continued up the creek toward the Simpson's cabin.

The wife of Fidel Buenrostro stood listening to the re-treating hoofbeats. Federico looked up at her, his face quiet but his eyes large. "Mamá," he said, "that man wore the stolen jacket of don Simón Ruiz."

"Yes."

"Why did he shoot our goat?"

"He is evil. Go into the house. Stay with your brother until I call you. The man may return."

Federico went to the door of the adobe. He stopped there to pick up the warm body of the dead rooster. Pressing it close and staining his own breast with the bird's blood, he passed into the house.

The Miwok watched him. Then she turned to the goat. The animal scrambled to its feet as she approached but held its one forefoot off the ground. Its cries increased in volume when she reached it, and it pressed its knobby head against her thighs, seeking comfort and ease from its pain. She spoke to it softly in the language of her own people. She thanked it for taking the wound that might have scarred her son. She praised it for its goodness and its usefulness. She asked it to cease crying, and told it that the stinging furrow in its side would soon be well, that it was neither deep nor serious.

When the animal was quieter, she left it and went toward the house. But as she would have gone in, the smell of smoke turned her back.

A glance upstream confirmed her fears. Quickly, she entered the cabin. Her two sons were in one corner. Federico had relinquished the murdered bird to his brother, and Joselito was now as blood-smeared from holding it as he. "¡Niños!" said their mother. "The evil man is burning the house of Misa Agnos and Mista Pito. The wind may bring the fire to us. We must prepare to leave."

At this, Joselito, who had been weeping silent tears into the rooster's feathers, dropped the bird and ran to his mother. She hugged him briefly, but sent him to roll up the blankets on the bed. Then she took up a large basket and went to fill it with acorn flour from her little pantry. Federico filled another with pinto beans.

Not many moments more had passed when the first men began to come from the town, riding fast to reach the fire before it could spread. Others came after them, some mounted, some on foot. The Miwok and her sons watched each new contingent anxiously. But Fidel Buenrostro was not among them.

"Mamá," said Federico, "I will go and see what is happening. I will walk among the people and listen to what they say. Then, I will come and tell you what I have learned."

"Yes," agreed his mother. "You will listen. You will not speak. First, you will clean yourself, or the people will think the blood from the bird is yours. They will think you are hurt."

Federico looked down at himself. Leaving the doorway, he knelt to scoop up a handful of sandy dirt and powdered the smears of blood, rubbed them away, leaving only smudges that would not draw a second glance.

As the boy got to his feet, he saw the Simpson's wagon rattle by on the road, its team of mules alternating between a stiff trot and an awkward gallop, pulling against each other as Uncle Peter drove them on through the uneven flow of traffic. Federico looked back at his mother. "You have seen?"

"Yes. When you return, bring Cindy. I will talk to her."

"I have heard." Federico trotted to the edge of the road and joined the general rush. When he arrived at the scene of the fire, he must push through a growing crowd of spectators. Dodging around, between, and even under the jostling men, he reached the front of the watchers' semicircle. There, he stayed crouched for a time to assess what he saw.

A relay line of men was passing buckets of water up from the creek to soak the ground in a broad belt around the burning building. Others were fighting smaller fires that had started in the dry grass from the showering sparks. The wind was light, but its direction was so variable, it was impossible to predict which way the flames would lean from one moment to the next.

Peter Simpson, his nephew, and his apprentice were among those who ran from place to place as needed, the boys with buckets, Uncle Peter with a shovel. Aunt Agnes, her face set and grim, still sat in the wagon. She had an arm around each of her two sons, not to comfort them or herself, but to prevent their getting in the way of the fire fighters.

Sydney sat beside them, her hands full of the reins, for the mules were uneasy so close to the breathy roar of the fire, its spitting crackle, and its streaming banners of hot flame.

Federico rose and let himself be pushed sideways along the line of spectators until he reached the wagon. Then he sprang lightly up the wheel and onto the seat next to Sydney.

He touched her arm as she turned to look at him. "I sorry, Cindy," he said.

"Me, too," she agreed and glanced at her aunt. Agnes Simpson was staring dry-eyed at the fire, not numb but offended, indignant with a careless Providence who had allowed this terrible thing to come to pass.

"You know how it start?" Federico asked Sydney.

"Nope. It might have been the cooking fire. We didn't put it out before we went to town. I was going to heat water on it to wash the noonday dishes with. But I don't see how the fire could have spread from there. We had stones around it, and the earth was all bare. And the wind hasn't been that strong."

"If you can come, Mamá will talk to you," the boy told her, his voice dropping to a softer note. "But only you, Misa Cindy."

"I'll come as soon as I can," she said. "You'd better go back home. She'll worry about you."

"I go now," said Federico.

But Aunt Agnes had turned to speak to Jacob beside her, and she noticed the neighbor boy. "Freddy!" she said. "Where did you come from?"

"Mamá, she send me," replied the boy. "See how you are."

"Where's your father? Why didn't **he** come?"

"He was in town. He doesn't return."

"What did he go to town for?"

"Talk to a man he knows."

"What man?"

"I don't know that, Misa Agnos."

Sydney was staring at her aunt. "What difference does it make?" she wanted to know.

Aunt Aggie's eyes narrowed. "I just wonder if Ben Rooster heard about how we found a big nugget today," she said. "Maybe he hasn't found any down the creek there for a while. Maybe he wants this spot for himself."

Sydney's stare lowered into a frown. "That's rotten, Aunt Agnes," she said.

"Yes, you'd better believe it's rotten! But I knew how it would be. I told your Uncle Peter we'd have trouble with that foreigner sooner or later. And now, you see, this has . . ."

"I meant what you said was rotten," Sydney interrupted, "not Ben Rooster."

Aunt Aggie closed her mouth. Then she opened it again. "I beg your pardon?" Her voice was icy.

"You should beg Federico's pardon."

Too angry to speak for a moment, Aunt Agnes locked eyes with her niece.

"You've got no reason to suspect Ben Rooster," said Sydney. "No reason at all."

"Haven't I!"

"Don't do it to him," said Sydney. "It would be mean and rotten to do it to him."

"Ma!" complained Tim. "You're pinching my arm off!"

"Mean . . . and rotten!" whispered Aunt Agnes. "Sydney Simpson, how dare you say such words to me!"

"What about Federico?" Sydney went on. "Do you want him to suffer because you started stupid rumors?"

"Freddy! Go home." Aunt Agnes spoke clearly to be sure the half-breed could understand her. "I want you never to come back here. Ever!"

Federico dropped promptly from the wooden seat onto the wheel, from there to the ground, and dived into the crowd.

Sydney looked after him for a moment, then thrust the reins into the hands of the cousin sitting nearest her. "Here, Jacob. Hold these," she said. And without another glance at Aunt Agnes, she climbed swiftly out of the wagon.

But she climbed right into the waiting arms of Daniel Perrin. "Sydney!" he exclaimed. "Where do you think you're goin'? There ain't nothin' you can do."

"Let me go." Sydney squirmed to try to free herself, but Perrin only held her the tighter. "What are you doing here?" she demanded, wedging her elbows against his ribs and prying at them. "Nobody asked you to come."

"I saw the smoke, like everybody else. I came to help."

"So, go and help. Let go of me."

"Hold still. I'm not hurtin' you. Tell me what happened. How did the fire start?"

"I don't know. Nobody knows. Only Aunt Aggie thinks she does. But she doesn't. And I've got to go warn Mrs. Ben Rooster. Now, let me go!"

"What are you talkin' about? Ow! Hey, you're a handful, ain't you? Will you quit your fightin' me? I'm not lettin' you go nowheres in this crowd."

"Sydney!" Aunt Agnes had had time to realize the impropriety, if not the outright danger of her niece's pushing through the spectators alone. She leaned over the side of the wagon to look down. "Oh! Thank heaven. Daniel! You stopped her. Sydney, come back up here."

Knowing the odds were now against her escape, and much preferring not to remain where she was with Perrin, Sydney surrendered to her aunt's command. Daniel climbed after her to the driver's box and planted himself firmly on the end of it. "Mrs. Simpson, I'm right sorry about this business," he said, gesturing at the burning cabin. As if to emphasize his words, the roof fell in, sending a fountain of flame and sparks on high. The onlookers drew a breath in unison at the sight. The fire-fighters paused to look up and move back. Sweat glistened on their heat-reddened faces.

"That fire was set," Aunt Agnes declared.

"Aw, no," protested Perrin. "That don't seem likely, Ma'am."

"Yes, it was."

"How do you know?" Daniel leaned into Sydney with the excuse of looking past her at her aunt. He reached an arm along the seat back to keep her from avoiding him.

"I know," said Aunt Aggie darkly. "It was our neighbor downstream. That foreigner. That Ben Rooster fellow."

"Ben Rooster! What makes you think that?"

"One of his little Indians was just here, spying on us. Nor hide nor hair have we seen of the man, himself. Why hasn't he come to try to help?"

"Well, maybe he's busy wettin' down his own place. The wind's pretty tricky today. And a fire on the loose is no joke."

"No joke," repeated Aunt Agnes. She stared at the walls of flame. "Everything we owned," she said. "And my mother's clock. How many hundreds of miles we carried that clock! I tended it like a baby. I padded the works so it would take no damage. It ticked the first time I wound it. Kept perfect time. Struck the half hours as well as the hours. Beautiful chime."

"I'm sure sorry, Ma'am." Perrin reached a little farther around Sydney. He touched her opposite shoulder with his thumb. She sat up straighter out of his reach.

"And all because Ben Rooster couldn't countenance our good fortune," mused Aunt Agnes.

"Miz Simpson, you better be pretty sure before you accuse the man," Perrin advised. "It may look to you like he's guilty, but the charge is mighty serious. And folks that know Old Ben are goin' to have a hard time believin' he'd do a thing like that. Why don't you just wait a little and see what other evidence turns up? I know you're grievin' your things. Clocks ain't easy to come by out here. And I reckon that wasn't all you lost that you hate havin' to lose. But as for the cabin itself, why . . . don't you worry. You got other neighbors besides Ben Rooster. We ain't goin' to let you and your family go without a place to live in. There'll be a collection taken up for you. There always is. Your cabin ain't the first one to burn down. It could happen to any of us at any time. And we know it. We'll all pitch in and help. I'll be glad to take some time out from my own claim and lend you a hand at rebuildin'."

Aunt Agnes made no reply for a moment but continued to stare straight ahead. Then suddenly, her shoulders sagged. She let go of Timothy and buried her face in her hands.

Sydney had listened to Perrin in surprise and relief. She turned to thank him with a look. But she found his face too close to hers. She found his eyes too avid. She turned back to Aunt Aggie, instead. But just as she put out a cautiously sympathetic hand, her aunt sat up again.

"Daniel," said Aunt Agnes, "would you drive us back to the parsonage? I guess there's no reason for Sydney and me and the boys to stay here. But you'd better tell Peter, so he won't wonder where we are and worry about us."

"Glad to, Ma'am." Perrin drew back from Sydney and climbed down out of the wagon. He shoved through the men and crossed the open ground toward Uncle Peter. Aunt Agnes and Sydney watched him go.

"That's one fine, young man," said Aunt Aggie, softly. "Sydney, if you would be a little nicer to him, you might be able to land him. I think he rather fancies you. And your uncle and I would be proud to have him as a nephew."

Sydney met her eyes. But seeing that Aunt Aggie was keeping back tears, her niece only shrugged and looked away.

CHAPTER TWENTY:

THE RETURN OF RUIZ

It was not known in the gold towns that the nephew of Silvestre had come back to the Mother Lode. Ruiz did not ride the roads. Mounted on a dark bay gelding and clad as a simple vaquero, he traveled eastward over open country. The only soul he met between his uncle's lands and those of Jack Sutherland was one of the American rancher's cowboys.

Ruiz had been moving up a dry draw, keeping to the edge of the brush in order to avoid being seen when from a rustling in the scrub emerged a wild-eyed steer. One of its long, heavy horns had been half broken off at the base, and blood ran down the side of its face. The animal bawled in pain and confusion, then charged into the heart of the brush.

Ruiz took down his new leather lariat and turned his bay in pursuit. He was working his way forward, making sure the steer did not pass him back toward the Valley, when he glimpsed a man riding along the rim of the draw. "¡Oiga! ¡Amigo!" he called. "¡Por ahí anda el novillo!"

"Speak English?" came the reply.

"The es-teer go that way! To you! I don't let him turn!"

"Right!" shouted the cowboy. And he spurred his horse in order to get well ahead of the wary animal before he rode down to the floor of the arroyo.

Together, Ruiz and the American rider cornered the steer against the steepening bank. It charged past the cowboy, but he swung his hemp and caught it by its one good horn, jerking it around. Before the noose could slip off, Ruiz closed in to rope its heels as it bucked and lunged, trying to free itself from the restraint. Turning the line twice round the pommel, Simón wheeled his bay, pulling the steer off its feet. It fell on its dangling horn and broke it off completely.

The American's lasso was tied to his pommel so that he could dismount and leave his horse to hold the line tight while he inspected the steer's injury. Then he looked up at Ruiz. "It'll be all right," he said. "Slack your rope!"

Simón rode forward, and the cowboy freed the steer's hind legs from the lariat. He was back in his saddle before the animal could flounder to its feet and twist itself free of the noose that still held its one good horn. Once rid of the rope, the steer shook its head at the two men and plunged back into the brush.

The cowboy nodded his thanks to Ruiz as he coiled his hemp. "Lucky how that horn broke off, wasn't it?" he said. "I thought I'd have to haul the critter back to camp and saw it off. It would have been a hell of a job. I'm sure glad you happened along just when you did."

"Para servirle," said Simón, touching the brim of his hat.

The cowboy appraised Ruiz thoughtfully. "You wouldn't be lookin' for work, would you?" he asked.

Ruiz shook his head. "Not now. Who you are working for?"

"Jack Sutherland."

"Ah. And you think that he gives me a job?"

"He might. The boss is always on the lookout for a good man."

"You are most kind. The patrón, he has other mexicanos that work for him?"

"Several. They've been comin' up from the Valley more and more often. Must be things are gettin' harder for the rancheros."

"Who are some of these men you say?" asked Ruiz. "Is possible I know them."

"Well . . ." the American thought a moment. "There's Juan Gómez. And Romero Moreno. Ignacio Pereda. Any of those sound familiar?"

Ruiz nodded. "Two, they have been the vaqueros of don Fernando Escobar."

"Escobar. Yes, that's right. They've been with us since last spring. There was another man, too. But he didn't last. Mariano García, his name was."

"¡No diga! Mariano García? I haven't know he work for don Fernando."

"Maybe he didn't. But he came here along about the same time. What's your name?"

"I am call Juan Solano. And you?"

"Baldy Hinkson." The cowboy grinned and doffed his hat to display an especially thick mop of curly brown hair.

"Mucho gusto," said Ruiz, unaware of the joke, and touching his own hatbrim again. "And have you hear, Baldés, that don Fernando is dead?"

"No, I sure hadn't. What happened? Was it an accident?"

"He is murder."

Hinkson whistled softly. "Do they know who did it?"

"Sí, Señor. But most of these men get away. Don Diego Silvestre take two that he catch to Sacramento. I do not hear yet what he accomplish there. But I think it does no good. The asesinos are americanos. ¿Me comprende?"

Hinkson shifted his weight in his saddle. "Sorry to hear it."

"Next you see Juan Gómez or Ignacio Pereda, you will tell them this? I know they wish to have news of their old patrón, even though that news is bad."

"Well, sure. Glad to oblige. Come to think of it, Pereda is stationed at the cow camp just south of here if you'd care to ride on over and tell him yourself."

"No, I thank you, Señor. My business is too urgent. I send Ignacio my regards with you. And my compliments to your patrón, Yak Sutterlan. I have hear good things about him. Some day, I hope I have the honor to meet him. Adiós, Baldés. Que le vaya bien."

"Adiós, Solano. Till we meet again." The cowboy shook his head as Ruiz disappeared up the brushy draw. "Now, why did I say that?" he wondered half aloud. "That hombre sure gave me a funny feeling. I reckon I ain't seen the last of him. Aw, hell. Some days, I think you're more than half loco, Baldy Hinkson."

Without a backwards look himself, Ruiz rode on, climbing the hills which rose more and more sharply before him and descending into the canyons between them where the afternoon shadows grew deeper and deeper.

When finally he stopped to make camp, he was only three hours' ride from Jackson. The evening was balmy. There was no need for a fire. Ruiz settled himself with his back against a tree and chewed on strips of jerky while he watched his horse graze the patch of green near a small spring.

Gradually, however, the scene before his eyes gave way to a more pleasant one in memory. He saw his uncle's peach grove in springtime, decked with masses of pink flowers above the emerald grass. He saw himself strolling through that fragrant fairyland by the side of a beautiful girl: a girl who did not chatter silly nothings as did the others of his acquaintance; a girl who turned upon him smiling eyes, dark eyes whose brilliance left him breathless. He saw himself gathering peach blossoms to heap into her arms. He saw her hide her face in their multitude and then look up at him. He saw himself lean to kiss her cheek, unable to resist its gentle curve. And then her lips. He saw her let fall the flowers to slip her arms about his neck. And for a moment, he folded close the loveliest girl he had ever seen, the only girl he had ever yet wanted to have for a wife.

But he had not asked her. The words had lain sweet on his tongue. But he had not asked her. Her answer had glowed in the warmth of her kiss. But he had not asked her. How glad he was now that he had not asked her!

Of course, he had known even then that if he wed the girl, he must accept the burden of the brother. And now, it was still worse. Now, had he been wed to the sister of Escobar, he would have been faced with the choice either of abetting a thief and a murderer or of killing his own brother-in-law. And yet . . .

Amanda herself was wholly ignorant of her brother's transgressions. Had she known of them, she might, indeed, have disowned him, as Ruiz had hinted to doña Graciela. But who was to tell her that Manuel was leading a wastrel's life in the Foothills, that he was admitting as his closest associates men whom his father would not have deigned to recognize?

And so, to delay his dilemma, Ruiz had spent the summer with his uncle's vaqueros, helping them round up herds of select beef to drive to the Gold Country for sale. He had overseen the loading of five grain carts. And he had made two drives to the hills, bringing back gold and urgent orders for more cattle.

Meanwhile, Amanda had gone home to take care of her father in his empty house with the help of a single servant girl and one aging vaquero who chose to spend his last days within sight of the Old Adobe rather than sell himself to the gringos for what little he was worth.

Don Diego and his eldest son, Francisco, had made frequent visits, bringing food and whatever else don Fernando would allow his daughter to accept. Had she been willing to accept Francisco, don Fernando surely would have moved with her back to the Casa Grande de Silvestre. But Amanda's memories of the peach grove were at least as poignant as Simón's. She received Francisco with courtesy but not with love. And don Fernando was too proud to impel his youngest daughter to marry of necessity.

And so, it had come to this. Ruiz thought bitterly of the rancher's death and wrestled with the ugly idea that had he obeyed his own true inclination and married Amanda, don Fernando would still be alive and sitting in the garden of the Casa Grande. He would have had the joy of grandchildren to look forward to, something he could again take pride in. And there would have been the pleasant journey to the south with the wedding party to spend several months with the Familia Ruiz.

And Manuel? What would Manuel be doing? Would Manuel have been content to come home and act the gentleman on the wealth of his in-laws? And even if he had, could Simón have borne with the daily sight of him? Was the pleasure of Amanda's constant company sufficient remedy for the poison of Manuel's?

Ruiz got up from his seat against the tree and went to quench his thirst at the little spring. "It is pointless to conjecture!" he reminded himself. "I cannot change the past. And what **must** be, **shall** be done."

But this wise philosophy did not prevent his thoughts from inevitably turning to his farewell to Amanda at the entrance of his uncle's house just after dawn that day.

She had not yet been dressed in mourning. But every gown she owned, except the one that she had on, was boiling in black dye. The smell of it curled his nostrils even in memory. Simón had not allowed her much time to speak to him.

He did not dare. He feared she would divine the true purpose for his returning to the Gold Country. He imagined she might read it in his eyes. When she gave him both her hands and looked longingly into his face, he only bent to kiss her fingers, pretending that he did not understand their pressure upon his, pretending that it was respect for her sorrow which kept him from taking her into his arms and offering her the hope she could not ask him for.

"You will keep Manuel from seeking vengeance?" she had reminded him.

"I have vowed it," he responded.

"Hasta luego, Simón. I will think of you."

"And I . . . of you, Amanda. Adiós."

* * *

Ruiz returned to the tree and cast himself upon his saddle blanket which he had spread out on the ground beneath it. "I will hope to find him quickly," he told himself. "I will not wait to prove his guilt. I will challenge him first and prove it later. ¡Ay! God give me strength."

CHAPTER TWENTY-ONE:

AT THE TOP OF THE STAIRS

It was noon when Ruiz rode into Jackson. He had been watching a heavy plume of smoke for an hour, wondering if some of the buildings in the town itself might have caught fire. It was a constant danger during the summer. The whole countryside was tinder dry. But the first rider he met on the road told him it was only a miner's shack. "They got it mostly under control, now," the man said. "It was right near the creek, so they was able to contain it. But the cabin itself burned to to a pile of ashes. Scary thing. Too near the town for comfort."

"No one is hurt?" asked Ruiz.

"Nope. The man that owned it wasn't there when the blaze started. Likely he left a cookin' fire untended. You just can't be too careful. Well, I'll be gettin' on. Good day to you."

Ruiz found the town's main street nearly deserted. Most of the populace at liberty to leave had gone to combat the fire, to see the extent of the destruction or to commiserate with the deprived miner.

Simón rode directly to the rear of the Eureka Dance Hall and dismounted, tied his bay to a slender tree that leaned toward the creek. Swiftly, he strode up the narrow alleyway to the closed door. He knocked on it three times. Then twice. Then once. He looked up at the little window on the second story. It remained tightly shuttered. But in front of him, the door itself suddenly opened. He sprang forward.

A quick-drawn breath confirmed that his summons had been mistaken for another's. He turned around in the passage to see the ugly servant girl cowering behind the door. "Violeta! I will not hurt you. Did you think it was Manuel?"

She nodded.

"He is not here?"

She shook her head.

"But he has been here recently?"

A nod, yes.

"¡Niña! Are you weeping?"

Yes.

Simón took the girl by the shoulders and drew her into the light of the half open door so that he could more clearly watch her face, now twisted as much with grief as deformity. "La Magdalena has beaten you!" he guessed.

Violeta shook her head.

"Ah! Your brother. It is your brother you weep for."

Yes.

Ruiz watched the tears dribbling down her cheeks. "Is he dead?" he asked softly.

Violeta nodded.

"Trudis!" came the voice of la Magdalena from the top of the stairs.

"Stay here!" whispered Ruiz. "Bolt the door. Let no one in unless I tell you."

"Trudis! Is that a man's voice? Who is there? Manolo? Is that you?"

Ruiz bounded lightly up the stairs. "It is I, Señorita!" he answered as la Magdalena appeared on the landing, silhouetted against the light. "It is Simón Ruiz."

"Don Simón! You have returned . . . so soon?" She backed off several steps.

"I have an urgent message for Manuel. Can you tell me where he is?"

The Rose of Jackson regarded Ruiz in silence for a moment. Then her tenseness relaxed and she came forward. "You have forced entry into my house only to look for Manuel? This was not gallant of you. Nor would I have expected such bluntness from so silver a tongue as yours." She approached him closely, looked up into his face with a little toss of her head. "Manuel Escobar is not here," she said. "Nor do I know where he has gone. Nor do I care. So!"

Ruiz removed his hat. "Señorita, were my message for him less heavy, less pressing, I would rejoice in your ignorance regarding Escobar. But the news I bear I wish him to hear from none but myself. And as bad news travels on the wind, it is necessary for me to find him soon. Or it will be too late. Will you at least tell me when was the last you saw him?"

"Yesterday," replied the Rose, tilting her head so that her black hair fell in a rippling curtain to her shoulder.

"And when he left you, did he ride north or south?"

"I did not ask him what he intended. It was nothing to me."

Ruiz sighed. "Forgive me. I had hoped he might be here. Or that you would be able to direct me to him. But I presumed too much. I will not annoy you further." He turned back toward the stairs.

La Magdalena caught his arm. "You truly have a message for him? It is not an excuse to find him for another reason?"

"Señorita! Of what do you suspect me?"

"I suspect you, Don Simón, of mistaking me for a vain and thoughtless woman. I suspect you of thinking I will betray Manuel to you for the price of a kiss."

"On the contrary. I thought you would tell me as a friend where I might look to find the son of an honorable man."

She smiled. "Vaya. Will you speak of honor to me, now? You would do better to offer me the kiss." The hand she had put on his arm slid to his shoulder. "There are not many men as candid as yourself and yet so clever. But you do not deceive me, Don Simón. And I know you will find Manuel, whether I tell you where he has gone or no. And what will you do when you find him?"

"I will tell him such terrible news as should recall him instantly to the Valley. I will repeat to him the words his sister bade me say."

"His sister. Ah! There is the reason for the difference I sense in you. You must not have seen her for some time the last you were here. Now, I may beg you in vain to remember it was I who sheltered you from Mariano García when he pursued you from the house of Paulo Gonzalves. And I who lay for two hours in your arms while he searched the streets. I who showed you the side door he has no knowledge of. Yes. Of course, I guessed the truth. And I guess it again. Now, tell me the news you are bringing Manolito from the Valley. And then, I will tell you where he is so that you shall still be the first from whom he hears it."

Ruiz frowned. "Your servant was weeping," he said.

"Trudis? She is a silly sheep. It takes so little to make her weep. A sharp look, an unkind word. The death of a sparrow."

"A sparrow! And how did the gorrión die? If he was murdered, I will avenge him."

"¡Ave María! Candid and clever! You are a dangerous man, Patrón. Tell me nothing, then. Leave me to guess. Manuel has gone to Mokelumne Hill. He will not dare to return to Jackson for some time. I warned him that you would not remain long in the Valley. There. Now pay me the kiss, and I will tell you who has followed him south."

"I will **ask** you to tell me," said Simón. "And the kiss you shall have regardless."

"You have not seen Paulo Gonzalves to know who he is or what he looks like, have you?"

"No."

"Yet it is important that you recognize him, first. For he will surely kill you if he can. So will Mariano García. But him you now know."

"Yes. Who killed the gorrión?"

"That, I do not know. Before heaven I swear that I do not. Nor do I know who sent the saddlebags to me. Little is told me. I am so often left to guess."

"What do you guess, then, Señorita?"

"Oh, Señor! Will you act on my guess alone? And suppose I am wrong?"

"Tell me how I may know Paulo Gonzalves. Give me some clue that I may look for to identify him."

"Paulo is taller than the others," said the Rose. "Taller than Manolo. Taller than you. And he is fond of fine clothes. When last I saw him, he was wearing a new jacket embroidered in gold. I noticed it was a little short in the sleeves." La Magdalena smoothed her hand back down Simón's arm. "Yes," she whispered. "I think it would fit you." She rose on tiptoe to touch her lips to his. And Ruiz allowed himself to savor their invitation, their admiration, their temptation.

"To keep long away from you, mujer," he said, "Manuel must drink himself into a state of insensibility. And if I only wait here for him to succumb to his longing, I will surely find him sooner than if I ride to Mokelumne Hill."

"You are welcome for as long as you wish."

"Say instead that I will still be welcome after I have met Manuel."

"Whenever you choose. But don't make me wait too long. I will not be taken for granted. That is a lesson Manuel has still to learn. He thinks I hold myself exclusively for him. That I languish in his absence. He is a conceited fool. I would yawn at the news of his death. Simón! I have never met a man like you. You excite me. You frighten me. Before, you were determined. Now, you are desperate. Is she so very beautiful, this sister of Manuel? No, don't tell me. I am already jealous of her. For I know she holds your heart. And yet, she has refused you! She is fickle, like Manuel. There is some other man she favors, now. But if she knew her don Simón is seeking comfort in the hungry arms of Magdalena Obregón . . .!"

Ruiz smiled. "And is it thus you judge the world in the shadows of your mirror? The heart you feel beneath your own is not so broken nor so desperate as you fancy it to be. Shall I invent a fantasy for you as well? Shall I believe that you have buried and mourned a young husband and yet refused the widow's lot? That life among your in-laws bored you, that your parents are yet grieving your departure from decorum as if it were your life you'd lost rather than your freedom that you've gained? Shall we pretend you are reluctant to face your mirror every morning for fear that what you see there will justify the censure of your family? And yet, every morning, the wicked glass reflects a Magdalena just as beautiful and full of pride and fire as it showed the night before."

The Rose of Jackson clung to Ruiz in terror. "Go!" she breathed. "Go before I can confess to you how close your guess is to the truth. Go before I can suspect you are an angel in disguise, come to find me out and shame me, to punish me with hopeless love. Oh, I was wrong about the sister of Manuel! It is you that have rejected her! Even now, she counts the beads of her rosary and prays heaven to send you back to her. Why don't you go?"

"I am no angel," said Simón. "Nor do I judge you. I only want to find Manuel. Him I have judged. Him I shall punish. And those men I learn have served him. Hasta luego, Señorita."

La Magdalena put both hands to her heart and fled into her parlor, shut the door behind her. Simón went quickly down the stairs.

The servant was still waiting at the bottom. "Violeta!" he said softly, knowing that upstairs, ears were straining to hear him leave. "Violeta, I want to find your little grandmother. Can you direct me to her house? Point in the right direction."

Violeta shook her head vigorously and laid her hands together, palm to palm, rolled her eyes to heaven.

"No harm shall come to her, I swear. Nor to you. Direct me. Quickly!"

She nodded, showed him her praying hands again, then held up one forefinger and crossed it with the other. She pointed up the street the way Simón had come.

"You mean she's at the church."

A definite nod.

"Gracias, niña. Your brother's death shall yet be answered for." And Simón opened the door, let himself out, traversed the alley toward the creek. He felt eyes watching his retreat. But he did not look back until he had cleared the buildings. Then, he saw the shuttered window close.

CHAPTER TWENTY-TWO:

THE CANDLES IN THE CHURCH

The little adobe chapel sat humbly at the north end of the dusty street, far enough removed from the town as to scarcely be a part of it. It was patronized exclusively by Mexicans, though there were Catholics of several nationalities in Jackson.

Ruiz dismounted before it, secured his horse, and entered. He stopped just inside the door to remove his hat and cross himself while he looked around the simple room. At its far end stood the altar, and to one side was a bank of candles. Only three of them were lit.

There were four people in the church. One was the priest. A young woman and her little girl sat on a rough bench pew, their heads devoutly bowed. Before the bank of candles, another woman knelt. Ruiz made his way quietly in her direction. He dropped to his knees beside her and bent to peer into her face around the border of the ragged shawl that covered her head. He could see only a wrinkled cheek and a drooping nose that nearly touched the moving, shriveled lips beneath. "For Thine is the kingdom," they were muttering in Spanish, "and the power . . ."

"And the glory," Ruiz joined in.

The old woman started but did not look up. "Forever and ever," she whispered in unison with him.

"Amen," said Simón.

Half blind, milky eyes turned toward him wonderingly. Mottled fingers, gnarled and stiff, put back the frayed edge of the shawl that brushed the wrinkled cheek. "God bless you, hijo," mumbled the old woman.

"And you, abuelita. May He give you great joy in your children and your grandchildren."

"My children. My only child is dead. And one of my grandchildren has gone to join her in heaven."

"The burden of sorrow is heavy," said Ruiz.

"God in His grace shall send me the strength to endure it."

"And for whom do you evoke the protection of the saints, abuelita?" Ruiz tipped his head toward the three candles burning brightly from the tiers before them.

"For my nieta, Gertrudis. She has no one but her old grandmother. And what power have I but the power of prayer to keep her from the same death, which took from me her poor simple brother only two days ago?"

"Tell me the name of the man who killed your grandson, abuelita," whispered Ruiz. "And I vow to you that he will not harm your granddaughter."

The half blind eyes widened. The wizened cheeks paled, and then two spots of color appeared there. "Who are you, Señor?"

"I call myself Juan Solano. And I call your granddaughter Violeta."

"Ah!" breathed the old woman. "It is you! But that was not the name she said."

"No. Nor is it a name known to Manuel Escobar. Nor to Paulo Gonsalves. Who killed your grandson, abuelita?"

The gnarled hand groped for his arm. "Can I trust you?"

"Before heaven."

"Come, then. My prayers have been answered. The saints have sent you. I will tell you what I know." And pulling herself to her feet, the grandmother of Violeta limped slowly toward the door, leaning on the steady arm of Juan Solano.

"My grandson is not the first one to be murdered by these men whose names you have repeated," she confided in a cracked whisper. "They came to Jackson together from Drytown early in the summer. They left that town to avoid the suspicion of a gringo judge named Curtees."

"What did he suspect them of?"

"They had hidden a band of robbers from the sheriff. One of the bandits had worked for don Manuel Escobar before he left the Valley."

"How did you learn these things?"

"Gertrudis learned them, listening to the men talk with that woman that she works for."

"Didn't they suspect?"

"They think it does not matter. They think my child cannot speak."

"Can she?"

"Yes. Well enough. And she is clever. God in His grace has made her look ugly and stupid only in order to protect her from harm. I have often told her so. I have told her that people with eyes that see beneath the surface will recognize her as the lovely child that she is."

"God in His grace has blessed her with a wise and caring grandmother," said Ruiz. "Tell me of Escobar."

"Yes. Gertrudis heard him say to la Magdalena that there were twelve men who had pledged themselves to serve him, but he mentioned by name only the portugués, Gonzalves, and the mexicano, García, and one other man, a chileno called Pío Pinto. These men have killed at least three Americans and have robbed many more. But then, they attacked a varón named Ruiz Silvestre. And for fear of him, they have fled."

"And for fear of him," said Simón, "they have murdered your grandson."

"Yes."

"Did you see them?"

"I begged them for his life while they cut his throat."

"Why did they not kill you?"

"They thought my fear would silence me."

"Which of these animals was the actual murderer?"

"El portugués."

"But Escobar was with him?"

"He sat watching from his saddle."

"No one else saw? Where did this take place?"

"At the door of my house. My neighbor saw them, I think. But he would not dare to speak. If Escobar found out, my neighbor would surely pay with his life."

"But there was a risk," mused Ruiz. "Why would Escobar chance so much in order to silence your grandson?"

"Alejo was simple. But he knew right from wrong, which is more than can be said for many who thought they were his betters. They feared he would betray them because he was honest. Because he was simple. Because he was brave."

"Señora. If I were to send you and your granddaughter to the Valley to protect you from these men, would you go? Would you leave the grave of your daughter and your grandson for the sake of Violeta? I would ask a friend to take you. Fidel Buenrostro. You may know him?"

"Patrón," replied the old woman, pressing his arm, "Fidel Buenrostro left Jackson this morning, riding between two other Mexicans. I did not think he went willingly."

Ruiz drew a quick breath. Then a long one. "What did they look like?"

"I am sorry, Patrón. I am an old woman, now. I can see well enough only to recognize those people already known to me. And not always them. All I can tell you is that one of the men with him rode a light-colored horse. The other was dark. Perhaps black."

Ruiz bowed his head in thought. "If you wish to go to the Valley, I will take you myself," he said then.

"No, Señor. The saints will protect us. Find Escobar. And the portugués. Their chileno and their bandoleros. It is not only my granddaughter's life you must save."

"Yes. I will go. God forgive my delay! Pray that I find them soon!"

Jackson's main street was filling with traffic again. The fire upstream was nearly out and the threat from it less urgent. Other business recalled most of the spectators if not those who had actually fought the blaze. To avoid them, Ruiz leaped his horse across the creek and rode on behind the buildings to the south end of town. Few people saw him or remarked his passing if they did.

Between Jackson and Butte City, he met three American riders. They asked him for news of the fire whose smoke still rose behind the shoulder of Jackson Butte. He repeated the report given him earlier about the miner's cabin and heard the inevitable opinion that it would take just one careless man to send all of Jackson up in flames, or any other town in the foothills. He agreed and rode on.

In Butte City, he asked if anyone had seen three Mexicans pass through town that morning, one on a light roan or a dun. He received two affirmatives and was directed on toward Big Bar and Mokelumne Hill.

Big Bar was a mining camp on the Mokelumne River. The man who ran the ferry there remembered three Mexicans crossing to the south side that morning. "They was a mighty silent party," he said. "It appeared to me the man in the middle was anxious about something. And the other two was grim-faced."

"The man in the middle, you say, he was the small one? And older? Grey hairs?"

"Yep. And he kept watchin' the feller with the scabby ear as if he'd like to tell him something. Are you goin' across after them? It'll cost you a dollar with your horse, or a pinch of dust if you ain't got the coin. Not many of us do, seems like."

Simón felt in his pocket for a sack of gold dust. "Last I come over this river, she cost me less," he said. "Seventy-five cents."

"I thought I remembered you from somewhere. I don't often forget a face, but I'm havin' some trouble placing yours."

"Do you remember what the third man look like?" Simón pressed a little dust between his finger and thumb and transferred it to the ferryman's palm.

"I sure do. He was a good-lookin' devil. Nigh as black as his horse. Eyes like a rat's. Are you sure you want to catch up to them three? If it was me, I'd sooner ride in the other direction."

"The man in the middle, he hopes that I catch them," said Ruiz.

The ferryman grunted. "I'll bet he does! Well, you'd better go on then. Good luck."

Simón led his bay onto the heavy planks of the ferryboat. Two miners afoot got on with him. And they were swung out into the swift current on the mule-drawn cables. The gelding shifted his weight uneasily and snorted. "Hang onto him," said one of the miners, eyeing the horse. "I ain't hankerin' for a cold bath."

They gained the opposite bank without incident, however. Ruiz remounted and spurred up the steep trail leading out of the river canyon. It was a long climb. He met no one. It was two hours past noon when he rode into the town of Mokelumne Hill.

And there, tied to the rail of the Grand Hotel, were a light roan and a black-bay. The coats of both horses were rough with dust and dried sweat. They stood with heads low over the hitching rack, each with a hind leg comfortably cocked. But there was no sorrel mare.

CHAPTER TWENTY-THREE:

THE HOTEL AT
MOKELUMNE HILL

The building before Ruiz was wide but shallow. Two
stories in front and three in back, it clung to the steep hillside
as if with both hands and its teeth. The door nearest the
corner opened into what was affectionately known as the
Court Room Saloon. It had seen many trials, some of which
had ended in hanging the accused from the porch roof, and
others which saw the entire proceedings turn into a friendly
drinking bout, including the judge and the jury, the plaintiff,
the defendant, and all of the witnesses.

The room was almost never empty. But two o'clock in the afternoon was one of its least busy times. The bartender was taking a nap. There was a quiet card game under way at a corner table. A yellow dog lay across the doorsill. Ruiz stepped over the animal as he entered. It opened one eye but did not lift its head.

Simón saw that all the card players marked his appearance with wary interest though none met his look. He went to the counter and reached across it to joggle the bartender's shoulder.

The man came awake with a jerk. "Uh! What will it be?" he asked. Receiving no answer, he rubbed one hand over his face from brow to chin and stared at Ruiz. "What's on your mind, amigo?"

"I look for a man," said Simón. "I have important thing to tell him. They say he comes here."

"Yeah? What's his name?"

"Fidel Buenrostro."

In the mirror, Simón saw one of the card players rise from the table. He was dark, almost black. His close-set eyes were small. Their glitter was hard. He came toward the bar with insolent casualness.

"There's a party of Mexicans stayin' here, right enough," said the bartender, "but they didn't all give their names. I don't recall a Fiddle Ben Rosco. Want to look at the register?" He got off his stool and might have reached under the counter, but the dark man slapped his hand down on the bar to warn him not to.

"Say, now . . ." objected the bartender mildly.

"Who are you?" the dark man asked Ruiz in Spanish.

Simón met his stare in the mirror and slowly turned around. "Who is it that asks me?" he countered.

"I am Juan Torres."

"And I am Juan Solano."

"You are lying."

"So are you."

"Why are you looking for Buenrostro?"

"He is a friend of mine," said Simón.

"Yes. We thought he was. But he would not confess it. I know who you are," the man added, his eyes glinting at Ruiz. "I was one of those who robbed you on the road from Ranchería."

"And you dare to tell me to my face?"

The outlaw smiled. "Patrón, this is not the Valley. I owe allegiance to none but my comrades . . . and to Manuel Escobar. You are looking for him, aren't you? You will never find him. We will not let you near him. Did you think you could walk right through us? Did you think we would step aside and doff our hats to you? I advise you to return to your rancho. Here you will stop nothing but a bullet."

"What have you done with Buenrostro?"

"Do you expect me to tell you?"

"Is Gonzalves here with you?"

"Perhaps." Simón saw Torres glance in the mirror at his associate whose left earlobe was ragged and scabby as if its tip had been shot off. At Torres' look, he rose slowly to his feet.

But before he could move out from behind the table, someone else came into the room through an open doorway at the far end of the bar. He was not especially tall, not much above average height. But he was taller than Ruiz. He wore a fine jacket of leather and wool, richly embroidered in gold. It was a little too short in the sleeves.

Simón felt his face heat with rage.

Torres smiled again. "Don Paulo!" he said, turning to greet the Brazilian. "Here is a man that is asking for you."

Gonzalves came forward, his look more curious than wary. He was at his ease. He feared nothing, no one. "Who is this?" he asked, looking Simón up and down.

"He says his name is Juan Solano," replied Torres.

"What do you want with me, Don Juan Solano de Tal?"

"I am looking for Manuel Escobar," said Ruiz. "But Torres tells me I must satisfy myself with the second in command. Is that you? Or Mariano García?"

Gonzalves switched a quick, inquiring look at Torres.

"This, Patrón, is actually don Simón Ruiz Silvestre," said the outlaw. And removing his hat, the man bowed in mock respect, including both of them in the gesture.

The Brazilian exclaimed under his breath and reached for the gun at his belt. But Simón lunged forward, catching his wrist and misdirecting his aim. The pistol went off, nicking the outer corner of the bar. The dog in the doorway yelped and sprang away.

Ruiz and Gonzalves wrestled for possession of the gun. The American card players had leaped to their feet at the shot, knocking the chairs in all directions. The man with the frayed ear was moving toward the open doorway, his back to the wall, his eyes busy. Torres had his own gun half drawn, but he, too, was keenly aware of the Americans and the possibility of their interference. He hesitated.

Then, the bartender rose from behind his cover and thrust the long muzzle of a rifle over the counter. "Hold it!" he warned. "I'll shoot the whole lot of you! Gonzales! Stand back! If you open fire again, I'll drill you right through."

"I am Gonzalves!" spat out the Brazilian, wrenching himself free of Ruiz, the gun still in his hand. He backed off a few steps, raising the weapon at Simón.

"Don't do it!" said the bartender.

"Why you protect him?"

"I just want to protect my mirrors and bottles, that's all. You gentlemen can take your little disagreement outside before you go on with it. Take it clear to Chile Gulch. Amigo," he said, darting appraising looks at Ruiz, "it appears you bit off more than you could chew. Suppose you go out, first. I'll give you five minutes headstart on Señor Gonsalvos and company. And don't say later I never done you no favors. Go on, man! Don't you know when you're outnumbered?"

Ruiz backed reluctantly toward the saloon door. Reaching it, he whirled and flung out of it. There was no one on the street. But eyes were watching from every door and window along the brow of the Hill.

At the corner, Simón threw himself down the steep path to the rear of the hotel. Halfway along its lower length was a closed door. Ruiz put his shoulder to it. It opened inward.

He stepped inside and looked around. He was in a storeroom. Crates and barrels, boxes and sacks sat this way and that in the semi-darkness. The door itself could not be made fast. Its hasp was broken. He left it and ran to a flight of stairs leading up to a second door. He feared to find it locked, but it also opened easily. He pushed through it and paused again.

He found himself in a corridor. Two doorways opened onto it. One was the kitchen's. The other led to a second hallway at right angles to the first. Sounds of running feet, curses in Spanish and English, banging doors, thumping and bumping issued from that quarter.

"Manuel!" Ruiz heard the voice of Gonzalves. Then a brisk knock. "Manuel! Are you there?"

A room door opened. Simón risked a quick look around the corner but instantly drew back. The Brazilian was standing in the hallway. "What is happening, Paulo?" asked the voice of Escobar.

"Ruiz is in Mokelumne Hill, looking for you."

"Already! Impossible."

"You heard the shot? The man accosted me. Then, he tried to disarm me. In the struggle, I fired my gun. The bartender interferred and sent him to Chile Gulch. Manuel, the gringos are unhappy with the disturbance. We must leave here immediately."

"This is most inconvenient, Paulo. Send the men on ahead of us. We will meet them at Chile Gulch. Or San Andreas, if you prefer."

"But I dare not stay myself, Manuel. The gringos blame me in part for what happened."

"Go with the others, then. I will join you later."

"What about Ruiz?"

"Has he not gone?"

"I do not know. I came instantly to find you."

"You would have done better to follow him."

"There is no time to search for him, now! The men are preparing to leave."

"Well, Ruiz is probably running before you. Catch him, if you can."

"As you wish."

The door closed. Footsteps retreated. Simón was about to slide around the corner when he heard a noise behind him. He whirled to see the man with the ragged ear come into the corridor from the cellar.

The outlaw saw Ruiz in the same moment. He crouched and drew a knife from his waist. Simón stooped to whip his own blade from his boot. But the outlaw changed his mind. He dodged back through the door. There was a bolt on it. Simón shot it across. Then he returned to the corner. He peered around it to be sure the way was clear before he went on to the door Gonzalves had knocked on. He rapped briskly.

The answer from within was a string of Spanish curses. But a moment later, the door was opened. Simón struck it wider to admit himself and stepped through it, his knife ready. He was greeted by a stifled cry from across the room and a surprised gasp from Escobar. "Ruiz!"

Simón caught the edge of the door out of Manuel's grasp and closed it, tripped its latch behind him.

Escobar backed away. His shirt was open down the front. His silver buttoned pantalón swung loosely around his legs, fastened only halfway down the outside of his thighs. On the rumpled bed behind him, a Mexican girl huddled herself into a knot against the headboard as if to disappear before the eyes of the intruder.

But Ruiz did not do more than glance in her direction. "Manuel," he said, gesturing at Escobar with his knife. "Alístese. You will come with me."

Escobar retreated another step. "How did you . . .?"

"Dress yourself. Leave your gun where it is. And your knife."

Escobar drew himself up with as much affront as he could affect. "Why do you meddle in my affairs?" he demanded. "Have you so little to occupy you that you must look to my misfortune for amusement?"

"You have yet to learn the full extent of that misfortune," replied Simón. "I have come in part to tell you. Your father is dead."

"Dead." Manuel made a motion as if to cross himself but did not complete the sign. "Don Fernando is dead. And so?"

"The news does not move you. I feared it would not."

"What do you expect me to do? Fall on my knees and pray for his soul? He is better off dead. He had nothing left to live for."

"Certainly he could no longer take pride in his son."

"¡Entremetido! Why do you plague me?"

"You are leaving with me. Button your shirt. Have you paid this puta for her services?"

"You have not allowed me time enough to enjoy them."

"¡Perro!"

"San Simón," retorted Manuel, his lip curling.

Ruiz left the door and crossed to a rickety table where Manuel's revolver lay. He put down his knife before he picked up the gun and added it to those at his waist. Then, he caught up Manuel's jacket and felt in the pockets, produced three sacks of gold dust which he tossed onto the bed. "Take them, mujer," he told the cringing prostitute.

Escobar stepped forward in protest. Ruiz seized the knife he had put down. Manuel stopped. Slowly, he buttoned his shirt. "Where do you intend to take me?" he inquired. "Back to the Rancho Silvestre? Will you offer me the consolation of your uncle's abundance?"

"Tell me what has become of Fidel Buenrostro," said Ruiz.

"Who? That cholo in Jackson whose mare was stolen?"

"Yes. Where is he?"

"I haven't the slightest idea. What makes you think that

I might have?"

"I wished to believe you had some control over the men who pretend to serve you. But I had forgotten. You are usually unaware of their actions. They robbed and almost murdered me without your knowledge. They sold you my horse for a tempting price. They may also take an honest miner from his family and drag him across the Mokelumne River to kill him where none will ever find him. But at least, they do not slaughter orphans without your sanction. That deed you have overseen yourself."

"What are you talking about?"

"The brother of the servant of Magdalena Obregón."

"Who has told you this lie?"

"Manuel, Manuel! Put aside your pretense. It is too late. I find you here among your rats in this basurero and you would have me believe you guiltless? Indeed, you may rejoice in the death of don Fernando. For it has spared him the shame of your depravity. Only your sisters are not so fortunate."

"My sisters," repeated Escobar. "You mean Amanda."

"She thinks you will seek to avenge your father."

"Avenge him! He has not merely died, then. He was killed."

"Amanda has charged me to say to you that you should content yourself with the love and respect of your family and friends for fear that you might also be killed in an attempt to redress the wrongs done your father. For you are all that is left to her."

Again, Manuel's lip curled in contempt. "Poor child!" he said. "But let her take heart. She will have Simón Ruiz Silvestre for a husband. What greater felicity could she possibly desire?"

"No," said Simón. "She will not have me."

"She has refused you! The girl has more presence of mind than I thought!"

"I have not asked her. I will not ask her. For I will never offend my father's name by linking it to yours!"

Manuel felt quickly for the gun missing from his waist, then relaxed. "Ah," he said. "You have come here to kill me."

"No," replied Ruiz heavily. "Only unless I must do so to prevent your escape or to protect my own life. I meant to kill you. I meant to challenge you as one may challenge his peer without loss of honor. But I will not show you so much courtesy. Instead, I will offer you only a final choice." Ruiz paused, the words tasting foul in his mouth. He had not intended this.

Escobar watched him. "I am at your mercy, San Simón."

Ruiz continued with an effort. "You shall swear to me upon your life that you will return to the Valley and comfort your grieving sister, show respect for your father's memory. If you do not, I will deliver you personally into the hands of Sheriff Phoenix and accuse you to him of your crimes. The gringos would be only too glad to hang you. But I prefer to spare Amanda the pain of such terrible news."

"Ever the gallant gentleman!" murmured Manuel.

"Don't goad me!" warned Ruiz. "Here." He tossed the jacket to Escobar. "Put that on. We are leaving."

"But what if I say I am ready to vow to you upon my life that I will return to the Valley?"

"I will go with you . . . to make sure."

"It will be a long and weary ride for you in such loathsome company as myself," predicted Escobar.

"It will. Alístese. Or I will take you half dressed."

Lingeringly, as if relishing the impatience and anger of Ruiz, Manuel obeyed.

The prostitute had watched it all in fascination. And when the two men turned at last toward the door, she dared to slide off the bed to her feet. "Señor Ruiz!" she said.

Simón caught Manuel by the elbow and checked him on the point of his knife. "What do you want, mujer?"

"All this gold . . ." She indicated the three buckskin sacks of dust still lying where he had tossed them on the bed. "Did you mean to give it all to me?"

"It is not mine to give you. But neither is it his. Do

whatever you wish with it. If you want it for yourself, that is your affair. But if your conscience troubles you concerning it, remember that it is enough to feed and clothe a dozen fatherless children. I leave it to you to decide. What more?" he added, seeing her eyes widen and her mouth half open as if to speak.

"If it will keep them from following you, I will pretend that he is still here with me!" she volunteered in a rush.

"My horse is standing on Main Street. So our departure cannot go unobserved. But it was a kind thought. And I thank you," said Ruiz. And then he reached past Escobar to open the door and prod him out of it into the corridor beyond.

CHAPTER TWENTY-FOUR:

DELAYED

Had it not been for the burning of Uncle Peter's cabin, Sydney might have made good her planned escape before Saturday, even without waiting for the return of Ruiz. But at the insistence of the Reverend Thomson's wife, she and her aunt must stay in the parsonage until a new house could be constructed on the claim. Sydney was often left to herself, since Aunt Agnes took greater pleasure in Ida Thomson's conversation than in that of her niece. Sydney would listen in unprotesting silence while her aunt bemoaned the loss of her furniture and the priceless clock, but she found little or nothing to say in return.

Amy also found Sydney dull company. She could not coax so much as a smile from her, much less a laugh. Sydney did not care to speculate in secret as to the strength of Daniel Perrin's ardor. She had no interest in the precise shade of Paul McCormick's eyes. Nor would she talk about Cecil's partiality. And Amy had but little interest in guns and horses. So, the parson's youngest left Sydney mostly to her own devices and turned as she always had to her sister, Susan Durham.

But even so, Sydney's plans for escape were thwarted at every turn. It was not possible, she found, to leave the parsonage alone. And even if it had been, she could not have ventured far along the streets in Jackson without attracting a numerous escort. The brown dress and grey, bibbed apron might as well have been an iron ball and chain.

She set herself to wait, therefore, until she could return to the creek. It was no easy thing. Daniel Perrin had kept his word about helping the Simpsons rebuild their cabin. And every evening, he came with Uncle Peter and Cecil and Paul for supper at the parsonage. Afterwards, he spent an hour in the parlor with the family. Aunt Agnes would not excuse Sydney from these nightly gatherings.

"I want you to be nicer to Daniel, honey," Aunt Aggie told her on Friday afternoon. "He's going to a lot of trouble for us, and I suspect that it's mainly on your account. You don't want him to think you're ungrateful?"

"He doesn't care what I think," said Sydney.

"Of course he does! But you want to look out, or you'll lose him to Amy. She's such a pretty girl, and she knows how to make eyes at the men. And Daniel's a good-looking boy."

"She can have him," said Sydney.

"I think he'd have to fight Paul for her, first."

"Fine."

"Do you know that if you had given Paul any encouragement, you could have had him? When are you going to wake up, honey, and discover that you're a woman?"

Sydney made no answer. Nor did she make any effort to be nice to Perrin that night. It made no difference. He sought her as usual after supper, though he must sit on a straight-backed chair to be near her, for she refused to understand her aunt's hints about there being plenty of room left on the sofa. She sat down in her usual place near the window where she could see the street and those who passed along it. But she watched in vain for a certain familiar face with eyes as black as bits of ebony beneath a wide-brimmed hat.

"Tomorrow," Uncle Peter announced, looking around the room in satisfaction, "the Simpson family moves back to the creek."

Amid exclamations of gratitude and approval, Daniel Perrin added, "It's a bigger cabin than the one you lost, Miz Simpson. And tight as a drum. If it weren't for your things bein' burnt, I'd say you'd find it an actual improvement."

"Thanks to you, I'm sure it is," agreed Aunt Aggie. "We are lucky to have had so much generous help."

"I like buildin' houses," Perrin professed. "I only wish I had a good reason to start another one."

"What sort of reason?" urged Amy, simpering at him from where she sat between Paul and Cecil on the sofa.

"Well, I'd like to be more settled than I am now. A man don't feel whole livin' by himself the way I do. He needs a family to belong to. You folks have all got each other. And that's a fine thing. The Simpson's cabin burns down, and they've lost a house, but they ain't lost a home. Because home is where your family is, whether it's a house or a tent or a wagon rollin' 'cross the prairie. Me, I live hereabouts, but I don't feel I've got a home."

"What you need, Daniel," said Ida Thomson, "is a wife."

Amy looked at Paul. He stirred as if to feel for her hand, but she turned immediately to Cecil on her other side. Paul frowned. Cecil met Amy's blue eyes with a start of surprise.

"Yes, Ma'am," answered Perrin. "But it ain't so easy for a man to find a wife here in the Gold Country. The single girls are mighty few."

"Fie, Mr. Perrin!" put in Susan Durham. "How dare you complain when you find yourself in the company of two such girls this moment?"

"I was about to say," explained Daniel, "that the ones there are can afford to be choosy. And it puts a man in a tough spot."

"For some men, that may be true," said Aunt Aggie. "But in your own case, Daniel, I feel certain it is only a matter of time before you find yourself busy building that new house."

"Time," Perrin repeated with a sigh, looking at his boots. "Time is the very thing I'm tired of wasting." His gaze shifted from his own toe to Sydney's and slid up the drape of her skirt to her knee. It paused there momentarily, then flashed to her face.

But Sydney was staring into the empty space between her own nose and the floor. Nor was she attending to the conversation. She sat quietly, her hands clasped in her lap, her thoughts turned inward. Her ears were deaf to all but one remembered voice, teaching her a useful word in Spanish with which she might command the intimate touch of a black mustache. The resulting sensation became so real she must draw two fingers under her nose to relieve its tickle. And it was only for fear this might excite suspicion as to the nature of her daydream that she glanced around.

To her dismay, she found the attention of the entire gathering upon her. She blushed scarlet. "What are you all staring at me for?" she demanded.

Amy burst into a peel of bright laughter.

Aunt Aggie smiled.

"A penny for your thoughts, Miss Simpson," offered Paul McCormick.

Sydney's blush deepened.

"I'll give more than that," said Perrin, attracting her reluctant eyes to his.

"I can think what I want to, can't I?" she said. "I don't ask you what's going through your mind."

"You don't have to," said Paul. "He's already as good as told you."

"He has?"

"Seems he's ready to build you a new cabin, if you want it."

"Why? What's wrong with the other one?"

"Dan'l," said Paul, "you'd better not be buyin' up the lumber for the new one just yet."

Amy controlled her continued amusement by turning her face against Cecil Simpson's shoulder. At the girl's touch, Cecil blushed as red as his sister.

"Mr. Simpson," said Perrin, addressing the silent Uncle Peter, "would you object to me inviting your niece for a breath of evening air on the front porch? I believe she's finding it too warm in here."

Uncle Peter cleared his throat. "So long as you stay on the porch," he said.

"Miss Simpson?"

Sydney looked desperately to her aunt for aid.

"Go ahead, honey," Aunt Aggie urged. "We can spare you and Daniel for a little."

"It's all right, Sydney," put in Mrs. Thomson gently, interpreting her hesitation as shyness. "The rest of us will still be right inside here."

Now feeling that it would be worse to remain in the room than to leave it with Perrin, Sydney rose and went to the door without further protest. Daniel pursued her closely.

The air on the porch was soft. The vibrant coral of the sunset was fading to pastels. Over the narrow valley of Jackson Creek, a ripe moon rose heavy and yellow. The walkway leading from the street to the parsonage was paved with rosy gold. Sydney stopped at the top of the steps, catching herself against the pillar of the porch. At the end of the walk, she could almost see a spirited, steel-grey horse held in check to wait for her. She could almost see its rider extend an arm to her. If she could run fast enough, perhaps he would actually be there when she got to the gate.

Instead, she was seized from behind, imprisoned against Perrin's broad chest, bound there by two arms as unyielding as the jaws of a metal trap. She turned her head away to avoid the accompanying kiss and felt it applied to the angle of her neck and shoulder. She squirmed uncomfortably.

"Sydney!" said Perrin, bending farther over her shoulder to try again for her cheek. "Don't think you have to fight me, anymore. Your folks don't expect you to. They've got no objection to my makin' love to you. Didn't you see that?"

"Lay off," said Sydney, trying to loosen his embrace with her elbows.

"I'll do more than build you a cabin," he offered. "I'll build you a two story, frame house. It'll have a big kitchen with one of those great big, black iron stoves. And there'll be a nursery upstairs."

"Let go," said Sydney. "I don't want any house."

"What do you want then, girl? You name it, and I'll get it for you. That little piece inside there, she thinks she's so cute and cuddly. But I'll take you over her any time. She's so stuck on herself, she'd never learn her duty to a husband. She'd expect to be pampered and petted like a kitten all her life. But you ain't full of such nonsense. You'd know how to back a man up. You're solid. You got both feet on the ground and your eyes wide open. I like that. It's how I am myself.

"As for looks, you ain't maybe the most beautiful girl I ever saw, but that don't matter. I ain't wantin' to marry a peacock. Handsome women are nothin' but trouble. I'm not sayin' you're plain," he added quickly. "I like the way you look. You've got a waist just achin' to be spanned. I never seen so small a waist on a woman. And I know it ain't laced in." He felt of it to prove his point. His touch made her flinch. She pried at his fingers only to have them catch hers and hold them. "Sydney!" he said in her ear. "You're everything I want in a wife. I'd marry you tomorrow. Tonight! But the parson's not due back till Sunday."

"Are you about done talking?"

"That's another thing I like about you. Yes, I guess I've said enough." He began to turn her in his arms to face him though she stubbornly resisted it. "When will you marry me, Sydney?"

"I won't," said Sydney. "Now, you let go of me, Dan'l Perrin, or I'll shout so loud for Uncle Peter the whole town will hear me."

To prevent this, or at least to postpone it, Perrin forced her further around against him and overlaid her mouth with his. But Sydney did not give in to him. When she found that her struggles were useless, she resorted to attack. Catching his upper lip between her teeth, she bit down hard.

Perrin released her in surprise and pain. But he recovered before she could get completely free of his grasp, and he caught her by the shoulders, held her out at arm's length. "You want to play rough?" he wondered, licking blood from his lip.

"Uncle Peter!" called Sydney.

"Shut up, girl!" Perrin hissed. "What's the matter with you?"

"Uncle Peter!"

Perrin let go and retreated a stride. He had not yet decided whether to hold his ground or make a run for it when Uncle Peter came to stand in the doorway. He looked past his niece to her suitor. "What's the trouble?" he asked. His voice was calm.

Perrin bowed his head and touched his sleeve to his lip. He said nothing.

"Dan'l's leaving," Sydney announced. "But he wants to talk to you, first. He's going to tell you why he can't help us move to the creek tomorrow. I'm going inside, now."

And Sydney pushed through the door, passing the open parlor to continue on to the guest bedroom which she was sharing with her aunt. There, she closed herself in and looked around in triumph at the darkening walls, savagely proud of having outsmarted Daniel Perrin.

CHAPTER TWENTY-FIVE:

FLIGHT

"Sydney, I want to talk to you." It was the fourth time that day Aunt Agnes had said it. But it was the first time she had actually had an opportunity to do it. The night before, Sydney had feigned sleep when her aunt finally came to bed after a long talk with Uncle Peter. And the following morning, there was no time for confidential conversation.

Right after breakfast, family and friends piled into the wagon to drive up the creek to the Claim. When they had admired the outside of the new cabin, Uncle Peter and the boys showed the women the inside. The furniture was rough, but surprisingly complete. Ingeniously stacked crates had been substituted for the lost cupboard. Slabs cut from a tree trunk and fitted with peglegs replaced the chairs. The iron bedframe had come through the fire well enough that Paul McCormick had merely sanded off its coating of charcoal and cut some wooden slats to support a new mattress. The mattress itself Aunt Agnes and Sydney had made at the parsonage: a canvas cover, stuffed with dry grass.

From the community at large, blankets, dishes, pans, soap, jerky, beans and flour had been collected. Aunt Aggie looked around her new house with a brave smile. "Daniel was right," she declared. "If it weren't for the clock, I'd almost say this was an improvement."

Just before noon, Ida Thomson and her two daughters returned home. Cecil and Paul took them in the wagon. The ladies feared that the Reverend Thomson and his son-in-law might come in early and find the parsonage empty if they lingered longer. But it was proposed and promised that they should come back to the Claim that evening, bringing the gentlemen with them. "I'll bet they bring more than the parson and the tax collector," young Jacob said wisely. "This is Saturday. Lots of people will want to come see our new place."

"Bright boy," said Paul McCormick.

"Sydney, I want to talk to you," said Aunt Agnes.

After lunch was eaten, and the new dishes were washed, and the men at the Simpson Camp had taken their gold pans down to the creek to try to make up a little for lost time, Aunt Agnes found her opportunity and repeated her intention.

"So, talk," said Sydney.

"Sit down, honey. It's about Daniel."

"Why should I sit down for that?"

"I want you to pay close attention."

"I am."

"Have you missed him?"

"Who?"

202

"Sydney, I vow you are the most exasperating . . .! Your uncle told me Daniel wouldn't be able to come here today because he had to make an important trip to Drytown. There is a man he needed to see there about some sort of business."

"There is?"

"But he said he didn't want to wait any longer to speak to your uncle for fear that his intentions toward you might be misunderstood. Sydney, he asked Peter's permission to marry you."

"What?"

"Why didn't you tell us yourself?"

"What did Uncle Peter say?"

"Well, of course, he said he would be proud to welcome him into the family."

"Oh."

"Honey, what is the matter? What are you hiding? And why won't you tell me?"

"I never told Dan'l I'd marry him."

"I know. He confessed as much to your uncle. But he says he won't give up, and he wanted to know how Peter and I felt about him before he approached you again."

"He's not so interested in how I feel."

"What did you tell him?"

"I told him, 'No.' "

"But why? Don't you want a husband? A place of your own? And children?"

"You can say whatever you want to, Aunt Aggie. I won't marry him. I won't."

"If he were too old for you or something, I could understand it," Aunt Agnes mused. "But he's made to order for you. He's young and hardworking and honest and handsome and thoughtful and attentive . . . You're not afraid of him, are you? Is that it? Is it a little overwhelming to be the object of so much attention? You've never been courted before. But it's all right, honey. You can let him kiss you if he wants to."

"Heck," said Sydney.

"Did he offer to, there on the porch?"

Sydney made no reply.

"If he did, you can tell me."

Silence.

"Don't be sulky, honey. It's so childish."

"I'm going to walk to the neighbors'," said Sydney.

"What neighbors?"

"Ben Roosters'."

"You know I'd rather you didn't go there."

"I want to see how they are. I'll be back before supper."

"Well . . . all right, then. You'll think about what I've said though, won't you?"

"Yep."

"Don't be too long. I don't trust those people. I'll send Jacob to fetch you home in a little while. Shall I?"

"If you want." Sydney had been sidling toward the door, and as she answered, she stepped outside. She looked quickly around. Uncle Peter and all the boys were at work in the creek. There was no one else to see her. She drew a deep breath and ran for the woody path.

To get there, she must cross a space of scorched ground. The black ash crunched and squeaked under her soft-shod feet. The acrid smell of it burned in her nose. But in another moment, she was among the fluttering willows. And then she was flying along the path, dodging trees, leaping rocks, running as if from pursuit, her heart pounding, her breath catching in her throat.

She did not stop until she could see the clearing around Buenrostro's adobe. Then she stumbled to a halt and sank down on the ground to peer through the brush as if it were enemies she had come to spy on rather than friends whose company she sought for solace. She wondered if the Miwok would still want to see her, talk with her. She wondered what Federico had told his mother the day of the fire. She wondered if Fidel had returned and where he was if he hadn't. She watched the white chickens walking here and there among the dry grass stems. She did not see the red and green rooster. Perhaps he was inside the house.

When her breath came easily again, Sydney pushed out of her hiding place and walked across the clearing to the corner of the adobe. The white goat struggled to its feet from where it lay on its chest. A dark line ran like a cut from its shoulder to its hip. The animal blatted, pulling at its tether. And in response to this warning, the Miwok appeared in the adobe's open doorway.

As the woman saw her, Syndey stopped again and waited for some indication as to whether or not she was welcome.

"Misa Cindy! Is you!"

"Can I talk to you, Miz Ben Rooster?"

"You come in. You come in. Good you come back. Have things I tell you."

"I'm sorry I couldn't come before."

"You here, now. We talk. You come in, Misa Cindy."

Surprised by the warmth and urgency of this reception, Sydney came forward to meet the Miwok who took her arm in both hands and drew her into the house. "I don't go and look for you in the town," she explained. "I don't leave my house for if Fidel come back. I don't know that Misa Agnos, she let me talk to you. I stay here and wait for you come back."

"Where's Fidel?" asked Sydney.

"No, I don't know," said the Miwok. "But is not the thing I tell you. The fire, he burns your casita."

"What about it?"

"This fire, he is start by someone. You sit down, here. Federico," she added to her son, "vigila la puerta."

"You mean, somebody set that fire on purpose?"

"Is a warning, man tells me."

"What man?"

"I don't know what his name. But he comes with the coat of don Simón."

"With it on? You mean, wearing it?"

"Mamá," said Federico softly from the door.

The Miwok signed Sydney to be silent. Together, they listened to the sounds of a horse being ridden into the yard.

Federico started up from the shadow of the doorway. And without a backward glance, he went outside. His mother stayed her second child with a look, then followed. Joselito ran to Sydney as she jumped up from her chair and hugged her round the waist, pressing against her for protection.

Before she could soothe him enough to be able to put him away from her, a man came in through the door. Federico and his mother were close behind. Sydney froze in surprise. It was Simón Ruiz.

But it was not the Simón that Sydney remembered. His clothes were covered with dust. There was a two days' growth of black beard on his face. His expression, before his astonishment swept it away, was grim. But Sydney's eyes found no fault in him. That she was actually seeing him in person before her was all that mattered.

As he saw her, he stopped in mid-stride. His look swept over her. She felt it almost as a warm flood of light. "Saidnay? Saidnay! Is you? You are here? How you are here?"

She worked to loosen Joselito's arms about her waist. But though the child recognized Ruiz, he was still frightened, and he clung as tightly as before.

Simón crossed the room in three strides to take Sydney by the shoulders and look at her in continued amazement. Even this did not dislodge Joselito. "Saidnay! I can't believe! Where is César? Do you not go to Seensome Bar?"

Sydney shook her head. Joy lit her sober face like a lamp. Beneath Ruiz' hands, her shoulders glowed and tingled.

"Misa Cindy is our vecina," Federico volunteered. He had come to stand beside Ruiz and watch their meeting with interest. "She live with Mista Pito and Misa Agnos and Pole and Yahco and . . ."

"We found Uncle Peter," Sydney explained, her voice sounding unfamiliar in her own ears. "He has a claim on the creek."

"Here?" exclaimed Simón, unconsciously squeezing her shoulders in emphasis. "Here in Yackson?"

She nodded. "We never left. See Saw got news of Uncle

Peter that same night. The next day, we went to his claim. Where have **you** been?"

She was immediately sorry she had said this, for Simón let her go and recoiled a step. "I mean, why didn't you come back before?" she amended. "Fidel said he thought you would. But he's been gone since the day our cabin burned down. Do you know where he is?"

Ruiz blinked. "**Your** cabin, Pecosa!"

"Señor," put in the Miwok, who had come to stand on his other side across from Federico, "tall man with your coat on, he comes."

Ruiz half whirled to face her. "Gonzalves! Does he hurt you?"

"He kill our gallo," answered Federico. "And he shoot our goat. And he say he will kill me if Mista Pito still here on the day he come back."

The Miwok nodded in reply to Simón's quick look. "Man say he kill See So, too, brother Misa Cindy. And he say that the Seensome, they leave Jackson, or he take away Cindy. I don't tell them. Is bad I don't tell them. But I stay here. I wait for Fidel, he come back."

"¡No, por Dios!" exclaimed Simón. Turning out of their midst, he went back to the open doorway. There, he stopped and stared out into the yard to where his bay horse stood exhausted, head drooping.

Sydney was finally able to transfer Joselito from her waist to the Miwok's. "Simón?" She went after him. He turned his head. "Did you catch up to the cholos?"

He studied her rapt face a moment before he answered. "Yes, Saidnay. But I make a mistake. And now, I wonder if I have make more."

"Why? What did you do?"

"I let Manuel live."

"You mean, you went after him, too? I thought you said he wasn't a bandit."

"I was wrong."

"Where is he, now?"

"I don't know. He escape me. I fear he comes here."

"Do you know where Fidel is?"

"No. I don't find him."

"Well, you don't have to worry about See Saw. He can look after himself. And nobody will find me. Because I'm leaving."

"You are leaving!"

"I'm running away."

Simón faced her more fully, a frown beginning in his eyes.

"I am!" said Sydney. "I won't stay! And if you had to live with Aunt Agony, you'd know why. And now, she and Uncle Peter want me to marry Dan'l Perrin. But I won't do it. He's . . . well, anyway, I was waiting until you got back from the Valley because I thought maybe . . . Simón? Do you remember what you said in the wagon about how See Saw and I could work for you, herding cattle?"

Ruiz cupped Sydney's chin in his hand. "And you still want to be my cowboy girl," he guessed.

She nodded against the warm pressure, suddenly breathless. "Will you take me away from here?" she managed to ask.

"¡Niña! You don't know what you say."

"Please, Simón! I can't stand it. See Saw knows that I'm miserable, but there's nothing he can do about it. Besides, he's happy enough, himself. He'd never miss me."

"Saidnay! Listen to me. This thing is not possible. You think that your brother, he does not care what becomes of you? You think Tío Pito does not throw down his shovel and pick up his gun? And this man who wants to marry you, you think he does not join in the chase? And they will all think Simón Ruiz is bandido."

"Well . . . Miz Ben Rooster can tell them that the man with your jacket on came and got me! They'll all chase after him!"

Ruiz dropped his hand from her face. But his eyes did not leave hers.

"She can tell them the whole story about how he burned our cabin and threatened to kill See Saw and Federico," went on Sydney. "Miz Ben Rooster knows what the man looks like, so she can describe him to them. What did you say his name was?"

"Gonzalves. Paulo Gonzalves. And there are also Juan Torres and Mariano García and a man with a cut in his ear whose name is Pío Pinto. There are eight more besides."

"You've been pretty busy, I guess," Sydney acknowledged. "Couldn't you catch any of them?"

"I catch too many at once. They almost catch me."

"I told you you'd need some help," she reminded him. "Why didn't you bring your uncle back from the Valley with you?"

"He is in Sacramento for another important business."

"Oh. Well, you'd better let Sheriff Phoenix help, then. Don't you think?"

"But, Saidnay, I can **ask** him to help if I decide is the thing I must do. I don't just carry you off and let la señora de Buenrostro tell lies to your family and the cheriff."

"But if you don't carry me off, I'll run away just the same. And then, they'll have to waste time looking for me instead of the bandits."

"Saidnay. You don't run away. You stay here."

"I wouldn't bet on it."

"¡Niña! Where do you run to? How do you go?"

"That'll be my business, won't it? Unless I go with you."

Ruiz looked out the door again. He stared at his horse. He stared at the wounded goat. He stared at the ground. He turned back to stare at Sydney. "Federico!" he said.

"¿Mande, Señor?"

"There is a horse in your corral. I will trade you mine for him. Bring him here. We put my saddle on him."

"¡Sí, Señor!" The boy slid between Ruiz and Sydney and ran for the corral.

"Saidnay," said Simón, his black eyes level and burning, "you are sure about this thing you want to do?"

The rebellious look cleared from her face. Joy dawned there once more. She nodded.

"Come here to me, Pecosa." He held out an arm. She stepped into its shelter and was drawn close against him. Thus made abruptly and uncomfortably aware of the arsenal at his waist, she repositioned two of the three pistols to make room for herself before she turned up her face. "Simón," she whispered, "otro."

The black mustache she had dreamed of was dusty. But its touch was still as thrilling. The growth of dark beard multiplied its tickle. And there was something in his kiss that she had not felt before. It lit her like a flame put to a candle and left her burning just as brightly afterwards.

"Bueno," he concluded, looking down into her eyes which opened to new depths, "I take you with me."

CHAPTER TWENTY-SIX:

LAYING A TRAIL

"I do not ask that you lie, Señora," Ruiz told the Miwok from the saddle. He steadied Buenrostro's red colt with one hand and held down the other to Sydney. "But neither do I say you must tell the truth. We will go toward Drytown. I have try to prevent the brasileño coming here by leaving for him a trail which I hope that he follows. Because I know he will be looking for me. I am the most dangerous enemy of these bandidos, now. Surely, Manuel will want me dead. And I hope that his men will leave you alone and the Familia Seensome while they look for me. I think it is what they will do. ¡So, potro!" he added to the red colt as the animal shied away from Sydney's skirts.

She had caught Ruiz' hand and put her foot in the stirrup to swing up behind him, but the horse had not carried two riders before, and the swishing cloth near his flank made him nervous.

Sydney let go and backed off.

Simón wrestled with the horse a moment; it shook its head against the reins and half reared. "Saidnay!" called

Ruiz, motioning her toward the corral. "Climb up there!"

She ran to mount the peeled poles. Simón released the colt into a capering canter and guided it alongside. But instead of taking the hand Sydney held out to help her on behind him, he leaned from the saddle and caught her round the waist, swept her on in front of him. She threw both arms around his neck to keep from falling. The horse bolted in fright.

Simón let it run straight up the hill behind the adobe, steering it clear of the trees and the rocks and urging it on when it offered to slow. He let it halt at the top to blow. "Pecosita," he said, directing his full gaze momentarily into Sydney's wide eyes, "now is your last chance to change your mind."

But she shook her head.

Ruiz touched his spurs to the red colt's flanks, and they were off again, running along the crest of the hill behind the town.

Riding strictly as a passenger was not entirely to Sydney's liking. While it was true that it afforded her an intimacy with Ruiz that could scarcely be improved upon, still her seat was insecure and rather uncomfortable. Had she let go of Simón, she felt she would have fallen off backwards. So by the time they were dropping down the shoulder of the hill toward the road to Jackson Gate, she had almost made up her mind to complain.

"Saidnay," said Ruiz, "there is someone that I try to see before we leave the town. Is an old woman who spend much of her time in the church. If she is there, I will tell her about Escobar and Gonzalves."

"Are they after her, too?"

"Perhaps. She has confess to me a terrible thing they have done. And they may delay long enough to silence her. Or punish her. I wish I had not hint to Manuel that she has told me."

"Another mistake?"

"Yes."

Simón looked down at the road. There was a rider moving along it, heading out of town. But there was no other traffic. After the supper hour, it would grow heavy. The miners would leave their claims for an evening's recreation in the dance halls and saloons, anticipating the even greater freedom of the coming Sabbath.

Simón urged the colt down to the road and across to the adobe chapel where he had met with the little grandmother of Violeta. He reined up before the door and let Sydney slide to the ground. The colt shied away. "Go inside, Saidnay," said Ruiz. "Wait for me there."

She obeyed, but she stopped just within, feeling strange and out of place. The chapel was dark and deeply quiet, for its walls were thick. The murmur of the priest at the altar only emphasized the stillness. There was no one else in the church. Sydney watched him. He must have been aware of her entering, but he gave no sign.

Then the door beside her opened, and Simón came in from the brightness outside. Removing his hat, he looked around.

"There's no old woman in here," Sydney informed him in a whisper.

"No? Then, I talk to the padre. Come." He took her by the arm. But Sydney dragged back, and Ruiz stopped to look at her. Noticing that she had nothing with which to cover her head, he put his own hat on it.

She allowed this without question, but still, she resisted when he tried to draw her after him. "Can't I wait by the door?" she wondered.

"Why do you want to?"

"We're interrupting him, Simón. He's praying or something."

"He is almost done."

She took a few halting steps, yielding to the insistent pressure of his hand. And once started, she let him guide her forward.

They did not, in fact, have long to wait. The priest caught Simón's eye and finished what he was doing perhaps sooner than he might have. Then he presented himself, asking how he could be of service.

Sydney stood uneasily beside Ruiz, only half listening to his rapid Spanish and wondering if Jacob had been sent to the neighbors yet. She wished that the priest would not look at her as if she had two heads. She thought about Aunt Agnes and what she would say when Jacob came galloping back to the Claim to report. Would the Miwok lie or tell the truth? Would Uncle Peter come after her? Would See Saw? How far would Simón take her? Clear to his uncle's ranch in the Valley? Or was there someone in Drytown he might leave her with? The only two names she knew connected with that place were Matthew Hindshaw of the freight office and Judge Curtis, the man that Simón had been trying to find when the bandits had robbed him.

She looked sideways at him, standing there beside her. He was not talking, now. The priest was talking. It seemed a lot to be saying about an old woman and the bandits. Simón must feel her gaze upon him, for he glanced down at her. "Saidnay? Is all right?" he asked softly.

She nodded. "Yep." He had beautiful eyes, she thought. So dark and so bright. She had never seen anything like them. She wondered if Amy Thomson would admire them. Of course she must. Anyone would.

Simón turned his attention back to the priest. Whatever the man had been saying, he appeared to be nearly done with it. He looked doubtfully at Syndey and made the sign of the Cross. She glanced again at Ruiz. What was going on? "Simón?"

"We go now, Saidnay." His voice was different. His look was different. She was not sure how.

"Simón?" She turned with him, moved back toward the chapel door.

"I have tie the horse by the creek. The bank there, she is steep. So, I think you get on without so much problem. From now to Ranchería, we ride on the road. I want to make more trail for the bandidos to follow. We hide from them, but not so well they think they have lose us."

"Did you tell the priest about the old woman?"

"Yes, I tell him."

"What did he say?"

Simón paused at the door of the chapel and felt in his pocket for a sack of gold dust which he put down on a stone receptacle before he ushered Sydney outside. There, **she** stopped, blinking at the change in the light. Ruiz took his hat from her head, returned it to his own. "We don't stand here, Pecosa," he said. "Remember, we are running away."

"Can I get on behind you, this time?"

The strange, guarded expression on his face grew more pronounced. "You don't like to ride in my arms?"

She found no way to answer this. She looked down at the toes of her moccasins. For the first time, she wondered if she had done right to ask for his help to get away from Aunt Aggie. The doubt grew swiftly toward regret. And shame. And mortification.

Simón took her face between his hands and turned it up so that he might look carefully into it. "Saidnay," he said. "I have just make you my wife."

"You did?" She frowned unhappily.

"Was not what you want?"

"You could have asked me."

"What you have say?"

"I don't know. But why didn't you ask me?"

"I fear you refuse."

"So what if I did?"

"So then I must leave you behind. I can't take you away if not to make you my wife."

"You still should have asked me."

"Yes. Maybe I should." Ruiz released her and went to untie the horse. Sydney watched him gather up the reins and step lightly into the saddle. The red colt snorted and shifted under him, but it stood. "Come, Saidnay. You ride behind me," said Ruiz.

"No," said Sydney.

"¡Niña! I don't leave you here!"

"No," she agreed, not moving.

Ruiz nudged the colt forward along the edge of the stream. Its feet sank into the wet sand, leaving deep holes which quickly filled with clouding water. The young animal moved uncertainly, snorting at every step. It stopped below where Sydney was waiting and lowered its head to blow at the water. Taking advantage of its distraction, Simón leaned to reach for her. But to his surprise, she hooked her arms around his neck again so that he must lift her on in front of him as before. The horse tossed its head and trampled the stream bank full of holes.

"Pecosa! You are not sorry?"

"Nope. Are you?"

In answer, or perhaps to avoid answering, Simón kissed his bride. And Sydney did not recognize the reserve behind the caress. For her, the world twirled off in a new direction. The water of the creek sang more sweetly. The air above it moved more softly. And life itself became more precious.

CHAPTER TWENTY-SEVEN:

THE ALARM

"Mista See So!"

Cecil looked up from his gold pan right into the eyes of Federico who was squatting above him on the stream bank. "Hello, Freddy. Where did you come from?"

"Mamá, she send me. Want to talk to you."

"Why? What's the trouble?"

"Misa Cindy."

Cecil stood up. "What's happened to her?"

"She gone."

"Gone! Gone where?"

"You come talk to Mamá, Mista See So. She tell you what happen."

"Don't **you** know?"

"Yes."

"Then, you tell me. Right now!" And dropping his gold pan in the creek, Cecil vaulted up onto the bank, catching the half-breed boy by the arm. "Talk!" he commanded.

Federico twisted in his grasp. "Mamá, she want to tell you."

"I want **you** to tell me. Why didn't your mother come, herself?"

"She scared to leave. Bad men might come again, kill our goat and our chickens. Or Papá, he come back and don't know where we are."

"What bad men? What are you talking about?"

"You hurt my arm, Mista See So."

"What's the matter, son?" called Uncle Peter from upstream.

"It's Sydney! She's gone!"

Uncle Peter threw aside his shovel. Paul McCormick had been working with him. He waited where he was, watching, while Uncle Peter stalked along the edge of the water. Jacob and Timothy would have followed, but Paul stopped them. "Wait, boys. Stay here with me for a minute."

"Where is she?" Uncle Peter demanded, coming to a halt before Cecil and Federico.

"I should have told you." Cecil squared his shoulders. "But in all that business of the nugget and the fire, I simply forgot about it. Sydney said she meant to run away."

"What!"

"I'm sorry I didn't tell you before. I guess I didn't think she would really go through with it. And then with Dan'l paying court to her . . ."

Uncle Peter bent a thunderous look on Federico. "What do you know about all this, you little savage? You always show up after the damage is done, don't you? Do you know where Miss Sydney is?"

The boy shook his head.

"He says his mother can tell us," said Cecil.

"Then, by heaven, we'll go and ask her!" Uncle Peter turned to beckon Paul McCormick. "Here," he added to Cecil. "I'll keep track of the boy. You go fetch our guns from the cabin. Tim! Jacob! Go to the house! Stay there with your ma till we get back!"

218

But as the boys ran to obey their father, their mother came from the cabin. "Jacob! What's happened?"

It was Cecil who answered. "It's Sydney, Aunt Agnes. I'm afraid she's run away."

"Run away!" gasped his aunt.

"Freddy says his mother can give us the particulars. Uncle Peter and Paul and I will go down there to see what she says."

"Run away!" repeated Aunt Agnes. "Oh, I don't believe that, Cecil. Why would she run away? Something else has happened to her. Those dirty foreigners! I'll bet they're back of this. You mark my words."

Cecil pushed by her toward the cabin. Timothy followed him. But Jacob lingered with his mother. And when she went on toward the creek bank, he tagged after her.

"What does he say?" Aunt Agnes asked, stopping out of reach of Federico and gathering up her skirts as if the boy were covered with filth and might soil her clothes. Jacob peered around her.

"He won't talk," said Uncle Peter.

"Freddy! You tell us this minute what has happened to Sydney!"

Federico regarded Aunt Agnes with large, dark eyes. He said nothing.

"What about Daniel Perrin?" Aunt Aggie suggested to Uncle Peter. "You don't suppose . . .? Sydney did act strangely this afternoon. And she said she was going to visit the neighbors. Could she have used it as an excuse to meet Daniel in secret? We don't know what all might have passed between them on the parson's porch. And why didn't Daniel come back into the house afterwards? Why was he so eager to know whether we would approve of him as her husband? Oh, Peter, can they have eloped?"

Uncle Peter hadn't thought of this. He turned the idea over in his mind. But then, he shook his head. "Sydney's not keen enough on him," he concluded. "But the boy himself is pretty impatient. It would be more likely that he spirited her away."

"Is not Mista Perrino who peer it away," said Federico.

Uncle Peter started and looked down at the boy. "Then, who did?" he demanded.

"Mamá tell you."

"**You** tell us! Tell us now!" Uncle Peter shook the half-breed by the arm.

"Mexican man."

"What's his name?"

"Gonzales! García. One of those."

"Did you see him?"

"Mamá see him. She tell you about him."

"Did she tell you what he looked like?" asked Aunt Agnes. But at this point, Cecil returned from the cabin, bringing the guns. He gave one to Uncle Peter. Sydney's old single-shot Cecil kept for himself.

"All right, let's go," said Uncle Peter. "Paul, you bridle the mules and the pony and ride after us. We may have to leave from Ben Rooster's. Jacob. Go to the cabin. Ma, you keep the boys home. We won't leave town without letting you know."

On their way down the creek, Uncle Peter related to Cecil what Federico had said. He kept hold of the boy by the arm, in case he tried to run ahead and prepare the way with his mother. "Their stories better jibe, by heaven!" he said.

Cecil made no comment. But as he sorted through in his mind what Sydney had told him of her plans to escape, he began to suspect that the man involved was not named García or Gonzales, either one. But he kept the thought to himself. As little as he trusted Simón Ruiz, he had not believed him enough interested in Sydney to abduct her. On the other hand, if she had asked to go . . . And Cecil wished in passing that he had not involved Uncle Peter quite so soon, that he had accompanied Federico to hear what the Miwok might have been willing to say to him alone. But it was too late now for that.

Mrs. Ben Rooster did not ask her neighbors to come in. She stood in her doorway with her arms folded and returned Uncle Peter's disapproving stare. Federico was sent stumbling to stand beside her. She laid a hand on his shoulder, pressing it in approval. "Why you bring guns?" she asked Uncle Peter. "No one here to shoot."

"Where is my niece?" demanded Uncle Peter.

"She gone."

"Where?"

"Man say Drytown."

"What man?"

"Man that take her."

"What's his name?"

"Gonzalves."

"What's he look like?"

"Tall. Not tall as you. Wear pretty jacket. Friend of other man, name García. Both men bad. Others with them. I hear them talk. One, call Torres. One, call Pinto. Have cut in ear."

"How did they know Sydney was here?"

"They not know. Come to tell me have my husband. Tell me they kill him if he don't do what they say. Tell me they kill Mista See So, next. Then my boy, Federico."

"Why?"

"Try to scare us. They think we maybe tell sheriff who they are. Don't want that."

"Well, that's exactly what they'll get! I'll have the whole county out after them. And if they harm a hair of my niece, I'll see them hang! How many of them are there?"

"Ten, two more."

"Who leads them?"

The Miwok hesitated. "Man name Escobar."

"Cecil," said Uncle Peter, "start for town. See if the sheriff's there. As soon as Paul brings the mules, we'll follow you."

"Paul had better go back to stay with Aunt Agnes and the boys, don't you think?" said Cecil. "What if these outlaws were to come again while we're gone?"

"By heaven, you're right. I'll send him back, then. Do you want one of the mules or the Indian pony?"

"I'll take Red Dog."

"All right. Get started. I'll be right after you."

Cecil ran for the road. "Sydney!" he whispered, letting his steps jar the separate syllables from his mouth. "If you've gone off with Simón Ruiz, I swear I'll kill the man! Sydney! Sydney! Oh, my sweet Lord!"

Sheriff Phoenix was in his office on Main Street. He looked up from the paperwork on his desk as the Simpsons came in, rifles in hand. Uncle Peter had overtaken Cecil half a mile out of town, and they had ridden the rest of the way together.

"Afternoon, gentlemen," Phoenix greeted them. "What's the problem?" He coughed dryly into his fist.

"My niece has been abducted is the problem!" said Uncle Peter. "And I expect you to help us find her and the man or men that have made off with her!"

Phoenix sat back and looked calmly from him to Cecil. "I've met you before, son," he said.

"Yes, sir. In France's Store in Rancheria."

"That's right. Your kid brother was with you."

"No, sir. I mean, Sydney's not my brother. She's my sister."

"Oh?" Phoenix considered. "It does seem like I've heard some sort of rumor to that effect."

"Rumors be hanged!" interrupted Uncle Peter. "My niece is gone! And I want to know if you mean to do anything about it!"

"Yes, sir, I do," replied Phoenix. "But I'd rather know as much about the situation as I can learn first. Suppose you two sit down and give me the details once over clearly. Son, you appear to be the most capable of that at the moment. You begin."

Uncle Peter straightened his back indignantly, but he held his peace. Cecil looked around for a chair and sank onto it, laid Sydney's rifle across his knees. "Sir," he said, "you remember those Mexican bandits that Señor Ruiz wouldn't tell you about?"

"I haven't had much opportunity to forget them. There's a report come from Tuttletown just this morning. They robbed the general store there, day before yesterday."

"How far away is Tuttletown?"

"Fifty, sixty miles by the roads. It's between Sonora and Angels Camp."

"I didn't come here for a lesson in geography!" exploded Uncle Peter. "My niece has been taken, I tell you!"

Phoenix looked up at him. "Mister, you just simmer down. I gather your nephew thinks this same bunch of bandits abducted your niece. It's possible, son," he added to Cecil. "Those men ride like demons. Besides, there's some evidence that they split into two or three groups now and then. What makes you think it might be them?"

"I don't, really," said Cecil. "I think my sister is with Simón Ruiz."

Uncle Peter spluttered at this, but Phoenix silenced him with a gesture. "What's your name again?" he asked Cecil. "Simpson, isn't it?"

"Yes, sir. Cecil Simpson. My sister is Sydney."

"Well, do you know, Cecil, that Simón Ruiz is what's thought of as high-class among the Spanish of this state? Before you accuse him of something this serious, you need more than a hunch to go on."

"I don't think he abducted her, sir. I think she probably asked him to take her. She was planning to run away, before. She told me she was just waiting for Simón to come back to Jackson so that she could propose some sort of scheme to him. Not only that, I think she's in love with him."

"How old is your sister, Cecil?"

"Eighteen."

Phoenix coughed again. "I see."

Uncle Peter sat down slowly on a vacant chair, his face a study.

"Do you know for a fact that Ruiz has been back to Jackson since he returned to the Valley?" the sheriff asked, next.

"No, sir. But I know that my sister expected him soon."

"How well did she know the man?"

"Scarcely at all. But she was taken with him from the start. And he encouraged her enough to worry me. My sister is . . . well, she can be pretty bullheaded. I tried to make her listen to reason. But I can't say she did."

"I understand. But I don't think you realize that for Señor Ruiz to steal her right out of the bosom of her family, so to speak, even at her request, he had to have a powerful motive. Why would he risk so much? Ruiz is not an easy man to deal with, but to my knowledge, he has never actually been on the wrong side of the law. He's made quite a parade of himself as one of the Old Guard Californios, what with his pride and his code of honor and his contempt for Americans. And it just doesn't make sense for him to involve himself in a scandal like this is apt to turn into. Son, your sister may be in love with him, as you say. And if Ruiz were able to take advantage of her willingness without its being found out, I wouldn't put it past him to be tempted. But just to whisk her away on impulse, knowing her family would raise the county to get her back . . . well, I find that hard to believe of the man. I won't completely rule it out," Phoenix added. "But I need stronger evidence than you've been able to give me before I act on it. Now, tell me about the outlaws you mentioned. How do they fit into the picture?"

Cecil recounted what the Miwok had said.

"Escobar!" mused the sheriff when Cecil gave the name as belonging to the leader of the bandits. "Now, isn't that an interesting idea! Do you know **him**?"

"No, sir."

"No proof of any of this, I suppose?"

"Only our neighbor's word, sir."

"And she thinks your sister was headed for Drytown, whoever she went with?"

"Yes, sir."

Phoenix coughed into his fist. "Well, we'd better go see what we can find out about her there," he concluded. "Do both of you have horses?"

"Yes, sir."

"Then you can either wait for me here or come along to the livery stable. My brother Sam runs it, and I have to talk to him before I leave. He serves as deputy in my absence."

"We'll go with you," said Uncle Peter.

CHAPTER TWENTY-EIGHT:

SAFE HAVEN

"And so, he came in and sat down in my parlor," Judge Curtis was saying. "And I vow to you the air around us fairly crackled with his presence! You can tell me nothing about Spanish pride and courtesy that I did not learn during that interview. I defy even your Joaquín Murieta to make a better showing."

Will Sutherland smiled and glanced at his father across the table.

"You ran right up against it, did you, Judge?" asked the rancher. The crinkles at the corners of his blue eyes deepened in amusement.

"I did, indeed. But I could wish to corner the man again. With his help, I'm sure Phoenix would be able catch the bandits that have plagued us on the roads all summer. If Ruiz would only work with us rather than in spite of us, I wager the entire business might be accomplished in a week."

"Well, I reckon you're the man to persuade him," said Sutherland. "But I'd sure like to be a fly on the wall of your courtroom, Dan'l Webster."

Curtis bowed his head to acknowledge the comparison. "You flatter me, Jack. Ellen," he added to the rancher's wife, "these biscuits are superb. I wonder if you would pass the honey this way, again. I can think of no more ambrosial combination."

Ellen Sutherland glanced around the supper table for the sweet-lipped pot. "Will," she said, spying it at her son's elbow, "give the judge the honey. He wants to cover up the taste of these bad buscuits."

Curtis was still protesting amid his hosts' gentle laughter when there was a knock on the front door.

"I'll get it," said Will. Scraping back his chair, he crossed the long room to see who it was. The door opened on a deep porch which ran the width of the house. And standing on that porch were two people Will Sutherland had never seen before. One was an American girl. The other was a Spanish man. Both looked travel-worn. Both looked wary.

"Perdón, Señor," said the Spaniard. "I am sorry I trouble you. I look for the house of Yak Sutterlan."

"You've found it," said Will. "Come on in." He stood aside for them to enter. Behind him, the others rose in anticipation.

But before any questions could be asked of the new arrivals, or any explanation offered by them, Judge Curtis exclaimed in amazement: "Don Simón!"

The judge was almost as astonished at being **able** to recognize Ruiz as that Simón had actually come. But at least, the unkempt growth of black beard, the dusty clothes, the third pistol and the hilt of the extra knife at his waist were ample explanation of how he had been occupied. The presence and appearance of his young companion, however, were not so readily understood.

The judge came around from behind the table, remembering at the last moment to discard his napkin. Jack Sutherland also came forward to greet his new guests. Ellen remained where she was a little longer.

"Señor Cortés!" said Ruiz, accepting the hand that the judge held out to him. "Is most fortunate I see you here. I have intend to impose on these friends you tell me with the excuse that I know you. But now, perhaps you do me the kindness of introduce me to them."

"It will be a pleasure! Only I am not acquainted with your, ah, . . .?" Curtis trailed off, looking at Sydney.

"My wife," said Ruiz. "Doña Saidnay Seensome de Ruiz Silvestre. Pecosita," he added to Sydney, "is Señor Cortés I tell you once I go to find."

Sydney looked at Curtis who was momentarily struck speechless. "You're the judge that lives in Drytown?" she asked.

Recovering himself, the magistrate bowed. "Yours to command, Ma'am." And then in his most gracious style, he introduced Jack Sutherland and his son Will and his wife Ellen who now came to stand between her tall men.

"Señora," said Ruiz, bending over the hand she offered in welcome, "you forgive us to intrude?"

"Nonsense," said Ellen. "You're not intruding. You must join us for supper. Will, bring in a bench from the porch. I will sit on it. You can fetch that stool from the kitchen for yourself. Señor . . . Mrs. Ruiz . . . please. I insist."

"We better wash up some, first," said Sydney, looking down at her bedraggled skirt and apron and inspecting her hands front and back. "We've been on the trail half the day. From Jackson," she added, and then looked up at Simón to see if she ought to have named the town. His reserved expression did not change.

Bursting with her curiosity but sensing that the situation was as volatile as it was unusual, Ellen Sutherland contained her questions and hastened to serve the needs of her guests. It was not until they were all settled once more around the table and the platters and bowls as well as the plates were beginning to look rather empty that she allowed herself the satisfaction of accosting Sydney.

"You've not been married long, Mrs. Ruiz?"

"Since about two o'clock," said Sydney. Again, she glanced at Ruiz for approval. Again, there was no reaction.

"Well!" said Curtis, feeling himself under some constraint to begin an examination of the case. "You have our warmest congratulations. Both of you," he added to Ruiz.

Simón lifted a lancing look into the judge's eyes. "Es muy amable," he said.

"Don Simón," pursued the judge, "I hope you will forgive us our astonishment. I assure you that you find yourselves among friends."

"Is what I have hope," agreed Simón.

"But are you not going to tell us what has been happening?" urged Curtis.

Ruiz applied his napkin to his mustache. "There are things," he said, "they must be done. I try to do them . . ." he stopped and looked at Sydney, then away.

"May I inquire," went on the judge, "what more you may have learned about the outlaws?"

Ruiz did not reply immediately but, "Yes," he said at last. "I have intend to tell you."

When he did not continue, however, Curtis tried another tack: "You are taking your bride to the Valley before you return to the fray?"

"No. I don't go back to the Valle again until the bandidos, they are stop, and the man who leads them is dead."

At this, the silence around the table, already attentive, thickened perceptibly.

"But this time," said Ruiz, speaking the words with an effort, "I tell you who they are, some of them. I ask you to help me."

"Indeed, I think it is the wisest course, Don Simón."

"Señor Sutterlan," said Ruiz, turning to the rancher, "I

do not wish to make problems for you. But I have bring my wife here because I do not know where else I take her so she is safe. She is in danger now from these bandidos. They suspect she knows who is their leader. And to keep the americanos from to learn who is that man, they have already murder a boy who is innocent, and perhaps a friend I have."

"Señor," Sutherland said evenly, "don't apologize for coming to us. Judge Curtis was hoping you'd be willing to join forces with us. We're doing you no favors. You're doing us one."

"You are good to say so, Señor. But still I must warn you. I am no longer chasing the bandidos. They now are chasing me. I have take their leader prisoner, and I have threaten him to try to make him do a certain thing. I offer him his life if he will swear to do it. And I tell him I betray him to the americanos if he fails. He has fail. And he knows I keep my word. To prevent this, he will kill me if he can. He may also try to kill anyone he knows I speak to. I don't think he trails me here. I have try to make him think I go to Drytown. And then, I had the plan to bring my wife to you to keep her safe while I find Señor Cortés and warn him what has happen. Instead, I find him here. For this, I am grateful."

"I'm glad you trusted me," said Sutherland.

"I know you are a friend of the magistrado," explained Simón, "if I trust him, then I must also trust his friends."

"How much of a lead do you think you had on these outlaws?"

Ruiz shook his head. "No mucha."

"Could they trace you as far as Drytown yet tonight?"

"Is possible."

"Will," said Jack, turning to his son, "why don't you take a couple of the boys and ride to town? Sniff around and see what you find. Though if the bandits are mostly after Señor Ruiz, it's likely they'll lie low until they've done their best to find him. I only wish there was a way to get word to Phoenix."

"Uncle Peter will tell him," put in Sydney. "He's probably in Drytown himself, by now. You see . . ." She stopped and looked at Ruiz.

He said nothing nor met her eyes.

"Before we left," Sydney went on, "Simón told my uncle's neighbor what had happened. And she said she'd tell Uncle Peter. And Uncle Peter sure will tell the sheriff."

"Well, that's good news," said Sutherland.

A silence followed this. Then everyone spoke at once. Sydney tried to amend her explanation. Simón offered to ride with Will to Drytown. Sutherland said Will ought to be careful not to hint to anyone that he had spoken to Ruiz. Judge Curtis asked Simón for the name of the outlaw's leader. Will asked his father which of the cowboys he ought to take. And Ellen told Sydney she was to think of the ranch house as her home for as long as it suited her. The muddle ended in laughter.

Before it could begin again, Judge Curtis firmly took the floor. "If I may make a suggestion . . ." he said and waited for their attention. "I do think Will ought to go to Drytown with a pair of good men as Jack has proposed. But I think there ought to be some trusted riders put on patrol here as well, to be certain that we are not surprised ourselves . . . in case don Simón has not wholly succeeded in misleading the outlaws. I do not think all the men should be told, however, particularly not the Mexican vaqueros, since they are more likely than the American cowboys to be linked to the bandits. Naturally, I do not assume that they are. But we cannot be too careful.

"Don Simón," Curtis continued directly to Ruiz who did not appear entirely pleased by this speech, "under no circumstances should you ride back to Drytown tonight. Your appearance there might, indeed, force the hand of the outlaw who is now your personal enemy. But it might also result in your death. Consider! You have chosen to trust me, and to trust the Sutherlands, with what you have already told us. But if we are to act in unison upon that information, you must allow yourself to be guided by our advice. Therefore, I beg you to content yourself with supplying whatever details are in your power to provide, and to stay here, quietly out of sight, at least until the actual location of the outlaws can be determined."

Ruiz' black brows drew low. His nostrils flared with a deep-drawn breath. "I have choose to tell you, yes," he said. "But I have not intend to run from danger and hide from my enemy like a coward! I come here so Saidnay is safe. Not so I am."

Curtis made a soothing gesture. "No one who knows you, Don Simón, could possibly consider you a coward. I am certain your enemy does not. But I appeal to you in the name of your bride. Surely you do not wish to leave her here alone to worry about you tonight, of all nights! Your paramount duty, as I perceive it, is presently to her."

"Hey," objected Sydney.

"Yes, Mrs. Ruiz?" inquired Curtis.

"The bandits robbed Simón, not you. But if they had, I bet you wouldn't be ready to just sit on your tail and let somebody else take over for you, either."

"My dear young lady!" said the judge. "I hasten to assure you . . ."

"I'll go back with you, if you want," Sydney told Ruiz. "Not like this, of course," she added, plucking at the skirt of her grey apron. "But if the Sutherlands can loan me some old clothes, I could pretend to be a boy, again. I don't care so much for staying here. And I might be some help. I'm a fair shot, remember."

At this, the astonishment of the judge and the Sutherlands exceeded the bounds of courtesy. But Simón answered her soberly. "Yes, Saidnay. I remember. But I tell you before. I tell you again. I know you are brave. I know you wish to help me. But I will not let you chase the cholos."

Sydney's gaze dropped to her lap. Her face contracted into the rebellious frown which it could adopt with such effect. But she said no more.

In the ensuing silence, Judge Curtis cleared his throat and rubbed the end of his nose.

"Amigos," Ruiz said then, tapping two fingers lightly on

the table edge, "I think that we must do as the magistrado has suggest. I have the obligation still to complete the business I have start with the bandidos. But since it is propose to go to Drytown only for find out if they are seen and if the Cheriff Finits is notify, my presence there is not necessary. Therefore I agree to this plan. You decide which men will go along, and I will give you the description of those outlaws that I know their names and what they look like."

CHAPTER TWENTY-NINE:

THE HEARING

When Will Sutherland set out for Drytown, he went armed with a rifle and pistol and was accompanied by two of the best men available. He took with him besides a succinct description of Paulo Gonzalves, Mariano García, Juan Torres and Pío Pinto as well as Manuel Escobar.

Jack Sutherland, the judge, and Ruiz accompanied Will as far as the front porch. Sydney stayed where she was at the table, her look still broody. But if Simón noticed her sulkiness, he gave no sign.

"Tell us, if you will, how your captive managed to escape you, Don Simón," Judge Curtis said when they had watched Will across the moonlit space between the ranch house and the bunkhouse door.

"He uses people who are inocente to defeat me," Ruiz explained. "He knows I will not sacrifice the lives of others only to take his."

"How so?"

But Simón did not immediately respond. He had seen Will re-emerge from the bunkhouse to move quickly toward the stable and corrals. One of the men who accompanied him Ruiz recognized. It was Baldy Hinkson.

"Is at the ferry crossing," Simón answered Curtis after a moment. "The chileno that I tell you name is Pinto has seen me in Mokelumne Hill just before I challenge Escobar. And Pinto follows to the crossing of the river. Ferry boat is on the other side, and we must wait. It comes across and brings two men with horses, three on foot. These people, they get off, and I am to get on with Escobar when Pinto opens fire at us from where he hides among some rocks. There is a big confusion with the pasajeros from the boat. Escobar, he take advantage to catch a man and steal his gun, threatens to shoot him if I interfere. El chileno comes down from the rocks, and he makes me get on the boat with all the other men who came across, only not the man that Escobar is holding. I learn who is this outlaw that has come to help his leader when Manuel talks to him.

" 'Well done, Pío,' he says in Spanish. I know from what somebody tell me earlier that one of the bandidos has the name of Pío Pinto. 'I don't forget this service that you do me,' Manuel says to him.

" 'And Ruiz?' asks Pinto. 'You let him go, Patrón?'

"Manuel looks at me. I have in my hands these guns I carry, but I don't shoot because I know the innocent people with me die. Yet Manuel sees it in my eyes that if he kills the man he uses to protect himself, I will not hesitate.

" 'Yes, we let him go this time,' says Escobar. 'But not next time. And next time will come soon. Hasta pronto, San Simón!' And then he signals to the ferryman to pull the boat across again.

"When we are in the middle of the corriente, Pinto cuts the cable. The boat almost turn over. My horse and the other two fall in the river. One is drown. But mine swims to the shore and people catch him there.

"Meanwhile, I look back and see that Manuel make the man that he has take get in the water to his neck. Then Escobar and Pío Pinto mount their horses and gallop up the road. I can watch them until they are far above the river. Until they pass a turn out of my sight.

"On the north shore," Ruiz continued, "people ask me questions. But I say I am surprise as they are by what happens. I say that I will talk to Cheriff Finits. That I will go to find him. But my horse, he is too tire to ride without some rest. Yet no one there will lend to me another horse. They say they bring the cheriff to Big Bar to talk to me. And so, I am delay a day. But the cheriff never comes.

"Meanwhile, some men ride west to the ford to see if they can trail Escobar and Pinto when they get across. Others, they prepare to mend the cable."

"Did you tell the people at Big Bar the names of the bandits?" asked the judge.

"No, Señor. At that time, I have still reserve the right to kill Manuel, myself."

"What changed your mind?"

"I see that the embrollo, he is always growing worse before my eyes. If I have only kill Manuel when I have had the chance, perhaps the things are different, now."

"You mean there at the ferry?"

"No. In Mokelumne Hill."

"May I ask what stayed your hand that time? Was it prudence? Or mercy? Or both?"

Ruiz was silent. Will and the two cowboys had long since saddled their horses and cantered off in the moonlight.

"What happened after the incident at Big Bar?" pursued the judge. "You're not assuming the outlaws are chasing you merely on the strength of Manuel's threat? He does not come across as particularly intrepid in your story. Would he not be more likely to actually postpone another confrontation?"

"Yes, he is a coward. But because he is a coward, he will want me dead as soon as his men can find me. I do not think he will come with them after me. But he surely sends Gonzalves. El brasileño knows well who I am. And he knows who to ask for news of me. Is for the lives of these people that I fear. All that may save them is the trail I have make for

Gonzalves to follow me easily without them. First, I stop in Butte City. I make it known there who I am and that I go on to Drytown to find my friend who is a judge."

"I am honored," said Curtis.

"Señor, I regret I have to call attention of the bandits to yourself. I have only hope to reach you in time to warn you."

"As, in fact, you have done. Please continue."

"My horse is so tire, I must leave him in Yackson," Ruiz went on. "And also, I wish to see how is the wife of my friend that the outlaws, they have take him and I have learn no news of him. I go to his house on Yackson Creek. His woman tells me that Gonzalves has not only threaten her but has burn the cabin of her neighbor. Los Seensome."

"Ah," said the judge.

"And there with the wife of my friend, I also find Saidnay."

"Ah," said the judge.

"My friend wife says Gonzalves has threaten to take Saidnay away when he comes back. And then Saidnay tells me she is too unhappy to live with her relatives. I tell her she must stay. She says she will not. But I know if she goes on alone, she goes into great danger. And is Saidnay I once tell you who save my life upon the road from Ranchería."

"Say no more, Don Simón. I comprehend perfectly."

"Señor, I must do what I think it is right."

"Naturally."

"There are others in Yackson, also, I wish I can offer some protection. For they would be in no danger had they not help me when I ask them."

"Don Simón," said Curtis, "it grieves me to see you laboring under such a weight. You are blaming yourself for more than can be the responsibility of any one man. When the scrupulous are forced to deal with the unscrupulous, it is unavoidable that those around you become involved. Your only error, as I see it, has been to attempt too much alone. And that error you have rectified. I am confident that Gonzalves and the rest will be apprehended soon. With the aid of a man as skilled and as determined as yourself, Sheriff Phoenix will have new advantage over them. But for tonight, you must rest your mind from a part of what troubles you. And I know that I speak for Jack and Ellen when I say you're in your own house here, as I believe the Spanish phrase is."

Jack Sutherland, who had been listening to Ruiz and Curtis in thoughtful silence, here interposed. "You know, there's nothing so bad that an hour spent in friendly company over a bottle of good wine can't improve it. Señor, you go back inside with the judge while I see to your horse. And if you'd like a wash and a shave and a change of clothes, you're more than welcome. Ellen will set you up. Then we'll open that bottle I've been saving for just such a good excuse as this is, and we'll leave the outlaws to Will and Phoenix for one night. What do you say?"

"Señor . . . I do not know how to answer you. But I confess I would be grateful for these generous attentions."

"No trouble at all," said Jack. And stepping down off the porch, he moved off toward the silent corrals.

Ruiz and Curtis stood together without speaking for a moment, watching the rancher go and musing separately over what had been revealed. Then, the magistrate turned once more to Simón. "I will ask you to forgive me for this next thing I am going to say to you, my friend, though I assure you that I do not say it to offend. Don Simón, what you have done in marrying this Simpson girl was perhaps the most feasible, if not the only possible thing a man of honor could have done under the circumstances. But it appears to be a misalliance of the most distressing kind."

"Señor," replied Simón, "I have put it out of my power to be offend. But you test the limit of my courtesy."

"I know. And again, I apologize. But I speak from a real concern for your future happiness. And hers. Do you intend to take that raw, uncultured girl back with you to your gracious, traditional world of Californio Society? Or will you attempt to adapt yourself to hers? Either way, I foresee difficulties so immense that even if it were a love-match, I would despair of your success. My boy, you must allow me to advise you before it is too late. Do not consummate this marriage. It still can be annulled."

"¡Señor!"

"I beg your pardon. But I cannot stand by and see you condemn yourself to such a union. Don Simón, I know you'll not deny that both your family and the girl's would have violently opposed this thing, had you consulted them. And in lieu of your absent parent, who would be both shocked and grieved, I counsel you not to commit yourself to a lifetime of regret. You have already answered your obligation. You have carried her safely out of harm's way without sacrificing honor. You need not sacrifice yourself."

"Señor Cortés . . ."

"Is there not some charming señorita in the Valley who is looking to the hills this night and wondering what has so long delayed you? Some lovely girl your uncle and your parents would be proud to welcome as the bride of a young man as dear to them as you must be? One who would wear the name Ruiz Silvestre as an adornment and in turn, lend still more grace and beauty to that name?"

"¡Basta!" exclaimed Simón. Then in a low voice, he answered, "Sí, Señor. There is one as you describe. But I have vow I will not marry her. For she is the sister of my enemy. I tell you this only because you have force me, for to speak of her in the ears of a stranger is a liberty I do not wish to take. But I have find that my affection, my respect for her, have come between me and my action. Is for her sake that I give Manuel another chance. Is for her sake that I close my eyes to what I plainly see when her brother stands before me in disgrace. And is partly for her sake that I am grateful of this chance to put myself out of the reach of her forever. I still shall kill Manuel! How then, shall I be husband to his sister? Yet if I do not marry her, what difference who I marry? For I know I don't forget her. But I do not punish Saidnay for what I blame myself. I try to be to her the best I can. I try to make her happy. She has been unhappy. I have never see her smile. With me, I vow she learns to smile. Or maybe she teach me. In any case, Señor, I do not repent what I have done."

Curtis sighed. "So be it," he said. "Shall we go in?"

CHAPTER THIRTY:

ELLEN'S INTUITION

If the judge had found Ruiz somewhat more communicative than he had expected, Ellen Sutherland found Sydney less so. "Your husband is a handsome man, Mrs. Ruiz," she had ventured as the others left the house with Will.

"Yep," said Sydney.

"How did you happen to meet him?"

"He was robbed by the bandits on the road near Rancheria. My brother See Saw and I were hauling freight to Jackson. We scared them off."

"I see." Without getting up, Ellen began collecting dishes from the table around her. "Where is your brother, now?"

"I don't know. He may be out looking for me with Uncle Peter by this time."

"Your folks didn't know about your plans to marry?"

"I didn't have any plans." Sydney reached for the plates nearest her and stacked them.

"Your brother and uncle will be pretty worried about you, then, won't they?"

"Maybe."

"Where do they live?"

"On Jackson Creek. With Aunt Aggie and the boys."

"Jack could send a rider with a message, if you'd like." Sydney made no answer.

Ellen rose to take her stack of plates to the kitchen.

Sydney followed, bringing hers. "Your parents aren't living?" Ellen surmised.

"Nope."

"Things must not have been very easy for you with your uncle's family."

"They weren't."

"But it's cruel just to let them worry about you, isn't it?" Silence.

"Would you object to Jack's sending them word that you're here with us and safe?"

"They'd come after me," said Sydney.

"Oh, no, I don't think they would. After all, you're married, now. And they can't do anything about that, can they?"

"Nope."

Ellen made another trip between the table and the kitchen. Sydney helped her. "We'll leave the dishes for tonight," said Ellen when the table was clear and the cloth was removed. "They won't go anywhere till morning, I guess. Let's sit somewhere comfortable, shall we?"

"I don't mind doing them now," said Sydney.

"Thank you. It's good of you to offer. But I'd rather let them stay right where they are. Come, Mrs. Ruiz."

"Call me Sydney. That other doesn't sound like me."

Ellen smiled. "It is you, though. So you'll have to get used to it." She led the way to the leather sofa and signed her guest to sit down. She chose a nearby chair for herself. "There'll be a lot of new things you'll have to get used to."

"I guess so." Sydney looked around the room. Then abruptly, she confided, "I don't feel married."

"It's too soon, yet."

Sydney looked at her hostess curiously. "How long did it take you?"

"Oh . . . a little while."

"Did you get married in a church?"

"No. At home." But rather than add anything further in explanation, as she certainly would have, were she talking to anyone else, Ellen only waited. For she sensed that Sydney was more likely to volunteer information than to respond to an interrogation, however well meant.

Sure enough: "We got married in a church," Sydney said after a moment. "It was a Catholic church. But I'm not a Catholic. Do you think it makes any difference?"

"Well, it might. Did your husband say anything to you about it?"

"Nope."

"What religion are you?"

"I don't know. Nothing, I guess. But my family is Presbyterian."

"Would you rather have been married in a Presbyterian church?"

Sydney shrugged. "Well . . . maybe I'd feel more married."

"Why don't you have a civil ceremony?"

"What's that?"

"When you're married by law instead of by religion."

"But it's too late, isn't it?"

"There's no reason I know of that you can't do both."

"Who would do the marrying? The sheriff?"

"No. The judge."

"You mean like Judge Curtis?"

"M'hm."

Sydney thought about this. Color showed in her sober face. "Could he do it right here? Tonight?"

"Yes, I think so. Especially if he knew it would make

you feel better. Do you want me to ask him?"

Sydney thought some more. She looked at Ellen several times before she nodded.

"Would you like to clean up for the ceremony? Take a bath? Wash your hair? Change your clothes?"

Sydney looked down at herself. "I've only got what I've got on."

"I'd loan you something."

"Would you?"

"Of course."

"That would be really nice of you, Miz Sutherland."

So it was when the men returned from the porch, the women were nowhere in sight. "Ellen!" called Curtis.

"Just a minute!" came the answer from behind a closed door.

The judge turned to Ruiz, but before he could suggest the obvious, Jack Sutherland came in after them from the stable. He had Simón's saddlebags over his arm. "Thought you might want these," he explained.

"Gracias, Señor."

"What is it, Judge?" asked Ellen, appearing from an adjoining room and closing its door quickly and firmly behind her.

"Where's our young wife?"

"She's taking a bath."

"Ah! Don Simón, it seems you have to stand in line."

"No, he doesn't," said Ellen. "This ranch boasts more than one bathtub. Jack, do you want to bring that one from the bunkhouse?"

"Sure." Sutherland leaned to deposit the saddlepack on the floor and went back outside.

"This is much trouble for you, Señora!" objected Ruiz.

"Not at all. And there's water hot enough to shave with in the reservoir at the side of the stove. Judge? Will you show him where? He can use Will's room for now. Excuse me, gentlemen. I promised Mrs. Ruiz I'd find her something clean to put on."

Even though his saddlebags were on the floor in front of him, it took a moment for Simón to recognize that this was an appropriate time to reveal what was in them. "¡Señora!" He lifted a detaining hand. "Saidnay has something is her own to put."

Ellen turned back. "Oh?"

Ruiz knelt beside the packs, unfastened one of the flaps, and took out the parcel which had filled that side since before he had returned to the Valley. He had come close to leaving it at the Casa Grande, but he had not wished its contents to be boiled in black dye. He stood up, and with a smile that Ellen Sutherland could almost have interpreted as wistful, he brought her the bundle, put it in her hands. "Is a surprise," he said. "Tell her that I buy for her in the store in Ranchería."

Ellen returned the smile warmly. "I'm sure it will mean a great deal to her, Don Simón."

It did. Sydney was out of the bath and standing on the bedside rug in a chemise which her hostess had provided. She was drying her hair, but she stopped to peer out from under the towel as Ellen came back in. "What's that?" she asked.

"A gift from your husband." Ellen put the package down on the bed.

Her freckled face a study of wonder, Sydney threw aside the towel and laid hands on the parcel. She held it a moment, then tore at the paper. Ellen was about to suggest she save the wrapping to put the dress in again later, but she closed her mouth on the words. She doubted that Sydney had received very many presents in her life. And she did not wish to spoil the moment for her with criticism.

Under Sydney's sunburned fingers, the package quickly gave up its contents. And at the first glimpse of soft ruffles trimmed with lace, her face flushed with pleasure. "It's just like a butterfly coming out of a cocoon, isn't it?" she said, shaking out the dress and holding it up in front of her. "You'd never have thought anything so pretty could be inside!" She turned sober but radiant eyes to Ellen. "Did he bring it from the Valley?"

"No," said Ellen. "He told me to tell you he bought it at France's Store in Rancheria."

"He did? He did! In Rancheria?" Sydney looked again at the dress. Suddenly she caught it to her and hid her face in its flounces.

Again, Ellen would have interposed. She wanted to take this girl to her heart . . . if only because she suspected that no one else ever had. But again, she merely watched and waited.

"I hope it fits," said Sydney, lifting her head and sniffing back her private tears which were more joyful than sad.

"Try it on. If it doesn't, we'll fix it so it will."

"Which is back and which is front?"

"Let me see. Here. This is how it goes. Oh, look! There was a belt with it. It fell when you shook the dress out. No, it's more than a belt. Oh, Sydney, this is really elegant."

"It is, isn't it?"

"I wish we were at the other ranch. I have a trunk of things there I didn't think I'd need down here. And there's a hoop skirt petticoat in it that would be right for this. Well, nevermind. It doesn't matter. Try it on."

"It's too tall in the shoulders," was Sydney's first conclusion when she had put the dress over her head, pushed her arms through its dainty sleeves and tried to make its neckline lie at a modest distance from her chin.

"You haven't pulled it down around your waist yet," said Ellen. "Let me help you. There. How's that?"

Sydney did not answer.

"What's the matter?"

"A part of it must be missing."

"Yes. The weskit. Put this around your waist and lace it up the front."

Reluctantly, Sydney accepted the wide, stiff, sculpted strip covered in emerald velvet. "I don't think it will help," she said.

"Turn around. Let me see what's wrong."

Still lacing the weskit, Sydney turned. And Ellen must bite back an exclamation of surprise. "Sydney," she said, "it's not the dress that is the butterfly. It's you."

"What?"

"You look positively stunning. A person could scarcely tell when you had on that awful old brown dress and faded apron, but you are a very pretty girl. I was going to offer to wash those things for you, but now, I think I'll tear them up. I have two or three dresses you can choose from to wear for everyday until you have a chance to get some others made. You realize, don't you, that you're not going to have to dress in rags . . . ever again?"

"Does it really look all right?"

"It looks more than all right. I may have to blindfold Jack. You haven't pulled the strings quite tight enough, yet. The weskit is meant to be snug."

"But isn't there any more to the top of it? I feel like my shirt's off."

"No. It's all right. It's meant to be like that."

"Is it decent?"

"Well, I don't suppose your Presbyterian aunt would think so. But what does she know? Don't put on those moccasins," Ellen protested when Sydney stepped into one of them. "They don't look right with it."

"But they're all I have."

"Go bearfoot. You have nice little feet. I wonder if that black eyed husband of yours knows what he's getting? He probably does," Ellen answered herself. "But you'll surprise him, just the same. Sydney, before we go back out there, I want to ask you something."

"What?"

Ellen fetched her hairbrush from the bureau. "Do you have any idea about what's in store for you? Do you know what it means to be married to a man?"

Sydney did not reply.

"You don't, do you?" Ellen gave her the brush.

"Aunt Aggie is married to Uncle Peter," Sydney offered.

"I've seen her a lot with him. But I didn't notice anything special about it."

"No, I don't suppose you did. But you said something about some boys, before. Are they your cousins?"

"Two of them are. Jacob and Timothy. The other one is my uncle's apprentice. His name's Paul McCormick. But he . . ."

"How old were you when your youngest cousin was born?"

Sydney brushed her hair and considered. "I guess I was about eight. Because Tim is nearly ten."

"You weren't allowed to help, then. You were too young."

"Help with what?"

"With the baby. Being born."

"Oh. But I've seen kittens born. And puppies. We had a dog once named . . ."

"Sydney. I'm sorry if I seem to be talking on about nothing, but there is a point to all this. Do you know . . . how babies are made?"

Sydney stopped brushing her hair.

"Do you know how kittens are made? And puppies?"

Slowly, Sydney shook her head. "I guess I never thought about it," she said. "Don't they just grow?"

"Once they're started, yes. But you have to start them."

"How?"

Ellen drew a deep breath and sat down on the edge of the bed. "I don't know why I began with this," she said. "Sydney, I just don't want you to be too shocked, is all."

"About what?"

Ellen studied the backs of her hands, then laced the fingers of one down through those of the other. "I've often wished I'd had a daughter," she reminded herself. "But I've never wondered how Jack told Will about such things. Maybe I should have asked him." She closed her fingers and looked up with a tight smile.

Sydney was watching her, mystified but fascinated.

"Had you thought about where you were going to sleep tonight?" Ellen asked her.

"Anywhere is fine. I don't want to put you to more trouble, Miz Sutherland."

"I don't mean it that way, Sydney. You'll have our guest room. Judge Curtis can sleep in Will's bed this time. No, I meant, did you think you were going to sleep with **him**?"

"With Judge Curtis?" exclaimed Sydney.

Ellen laughed. "When I said you'd be shocked, I didn't mean you'd be **that** shocked. No, not with Judge Curtis. With your husband."

"With Simón? You mean right in the same room?"

"I mean right in the same bed. And don't ask me if there aren't enough here to go around. Your aunt and uncle sleep together, don't they? Well, so do Jack and I. It's part of the reason that people get married."

"It is?"

"It's usually most of the reason, at least to begin with."

"That wasn't why Simón married **me**," Sydney declared with conviction.

"Perhaps not," said Ellen. "But from what little I know about Latin men, high class or no, I'd guess that he expects to include it." She paused and sighed and looked away for the inspiration to continue. But when she turned back to Sydney, she saw that she already had said enough.

"It's all right, Sydney," Ellen told her softly. "If you love him. And you do love him, don't you?"

Sydney flashed a look at her, then down. She nodded. "It's a . . . funny thing," she said, her voice unsteady. "When I'm with him, I feel . . . warm. All over. And when I'm really close to him . . . I mean . . . when he . . . do **you** think he has beautiful eyes, Miz Sutherland?"

Ellen clasped her hands more tightly together. "They're very expressive," she agreed.

"They're beautiful, though, aren't they?"

"Yes."

"Do you feel all warm when you're with Jack?"

"Sometimes."

"He has nice eyes, too. Only, they're blue. And crinkly at the corners. He's a nice man. I like him."

"Thank you, Sydney. You're very sweet. Shall we go back to the living room?"

CHAPTER THIRTY-ONE:

POR LO CIVIL

Of the assorted company which reassembled in the ranch house sitting room, Judge Curtis was at once the most surprised and yet the least impressed by Sydney's new appearance. During the absence of his hostess and his fellow guests, the magistrate had tried to engage Jack Sutherland's sympathy for Ruiz' plight.

"There ought to be a law against such ill-paired marriages!" he grumbled. But he spoke in an undertone to avoid being overheard from behind the two respective doors.

"I believe you're bothered by it, Judge," returned Sutherland with an easy smile.

"I am. And so should you be. I cannot imagine a less promising alliance."

Sutherland stretched an arm out along the sofa back and crossed his legs in front of him. "Oh, I don't know. It appears to me those two already have some understanding built up between them. She looks to him for guidance, and he lets her use her own judgement. But he can put his foot down when he has to. I call that a fair start. There's a lot of couples take twenty years to get that far."

"Rubbish, Jack! They represent opposite poles, I tell you. Can you imagine that girl trying to cope with the kind of society he comes from?"

"She might blow a breath of fresh air into it."

"She would embarrass him every time she opened her mouth."

"He hasn't made **us** any apologies for her."

"He has made **me** one."

"You must have pushed him for it."

"He confessed to me that he has purposefully used her to lock the doors of his own kind against him. He is chastising himself for what he considers his ineptitude."

"How's that?"

"Ruiz sees it as his bounden duty to exterminate this scoundrel Escobar he talks of. But he can't bring himself do it because he's just too decent to shoot the fellow down in cold blood. So, as a penance, he means to ostracize himself and alienate his family with this marriage. Why, he has made his return to the Valley virtually impossible. Yet how can he live among Americans? He can't scratch the ground for gold or hire himself out as a vaquero for a living. His pride would kill him."

"Well, but the man's rich, isn't he? Maybe he'll buy up some land hereabouts and run a few head of cattle. I'll bet the vaqueros would fall all over themselves signing on to work for him. And in that case, this little gal he's married will be just the wife he needs. She's not quite grown up yet, but in a few more years I'd guess she'll be a real force to reckon with. And with her solidly behind him, he stands as good a chance as any American rancher that's just beginning. Better. He's been raised to it. And his uncle won't desert him entirely, no matter who he marries. No, you're all worked up over nothing, Judge. You're too used to looking at things in terms of the law, where one thing's right and another thing's wrong."

Curtis shifted his weight abruptly in his chair. "Not at all," he said. "The law allows for loopholes."

"Then, you better allow one for don Simón."

"But I hate to see him pollute himself," mourned the judge. "He's such a perfect specimen."

Sutherland chuckled comfortably. "You should have stayed back East and raised that family you never had and always say you didn't want. You could have turned out a dozen such specimens as he is."

"Yes, and they'd all have disappointed me as soon as they were old enough to think they could use their own heads! Don't wish any such fate as that upon me."

"You've not been disappointed in Will, yet, have you?" As he asked this, Sutherland glanced toward the door which opened to admit Ruiz into their company once more.

"He is your son, Jack, not mine," said Curtis. "And therefore, his base is solid and his eyes have not been clouded. Will listens to my advice with great patience. But he almost never takes it. Don Simón!" the magistrate added to Ruiz. "You look a different man!"

"Only the surface, he is change, Señor," replied Simón. He glanced down at himself. Will Sutherland's blue and white checked shirt fit him well enough except for the length of the sleeves. A pair of leather arm bands had remedied this. But at his host's insistence, the borrowed trousers had been permanently shortened. Their raw cut edge brushed the instep of his newly cleaned boots. The large-roweled spurs he had put aside, however, together with his hat, the three pistols and the two knives.

"I have hear that a certain bandido known to el señor Sutterlan also used to disguise as the americano," said Ruiz.

Jack's brows lifted. "I hate to tell you, Don Simón, but you're not liable to fool folks quite so easily as Joaquín did."

"Ah, no? Pues, is good I do not think to try it, then." Simón rubbed his freshly-shaven chin and cast about him for a place to sit.

But now, the other closed door opened, and Ellen Sutherland led from it a blushing and uncertain butterfly who looked no more Spanish in her new finery than Ruiz looked American in his borrowed dungarees. Yet neither the white dress, with its yards of lace and ribbon, nor the girl who wore it were any the less lovely for that.

"Well!" said Jack, pushing himself onto his feet.

"My dear young lady!" exclaimed the judge, bouncing up.

But Sydney scarcely noticed them. It was the approval of Simón she sought. She watched him anxiously as he came toward her, nor was she satisfied merely to see the admiring light in his dark eyes, the smile flashing white beneath his black mustache. Even when he took both her hands and kissed them, she continued to watch his face for reassurance.

"Saidnay, you make this dress to be beautiful," he told her.

She found nothing to say in reply.

"You do not like?"

She nodded. "Simón? Did you really buy it on purpose for me?"

"Of course I do, niña."

"But you didn't even know where I was then, did you? I mean, didn't you think I had gone to Simpson's Bar?"

"I would have find you, Pecosa."

"You would? Really?"

"I remember I promise to say goodbye to you a second time. And to keep that promise, I must first find you a second time."

The anxious look faded from Sydney's face. And then, she smiled. It was not a large smile. It did no more than tilt the corners of her lips. But it changed the whole aspect of her countenance. And to catch a taste of its fleeting sunlight, Ruiz bent quickly to kiss it before it disappeared.

"Judge Curtis," said Ellen briskly, distracting the others' attention from Sydney and Simón for a moment, "we have a favor to ask you. Or rather, a service."

The magistrate bowed. "I would be honored, I'm sure."

"Sydney has confided to me that she feels a little uncomfortable about her wedding. I can imagine it was rather
hurried. When you are not only eloping but trying to keep
out of the reach of a band of outlaws at the same time, there
isn't much space left for the niceties. So, I have suggested to
her, and I suggest to don Simón, that we have another ceremony. Right now. Just so she can feel better about it all. A
woman is only married once. It ought to be something she
can think back on with pleasure. Judge," Ellen concluded,
clasping her hands and letting them fall forward in an unconscious gesture of appeal, "I told her you would marry them
again."

Curtis did not immediately reply.

Jack Sutherland coughed slightly to mask what might
have been amusement. "Ellie, maybe you'd better ask don
Simón how he likes the idea of marrying the same girl twice,"
he said.

"I marry her three time, if she wants it," declared Ruiz
in an effort to coax another smile from his bride. But Sydney
was too embarrassed.

There was another moment's silence.

"I . . . ah, didn't bring my books with me," said Curtis.

"Oh, I'm sure you can remember the right words to say,"
urged Ellen.

"And there must be a record of the ceremony," mused
the magistrate. "I suppose I could write up some sort of certificate that would serve the purpose. But . . ."

"I'll get you the paper and ink." Ellen whisked away to a
massive desk against the wall at the far end of the room. She
returned with the required items and put them down on a
little table beside the chair from which Curtis had risen.

"Hem! Yes. Well . . ." The judge sat down again with
more reluctance than dignity and felt in his pocket for his
pen. But once he was well begun, the momentum of the task
itself carried him on. The others gathered around his chair to
watch him write.

"I am not going to mention here that you were actually married previously," he told Simón who had drawn Sydney close to the table with him. "I fear it may cause unpleasant speculation. Although there will be something entered on the chapel's records to that effect, no doubt. Which church was it? San Gabriel?"

"No, pues, I do not know the name of it," Ruiz admitted. "Is the capilla de adobe along the road close to town of Yackson."

"That's San Gabriel." The judge wrote on. The whisper of his nib was plainly audible. When he had finished, he read over what he had written. "Where would you like us to stand?" he asked Ellen.

The rancher's wife looked around the big room as if she had never really seen it before. But she chose for them to remain more or less where they were, with the judge standing to one side of his chair and Ruiz and Sydney before him. She stationed Jack on the other side of Simón and took up her own position across from him so that they formed a little semi-circle around the judge. Then Ellen smoothed her skirts and folded her hands in front of her to signal to the magistrate he might begin.

"Dear friends," said Curtis. "We have gathered here in the presence of these witnesses to join together this man and this woman in legal matrimony. Marriage is a lawful and an honorable estate. It is not to be entered into lightly. Nor unadvisedly." The judge paused. He looked at Simón.

Ruiz neither stirred nor changed expression.

"If there be any man present who knows of any just cause why these two may not be joined in marriage, I require him to make it known, or to ever after hold his peace." The judge came to another full stop. He looked at Sutherland.

The rancher's blue eyes twinkled at him, but Jack repressed his smile. He was silent.

Curtis turned back to Simón and Sydney. "Together, you are about to assume a new identity, a new commitment, a new responsibility. You are about to pledge to each other undying devotion and fidelity. If there is any reason why you should not do so, I charge you now to make it known."

Ruiz' brow betrayed a furrow of impatience. But still he waited.

"These vows you take must be kept inviolate," pursued the judge. "For henceforth you will no longer be twain, but one. Your paths will be no longer divided but parallel. And no storm of life, no temptation of the flesh, must come between you. It is into such a union as this that you will now be joined." Curtis paused a third time.

Then gathering the whole force of his authority into his gaze, he directed it into the proud look of Ruiz. "Do you, Simón Ruiz Silvestre, take this woman to be your lawful wedded wife, to honor and to cherish her; and do you promise, forsaking all others, to cleave to her and to her only for so long as you both shall live?"

Simón's presence expanded tangibly as he made answer: "¡Sí, Señor!" And Curtis searched his gaze in vain for a hint of regret or shame.

Then the judge turned to Sydney and looked directly into her eyes. But though he found there both the ignorance and the innocence that he expected, he also saw a depth and a comprehension that surprised him. Her brown eyes were round and solemn. No brown eyes were ever so solemn. And when Curtis spoke again, it was with more tenderness than he had intended.

"Do you, Sydney Simpson, take this man to be your lawful wedded husband, to honor and to obey him; and do you promise, forsaking all others, to cleave to him and to him only for so long as you both shall live?"

Sydney nodded. "Yep," she said. "I do."

Curtis drew a concluding breath. "By the authority invested in me by the State of California, I now pronounce you man and wife. May this union be a fruitful one. God bless you both."

CHAPTER THIRTY-TWO:

MAN AND WIFE

"You shall sign it, also, Ellen." Judge Curtis put the pen into her hand and pointed at the bottom of the certificate of marriage that he had drawn up beforehand.

The rancher's wife wrote her name below her husband's which he had just put there as a witness to the legality of the proceedings. "It was a beautiful ceremony, Judge," she said.

"What we need now," put in Sutherland, "is that bottle of wine I promised don Simón."

"What bottle of wine!" exclaimed Ellen, rising upright to look at her husband in astonishment.

"Oh, didn't I tell you? I wasted a dollar on some port

last time I was in town. I figured we'd have it to celebrate your birthday."

"My birthday!"

"I know it's not till November," Jack admitted. "But port keeps pretty well if you don't uncork it more than once a week."

"John Beuford Sutherland! You promised me faithfully never again!"

"It's only port wine, Ellen. And the cork hasn't been out of it once, yet. So help me, hallelujah."

Ellen looked long at her husband's half guilty, half hopeful expression before she suddenly relented: "Well, you'd better go and get it, then."

Jack strode to the door. "It's in the stable," he explained to no one in particular. Then he went out.

"What we really need is some music," said Ellen. "Or something. Judge! You play the guitar . . .!"

But Curtis raised both hands and shook his head. "My dear, I am no musician."

"Nonsense! I know you do! You've played it for us right here in this room. I think the guitar's in the bunkhouse. Jack! Jack!" She ran to the door and jerked it open.

Sutherland was already halfway to the stable. But he heard her and turned. And as she saw him, it seemed to Ellen that he looked younger, somehow. Perhaps it was the way the moonlight silvered his shoulders. But he looked as she had not seen him for nearly twenty years. She went out onto the porch.

"Jack . . .?"

"What is it?" he called back. Even his voice was younger. Further obeying impulse, Ellen went down the low steps and started toward him across the open space. The summer dust lay softly white beneath her feet. The corral poles cast a basket-weave of shadow on the ground. From a nearby hilltop, a coyote burst out in a wild tenor. And Ellen let herself be startled by the familiar sound. She ran. She ran until Jack caught her off her feet and swung her round. Nor did he let her go again when he set her down. For Ellen had cast both arms about his neck and kissed him. "Oh, Jack!"

"You're as silly as I am, aren't you?" he demanded, holding her close.

"Is it silly? I suppose it is. But it just . . . brought it all back so! Didn't it?"

"Mrs. Sutherland, this night is not over yet."

"Jack, where's the guitar?"

"How's that again?"

"I came out here to tell you to look for the guitar in the bunkhouse."

"That old thing? I haven't seen it for weeks. If it's anywhere, it's probably in Will's room. What do you want it for?"

"I feel like dancing! And I remember that the judge played for us once."

"Then, I'm sure you made him promise to do it again before he knew what he was getting into. I never saw a justice look so floored! I think he'd have rather married a steer to a fence than to join those two young lovers in 'legal matrimony'! Ha, ha, ha!"

"Shh! He'll hear you."

"Well, you better trot back inside there and rescue him from the 'ill-paired' company of Mr. and Mrs. Unadvised. He'll be squirming like a branded calf!"

"Jack! Will you look in the bunkhouse for the guitar?"

"Yes, Ma'am! Will you give me another kiss like that last one? Mmm! Ellie, I haven't seen you look so downright pretty since before Will was born. I wish we knew more young folks wanting to elope. I'd witness as many weddings as they'd bring to our door."

"Oh, go along with you. You can't take your eyes off doña Saidnay Seensome de Ruiz Silvestre, and you know it!"

"Who? You mean that little freckle-breasted, brown-eyed angel that'll take our perfect specimen on a trip to heaven tonight?"

"I really feel for her, Jack. She hasn't the faintest

notion . . .!"

"Did you?"

"Oh, go find the guitar."

"And the port?"

"Bring both bottles," said Ellen. "It's likely we'll need them."

"My darling wife, I swear to you there's only one. Besides, it's only the judge that really needs it." And Jack kissed her again.

But when Ellen returned to the house, she found things more amicable than Jack had insinuated. Curtis was back in his chair, and Ruiz was on the sofa with Sydney who was nestled against him inside the circle of his arm. They were both listening politely while the judge recounted the sad case of Port Wine, the notorious tippler of Rancheria.

"He's been given some pretty tempting offers to sell his claim," the magistrate was saying. "And it's truly a wonder he doesn't. He only works it the absolute minimum the law allows without having to forfeit his ownership."

"I'll be right with you," said Ellen as they all looked up. "Please stay where you are," she added, for the men would have risen. "I'm going to look in Will's room for the guitar. Jack thinks that's where he saw it last. Oh!" she added, pausing uncertainly. "I forgot that your things are there, Don Simón. Do you mind if I go in?"

"Señora," said Ruiz, kissing Sydney's hand as he took his arm from behind her, "is not that I mind. But you must let me help you to look for it." He got quickly to his feet.

Ellen would have protested. It meant leaving Sydney to face the judge alone. Or the judge to face Sydney alone. But Ruiz came forward with so firm a step that Ellen felt it less awkward to allow him to accompany her than to try to send him back. Taking the kerosene lamp from the dining room table, she went on with him to her son's room.

There was no disorder. The tin tub had already been taken outside and emptied. Ruiz' soiled clothes were folded under his hat on the end of Will's bed. The three pistols and the two knives lay in a neat row on the dressing table. The

spurs were beside them. They gleamed in the lamp-light. Ellen peered around at the shadowy corners of the room.
"There!" she said, pointing to the fretted neck of the instrument which leaned against the linen chest.

Ruiz went after it. As he brought it back, he tucked the
guitar's scarred belly under his arm and tried its strings with
his thumb. They were sadly out of tune. But when he would
have tightened them, Ellen put out her hand to hush the
sound. "Leave it," she said softly. "And don't you dare let the
judge know you can play it."

Ruiz lifted inquiring eyes.

"You can't dance and play at the same time, Don Simón," she explained.

"¡Ah, ya! Le comprendo. You are most thoughtful of
me and my Saidnay, Señora. And I say to you now how much
I thank you for what you have done." Holding the guitar flat
to his side to keep any whisper of music from escaping its
rusty strings, he gestured Ellen to precede him back to the
living room.

But she stood where she was. "Your Sydney," she said,
determined to sound the man for what lay under his polished
surface, "is a very brave and beautiful girl."

"I am honor you say so."

"But she is . . . inexperienced! In some ways."

"What do you wish to say to me, Doña Elena?"

Ellen sighed. "I know you'll be good to her. I've watched
you. You are tender with her. And it's what she needs. You
think this is none of my business, I'm sure. But Sydney has
no mother to be concerned for her. And I gather that her
aunt has been a poor substitute. Don Simón . . . forgive me.
But I worry about her."

"Señora," Ruiz said soberly, "that which the magistrado
has ask me to promise before you in this ceremony of marriage, what more I can say to assure you? I do my best to
make her be happy. The rest, he is in the hand of heaven."

"Yes. Yes, I do believe you will try with her. Thank you.
Forgive me, again."

Ruiz smiled. "You remind me my tía. My own aunt. She

will also like Saidnay. I think you forget: my wife has new parientes, more relatives who will be concern for her."

Ellen nodded doubtfully. "I'm certain . . . they will."

"We go back now, Señora. I talk to you more later if you wish me and there is opportunity."

"Yes," agreed Ellen. "Of course." And she led the way out of the room.

When Jack Sutherland rejoined the company, the judge was still attempting to tune the guitar. "I shall have to play it as it is, I'm afraid," he said. "Or not at all."

"It'll sound all right after a glass of port," said Jack.

"Well, we shall see . . ." Curtis sat forward in his chair, and wrapping himself around the battered instrument, he struck the strings in a series of swift motions which filled the room with a ringing cadence and brought Simón instantly to his feet from where he had resettled himself beside Sydney. Snapping his fingers first over his head and then behind his back, Ruiz added a dramatic rhythmn of heel taps to counterpoint the judge's continuous chording. "¡Por Dios!" he cried when Curtis ended. "Where you have learn to do that?"

The judge flushed with modest pleasure. "Unfortunately, what you have just heard is the extent of my expertise in that direction," he said. "The rest of what I shall offer you is much more prosaic. And much more American in flavor. Mrs. Ruiz," he added, turning politely to Sydney, "would you prefer a waltz or a polka?"

"It won't make much difference," she said. "I can't dance."

No one responded for a moment. Everyone looked at Sydney. She sat alone on the big, leather sofa, the beautiful skirts of her Spanish dress spread out beside her, one finger tracing a satin ribbon across her knees, her eyes downcast, her face quiet.

But then before she knew how it happened, Sydney found herself standing on the open floor. Simón's half embrace held her there, and all the voices around her were urging her to let him show her what to do.

"Play the baltz you say so, Señor," Ruiz instructed the judge. "Pecosita, come up on my toes."

"What?"

"My toes. Stand on them, niña."

"You want me to step on your toes?"

"¡Sí, sí! No, stand on the top of them. ¡Ea! Like that. I will dance underneath you until you feel the way that it goes."

But the first step he took dislodged her.

"No, Saidnay! Don't try to stay still where you are. Move with me. We try again."

"I feel stupid doing this."

"You are not stupid, muñeca. Here. I walk with you. I walk only forward. You let me carry you with me. ¡Eso! See? Is not so difficult. Señor Cortés, if you will play again, now . . ."

"Come on, Jack," said Ellen. "She'll do better without us watching her. Go ahead, Judge. Mr. Sutherland . . .? I just invited you to dance with me. Do you remember how? Or do you need to stand on **my** toes?"

The rancher rose from his chair. "I may stand on them some without needing to," he said. "It's been several years since they let me out of finishing school."

"You mean turned you out of school . . . without finishing."

"Don't sass me, Ma'am. I'm powerful mean when I get roused."

"How many years ago was that?"

"I thought you'd remember."

Ellen laughed and slipped into his arms. And he whirled her away around the room.

Seeing them, Sydney dismounted from the slippery toes of Simon's boots and stood in his way to stop him. Without speaking or moving, she watched the Sutherlands waltz. Ruiz enjoyed her intent expression for a few moments before he interrupted her concentration. "Payasita . . ." he said softly.

She looked up.

"You don't have to do it, niña. If you don't want to."

"But I want to!" She returned her attention to the Sutherlands' demonstration.

Ruiz caressed her hand inside his own to distract her again. "The way to learn is to do it, Saidnay!" he insisted. "When you only watch, you only learn how well the others can do it."

"They make it seem so easy."

"Is not the first time for them."

"It looks beautiful, doesn't it?"

"It feels beautiful." He moved his hand on hers. "And is this the way you are with everything, Pecosa? That you must put your whole heart in?"

Her eyes lifted back to his.

"Saidnay," he whispered, "come with me outside."

"Don't you want me to learn to dance?"

"Another time, I teach you. Now, I want that you give your heart only to Simón Ruiz. And nothing else." They had been near the door when Sydney stopped to watch the Sutherlands. Simón drew her to it and through it and closed it softly behind them.

Jack saw them go. "We've lost our lovers," he said in Ellen's ear.

"Already?" She looked back over her shoulder. The room was empty. Only Judge Curtis still sat as before on the edge of his chair, bending over the old guitar, his greying head bowed to his work, his fingers moving nimbly on the rusty strings. The unopened wine bottle was on the table at his elbow.

"Well . . ." sighed Ellen, "we don't care, do we? Waltz me around again, John Beuford. The night is young, and so is my heart. And I declare, you do dance divinely."

"You want to look out how you praise me, minx. You'll be turning my head, next."

"I love you, Jack."

"Shall we send the judge to bed?"

"No. Let him play. I don't suppose he'll last much longer."

"Neither will I."

Ellen felt of the iron-hard muscle in her husband's arm.

"You just let me know when you're beginning to feel faint," she said.

"I love you, Ellie. Will you marry me?"

"Twice."

Sutherland leaned to kiss his wife's ear. "I'll hold you to it," he promised.

CHAPTER THIRTY-THREE:

CUTE AND CUDDLY

The moonlight was softly muted in the shadow of the porch. On the single bench remaining there against the wall, Sydney sank down with a small sigh beside Simón. But it was not a sigh of happiness, although she gave herself readily into his arms and let her head drop on his shoulder.

"What is it, Payasita?" asked Ruiz, recognizing her silence as more pensive than blissful.

"Nothing much. Simón . . .?"

"I am here with you, Saidnay."

"Will See Saw be worried?"

"This is what it is, then? Yes. He is worry. But no more than an hour ago."

"It **was** cruel what I did to him, wasn't it?"

"What you have done to him?"

"Of course, I told him before that I meant to run off. He probably forgot. I bet he remembers, now."

"I am sure that he does."

"Do you think Miz Ben Rooster told him the truth? Or the lie?"

"I don't think that it matters, Pecosa. Either way, he is worry."

"You think he'd still worry if he knew I went with you?"

"I hope not so much as if he think you are captive of the bandidos. But yes. Your brother is worry to think you are with me."

Sydney sighed again.

"Is something you should have consider about before, niña."

"I did. I considered about it a lot when I was making up my mind to run off."

"And then?"

"Then, I figured I could stand having See Saw worry over me easier than I could stand staying there with Aunt Aggie and Uncle Peter and Jacob and Timothy and Paul Mc-Cormick. And Amy Thomson."

"Who is this?"

"The parson's daughter. Paul and See Saw are both gone on her."

"César is in love with someone?"

"Well, pretty much. But I don't think he stands a chance against Paul. He's just making a big fool of himself for nothing."

"What she is like, this Emmie Topsaw?"

Sydney stirred against Ruiz in disgust. "I don't know exactly. But I guess she thinks she's pretty cute and cuddly."

Ruiz smiled. "Is César who say this about her?"

"No. Dan'l Perrin said it. I wish he'd marry her. It would serve him and Paul and everybody right."

"What is cadda-lee?"

"Hm? Oh, cuddly is, well . . . something you like to hug. Something soft and warm and snuggly, like a puppy or a kitten or a . . ." She stopped, suddenly much embarrassed.

"Or a Saidnay?" suggested Ruiz, closing his embrace about her and pressing her warmly yielding waist to his.

"What?" she breathed. A spot of heat burst under her ribs and swept to the top of her head, the ends of her fingers, the tips of her toes. "I'm not . . . cuddly," she protested.

"Even Daddy used to say . . ."

"What has he say, mimada?" murmured Ruiz, nuzzling into the clean softness of her hair.

". . . That I was all knees and elbows," she finished with difficulty.

He felt for her arm, and cupping her elbow in his hand, half lifted it, half bent to it and laid his lips into its inner angle. Another star exploded under Sydney's velvet weskit.

"Soft," mused Ruiz, moving up her bare arm a kiss at a time. "Soft like a baby." Reaching the lower edge of her lacy sleeve, he pushed two kisses up under it before he transferred to the top of her shoulder and continued on. By the time he had gained her throat, the pulse there was clearly sensible. "Warm," he said. "Yes. She is warm like the sunshine."

He lifted lightly to her lips and played with their willingness, teased them to a tingling sweetness. "Saidnay!" he interrupted himself to whisper. "Is this way I want you to feel in my arms. Tierna . . . ¡Ardiente! But give to me all of you. All those thoughts in your head. Make them all about me. All this warm heart that I feel in your breast, it all must be mine. Saidnay! You are beautiful. Beautiful not like a rose. Beautiful not like a garden of roses. But beautiful like the long sight from the side of a mountain. Beautiful like the new wind of the morning. Like a deer leap away from the edge of a stream. This girl with the brown eye and the smile that I kill for, she is more than I let myself think."

Unable to answer him, Sydney could only listen in breathless wonder. Only twine her arms tightly around him. Only return every kiss that he put to her lips until she could not go on living unless he gave her the next one in time.

And then, Ruiz half rose from the bench onto one knee, lifting her with him. Bracing himself with the other foot on the boards of the porch floor, he bent her back over his arm and settled his mouth into hers as if never to leave it again.

And Sydney would have received him as hungrily as he sought her but for the hand that he slid from her waist to her thigh and back up at an angle to press her still more tightly into him. The strength of his kneading grip enforced a frightening intimacy she did not think she ought to feel. She took her arms from around him and tried to push him away. It was as vain an attempt as if she had tried to push off a tree she was tied to. But at least, he acknowledged her objection.

"Is all right!" he assured her, leaving her lips in order to speak. "Saidnay . . . is all right."

But still, she resisted him.

Ruiz held her another moment so, then relaxed, released her, raised her and himself to stand fully upright. "Come, niña," he said, "we go in. We stay on this porch, I have it all to do over."

Surprised, puzzled, regretful, Sydney lagged back, reluctant to leave the moonlight and the shadows and the new sensations she wished she had not protested. She didn't want to see the judge again. She didn't even want to see Ellen Sutherland again, however kind and understanding she might be.

But the long sitting room was vacant. There was no one in it at all. The lamp still burned on the table. The battered guitar leaned against the sofa. The bottle of port wine had been uncorked, but only the judge's glass had been filled. Of the three doors that opened on the sitting room, two were closed. The third one stood invitingly ajar.

Ruiz led her toward it, retrieving the lamp on the way. Sydney's reluctance acquired new weight. She looked at the sofa, at the judge's chair as she passed them, and wished that they had not been empty after all. She thought of telling Simón that she was not sleepy. She had not decided for or against this yet when she found herself actually in the guest room.

Simón closed the door and glanced around. Choosing the bureau as the best place for the lamp, he left Sydney where she had stopped and went to set it there. Then he turned back. "Ven, Pecosa," he said, beckoning her with the fingers of the hand he reached out to her. But at the same time, he moved to the bed and sat down.

Sydney stood looking at him, half inclined to return to the relative safety of the porch. There was nothing she wanted more than to spend a whole night in the arms of Simón. But she was not quite prepared to spend it in bed with him, no matter what Ellen Sutherland had said.

Still, Ruiz waited, holding out his hand. And slowly, cautiously, Sydney moved toward him. The very deer he had envisioned at the brink of the stream could not have approached him with more deliberation. She stopped again just out of his reach. He turned up the palm of his hand to request hers. "La manito, pues," he said.

Hesitantly, she complied. His grasp was warm and steady. It guided her gently to the bedside, seated her next to him softly. It did not leave her hand until she was settled. Then, it slid up her arm. They both watched its progress. When it reached her shoulder, she had only to turn her head in order to receive his kiss. But she did not.

Ruiz watched her half averted face, comparing it to another in his mind's eye. He tried to feel regretful. He could not. Certain that she was not watching him, he dropped his gaze to her bosom and tried again. Here was not the rich, creamy skin, as flawless as a peach petal, of which he had dreamed since spring. But it made no difference. The rapid flick of pulse and the swell and fall of breath was just as tempting here. More so! Nothing but their own sweet shape pushed up these speckled fruits beneath the cloth and lace which only partly draped them.

No. If he were to count his loss as greater than his gain, it would not be beauty that he mourned.

He took his hand from Sydney's shoulder to touch her face and turn it round. He needed only a full look from her eyes to finally convince him. He had made small sacrifice. He could still manage a twinge of pity for Amanda. But there was always his cousin . . . Francisco would not be sorry to learn Ruiz had forsaken the daughter of don Fernando. Francisco would find a way to comfort her. Francisco could be father and brother and lover and husband to her. And meanwhile, Manuel Escobar had lost his only power to wound his adversary.

"Payasita," whispered Ruiz. "Te quiero."

She frowned slightly. "That's not fair."

"What is not fair, cervata?"

"You say all these things, and I don't know what they mean."

"I have just say that I love you, Saidnay."

"You did?"

"Por cierto."

"What?"

"I love you, muñeca."

"What's moon yay ka?"

"Is what you are like. Small and cute and cadda-lee."

"You've been saying that all this time? And what else? What's pay coza?"

"Is these little bits of sweetness all over your face. And everywhere else that I see you."

"Freckles? You've been calling me 'Freckles'!?"

"Is that how you name them? Fray-cose?" His eyes returned to her breast. "I am not satisfy till I have kiss all of them."

She started and covered herself with both hands. "**All** of them?" she repeated, aghast.

"Everywhere," he agreed.

Her face burned under its multitude. "It'll take you ten years," she declared.

"Then, is better I get started." He kissed three on her cheek he had somehow missed before.

"What'll you do . . . when you're done?" she wondered, pressing her hands still more tightly to her breast as he tried gently to pry them away.

"Start over," he whispered. "Pecosa . . . Cervata . . . Payasita . . . es tanto que te quiero." And succeeding in lifting one of her hands, he carried it to his neck and hooked it there before he began in earnest on the pleasant task he had set for himself which was to take him the next ten years.

CHAPTER THIRTY-FOUR:

THE LAZY Q

"William! This is a pleasant surprise," said John Dynan. He looked young Sutherland up and down with unalloyed satisfaction. "This night portends, my boy. So it does. Come in. Come in! Who is this with you? Hinkson, is it? And Sherill? Come in, gentlemen! And what can it be brings all three of you to Rancheria at this particular moment in the course of human events?"

Will took off his hat as he passed by the hotel's proprietor into his private parlor. The two cowboys jostled after him. But all three of them stopped on the edge of the carpet, mindful of their dusty boots. "Evening, Mrs. Dynan," said young Sutherland, inclining himself in her direction. "Hope we aren't distubing you."

The lady looked up from her chair where she sat with her needlework. She offered the visitors a sweet smile.

But it was John Dynan who answered Will: "Not at all, my boy! Dolly is always pleased to have company. Aren't you, my dear? And such an evening it has been for company!

If we can count four o'clock as belonging more to the evening than the morning."

"Yes, sir," said Will. "Actually, we're on the lookout for Sheriff Phoenix, and we were wanting to ask you for news of him. We were told in Drytown that he'd talked to you, today."

"You hear that, my love? It's the sheriff he wants! It portends. It portends. It so happens, my boy, that we have been visited by the good officer and two individuals surnamed Simpson. Related, of course. Uncle and nephew. The most shocking business! Have you ever chanced to meet a Spanish dandy known to the local populace as don Simón Ruiz?"

Will frowned and turned his hat in his hands.

"Ha! I can see that you have. No need to deny it. And would you believe, my lad, being ever so slighty acquainted with this Spanish gentleman as you may be . . . I say, can you believe that he has actually abducted and carried off the niece and sister of these two Simpsons I have just mentioned?"

"No, sir," Will admitted. "I can't."

"Well, such does seem to be the case. At least, there is a suspicion of it. A strong suspicion. Sheriff Phoenix sat in this very parlor not five hours ago and required me to relate to him every pertinent detail I could dredge from my memory in reference to this same Simón Ruiz. And I trust I was able to enlighten him as to the latent discrepencies in the man's character."

"But do you know where the sheriff is now, Mr. Dynan?"

"The sheriff, William, is following a fresh scent in the direction of the Lazy Q. It is believed by several citizens of this town that the unfortunate niece and sister of the aforementioned Simpsons may have been taken there."

"To the Lazy Q?"

"I know it sounds improbable, my boy, but remember! Many a hidden gulch and gully lies between here and the Q."

"Mr. Dynan, I just don't think . . . "

"No, of course not! Who **would** have thought it? That even the most brightly polished of these hispanic exiles should conceal so vile a spot of tarnish. Our women are never too closely protected from such men. And I shall take heed. My wife is not to stir from her hearthside without . . ."

"I'm sorry, Mr. Dynan," interrupted Will, "but it's pretty urgent that I find Phoenix. He was headed for the Q around four o'clock, was he?"

"Nearer to five, I should think, by the time he left here. Wouldn't you say so, Dolly? And then he stopped off across the street to talk to Albert France as well. He may have been there another ten minutes. Not more. I'm sure that Albert had little to add to my remarks, for he knows no more of Ruiz than I do."

"Who was it told the sheriff to try at the Q?"

"Well, now, let me see . . . Dolly, do you recall? There were several witnesses who swore to having seen a Spanish man of apparent substance, mounted on a fine horse, and dressed in costly clothes such as Ruiz habitually wears. He was accompanied by two or three others, also well mounted and equipped."

"One of them was dark, was he?"

"You have seen them yourself!"

"No, sir. I'm only asking."

"Indeed you are. Yes, I believe one of the men with Ruiz was reported to be very dark. Black, in fact. A body servant, no doubt. The man is known to have incredible wealth. Why, in France's Store . . ."

"Did anybody talk to them?"

"I was just coming to that," said Dynan. "But you must not stand waiting in the door as if you were not welcome here. Sit down! Please! Make yourselves comfortable."

"No, thanks just the same. We didn't mean to stay. We won't take up much more of your time, sir. Who talked to the man with the fancy clothes?"

"Several of the local Mexicans, I believe. But only one of them could be located afterwards to answer the sheriff's questions. And he is a worthless ne'er-do-well named, ah . . . Dolly? What is the actual name of our local tippler? The one everybody refers to as 'Port Wine'? Oh! Núñez. Emilio Núñez. That's it, isn't it? I am surprised I remember. Anyway, the man was relatively sober, for once. Let me see, it's the end of the week. And Núñez usually depletes his supply of port wine by Friday afternoon, and he does not become desperate enough to work his claim again until Monday. But on Tuesday, he generally has the gold dust to buy spirits enough to carry him over until the following Friday, and so on and on.

"At any rate, he was fairly coherent. But I fear the man's mind must be permanently muddled. He was loud in his praise of Ruiz and denied several times that the "Patrón" could have abducted the Simpson female. But he was just as definite about the direction taken by the Spaniard's party, as I indicated."

"Did the sheriff seem to think it was Ruiz he was after?"

"You need not even ask me, William. What Sheriff Phoenix thinks is seldom divulged until he has positive proof either for or against. But the mere fact that he has taken up the trail to the Lazy Q speaks plainly enough for his thoughts, I should say."

"The Simpsons went with him, did they?"

"Oh, to be sure! The girl's uncle, in particular, was ardently in favor of immediate pursuit."

"That's understandable, I guess. Thanks, Mr. Dynan. We'll ride over that way ourselves and see if Phoenix made it as far as the Q. Goodbye, Mrs. Dynan. Baldy? Sherry?"

Both the cowboys bowed again to the lady who smiled at them cheerfully. She even went so far as to put down her needlework in order to wave a winsome farewell. Baldy Hinkson shivered in the warm night air as he and Sherill strode back down the steps of the hotel with Sutherland. "Brrr!" he said. "I don't think much of that outfit. Them two give me the chilblains."

"At least the pump don't take much priming," said Sherill.

"Boss, you ain't been exactly overflowin' with facts, yourself," Baldy complained to Sutherland. "Are we lookin' for outlaws from Brazil or wife-snatchers from Mexico?"

Young Sutherland stopped on the bottom step and looked up and down the busy street. Light flowed out from nearly every door. Shouts and laughter and a thin tinkle of piano music were occasionally audible above the continuous shuffle of booted feet on the boardwalks, the constant flow of men's voices, and the thudding of horses' hoofbeats, the jangle and squeak of harness, the rattle of carts and buggies. Without answering Hinkson, Sutherland moved on to untie the reins of his horse from the hitching rack and slide between the close standing animals to climb back into his saddle.

"Sherry," Hinkson said aside, "how's this whole dog-gone goose chase strike you?"

"Baldy," replied Sherill, "I'm reservin' my judgementals."

"You ever knowed our Will to be so tongue-tied?"

"Nope. But I ain't ever knowed him to push another man for his reasons, either. Come on. You and me got a date with the Lazy Q."

Once they were well out of town, Will Sutherland turned off the road and led his companions at a steady pace across the open, rolling country. The moonlight was hard and bright around them; no rider could have escaped their sight without resorting to the brush-choked draws or willow-grown creek bottoms. And these, they carefully skirted. Will wished to find the sheriff, not the outlaws. They rode in silence, Will slightly ahead, Hinkson and Sherill at his flanks.

They were within two miles of the Lazy Q headquarters when they saw the yellow spark of a campfire winking among the trunks of a stand of live oak near the top of the next rise. Will turned his horse quickly aside, motioning the others to follow suit. They continued on around the crown of the hill, keeping its crest between them and the light until it appeared again, much closer and brighter than before.

Will slipped out of his saddle and was immediately joined by Hinkson and Sherill.

"Reckon it's them?" whispered Baldy.

"Well, it's somebody or other," replied Will. "But we'll have to get closer than this to find out who."

"They'll sure see us coming," warned Sherry.

"We could circle around and come up on the far side of that knoll," said Baldy.

"Yes. I think we'll try it," agreed Will.

"Won't they have posted a watch on the top?" wondered Sherill.

"Maybe. But if they offer to chase us, we can run for the home ranch. And they'd be less likely to follow in that case. Let's go."

The three men led their horses for a short way to be sure that when they remounted, they would not be visible to anyone by the campfire. It took half an hour's careful reconnoitering to gain the far side of the knoll without betraying themselves to view. They found the slope there much longer and steeper. There was no cover except an occasional outcropping of stone, starkly black and white in the moonlight.

Will drew rein. "Baldy, you stay here and keep us covered," he said to Hinkson. "Sherry and I will try to ride up as far as that second big bunch of rocks. Then, I'll go on alone on foot. If they're keeping a lookout, the chances are good we'll all have to dodge some lead. But if not, I'll crawl right on over the top and count noses."

Hinkson pulled his rifle from his saddle scabbard. "And if it turns out to be the sheriff and the Simpsons?" he asked.

"Then, I'll yodel for you. Sherry?"

It was not the sheriff. And those around the campfire felt secure enough in their numbers and with the steep bulk of the hill between them and the Lazy Q headquarters that they had posted no watch. There were fully a dozen. Will counted twice to make sure. Then he returned to where Sherry waited, holding their horses below the jutting rocks.

"Well?" the cowboy greeted him softly.

Will nodded. "Now, we ride for the Q!"

* * *

Phoenix and the Simpsons had retired for the remainder of the night when the three riders from the Dry Creek Spread dismounted at the corrals outside. Old Tom Quincy, the owner of the Lazy Q, opened the door of his log cabin in his suspenders, not bothering to put on a shirt. "Who is it this time, hey?" he demanded, offering his visitors the muzzle of a sixgun.

"Evening to you, Tom," said Will.

"Evening? More like morning by now! What the hell do you want? Oh. It's Sutherland's stripling. Ain't it?"

"Yes, it is. Sorry to rouse you, Tom. I'm looking for Sheriff Phoenix. Is he here?"

"Reckon he is."

"Well, I need to talk to him."

"Can't you fellers do business by daylight? Why do you all have to sneak around in the dark like a goddam bunch of lost haints? Well, come on in, then! What are you standing there for? How many with you?"

"Sherry, Baldy . . . you boys know Old Tom, don't you?"

"By reputy-tation!" said Hinkson, pulling at his hatbrim and grinning at the rancher's sour look. "Howdy, Mr. Quincy."

"Go to hell," said Tom. "Sheriff? These boys are your look out. I'm going back to bed."

"Will!" said Phoenix, coming quickly across the raw boards. He coughed drily.

"Sorry to get you up, Sheriff. But I didn't think it ought to wait till morning."

"Come in and sit down."

"No. I'd like your ear in private, first. Boys, you'll have to forgive me. I don't know how much of what I've got to say ought to be made wider known. I'll let the sheriff decide that afterwards. You'll excuse us?"

"It's your business, Boss. You want us to unsaddle? Or might we be headin' back for the knoll again tonight?"

"Just loosen the cinches and slip the bridles. If we do stay on here, I'll finish bedding the horses down myself. Sheriff . . .?"

CHAPTER THIRTY-FIVE:

A CONSOLIDATION OF FORCES

Phoenix followed Will to the far side of a tall pine that Tom Quincy had spared to stand sentinel beside his cabin. "Baldy and Sherry and I have sighted the outlaws," said Will as he halted with the sheriff inside the straight, black shadow of the tree. "Did you locate them yourself before you came on to the Q?"

"No," replied Phoenix. "There wasn't a sign of them. Where did you run across them?"

"On a hillside three or four knolls over. I counted twelve men. If you want to try to surprise them, we'll sure help you. But before you decide one way or the other, I think you'd better know that the Simpson girl and Simón Ruiz are guests at my folks' ranch on Dry Creek, tonight."

"Hm!" grunted Phoenix. He rubbed the back of his neck. "The girl's all right, is she?"

"Seems like it. Ruiz has married her."

Phoenix let out a sharp breath of surprise that brought on a whole series of coughs. He jerked a handkerchief from his back pocket and clamped it to his mouth. Even when he took it away, he drew two or three more broken breaths before he could speak. "Damn," he said quietly.

"You all right, sir?"

"Oh, it's this same raw throat and tight chest I've had for a couple of weeks. Nevermind. I guess I'll survive. You're sure about the marriage?"

"Yes, sir. And also, Judge Curtis is staying over at my parents' invitation . . ."

"Hm!" grunted Phoenix again. "I imagine the judge will take care of all that end of the business, then."

"Yes, sir. I think he will."

"I wonder how much Ruiz confessed to him about the bandits?"

"He told all of us everything he said he knew. And he offered to talk to you, besides."

Phoenix looked up at the stars among the branches overhead. "Everything he knew . . ." he mused. "Too bad you couldn't bring him with you. But that would have left the girl, I suppose?"

"Well, he said he would come, anyway. But the judge talked him out of it for the sake of the bride."

"The judge talked him out of it for the sake of the

bride!" echoed Phoenix. And then, he began to chuckle. The chuckle turned back into a cough. Resorting to his handker-chief once more, the sheriff leaned against the pine and waited for his amusement to wane enough for him to be able to draw a free breath.

"You sure you're all right?" asked Will again in some concern.

This renewed the officer's amusement. But he mastered it. "Let's get back to the outlaws," he suggested. "There were twelve of them, you said?"

"Yes, sir."

"How far from here?"

"About two miles. Toward Drytown. They were just climbing into their bedrolls. I saw the black man clearly. And the one with the fancy clothes. He's a Brazilian, according to Ruiz."

"Is that a fact? What's his name?"

"Paulo Gonzalves."

"Mm! Yes. A Brazilian, is he? And did Ruiz mention a Manuel Escobar?"

"Yes, he did, sir."

"Good. Could you tell if **he** was with this bunch you saw?"

"I think not. I saw no one answering to the description Ruiz gave us. But don Simón did say he didn't expect Esco-bar to be with them."

"No. Likely not. We'll have to catch him with a different rope. It's a damned shame there aren't more men on hand to help out tonight," Phoenix added. "I'm afraid the odds are pretty much against us."

"Aren't any of Old Tom's men here?"

"Only one. A German immigrant named Eichelberger. I doubt he's ever held a gun. And I can't even be sure Old Quincy would agree to go with us. Though I've heard he's a crack shot."

"What about these Simpsons?"

"Well, now, I'll tell you . . ." Phoenix trailed off. Then,

"The boy seems reliable," he said. "But I don't know, Will. There's only you and your cowboys and this younger Simpson and me . . . and maybe Tom. That's still two against one in the bandits' favor. And all our horses are tired. I don't like it."

"But we'd have the advantage of surprise, Sheriff! I was able to walk within a pebble's toss of their campfire. They're not keeping any kind of watch."

"All right, we'll try out the idea on the others and see what they say. But I'll tell you this. I won't lead fewer than five men. And I want no pressure put on anybody. These outlaws are more than just thieves, remember, Will. They're killers. They won't only try to scatter and hide from us. We can expect a fierce defense."

"Will you tell the Simpsons about their girl, first?"

Phoenix nodded. "And thanks for your persistence, Will. It's not every man would have trailed me this far. And you've run some risk, besides. I may just reward you with worse. If you want to stay with this thing, I'll deputize you."

"That would suit me right to the ground," said Will.

They found the Simpsons up. They were sitting around a rough-hewn table with Hinkson and Sherill and the German Eichelberger and Old Tom Quincy. The owner of the Lazy Q had abandoned his third attempt to get some sleep that night and had relit the fire to heat a flame-blackened coffee pot. "If you can't lick 'em, join 'em," he'd muttered.

"Mr. Simpson . . . Cecil . . ." said Phoenix as he came through the cabin door, "this is Will Sutherland, the son of the district's first rancher. Both Will and Jack are well known for their upright dealings and their solid worth. If either one of them was to tell me it had snowed on the flats in the middle of August, I would know that it had. No, it's all right, Will. I say it because the news you've brought us is liable to be questioned. And I want to assure these gentlemen beforehand that your word on a thing is as much proof of it as I need."

"You've found Sydney!" guessed Cecil, starting from his

chair.

"Yes," said Will. "And she's fine. She's at my dad's ranch."

Cecil traded a quick look with Uncle Peter. "Where's that?"

"Little more than half a day's ride from here. On the creek below Drytown."

"How did she get there?"

Will glanced at the sheriff. Phoenix nodded. "Her husband brought her," said Sutherland.

"Husband! Then, it **was** Perrin!" exclaimed Uncle Peter, greatly relieved. "By heaven, Ma's hunch wasn't far wrong! And Dan'l told us he was going to Drytown! He must have seen the outlaws when they passed through with Sydney. And rescued her! How did he manage it?"

But Cecil was watching Will's face. "No, Uncle Peter," he said, putting out a hand to silence him. "It wasn't Dan'l. Was it?" he asked Sutherland.

Will shook his head.

"Was it Simón Ruiz?"

"Yes. It was."

"**He's** her husband? He's her **husband**? He **married** her?

"Yes, he did."

Cecil sank bank onto his bench. "Oh, my sweet Lord!" he breathed.

But now, Uncle Peter jumped up. "My niece has married a Greaser?" he demanded fiercely. "And nobody stopped her?"

Will's face reddened. "Mr. Simpson," he said, "it wasn't our place she ran off from."

"Gentlemen," interposed Phoenix, "arguing won't change the facts. Mr. Simpson, it seems to me you ought to be glad the girl's safe."

"Safe!" cried Uncle Peter. "If this almighty son of a first rancher had told me she was dead, I might have more to be glad about!"

"Uncle Peter!" said Cecil.

"The hunt's over," went on Simpson, ignoring his nephew. "I don't want to find her, now. Cecil and I will go back to Jackson in the morning. And if she ever asks you about us, Mr. Sutherland, you just tell her that as far as we're concerned, she's dead. As dead as her daddy that'll be turning in his fresh grave on the mountain!"

"Uncle Peter!" shouted Cecil, leaping back to his feet. He stared at his father's brother in great dislike. "Sydney may be dead to you, but she's not dead to me!" He whirled on Will. "I want to see her! If you're going back, I'll go with you. Will she still be at your place tomorrow, do you think?"

"She's likely to be there quite a while. Don Simón has asked my folks if he can leave her with them while he helps catch the bandits that everybody still wants caught. He would have come with me tonight, except your sister threatened to come with him."

Cecil sighed. "That sounds like her," he admitted. "But then, it **was** Ruiz she left with from Jackson? The outlaws never got hold of her at all?"

"The outlaws are after don Simón," answered Will. "But he lost them near Drytown. He was afraid they might be able to follow him to my dad's place. But they didn't. Because Baldy and Sherry and I have just seen them not two miles from this cabin. And I'm not going home myself until they're caught. I've offered my help to the sheriff. And if you'll join us . . ."

"No, Will," Phoenix reminded him. "Cecil wants to see his sister to be certain she's all right . . ."

"I ain't never heard the like of this!" Old Tom Quincy put in suddenly. He swung his right leg off the bench and stamped his foot on the floor as he rose. "You mean we been sittin' round here jawin' about some dizzy female that's gone off and got hitched while them damn bandits are makin' theirselves to home on my property? Ike, go help these men saddle some fresh horses. And one for me and one for yourself. Move, you German jackass! Simpson, you and your nephew can argue over the girl later. Right now, you're goin' after bandits with us."

"Hold on, Tom," said Phoenix, "these men will make up their own minds."

"Will they! Then, they'd better make 'em up quick! They're on my land. And they'll either help me chase them bandits off it or get off it theirselves! And that goes for any long-winded lawmen as would rather talk than shoot."

"Quincy, you'll keep a hold on your temper, or you'll be in some trouble yourself," said Phoenix. "When I go after a dozen well-armed men that are known murderers, I don't want any hotheads with me. So if you want to be a part of the posse, you'll remember that I'm in charge of it. We want to **catch** these bandits, not just herd them like stray cattle off the range of the Lazy Q! Will has offered in good faith to go with me and try to surprise them. He knows where they are and can lead us there. Who else wants to be a part of this expedition?"

"Count me and Sherry in," said Baldy.

"No. Every man offers himself."

"I'm with you," said Sherill.

"I'll go!" said Cecil.

"What about your sister?"

"This man's said she's all right. She is, isn't she?" he insisted, turning again to Will Sutherland.

"As far as I know. She ate quite a lot for supper. She told us that you were probably out looking for her and she thought you probably told Phoenix she had run off. She didn't seem sorry at all."

"The little bitch!" muttered Uncle Peter.

Without warning, Cecil sprang at him. But Will and Phoenix both jumped to interfere. "Easy, son!" said the sheriff.

"It's my sister he's calling that!"

"Are we goin' after bandits, or ain't we?" demanded Quincy.

"I am!" said Cecil, allowing himself to be backed a step away from his uncle. "And afterwards, I'll go home with Will Sutherland, if he doesn't object to my company. Simón Ruiz offered me a job once, herding cattle for him. I mean to take him up on it!"

Uncle Peter pointed a finger at his nephew. "You leave without my say-so, and you'll never be welcome back," he warned.

"Too bad!" said Cecil. "I guess you'll have to find your own nuggets from now on!"

Uncle Peter's face flamed red. "Now, you just listen to me! I've held my tongue about this till now! But it's your sister that I blame for our cabin's burning down! If she had been paying attention to her duties the way any other girl would have, she'd have been sure the fire she meant to boil water on was out before we went to town that day. I've not said a word about it," he added as his nephew's face went white, "but if it hadn't been for Sydney's carelessness, that eighty-five dollar lump you found might have done the whole family some good. As it was, I had to spend it all for lumber and nails. And if it weren't for the generosity of the folks around Jackson, I'd still be owing for that. But the cabin itself is not the worst of it! Ma's clock . . ."

"Oh, shut up about the clock!" cried Cecil. "I'm glad the damn thing burned! It had a bong like Doomsday! It wouldn't let me sleep for more than half an hour at a stretch! I was ready to jam up its works! But I'll replace it for Aunt Aggie. I'll save up every penny of all the wages I earn until I can buy her another one. Don't worry! I won't bring it to her in person! I'll send it. And if you don't like it, you can throw it in the creek!"

Uncle Peter's face closed. Its color drained away until it was as white as Cecil's. He said nothing more but picked up his rifle and went to the door, retrieving his hat from a peg beside it.

"Wait a minute, Simpson," said Phoenix.

Uncle Peter turned.

"There's a dozen outlaws within two miles of this place. I don't think you ought to go back to town alone."

"I will do what I please," said Uncle Peter.

"Your mule is pretty tired. Why don't you stay here until morning? You can lock yourself in the cabin. I think Tom will let you use it for one night."

"Don't burn it down is all," growled Quincy.

Uncle Peter made no answer. He opened the door and went out.

"Keep to the roads!" Phoenix called after him.

CHAPTER THIRTY-SIX:

THE ADVENTURES OF GEORGE DURHAM

Monday, August sixth, long had dawned as fair as the day before it when George Durham, the county's Foreign Tax Collector, set out on his rounds through the China Camps between Jackson and Drytown. He had not had a restful Sunday. In fact, he'd had no rest at all since he had returned to the parsonage with his father-in-law on the afternoon of the fourth.

First, he was obliged to attend the house-warming of a new member of the Presbyterian congregation whose family had become virtually the sole topic of conversation at the Thomson's. Durham's wife, Susan, and her sister, Amy, and her mother, Ida, could not talk about these people fast enough. But George was able to glean several pertinent facts from the multitude provided him:

The head of the new family was a man named Peter Simpson. He had found a large nugget. Then, his cabin had burned down. The community had helped him construct a new one. Daniel Perrin, a young man with whom Durham was already somewhat acquainted, had helped in particular. This, because he, Daniel, wanted to marry Peter Simpson's niece. And in the meantime, Amy had enjoyed the company of Peter Simpson's nephew, variously known as See Saw and Cecil, and Peter Simpson's apprentice, named Paul McCormick.

Both of these young men were attractive and manly. Paul was favored because of the color of his eyes. See Saw because of the quaintness of his smile. Peter Simpon's wife, a robust woman of great spirit and courage but rather too talkative and opinionated to be considered really amiable company, was also occasionally referred to in conjunction with a lost clock.

Thus informed, George drove with his wife's family to the Simpson Claim, only to find there was to be no housewarming after all. For a new calamity had occurred. Peter Simpson's niece had been abducted by Mexican outlaws. The girl's brother and uncle had engaged the county sheriff to help them search for her. The matter seemed to be vaguely related to the recent disappearance of the Simpson's neighbor, Ben Rooster, who may or may not have run off to avoid paying his taxes, knowing that Durham was due back in town.

Enlarging on this idea, Mrs. Simpson waxed vehement on the unpredictability of all foreigners and asked Durham more than once how he could possibly deal with them on a daily basis. George replied that duty was duty, and he hoped he would always be prepared to perform his own.

Paul McCormick concurred that this was the attitude which all men of good character must espouse. Then, he said that he felt he was fulfilling **his** obligation by staying at the Claim to guard and protect Mrs. Simpson and her boys in the absence of Mr. Simpson and his nephew. This duty might not be so glamorous as chasing outlaws, he said, but it was fully as needful. Amy declared it was not only needful but noble.

Most of this conversation had taken place around the site of the razed cabin while the various members of the company poked at the ashes and re-envisioned the roaring flames which had demolished it. Then, Amy noticed a little path leading into the willows. With an exclamation of delight, she had proposed to explore the first two or three of its twists and turnings, and to this end, she ran gaily off.

Expressing his concern for her safety, for daylight was soon to fade with the setting sun, Paul McCormick volunteered to go after her and bring her back. When he did not immediately return, Susan suggested to George that he had better go see what was keeping them.

Durham complied but took his time. The respite it afforded him from clattering tongues was conducive to loitering among the softly lighted timber. And when he actually came upon Amy and McCormick standing together at the fifth bend in the trail, he discreetly retraced his steps a short distance before alerting them to his approach. For he had seen one of McCormick's hands massaging the girl's waist, and the other one crushing a cluster of golden curls behind her tilted head. And by the time George had extracted the wooing pair from the woods, the Reverend Thomson felt it was time to return to the parsonage for the night.

Not to sleep, however. The entire episode of Sydney Simpson's disappearance must be discussed and speculated upon until all hours, first among the family at large, and then between sister and sister, and mother and daughter, and father and son-in-law, and finally, husband and wife.

The Reverend Thomson became so inspired by the topic, he decided to write it into his sermon for the following morning. And though he had already gone to bed, he got up again in order to work on it. The resulting oration was spiritually invigorating. It evoked Divine protection for all who strayed beyond the reach of their friends and families and praised the courage of those who sought to return the wayward to the safety of the fold. At the same time, they were exhorted to shun the ungodly and distrust the papists and turn away those whom the devil had plainly marked as his own. Durham was moved by it. But he found it somewhat less uplifting when he heard it for the second time the next day in church. Susan must nudge him occasionally to keep him from nodding off.

After the service, when all the congregation had departed, (with the exception of Mrs. Simpson and her sons and Paul McCormick, who had been generously invited to stay for dinner) Durham had looked forward to a good meal and an afternoon nap.

Instead, Mr. Peter Simpson had arrived at the parsonage on a weary mule. And what he had to say about the wayward and the papists bordered on the ungodly. He even referred to the county sheriff as a meddling moron and vowed that the bandits would die at their ease of old age before Phoenix ever blundered upon them.

As for his nephew, Simpson indicated that the boy was an ingrate as undeserving as his sister who had not been satisfied with burning down the family's cabin but now must disgrace them by eloping with a Mexican and causing her brother to quarrel with his only remaining relative. And while Peter Simpson had never been one to speak ill of the dead, he hinted that had his departed brother taken the good advice of his relatives, he would either have remarried or sent the unruly girl to live with her aunt at an early age, and then this ultimate tragedy might have been averted.

It was well into the afternoon before the Simpsons returned to Jackson Creek. And it was midnight before the Thomsons had fully exhausted the subject and themselves and had once more retired to their various rooms to await the morning.

And so it was that George Durham set out for the China Camps to the north of Jackson rather later on Monday than usual. But his troubles were far from over. He was to discover that the Celestials had no money with which to pay their taxes, and through no fault of their own. They had all been robbed. Everywhere he went, he met with a similar story. The thing was uncanny.

Over and over, he was told that a band of Mexican
outlaws, led by a tall man wearing a fancy jacket, had attacked the day before and had taken all the gold. These tireless thieves had supposedly made their way from camp to
camp, looting, pillaging and terrorizing the Orientals, tying
them hand and foot and threatening to kill them if they did
not give up every sack of dust and every coin they owned.

By the third time he had heard this tale, however,
George was beginning to wonder whether the robbery had
actually taken place more than once, whether the other
camps had only learned of it and seized on the excuse. In any
case, he had grown heartily weary of the whole affair long
before he reached the town of Rancheria.

"George!" Albert France greeted him when Durham
pushed into the General Store late that afternoon. "Is it the
second week of the month again already?"

"Hello, Albert. Do you know if Constable Cross is in
town this afternoon?"

"He's gone on over to Drytown, I think. Why? What's
the trouble?"

"Not much, really. Or so I suspect. But I've had a few
reports of bandits through the China Camps today, and I
wondered what Cross might know about it."

"No more than the rest of us, or I'd be much surprised,"
replied the shopkeeper. "Are you just come in from the
camps?"

"Yes. I suppose you've heard the latest news concerning
these infernal outlaws and their escapades?"

"I know they rode right through Rancheria late Saturday afternoon," said France.

"In broad daylight?"

"It seems too cheeky, doesn't it? But you can't beat these
bandits for brass. And it wasn't known for certain who they
were until the sheriff showed up several hours later. You see,
Phoenix had a man named Simpson with him. And he . . ."

"Yes, I know," said Durham.

"Oh. You've heard that story already, have you?"

"I have. Where's Phoenix, now?"

"Why, still on the heels of the outlaws, as far as anyone knows."

"But Simpson is back in Jackson," George confided. "Does anyone know that?"

"No! Did he find his girl?"

"I wasn't too clear on that part of it," Durham admitted. "But I know he's dropped out of the chase. Only his nephew is still with the sheriff."

"Well, now that's an odd thing! Isn't it?"

"Albert," said Durham, "you know I've never been one to repeat idle talk."

"I know it, George. And I've always admired you for it. There's nothing more vicious than gossip. And why folks will go on about a thing they know nothing of themselves is more than I can say. Take John Dynan. And it's not that I would ever speak a word against him. John's a good man. But I'm stating no more than the facts when I say he's too fond of peddling his neighbor's business. Just the other day, he asked me point blank if I'd topped my profits from last year, yet! Well, all I told him was that I didn't expect to die a pauper."

"You'd have done better to complain of the year's being a poor one," said Durham, "what with these Mexican thieves growing bolder by the day. You're in a pretty vulnerable position, here."

"Oh, I really don't think I'm in much danger."

"That's what Tuttle thought. You've heard what happened to his store in Tuolumne County?"

"Well, but Tuttle doesn't cater to the Mexicans as I do. Many of my best customers are Mexican! These outlaws wouldn't rob me. They've no grievance against me as they had against Tuttle."

"I wouldn't be too sure, Albert. I'd take precautions."

"Oh, I do. I do! I lock the place up tight every evening. And Sam Wilson serves me as a night watchman. I'm not to be caught unawares. I'm safer than you, anyway, George.

There you are, roaming around the countryside with your pockets full of gold . . ."

Durham frowned. "It is county gold," he reminded the shopkeeper. "And I must do my duty."

"But that duty is an affront to the Mexicans," France reminded him pleasantly. "And you could be easily overpowered by so many armed men."

"I assure you the thought has never even occurred to me."

"You are a brave man, George. I would not have so much nerve, myself."

"Well!" said Durham. "I only stopped in to ask you about Constable Cross. I must get on. Good afternoon, Albert."

"Stop by again on your way back to Jackson!" France called after him. "By that time, the new shipment of linens ought to be in. I remember you said your wife wanted several items!"

"Yes. Yes, I'll be sure to do that, Albert. Goodbye." And cocking the set of his bowler hat, George Durham returned to the road which was to lead him not only over the hill to Drytown but right into the laps of the outlaws.

CHAPTER THIRTY-SEVEN:

PRECISELY TWO O'CLOCK

The woody draw halfway between Rancheria and Dry-town had been given the unpleasant name of Murderer's Gulch in reference to the various acts of crime and violence which had taken place there over several seasons. And although George Durham had never encountered in it anything more alarming than the raucous jeering of a pair of acorn woodpeckers, today he approached the broad strip of brush and timber with his mouth dry and his palms wet.

Ordinarily, he would have been grateful for the deep shade of the gulch. The afternoon sun was fierce. But Durham found no relief there, this time. And he moved his horse along at a quick clip.

At the center of the gulch, the trail dipped across a dry wash, rough with loose stones and forest trash. From there, it rose to a wide bend, then on to the edge of the belt of woodland and into the sunlight of the open road once more. Durham was just beginning to relax and to congratulate himself on his usual good fortune and on his own, unswerving, high courage, when he caught sight of a cluster of horsemen at the far end of the draw's shady passage. George pulled his mount to a walk. Then a halt. He sat in his saddle in the middle of the roadway, listening intently for the sound of their voices in the hope that he might be able to tell from this distance whether the riders before him were friend or foe.

"¡Que vaya al diablo!" he heard one of them say.

"Dirígeme tú, que bien conoces el camino al infierno," came the retort.

"¡Cállense, amigos!" interposed a third voice, thick with an accent less familiar to the tax collector's ears. "Por ahí se acerca algún cristão."

George saw the horsemen shift position to peer down the trail at him. "¡Cristiano!" some one of them echoed. "Será el diablo mismo. ¡Pío pío! Reza un Padre Nuestro. ¿No tienes mucho miedo?"

Amid a chorus of rough laughter, one of the riders reined his horse sharply into that of the last speaker. The other retaliated, and the two men locked arms, wrestling each other from horseback.

It was during this moment of the bandits' distraction that George Durham ought to have made his escape. For that these were the very Mexican outlaws of which he had repeatedly been warned now seemed certain. Yet George was not a man to be easily diverted from the path of his duty. And he as little liked the thought of returning to Rancheria with nothing more to report than a sighting of what might have been bandits in Murderer's Gulch. Besides, he carried no money. He had no valuables more than his horse and his pocket watch. And the laughter of the outlaws goaded him. He knew it would increase were he to turn tail and gallop off. Drawing a breath and setting his jaw, George Durham rode forward.

At his approach, the two wrestlers broke apart, and the others drew into a tighter knot, completely blocking the road. There were eight of them. The apparent leader of the group, a tall man with a fancy jacket, pushed his horse into the center of the trail.

Durham's horse slowed of its own accord, so that George must prod the animal with his heels to try to pass the outlaw chief. "Boas tardes, Senhor," said the brigand, riding into his way to stop him. "Que faz por aquí?" His voice bore a hint of the nasal, and his words were slushy.

"I don't speak Spanish," said George. ("Either," he refrained from adding.)

"Não?" The tall man looked to his followers in mock surprise. "Não fala espanhol!" he exclaimed.

"He will speak chino," declared the man they had called Pío.

"Sim? Why is that?"

"He is exactor."

"Não diz! O Colector? What you collect today?" the chief demanded of Durham.

"Nothing," said George. ("Thanks to you," he did not say.)

"No-shing! The Chineesh, they don't pay you?"

"No, they didn't," said George.

"You ash them? Politely?"

"I asked them," said George.

"¡Qué cochinos! ¡Ingratos! ¡Presumidos de chinos! No luck wish them, eh?"

"None at all."

"I tell you, Senhor, nesh time, you take **me** along. I show you way to collect. Eh? Eh? Where you go, now?"

"I'm going to Drytown."

"Dry town. Why you go there? For the chinos who live there? Or for the chilenos, like my friend, Pío? Or perhaps mexicanos, like my friend, Juan?" He introduced those he referred to with eloquent motions of his hand.

Durham looked from one face to the next and wished he had turned back, after all. But he sat up straight in his saddle. "I am not going to Drytown to collect from the denizens of Chile Flat," he professed. "I am going in search of Constable Cross. I was told I might find him there. Have you seen him today, yourselves?"

The Brazilian showed insolent surprise. "You ash **us** for news of him, Colector?"

"Yes. Why not? You seem to have been watching the road. And Constable Cross must have come this way . . .?"

Gonzalves shook his head slowly from side to side, grinning at George. Like a full-bellied tiger which may condescend to play with its prey, the outlaw humored the Tax Collector only for his own amusement. "No one, he has come from Ranchería since we have stop in this place to rest," he said. "But we are not here so long, yet. Que horas são?" he added, gesturing at the watch chain spanning the front of Durham's waistcoat. "What time you have, Senhor?"

George felt for his watch with some reluctance. The other outlaws had gradually encircled them as they spoke, cutting off all possible escape. But Durham did not look around. To what purpose? Slowly, he produced the watch and opened its gold case. The snowy face of the little clock shone up at him, its delicate black hands and elegant numbers suddenly dearer and more beautiful than he had ever seen them. "It is two o'clock," said George. "Precisely." He snapped the gold lid shut.

"Tão tarde!" exclaimed Gonzalves. "You are certain? Let me see." He held out a hand for the timepiece.

With a disinclination which further slowed his deliberate movements, Durham unhooked the watch chain from his buttonhole and put his little treasure into the outlaw's open hand.

Gonzalves carried the piece close to his chest and examined its gold case with evident admiration, then felt around its edge for the spring release. Juan Torres, the man nearest him, reined closer to see better. Together they looked down at the pristine face of the pocket watch. "Está bello," said Torres.

"Sim!" the Brazilian agreed. He glanced up at Durham. "He always keep good time?"

The Tax Collector nodded.

"Two oh cloak," said Juan, still looking at the watch face. "¿Ves? Ahí dice. Las dos en punto."

"Colector," the Brazilian said to George, all comedy disappearing from his countenance. "Two oh cloak for you is to be a time you can always remember. Is to be the time you say your thanks to God each day. For is the time I let you go. And so you don't forget, I stop this hour for you." And with a deadly grace, the Brazilian drew one of the pistols from his waist. Balancing the watch a moment in his hand, he tossed it high into the air. Quicker than thought, Torres also drew his gun. And Pío Pinto, half a heartbeat after him. Three shots broke the stillness in Murderer's Gulch. The gold pocket watch exploded. Its several pieces hit the road among the horses' restless feet.

"¡Aléjense!" commanded the Brazilian, waving the other outlaws away from the Tax Collector. "Dismount, Senhor," he told Durham. "Pick up the relógio. You take it with you. Then I am sure you don't forget."

George obeyed him as calmly as he could. But his hands shook so that he could scarcely gather up the pieces.

"You ash us news of the constadable," said the Brazilian, watching him flounder in the dust. "Now, I ash news of you. Where is the Sheriff Finish?"

George stood up, holding the remains of his watch. A thin ribbon of sweat glistened from his temple to his chin. But he answered quietly. "If I knew the location of the sheriff, I would not be looking for the constable. But I had presumed that Phoenix was chasing a group of outlaws known to frequent these roads. Because at last report, at least, he was."

"You tell the constabable when you find him, Colector, that if the sheriff want the outlaws to leave in peace the roads near Ranchería, all he have to do is let us have the man his name is Simón Ruiz. Compreende-me?"

"Ruiz?" repeated Durham. "But he . . . Isn't he . . .?" (George kept himself from saying, "one of you?")

"You know where he is, Senhor?"

"No! I mean, first, I heard that he had gone back to the Valley. And then, there was some rumor about his return. But I truly did not pay it much attention."

"Now, you pay attention, Colector."

"Now, yes. I pay attention."

"¡Móntese, pues! Get on your horsh. Tell your Constabable, your Sheriff Finish, everyone you meet, the bandidos look for Simón Ruiz. We find him, we leave here. If not, we look for him. We ash for him. And we do not ash politely. Go. Go! Before I change my mind and kill you!"

George scrambled back into his saddle. And when the outlaws parted before him to let him pass, he was not too proud to whip his horse to a run.

CHAPTER THIRTY-EIGHT:

BACK AT THE RANCH

The morning that dawns on Happiness is a rare rising. And for Sydney, that first of all happy mornings that were to dawn for the rest of her life was Saturday, August fourth.

Waking itself was delicious. For she slipped from a pleasant dream involving the sunlit fields near the Old Indiana Homestead into a even more pleasant reality. She found that she lay inside the protective embrace of the man she loved the best in the world. And this was a luxury she had not enjoyed since the age of six when her father had weaned her from his bed.

For a little while, Sydney pretended she was back there again, that the arms about her were Eli Simpson's, and that all the warm strength lying dormant against her was his. "Another bright, blessed day has caught up to us, Sydnipper," he would say in a moment. "Pile out and take hold of it."

And then, before her half conscious mind could turn toward sorrow, before she could do more than vaguely envision the cold, smothering weight of the grave high up on the mountain where Eli forever lay still, the man whose arms actually held her awoke. And his method of rallying her from slumber put all thought of her father aside.

Nor was it until she was thoroughly convinced that the word "cuddly" had been invented specifically to describe Sydney Simpson de Ruiz Silvestre would her bridegroom even consider getting up. Breakfast was, apparently, the last thing on his mind. Though it was not the least of her own thoughts.

When finally they did come to the kitchen table, it was halfway to noon. And the steak and eggs and thick slabs of gold-crusted bread which Ellen Sutherland served them twice over tasted like food for the gods.

Sydney was rather shy of her hostess that morning. The strange and frightening thing that Simón had done to her the night before was not something she thought Mrs. Sutherland ought to know about, even though the gentle light in Ellen's grey eyes clearly said that she already did.

The conversation, what little there was, was carried on entirely by Ellen and Simón. Asking after Jack and the judge, Ruiz learned that Curtis had returned to Drytown in anticipation of his duties on Monday and that Sutherland had ridden with him. Knowing the magistrate was one of Simón's intended confidants, the outlaws might well be on the lookout for him, and Jack had not thought it wise for Curtis to travel unaccompanied. Besides, Will's continuing absence might be accounted for in town. While in all probability, the rancher's son was only gone in search of Sheriff Phoenix,

Jack preferred to learn that nothing more alarming was keeping Will from coming home with the news he had been sent to bring.

"Is I who should look for him," said Simón, his brow furrowing with concern.

"No," said Ellen quietly. "Jack asked for you to wait until he comes back before you decide what to do next. He promised he wouldn't let himself get tied up in whatever's going on but would come straight back and tell us. I'm sure he won't be much longer."

Ruiz sighed. And as a means of distracting himself, he reached for a well worn newspaper which lay on the end of the table: the Jackson Sentinel.

"Do you read English?" Ellen asked in surprise and admiration.

"Oh, well . . . a little, Señora. Enough to make sense of him if I study a while. See, here it say something about fire near Yackson. Saidnay! Is about your Tío Pito."

Sydney scrambled from her chair to look. Simón moved over in his own seat to accommodate her beside him, encircling her with one arm and sharing with her a hold on the half folded newspaper.

" 'Due to the combined and immediate efforts of the citizens of Jackson,' " she read, " 'the town's annihilation by fire has once again been averted. For the unfortunate individual whose residence was devoured by hungry flames, there remains, however, only the consolation of his neighbors' good will. Reconstruction is to commence immediately. It will be funded in part by a lucky find which took place minutes prior to the fire's breaking out.' "

Sydney paused. "They get all tangled up in their words, don't they?" she observed. "It would be easier if they just said it. 'A gold nugget, weighing nearly ninety dollars . . .' (Eighty-five dollars and forty-two cents," Sydney amended,) " 'was extracted from the claim of Mr. Peter Simpson and was taken by him and his entire family to the Wells Fargo Office for appraisal and conversion to a more convenient currency. No one was by, therefore, to check the spreading of a cooking fire which was inadvertently left burning.' " Sydney looked up at Simón. "Gonzalves probably threw a couple of those sticks through the window," she said. "Do you think he would have burned the cabin down if he hadn't found the fire still going?"

"It does not matter, amorcito. What matter is, you are not there when he comes. Is for that I thank God."

"Why? What would he have done if I'd been there?"

"No, Saidnay. I do not even say so."

"Would he have carried me off, like he told Miz Ben Rooster?"

"Seguro."

"And then, would you have come looking for me?"

"Sí, muñeca. Por su puesto."

Picturing the rescue, Sydney smiled. But Simón frowned, and seeing him, she sobered instantly. "Would he have killed See Saw?" she asked.

Ruiz was saved from having to agree with this unpleasant speculation by the sound of approaching hoofbeats announcing the return of Jack Sutherland.

The rancher greeted his wife and his guests with mixed news. "Will and the cowboys went looking for Phoenix, all right," he said, mostly to Ruiz who came out onto the porch to watch him ride up and dismount. Sydney came, too. Ellen stopped behind them in the doorway.

"The bandits rode straight through Rancheria and Drytown and then off in the direction of the Lazy Q. That was yesterday afternoon. The sheriff and the Simpsons were hard after them. So, Will and Sherry and Baldy rode on in hopes of finding Phoenix at the Q. But whether or not they found him, and whether or not Phoenix found the outlaws, there's been no word, as yet.

"The judge sends his regards and his regrets," Jack added to both Simón and Sydney. "I guess his desk is piled pretty high with papers he thinks he has to work on before Monday. Or maybe he wants to get the bow out of his legs

before he swaggers into court. Curtis doesn't ride any distance anymore with quite the ease he used to. The pair of
you've had breakfast, have you?"

"A really good one," answered Sydney, attracting more
of the rancher's attention than he had given her, yet. His blue
eyes twinkled at her.

"Well, that's fine," he said. "Ellie?" he called to his wife.
"Is there any coffee left in the pot?"

"I'll warm it up," she answered.

"I'll put my horse in the stable, then." But as he turned
to leave the porch, Sutherland glanced meaningly at Simón.

Ruiz lay a light embrace around Sydney's shoulders.
"Con tu permiso, amor," he said. Releasing her, he went
down the steps. Nor did he look back. Sydney stood where
she was, watching him catch up to Sutherland and walk on
toward the stable with him. The rancher's horse followed
them, dragging its reins.

"Sydney . . .?" said Ellen from the doorway.

Sydney did not answer. She put out a hand to the nearest porch post. Ellen waited a moment longer; then she went
back to the kitchen.

"There is something else you wish to tell me, Señor?"
Simón inquired of his host when he and Sutherland had
gained the corrals without Jack's having spoken again.

Sutherland nodded. "It's not too pretty. But you're
probably already braced for it: Your bride's family think that
you've abducted her . . . and with the worst intentions."

"Yes, I have fear that they might," agreed Simón.

"Besides that, there's a lot of talk about how you
refused to betray the outlaws to Phoenix in France's Store in
Rancheria. And how you didn't pay right off for that pair of
pistols you bought. And folks have invented some ugly reasons for it all. I guess you didn't tell anyone but Curtis you'd
been robbed. So, now they're saying maybe you attacked
somebody and were bested. That idea seems to have been
started by a man named Williston. Boston, they call him,
mostly. He's got some sort of axe to grind, I reckon?"

"Bastón! He is not still in jail?"

"No. Was he in jail?"

"Cheriff Finits put him in for how he attack the wagon of Saidnay and her brother."

"Hm! No. That part of the story seems to have got left out. But it'll all be put to rights eventually. That I can promise you. Judge Curtis will be able to turn it all around just by saying what he knows about you. That certificate of marriage he wrote up and we all signed will make some difference, too.

"But the judge won't gainsay the gossip yet because he thinks it's best for you to go on lying low. The sheriff has his hands full enough without worrying that his star witness might be lying dead somewhere. I'm sorry, Don Simón. But it appears that circumstances have made you a kind of prisoner, here. Of course, there's nothing to keep you from taking your wife and your horse and riding away if you choose to. But I'm asking you now for your word that you won't."

They had stopped at the stable door. Sutherland's horse went on inside by itself to glean wisps of hay that had been dropped between the stalls. Buenrostro's red colt neighed a greeting.

"Señor Sutterlan," said Ruiz, "I have choose to trust you. I come here and you take me in. You show me and my novia great kindness. I believe you are sincere. When a man has ask for help, he is too ungrateful if he does not take the help is given him. I will stay here. But only until I can be of more service to you in another place. My life, Señor, does not mean so much to me that to protect it I will sacrifice both honor and service. For then, it would be worthless. You understand me?"

"I do. And here's my hand on it. And I want you to know, Don Simón, that when this business of the outlaws is over, you and your little Sydney are to come back to visit us whenever the notion takes you. You'll always be welcome here. And I mean that. You won't forget I said so, will you?"

"I remember, Yak Sutterlan. Y se lo agradezco."

CHAPTER THIRTY-NINE:

THE STORM BREAKS

Sunday passed. Monday dawned and dawdled on. For Simón, who had but little practiced the exacting art of patience, these two days sounded fully all the depths of his endurance. And in his effort to sustain a calm, unruffled surface, he retreated farther and farther into courteous reserve.

Sydney spent her second and her third nights of new happiness in uninterrupted slumber. Simón spent them awake, watching the moonlight's stealthy creeping after shadows on the wall while he tried on several sizes of regret and should-have-done's.

He thoroughly examined the entire subject of Amanda. He met Manuel in a variety of ways. Some of these confrontations ended in the death of Escobar, some in his own, and one of them in neither. None pleased him.

Yet less and less he liked the thought of Manuel's death at the hands of the Americans. The son of Escobar dangling by a rope from Jackson's Hanging Tree was an image to appall. That Manuel deserved to die was not the question. But the indignity of such an execution would be far worse than death itself. And for all his guilt, his insolence, his villainy, his cowardice, Manuel was gente de razón. He still was don Fernando's son, the brother of Amanda, and the neighbor of Silvestre. That he be hanged just as irreverently as any nameless dog was barbarous. And hang he would if Phoenix caught him. Of that there was no doubt. The task of Simón Ruiz, therefore, was still unchanged. Only the reason for it altered. Now, it was to save Manuel from the ignominy of the hangman's noose. And Amanda from the pain of that disgrace. And don Diego, and himself. And every proud and landed family of California under seige. And in the silent depths of night, Ruiz renewed his vow to visit swift, appropriate death on Manuel Escobar.

Tuesday's sunrise caught Simón in restless sleep. Exhausted by his wrestling with angels, he had at last allowed unconsciousness to take him. He was reawakened by a light touch on his chest. He started, opened his eyes, and threw a hand up to defend himself, only to see Sydney drawing back from him, her hand also lifted.

Reminded poignantly of the first time he had seen her, when he had wakened on the road from Rancheria, Simón relaxed and smiled. "¡Ladroncita!" he accused her. "Sí, que sí lo eres. Me has robado todo, todo. Futuro, pasado, y corazón." He reached up to take her hand and draw it down again. "I am sorry, Pecosita. I was dreaming with the cholos. Have I frighten you?"

She shook her head.

He lay looking up at her, watching her thoughts in her eyes, amused to know they would surprise him, were she to put them into words. But she said nothing, and his attention wandered from her quiet face with its mass of merry freckles to her near shoulder, whose thin, fine skin was also spattered liberally. The loose neck of her chemise had fallen down the arm she propped herself upon. Simón traced its column and the contours of the breast that nudged it softly beneath the loose cloth. He would have caught away that cloth to afford himself full sight of what it veiled, but she flinched at his gesture, and he lay back. "Tell me, niña," he prompted her, "what you think so hard about. Why you look at me as if you never see Simón Ruiz before. You are sorry, now, to be my wife?"

"Nope."

"Nope-y. Yupp-y," he mimicked her. "My pecosita has not say more than these two words since I have make her mine. But I know there are more thoughts than that inside this head you have. Say what it is you think so much."

"Different things," Sydney said reluctantly.

"Tell me one of those things," he insisted.

"I think . . . I didn't know anything before at all."

"About what, Payasa?"

"I . . . just wanted to be with you, before. I didn't exactly want to be your wife."

He did not respond to this.

"I didn't want to marry anybody," she explained. "I didn't think I'd like it much. I'm still not sure. But there's a difference, now."

"What is the difference, amor mío?"

"It's scary," she confided. "Simón, I . . ."

"What is the matter, Saidnay?"

"I'm with you almost all the time. But I'm not with you enough! Of course, I know you're worried about the outlaws. But it's not because of that. And it's not because you don't talk to me. Because you do. And I never knew I could feel so good as I feel when I'm close to you. But . . . something's wrong. There's something that's not like it was. And I want it back."

He watched her, uncomprehending.

"Simón, do you remember how it felt when we were riding in the freight wagon? Do you remember how you explained things and gave me your gun to shoot at the rock and how I saw your horse under the tree, and you told Manuel I was your friend?"

"Of course I do, Saidnay."

"It's different, now, isn't it?"

"You are my wife," he suggested.

"That doesn't matter. It's not what I mean. Or anyway, I don't think it is. It's that I'm not your friend anymore! Am I?" she said, more certain, now, that she had found the key to her puzzle. "Before, we were two people. You were a person, and I was a person, and we talked about things. But now, you're not anybody. And I'm not anybody. And there's nothing to say! But if I don't see you and I don't hear you and I'm not close to you, I get scared!"

Ruiz sat up slowly, not to startle her, and leaned to gently taste her lips, to test their appetite, to enjoy their accommodation. But he found in them a hunger whose depth he had not touched before. Heat swept him. He seized her in both arms and bore her over backwards under him.

But she struggled with him, trying to deny him even while she asked for him. And the moment he left her mouth, she gasped out, "Don't! It's not fair!"

"Ah! What is not fair?" he demanded, rising with an effort far enough above his own passion to be able to respond to her verbally.

"Simón, I want that other thing! The thing you stopped giving me when you married me in Jackson."

"But what that other thing is?" he wondered, baffled and growing angry in his inability to understand his bride's simplicity.

"I don't know!" she retorted, meeting his anger as instantly as she had met both his tenderness and his desire. "I don't know any word for it. Maybe it doesn't have a name. But if it were bread, you'd be giving me cake."

"No, I don't understand you, mujer!"

"And if it were cake, you'd be giving me frosting!"

"What is frossie?"

"And I love cake, and I love frosting, but I can't live on them!" she finished desperately.

Simón buried his face in her bare shoulder and felt it melt into a still more enticing softness as he kissed it. "Saidnay . . . Saidnay! What I should do with you?" he mused.

"Where I should put this payasita so she stay contenta for a while?" He lifted back to look at her.

"What's pie-yuh-see-saw mean?" she demanded, frowning up into his eyes.

"I don't know the word in English," he evaded. "Change your face at me, amor. This wrinkly in your fronthead gives me pain." He smoothed his fingertips across the pucker in her brow, but it did not relax.

"Simón . . .?"

"Ask me, muñeca."

"Do you wish I'd stayed with Uncle Peter and Aunt Agnes?"

"Saidnay . . ."

"You do, don't you?"

"No, I don't wish it. You are not happy with them. I want that you are happy. I wish there are no bandidos to get in the way while I make you to be happy."

"But it's not the bandidos that are in the way!"

"Niña, I . . ." He stopped. And froze. And then he threw aside the sheet and whirled out of bed, caught up his drawers and stepped into them hurriedly. Still tying their drawstring at his waist, he went around to the window and threw back the shutter. Daylight blinked bright in the room.

Sydney caught the sound of galloping hooves. She dropped lightly to the floor and ran to join Simón at the window. But he put her away from it and closed the shutter, brushed by her to return to the bedside and finish dressing. Sydney stared after him for a moment before she swung the shutter wide and looked out for herself.

She saw a horseman riding toward the ranch house at a run, dusting his mount's neck and rump with his hat to urge it on. But there was no one chasing him. When she was sure it was an American cowboy and not a Mexican bandit, she closed the shutter and turned around.

Simón had his shirt on and was buttoning his pantalón over his hip. His garments were clean. Syndey had washed them the day before. Ellen had offered to help, but Sydney jealously refused to let her touch them, even though it meant giving up an hour's precious time with Simón. She was glad he was putting them on again, now. He didn't look right in Will's things.

Ruiz ducked a quick glance into the mirror above the bureau and ran both hands through his hair. It fell into place like a crow's wing closing. Catching up the three pistols that lay on the dresser top in front of him, he thrust them into his sash, one after the other. Then, he strode to the door, jerked it open, and went out.

Sydney now flew into action. Ellen had loaned her a dress of bright green gingham and a snowy apron with ruffled shoulders. She put them on with such haste her fingers fumbled and slowed her down. The apron's sash she tied in back with an impatient half bow. Nor did she consult the mirror before she left the room.

On the wide porch, Ruiz and Jack Sutherland together awaited the rider. It was Baldy Hinkson.

The cowboy leaped from his saddle as his steaming horse slid to a halt. "Boss!" he cried, centering on Sutherland. But an instant later, he had recognized Simón, and he stopped to reconsider and catch his breath. Deciding it made no difference, he rushed on. "Boss, there's a hell of a thing! In Rancheria!"

"Come on inside, Baldy," Sutherland said evenly.

But Hinkson shook his head. "No time! You got to come! I've rode like hell to get here soon's I could just so's you'd come in time. You've got to saddle up right now and head back with me! I'll tell you why on the way." He looked uneasily at Simón. "Howdy Solano," he said and brushed his fingers past his dusty hatbrim.

But then, Sydney came out onto the porch. And in the time it took him to look from her to Ruiz and back again, Baldy put the truth together. "Ma'am . . ." he said to Sydney. "Miz Sutherland," he added as Ellen joined them. "I'm sorry, but there ain't no time for more than 'howdy', now. Boss," he urged Jack again, "you got to come!"

"Where's Will?" asked Sutherland, not moving.

"Gone with the sheriff off towards Injun Diggin's. I'd have gone with him, but he asked me to fetch you to Rancheria."

"Is it the bandits, Baldy?"

"Yes, sir. Damn right it's the bandits. 'Scuse me, Ma'am . . . Miz Sutherland. Boss, will you please come?"

"You'll tell me why, first," said Jack. "Come up on the porch."

"No, sir. No. There ain't no time for talkin'. There's some folks have been murdered . . . butchered! God, it's awful! And half the county's already come to town. The other half will be there soon enough. And it looks like they're fixin' to hang every Mexican in Rancheria. Boss, you got to come!"

"I'll get my hat," said Sutherland, and he turned back toward the house. He was confronted squarely by Ruiz.

"¡Señor!" said Simón.

Jack locked eyes with him. Then he nodded. "Come with us," he said. He would have entered the house, but Ellen had already gone after his hat and his rifle. She met him with them in the doorway.

"Be careful, Jack," was all she said.

Sutherland looked at her while he put on his hat and took his gun from her hand. Ruiz and Baldy waited for him at the bottom of the steps.

Sydney had witnessed everything in anxious suspense. But as the three men started for the stable together, she ran after Ruiz, her uneven apron strings fluttering behind her. "Simón!"

He stopped and turned. In her haste to check him, Sydney ran right into him. She caught herself against him, seized his arms. Jack and Baldy looked back, halted.

Sutherland waved the cowboy on toward the stable. "We'll saddle a horse for you, Don Simón," he said and followed Hinkson.

"Saidnay," said Ruiz, "I am sorry. I must go. I know you are safe here."

"But I'm going with you!" she informed him, holding on.

"No, niña. No."

"I won't stay here without you!"

"Yes, you stay here, Saidnay."

"No, I won't! I won't!"

"You do. You will!" He broke her grip with a quick motion but only to pick her up off her feet and carry her bodily back to the porch.

Sydney squirmed and kicked. "I won't!" she declared. "The judge said we wouldn't be divided! No storm would make us not be parallel! You promised him you'd cherish me! You can't cherish me if you're in Rancheria and I'm here!"

Simón bore her up the steps. He set her down at their top and took her by the shoulders. "Saidnay!" he said, burrowing the full force of his gaze into her rebellious eyes. "You will do what I tell you. I am your husband. You will obey me. That is what **you** have promise the magistrado."

But when he released her, she threw both arms around him and pressed her cheek tight to his chest. "I won't let you go," she said. "You promised to cherish me. I bet you don't even know what it means!"

"You don't know what he means to obey!" countered Ruiz. He reached back to take her wrists and unwrap her embrace by main strength. He held her out away from him. "But this time, Saidnay, you obey! And you promise to stay here. Tell me, 'Simón, I stay here.' "

"No! Simón, I won't stay here!"

He stared at her in frustration, then caught her against him again, sought her mouth with his, kissed her hard and roughly, overrode her attempts to retaliate until she suddenly stopped fighting and pushed herself into him, gathered his kiss into hers, and buried herself in his arms.

For a timeless moment, the bandits evaporated. Manuel Escobar ceased to exist even without the help of a rope or a knife. The ranch house porch disappeared from around them, over them, under them. Then, Ruiz tore his mouth from hers. "You stay!" he exclaimed. He took her hands from his sides and applied them to the porch post. Pressing her wrists as if to tie her with the invisible cords of his will, he left her there, strode down the steps and on toward the stable.

Sydney stood gripping the post with both hands, watching him go.

CHAPTER FORTY:

BLOODY MURDER

"Go ahead, Baldy," urged Sutherland. "There's nothing you can say to me that you can't say to don Simón."

The three men were riding abreast across the rolling rangeland, the rancher between Ruiz and Hinkson. After the first fast mile and a half, Sutherland had slowed the pace in order to save the horses and to be able to listen to what the cowboy had to say.

But Hinkson was leary of talking openly before Ruiz. And his former excitement had cooled in consequence. "Me and Sherry and Will found Sheriff Phoenix at the Lazy Q," he began. "That was late Saturday night. But before that, we run across the outlaws camped out a couple of miles from the Q's headquarters. So, Will told the sheriff about them. And about how the Simpson girl . . . Miz Reese, I mean, was all right. And married. And so on." He looked at Simón and away again.

"The lady's brother took it pretty well," Baldy told the horizon. "But her uncle wasn't too happy about it. Anyhow, he called off the search and went home."

318

"He went home!" repeated Sutherland.

"Yes, sir. He saddled his mule and rode off. The younger feller, Cecil, was for comin' to see his sister, but we needed him to help us try to surprise the outlaws. So, he joined the posse, instead."

"Did the family send Mrs. Ruiz any message?"

Baldy glanced across the neck of Sutherland's horse again before he answered. "Nope. But things was kind of too riled up for such as that. Her brother did say you'd offered him a job once, Señor," he added to Ruiz. "And he said he might take you up on it, yet."

Simón gestured acknowledgment. "When he wish," he agreed.

Baldy wiped his dusty face on his dusty sleeve. "I don't reckon you'll be lookin' for work around here too soon yourself, in that case, will you?"

Simón returned his glance with the suggestion of a smile. "These things, they are hard to know," he said. "Someday, perhaps, I do."

"Well, anyway, your . . . uh, brother-in-law went with us that night to try to catch the bandits. And it's damn bad luck we didn't, because then, this god-awful massacre at Rancheria would never have happened." Baldy unhooked a canteen from his saddlehorn and drank from it.

"How many are dead?" asked Sutherland when the cowboy had recorked his water boot.

"Boss, I don't really know. But Miz Dynan for one. And John Dynan's wounded."

"The bandidos kill the señora de Dino!" exclaimed Ruiz. "¡La mataron! ¿La mataron?"

"Yep. And Dynan may lose his mind over it. He was ravin' so loud, you could hear him outside above the noise in the street. He'd been shot hisself, and they're goin' to have a hard time keepin' him quiet enough so's he'll recover. But I reckon he will. He took a ball in the belly, I heard, but they say it went right on through without hittin' much else. And that's a whole lot better than can be said for the shopkeeper.

Albert France was hurt powerful bad. They're goin' to try to save him, too. But it don't look so hopeful. Maybe if Doc Shields gets to him in time, he'll make it. I don't know. If he would have just laid low, the bandits might not have bothered with him. But they blew open his safe to rob him, and like a fool, he ran out to try to stop them. I guess he grabbed up an axe. But they took it away from him. And used it on him. He was conscious when I saw him, but I reckon he'd rather he weren't."

"Good God!" muttered Sutherland. "Who else that we know, Baldy?"

"Sam Wilson, France's night watchman. And Old Dan Hutchinson, France's clerk. There was some others, but I didn't recognize the names. Reynolds Somebody. Or Somebody Reynolds. And a Jesse Hindshaw. He's maybe related to the freight clerk in Drytown. You know him?"

"No. Anybody else?"

"Well, there was an Injun found dead in France's Store. I don't know which side he was fightin' on. Likely he didn't, either. But he died for it. Oh, and Buckshot Hayes. You remember Buckshot, don't you? He worked at the Lazy Q last year. Anyway, he was with Sam Wilson, lyin' dead across the top of him behind the counter in France's place."

"Hayes . . . yes."

"He's the only one not apt to be much missed by anybody," suggested Baldy. " 'Cept maybe Boston Williston. I guess he had some use for Hayes. Anyway, Boston's set on makin' a bad situation worse. He's advocatin' a mass hangin' of all the Mexicans in town and an open war on the rest in the state. If it weren't for men like Judge Curtis and Mr. Clark, and a few others, I wouldn't even have bothered to fetch you. The mood is mighty ugly. I ain't even sure it's the best idea for Señor Ruiz to be comin' with us."

Jack looked at Simón. Ruiz returned that look with fire in his eyes. The wind ruffled the black hair that lay aslant his brow. He had left the ranch without his hat. Sutherland felt suddenly older as he looked at him.

"No," Jack told Hinkson. "We're apt to need an interpreter with a steady nerve and a level head. And I don't know any man who answers that description better than don Simón. Let's move along a little faster, again. I'd like to think there'll be somebody left to interpret for by the time we get there." He lifted his reins and nudged his horse.

In the kitchen of the ranch house on Dry Creek, Ellen Sutherland had finished washing the breakfast dishes. Drying her hands on the dish towel, she made her fourth trip to one of the windows that opened on the front porch.

She saw that Sydney had at last let go of the post. She was sitting on the top step, instead, tracing with one finger the star design of white shells on the toe of her moccasin. But as Ellen was about to move away, Sydney abruptly sat up straight. Then, she stood up. Raising her arms, she plunged both her hands through her tousled hair before she turned around and came to the door.

Ellen was hastily wiping the clean tabletop with the soiled towel when Sydney entered the house. The rancher's wife looked up, a gentle word ready. But Sydney did not even glance at her. She walked across to the door of the guest room and went in, closing it firmly behind her.

Ellen sighed and dropped the towel across a chair back. She stood looking at the closed door, debating. Shaking her head, she sat down at the table and studied the backs of her hands while she listened for noises from the guest room. There were none. Eventually, she got up and returned to the kitchen. This was the morning she had been saving to make butter. There was no good reason not to use it as planned.

In the guest room, however, Sydney was not lying face down on the bed nor staring out the window with her chin in her hands. She was changing clothes. Will's shortened trousers were still too long in the legs for her. But she let them drag to half hide her mocasins. The belt was not quite long enough to go around twice. She tied it in a knot through the buckle to hold it.

From the skirt of the drab brown dress which Ellen had washed, prepratory to cutting the ugly garment into dusters,

Sydney tore a long, wide strip. She was afraid Mrs. Sutherland might hear the cloth ripping and come to investigate. But Ellen had gone after the bucket of milk hanging in the well, so she was none the wiser.

Sydney discovered she was more reluctant to bind herself than before. But she did it thoroughly. Next, she put on the blue checked shirt and tied up its sleeves with the leather arm bands. The cloth fell back down over them clear to her elbows.

Her disguise complete, Sydney stepped in front of the mirror. Satisfied with her image in front, she turned sideways, then completely around and peered back over her shoulder at the glass. With relief she saw that Will Sutherland's pants hung shapelessly from her waist.

But the look of her own face caught her attention, and she went to peer in closely at the familiar reflection. There was definitely something different about it. It was prettier. She tried scowling. Even this did not wholly erase the new charm of it. And when she let her face relax, it settled into a softer expression than she had ever met in a mirror. The very freckles over-populating the available space on her cheeks and brow and nose and chin were no longer repulsive. They had become "bits of sweetness." This memory embarrassed her, and her glance fell from the glass to the dark hat lying on top of the bureau.

She had not thought about the hat before, though she had known it was there. If Simón had asked her where it was, she could have told him exactly. Now, she picked it up and put it to her cheek.

Another thought occurring to her, she flipped it upside down and ran her finger inside its inner band. It was with some satisfaction that she encountered a row of coins. She took one out to look at its burnished gleam. Carefully, she replaced it. And then she put the hat on her head and looked in the mirror, again.

The dark crown settled loosely around her ears, and the soft brim drooped low over her face. It was a perfect mask: the only thing her new disguise had lacked. How to keep it from flying off in the wind was the only problem. She must fashion some kind of tie-down for it. Well, there would be plenty of leather strings in the stable . . . She went to the bedroom window and turned back the shutter.

In the kitchen, Ellen heard the hoofbeats. She straightened in surprise, let go of the churn staff and ran to the kitchen door. In the first moment of her astonishment, she did not recognize the rider who lay low along the neck of Buenrostro's red colt. Then, she recognized the shirt. "Oh, my stars! Sydney!" she cried, running down the back steps. "No, Sydney! Wait! Stop! Sydney! Come back!"

But the red colt, fresher from its day of rest than either Jack Sutherland or Simón Ruiz had expected, raced on, as eager to return to its home by Jackson Creek as its rider was to get to Rancheria.

CHAPTER FORTY-ONE:

THE BLACK OAK AT RANCHERIA

"Didn't you hear what he said?" Boston Williston jutted his jaw at Judge Curtis. "Jimmy swears he saw this stinkin' Greaser in the street last night, runnin' around with the rest of them!"

An urgent, growing crowd pressed a tightening ring around the tree at the corner of Dynan's Hotel. Over its lowest heavy limb had been thrown a rope whose hungry noose dangled among the heads of the protagonists debating in the tree's thin shade. On the ground between the judge and Williston knelt Emilio Núñez, the town's unhappy tippler. He was not tied. His hands were bound together only in desperate supplication. "Oh, no, su merced!" he cried. "Is not true! Port Wine, he is home! Home in his bed! You ask his woman. ¡Que Dios me mate si les miento! Oh, if you hang him, Señores! Oh, Señores! You hang a man innocent. Oh, not to hang me! I will reform! Never, I drink another small drop, long while I live! What else I have done that you hang me, caballeros?"

"Mr. Johnson," said Curtis, turning to the man standing beside Williston. "What precisely did you see Emilio doing?"

"No, he does not see me at all!" insisted Port Wine. "I am not there! I am in bed with my woman! You ask her. Not to . . ."

"Shut up, you crawlin' dog!" Boston told the abject Mexican, aiming a kick at him. "Everybody knows you talked to them murderers when they rode through here two days ago. And Jimmy seen you leadin' them along the street last night toward this hotel. Didn't you, Jim?"

Johnson nodded. "That's right. Damn right I did. I looked outside and I seen him with them. And he was shoutin', 'Viva México'. I heard him."

"Hang him!" prompted one of the crowd. "What are we waitin' for?" A gutteral chorus seconded the motion.

"Not so hasty, gentlemen," said Curtis, warding Boston back as Williston reached for the noose. "Mr. Johnson, you claim you saw the bandits on their way to the hotel? Were they mounted or on foot?"

"Huh? Why, they was sneakin' along from house to house."

"But did you not attempt to raise an alarm?"

" 'Course he didn't!" Boston answered. "If Jimmy had put more than his nose out, the outlaws would have killed him."

"Does your house have a rear exit?" inquired the judge, looking only at Johnson.

But before Jimmy could respond to this implication, there stepped from the front door of the hotel a tall, imposing man whose red-blond hair and beard burned bright as autumn. The crowd was as close on the porch as anywhere, but way was immediately made for him. And the noise fell into silence as he looked about with a commanding eye.

"Friends!" he called in the far-reaching tones of a practiced orator. "I regret to inform you! Our good neighbor, Albert France, has died of his wounds!"

There was a short silence. And then a roar of rage arose from the tight-packed crowd. In the middle of the street, a group of some thirty Mexican men had been imprisoned inside a rope corral. Now, they were brought forward, rope and all, by the jostling mob of Americans that converged upon them. They were halted and held before the black oak tree.

Seizing the brief lull which followed this delivery to the gallows, the red-haired orator on the porch again called out to the assemblage: "Friends! In the name of those who have died at the hands of unreasoning hatred, let us temper our anger with justice! Let us not crown atrocity with inequity! Let us not stoop to the despicable tactics of these inhuman brigands against whom every righteous soul must experience the most violent outrage!"

"Clark, we're tired of speeches!" Williston shouted as the orator directed a penetrating gaze around at his restless audience. "What we want is action! We ain't goin' to take these here dispittle atroci-trees sittin' down. We aim to hang the guilty. And we ain't waitin' for you nor anybody else to give us the go ahead!"

"Mr. Williston!" replied the orator, motioning imperiously for silence. "If it can be ascertained that all those you intend to hang are indeed guilty, I will myself haul on the avenging rope. But you are denying these prisoners the right of fair trial. Mexicans they may be. Yet as you are an American, you must hold sacred the American tradition of legal law and order! Justice, Mr. Williston, knows no bias. Her eyes wear the blindfold of impartiality. What evidence have you against these men? And of what do you accuse them? They are not outlaws. They are well known citizens of this town.

"Suppose you were to find yourself to be just such a citizen in some foreign land," the orator went on. "And suppose that a small group of your countrymen had committed some horrendous crime. Should you be held responsible for that crime yourself, merely because you share a common nationality with the criminals? What man," he called, sweeping an eloquent hand at those before him and around him, "what man among you can produce any telling evidence against these captives?"

"I can!" cried a dark-bearded miner, forcing passage for himself among the multitude.

"Indeed, sir! And who are you?"

"Isaac Roberts! And I'm an eyewitness to what happened last night."

"So, you were abroad then, Mr. Roberts?"

"Abroad! Hell, no. I was right here in town. And that's more than you can say yourself, Bill Clark!"

"What exactly did you witness, sir?"

"I seen this Greaser here!" Roberts turned to the rope enclosure and seized a man by the shirt. "Him and another . . ." Roberts' eye darted from face to face among the prisoners. "There! That one, there! He come out of his house and set a lighted lantern in the street as a signal to the bandits. And this other one was with them when they passed the light. I saw him plain as day."

"Where were you, Mr. Roberts?"

"I was where I could see what was goin' on."

"But what was your actual location?"

"What's that got to do with it?"

"Answer the question, sir, or we may suspect you of duplicity."

"Suspect me!" cried Roberts, his face heating. "I ain't done nothin' you wouldn't have done in my place! All right! So, I hid under the boardwalk! And if you had looked behind you and seen half a dozen outlaws comin' up the street and another couple of three comin' from the other way, I bet you'd have looked for a handy hole to crawl into, too, and thanked God if you'd found one!"

"Cowardice, Mr. Roberts," said Clark, "is not a criminal offense. You are acquitted. Did you see any others of your Spanish neighbors while you were peeping from your hideaway?"

"Don't you laugh at me!" Roberts shouted, pointing his

finger at Clark. "You asked for evidence. I gave it. This man here and that one there are guilty. And I say they ought to hang for it!"

But this convincing appeal was upstaged by a disturbance from the outskirts of the crowd. "It's Sutherland!" someone shouted. "He's caught another one!"

There was a rippling wave of movement in the street. Heads turned. Hatbrims tilted. At its outer edge, the assemblage split to allow three riders to approach the black oak tree. Shouts of fierce approval greeted them. Hands reached up. If Simón Ruiz had not now been riding between Jack Sutherland and Hinkson, he might have been dragged from his horse.

"Back there!" shouted the rancher, sweeping his arm to clear the way in front of them. "Baldy!" he called across to Hinkson. "Was it this bad when you left?"

"No, Boss! But like I told you, more folks was comin'!"

"I've never seen such a mob. Judge!" Jack bellowed, cupping his hands around his mouth to project his voice above the noise.

Curtis signaled with one hand in answer.

As they moved on, the crowd parted reluctantly before the three and closed in immediately behind them. But the noise diminished as they went, and when they had drawn rein beside the oak, it was quiet enough for what was said there to be heard by many.

"Judge," said Sutherland, "what little we're able to do here, we've come to try to do. Mr. Clark," he added to the speaker on the porch, "this gentleman is a personal friend of mine: don Simón Ruiz Silvestre. You'll have heard of him, I think."

"Ruiz!" exclaimed the orator in a voice the whole street heard. And a new crescendo of noise began. This time, the Mexican prisoners joined in, calling to Simón in Spanish. Emilio Núñez, who would have risen from his knees in his desperate gladness at the sight of the Patrón, groveled where Williston had forced him back down again.

Simón himself looked around at the hostile crowd and at the roped-in captives with no sign of dismay or fear. And riding forward from between Sutherland and Baldy into the small space left clear beneath the tree, he caught at the dangling hangman's noose, drew one of the knives from his belt and cut the rope in two, cast the loop at Boston's feet.

"¡Señores!" he cried, staying Williston with a gesture of his blade before turning on the crowd. "Do you kill the chickens because the hawks have raid your flock? The cattle because the wolves are gone? Your friends because your enemies have dare to walk among them? Save your rope for Paulo Gonzalves! For Mariano García! Juan Torres! Pío Pinto! **They** are your enemies! They are **my** enemies! And I have swear to bring them to you! Cheriff Finits chase them! With my help, now, he catch them! Before this magistrado, Simón Ruiz has pledge his word!" And with a flourish, he sheathed his knife.

But that the multitude did not instantly overwhelm him was due more to the supportive presence of Sutherland and Curtis than to Ruiz' eloquence.

"Señor Cortés," Simón said then, still in a voice that carried far beyond the immediate group beneath the oak, "if there are any mexicanos here who have help the bandidos, I will find out for you." And bending a stern gaze upon Núñez, he said something to him in Spanish.

Port Wine's response was so rapid and so garbled that even Simón must ask him to collect his wits and try again. Williston and Johnson exchanged looks meanwhile, and at Boston's nod, Johnson went to lower the rope and begin to tie a second noose in the free end of it. Curtis watched him, reluctant to interfere, knowing that the resulting wrangle would surely distract the attention of the assemblage from Ruiz' efforts to establish the innocence of his countrymen.

Núñez had little to report. When he had told twice everything he knew, Simón gestured him to silence and turned to the two men that Isaac Roberts had brought forward from the rope enclosure in the interim.

One of these two only shook his head. The other spoke for both. He spoke well and clearly. Ruiz heard him out, then turned again to the crowd. "¡Caballeros!" he called. "The man you think has put a signal in the road? He has hear a noise and go outside to see what make him. He catch sight of the bandidos and leave the lantern there so they don't see to follow him while he run to warn his friends. Other man come to meet him, but bandidos, they catch this one and make him walk with them so he tells no one they are there."

"Well, sure they're goin' to say that!" Williston strode forward to plant himself between Ruiz and Emilio Núñez. Port Wine's eyes rolled fearfully toward Johnson who held the new-tied noose. Boston threw back his head to look up at Simón. "They're lyin' to save their skins!" he said. "And who invited you to try to help them do it?"

"I asked him to come!" Sutherland informed the freight driver. "And I know Señor Ruiz to be a man of honor."

"You don't know nothin' of the sort!" argued Isaac Roberts, confronting the rancher as belligerently as Williston had challenged Ruiz. "The word is, this fine and honorable Greaser friend of yours is one of the outlaws hisself! He's likely tryin' to save the necks of these three 'cause they're a part of his band! He ought to hang as high as any of them!"

"You're wrong," said Jack.

"Like hell I am! It's you has had the wool pulled over your honest eyes, Jack Sutherland! I ain't sayin' nothin' else against you. The whole county knows you're white clean through. But you can be as easy hoodwinked as the next man! Maybe easier! You're too apt to believe the best report about a feller, no matter who he is . . . and overlook the worst."

"I've heard no bad reports of don Simón," answered Jack. "Except some vicious gossip that I know positively isn't true. He's no more a bandit than you are yourself."

"Señor," Ruiz said to the miner, "what proof do you like so I convince you I am not bandido? That these other men you have accuse are not bandidos?"

"Where were you last night?" asked Roberts.

"He was staying at my ranch," answered Sutherland. "At my invitation. And had been since Saturday evening."

Roberts grunted. "That don't prove he ain't mixed up with the bandits. Why didn't he answer Sheriff Phoenix that time in France's store?"

"Because, Señor, I know nothing I can tell the cheriff," Simón replied. "I do not know the bandits then."

"**Then . . .!**" Boston triumphantly repeated, putting himself back into the debate. "But you admit you know them now?"

Simón looked down at the freight driver with disdain. "I know only those I tell you and the magistrado. It take me all this time I use to find out what I know of them. But this I know I can prove true. What do you know of these men that you accuse?" Ruiz gestured at the Mexicans.

"We know what Isaac has told us!"

"Yes," said Roberts. "And I seen them with my own two eyes, conspirin' with the bandits."

"You see **one** with the bandidos," Ruiz corrected him. "And he is their prisionero. These men have swear to me they tell the truth. They say they live here two, three year. They ask if anybody know them ever to cause trouble or to ever speak unfriendly of Americans."

"How would I know? I ain't never bothered with such as them," returned Roberts sullenly. "They might have been hatchin' some sort of scheme as this for months. They could have talked about it right in front of me, and I'd never been the wiser. I can't understand a word of that lingo all you chili-eaters speak. I don't even know they've said just now what all you said they said. You could be makin' the whole thing up. All I know is what I seen with my two eyes as plain as day. And that's enough for me."

"Roberts speaks for the rest of us!" concurred Williston, appealing to the crowd. "We've put up with these damn

Greasers long enough, now, ain't we? We've caught these three red-handed. And we'll hang them. Won't we?"

"Hang them!" came the vicious chorus. "Hang them!"

The hostile uproar continued, drowning out both Clark and Curtis who would have intervened again. But with the clear consensus of the crowd behind him, Boston could be delayed no longer. He whirled around, strode to lay rough hands on Núñez.

"Put that halter on him, Jim!" he commanded. "Let's string him up."

Port Wine struggled wildly, but Boston set a knee in his back and pinned his arms behind him. Johnson had some trouble fitting the noose over the Mexican's head. The loop was too small. He must tug at its sliding shank in order to force it down over Emilio's ears.

And then, before Jimmy could do more than pull the rope snug around the prisoner's neck, Simón vaulted from his saddle and came to interfere. Forcing his way between Boston and Johnson, he seized the rope a second time. "No!" he cried. "You don't hang this man!"

"Like hell we don't!" retorted Williston. He caught Ruiz' arm by the wrist. "I've had enough of you and your high and mighty ways! Let go, or you'll be the next we hang today!"

Simón might have thrown him off, but as Boston released his prisoner's arms, Núñez grabbed Ruiz around the knees, hobbling him with a frantic grip. "¡Patrón!" he sobbed. "¡Que me van a ahorcar! ¡Sálveme! ¡Ayúdeme! ¡Socorro!"

Here, Isaac Roberts joined the struggle, seizing Ruiz from behind to pull him away while Boston stooped to loosen Port Wine's hold. Jimmy Johnson ran to take the other end of the rope. Two men from the inner edge of the crowd jumped to help him. Together, they threw their weight on the line and Núñez seemed to leap from his knees into the air. Scratching vainly at the noose around his neck, choking, twisting, lashing out with his legs, he jerked higher and higher.

Williston and Roberts and Ruiz moved back involuntarily, their eyes fastened on the spectacle, unable for a terrible moment to look away until, recovering his senses, Ruiz took advantage of the others' distraction to wrench himself loose from Roberts. Drawing his knife again, he sprang toward the three who were still hauling on the rope.

Seeing him, they let go. But one of them had already tied the line fast to the tree, and Núñez fell only half his height, to be brought up short with a final jerk that broke his neck. Ruiz reached the rope seconds too late and slashed through it with his blade. Port Wine dropped to the ground in a lifeless heap.

With a curse, Isaac Roberts charged Simón, and catching him off balance as he turned around, seized one of the matching pistols from his waist sash.

Ruiz threw himself sideways in an attempt to dodge the point-blank range of Robert's aim. The miner followed his movement unerringly, cocked the hammer and pulled the trigger. Ruiz staggered back in horror. But there was no explosion. The gun had not fired.

Puzzled, Roberts turned the pistol in his hand to look at it, pointing it at himself in his unthinking surprise. And then, the gun went off. The bullet that Simón had imagined he felt burning through him bored through Roberts instead, killing him instantly. The miner collapsed without so much as changing expression. He lay beside Núñez, staring in glassy-eyed astonishment high into the branches of the black oak tree.

CHAPTER FORTY-TWO:

SHORT RESPITE

"Misfire!" gasped Ruiz. "She misfire!" Breathless with his shock and horror and relief, he allowed Sutherland and Curtis to come to his rescue.

The judge planted himself in front of Simón, stopping Boston. For the freight driver had taken the reata from Ruiz' saddle to come after him with it. "Stand off!" commanded Curtis.

At the same time, Jack Sutherland dismounted and took Ruiz by the arm. "Don Simón!" he urged. "Get on my horse! You can't stay here!" He pulled him a few steps toward the animal. "Baldy! Go with him! Get him out of here!"

But as Simón was about to climb into the saddle, Boston whirled a loop at him over the magistrate's head. The braided line struck Ruiz' shoulder and knocked off Curtis' hat. William Clark, the red-haired orator, vaulted the porch rail to come to the aid of the defense.

Simón was only partially aware of all that went on around him. His ears roared with the hostile noise of the crowd. His eyes wandered from Sutherland to the bodies beneath the tree. He saw a woman burst from the ring of spectators, squeezing out from the line along the hotel wall, and run to throw herself hysterically on top of Núñez. A pair of ragged children that Ruiz remembered followed her uncertainly, stopping below the porch to hug each other and stare about in terror. Clark almost ran over them.

The two Mexicans that Roberts had accused were hustled forward by half a dozen Americans, and Williston turned away from Curtis to receive them, giving Ruiz a chance to mount Jack's horse.

"Boss!" shouted Baldy. "You'd better come with us! I can't keep 'em from draggin' him off the other side!"

"Go ahead, Jack," agreed Curtis. "Clark and I will hold the fort. William!" he called to the orator. "Bring that horse!" He left Sutherland to go to the aid of the Mexican children.

Automatically, Jack stooped to pick up the judge's hat. But when he straightened, Curtis was already out of reach, and Clark was approaching him, instead. "This is a sad day for us all, Mr. Sutherland," the orator observed.

"Do what you can," replied Jack. Still holding the judge's hat, he mounted Ruiz' horse. "I'll be back," he promised.

The retreat of the three riders was more easily accomplished than any of them expected. Whether it was Sutherland's determined presence or the fascination of what was going on beneath the black oak tree, there were few among the spectators who objected to their passage. Jack cleared the way before them with motions of the judge's hat. And they reached the ragged outskirts of the mob without mishap.

Baldy looked back. "My God!" he said. "They've already hung another one."

Ruiz turned in his saddle. The Mexican who had left the lantern in the road was dancing in midair on the end of Simón's leather rope. Ruiz would have reined his horse around, but Jack and Baldy stopped him. "You did what you could!" said Sutherland. "If you go back, you'll die with them to no purpose!"

As if an invisible hand had laid hold of his vitals and twisted them inside him, Ruiz was suddenly bent double across the pommel of his saddle. The world swooped out of balance. He clutched at the horse's mane to save himself from falling while he gagged and retched. He felt Jack put the judge's hat on his head in order to have a hand free to steady his shoulder. "Easy, son!" the rancher said.

"There goes the third one," reported Hinkson. "Where are they gettin' all the rope?"

"Shut up, Baldy."

"Sorry, Boss."

"Simón!" said Sutherland, his hand still firm on Ruiz' shoulder. "It's not your fault! Do you hear me?"

Painfully, a little strength flowed back into Ruiz' arms. He pushed himself upright and raised watering eyes to blink at the black oak tree. He saw the second man swinging by his neck from the hotel's porch roof. He saw the first still thrashing above the heads of his executioners.

Then Baldy Hinkson put himself in the way of Ruiz' view. The cowboy's face was as moist and colorless as bread dough. "I'm sure sorry, Juan," he said. "But it's like the boss says. It ain't none of it your fault."

"Is much of him . . . my fault!" Simón answered hoarsely. "You should have . . . leave me there!"

"Aw, no!"

"Simón!" Jack pressed Ruiz' shoulder to get his attention. "Look at me! There's still much to be done! The outlaws are still to be caught, as far as we know. And it's them that are responsible for all of this . . . Manuel Escobar! And Phoenix needs you to help corral him. He can't do everything alone. Nobody can!

"And listen," Jack went on. "This dirty business is not apt to end here at Rancheria. I'm afraid it's just well started. We saw something like it two years ago in the wake of Joaquin's death. There was an effort made then to clear all the Mexicans out of the Gold Country. And I suspect there'll be another effort, now. If you want to avoid being rounded up with the rest, or worse, you'll have to keep off the roads and out of sight. Are you hearing me? It's not just for your own sake I'm saying it. The county needs you. Whether it knows it or not.

"Now, I'm going to see if I can keep them from hanging all thirty-odd of that luckless bunch by the tree. You can go back to the ranch before you look for Escobar, if you want. Or send Baldy, if you don't think you should spare the time to go yourself. Either way, you don't need to worry about your bride. We'll take good care of her for you. We mean to stand by you. All of us."

Ruiz nodded his comprehension and his gratitude. Reaching up, he gripped Jack's arm in return. "I look for Manuel," he said. "You see the cheriff, tell him. And tell my Saidnay . . . I come back. Hasta luego, Yak."

Sutherland pressed Simón's shoulder a final time before he turned his horse back toward the crowd in the street. Ruiz kicked his mount in the opposite direction. Baldy Hinkson followed him. Neither of them noticed Buenrostro's red colt tied to a bush among the growing number of horses and mules and carts and buggies that crowded the side streets.

The two men rode in silence. For Simón, the retreat was as humiliating as it was necessary.

A mile out of town, the landscape lay wide around them in comforting quietude. The summer day had draped the Big Valley beyond the hills in a warm haze. While near at hand, the bubbling notes of a meadowlark rang as pure and sweet as if the madness of men were of no consequence.

Baldy pointed to a spinney of young live oak, Ruiz agreed with a nod, and they rode up to dismount in its shade. Both wished to rest. Neither would have admitted it. They sank gratefully onto the dry grass to pass Baldy's canteen back and forth between them and soothe their troubled hearts by absorbing the sight of the clean, uncluttered countryside.

But they did not sit long. Ruiz was acutely aware of time's swift flying and of the urgency for action. He had picked himself up to return to his horse, when he caught sight of a steadily moving black dot on the rolling swells of land before them.

Baldy saw it, also. "What the hell's that?" the cowboy wondered aloud, loosely interpreting Simón's own thought.

They watched a little longer before Ruiz recognized the growing shape, unfamiliar only because it was traveling overland. "Is a buggy," he said.

"By God, you're right! Let's go."

Squaring their hats and gathering up their reins, the two men remounted and rode to meet the vehicle. Their unspoken suspicions were soon confirmed. It was Ellen Sutherland. But the rancher's wife was alone.

"¡Señora!" cried Ruiz as they came up. He swept off the judge's hat that Jack had put on his head.

"Miz Sutherland!" exclaimed Hinkson, also doffing his dusty felt.

"Where's Jack?" was her response. "Is he all right?"

"He was when we left him," said Baldly. "I don't think he runs much risk himself, Ma'am. But Solano, here . . ."

"Where is Saidnay?" demanded Ruiz. "You have not leave her, Señora!"

"Don Simón," answered Ellen, her hands tight on the reins, her face pale with guilt, "I must tell you . . . but please, if you are angry, be angry with me, rather than Sydney. She did not disobey from willfulness, I know, but only

because she could not bear to be parted from you. And
I . . ?"

"She run away!"

"Yes, I . . ."

"She follow me here?"

"I'm sure she meant to. She put on Will's clothes, the
ones you wore, and I think she climbed out the window and
ran to the stable. But I didn't see her leaving until it was too
late to try to stop her."

"¡Ay! Dios mío, ¿qué he hecho que así me castigas?"
Simón asked the broad skies. Then, he pulled his horse violently around.

But Baldy pushed into his path. "Hold on, Juan! You're
not thinkin' of goin' back to town to look for her there?"

Ruiz' eyes blazed at the cowboy. "¡Quítese!"

"No, sir! There ain't no way I'll let you go back there.
Don't you know it's by a fly's whisker that you missed dyin'
just now? You think that locoed lynch mob would let you
pass free among 'em again? Let me go find her for you. You
stay here with Miz Sutherland."

"No," said Ellen, leaning forward on the buggy seat.
"I'm going to Rancheria myself. I will find her. It was my
fault she left the ranch. I should have spoken to her, tried to
comfort her."

Ruiz' horse, baffled by the urgent pressure of its rider's
legs, the rain of kicks from his heels while it was blocked by
Hinkson's mount, suddenly reared up. Baldy's animal turned
out of its way. Taking advantage of the moment's space,
Simón's horse charged forward. But Hinkson spurred immediately after it. The two men pelted back the way they had
come, shouting as they rode.

"No! Juan! Don Simón!"

"¡Déjeme! ¡No se meta!"

"They'll hang you, sure!"

"¡No tienen por qué!"

"Damn it, man! Listen to reason!"

Ellen's buggy jolted after them.

"You don't even know for sure she's there!" cried Baldy. "Now, hold up! You're goin' off half cocked!"

By the time they had regained the live oak grove, Simón had slowed. Yielding to the cowboy's continued appeals, he again drew rein in the shade to hear the rest of Baldy's reasoning.

"I don't know so much about women, I admit!" Hinkson said. "But I reckon once this little gal of yours has rode after you clear to Rancheria, she won't just sit there countin' Mexicans while they hang 'em from the hotel roof! Like as not, she seen you leave. And she'll be on your tail again as soon as she can worm her way back through that crowd to her horse. If you want her to find you, all you have to do is sit tight and watch out for her. She'll sure think you meant to go back to the ranch, won't she? And meanwhile, me and Miz Sutherland can search for her, besides."

"She avoid you," Simón replied coldly. "She know you prevent her to follow me."

"Well, she may avoid **you** for the same reason until you're far enough away that she thinks you won't send her back."

Simón saw the truth of this at once. Gripping his pommel, he turned his gaze from Hinkson and closed his jaw down on the rest of the angry words he had meant to say.

"It's a damned shame," Baldy offered.

"Shame, Señor! You speak to me of shame! You see me in a shame I have never feel before. ¡Ay, por Dios! Each thing I try to do him, something else go wrong."

"Well, you ain't alone in that," Baldy observed. "I've had my own spells when nothin' went right. Not long ago, I bought me a new rope 'cause I feared my old one was about to bust. But the first time I used the new one, my saddle cinch broke instead, and the steer I'd caught hauled my riggin' through a couple miles of rocks and brush. He pulled my saddle to pieces and tied himself up in the rope so bad I had to cut it to get him loose when I finally found him. But I'll tell you what: it could have been my neck as well as the cinch that broke that day. So, I ain't goin' to curse my luck too hard."

Ruiz bowed his head, hiding his face beneath his borrowed hat. "What I do now?" he wondered half aloud.

"What were you goin' to do before?"

"I find Manuel Escobar."

"Then, if I were you, I'd go ahead."

Ruiz looked up. "And my Saidnay?"

"If she was here, what would you do?"

"I send her back to Sutterlan Ranch."

"You think she'd go? Or would she run off again as soon as folks looked the other way?"

Ruiz frowned. But he could not answer this.

"Juan, I hate to say it," Baldy concluded. "But it appears to me your woman has got you right over a barrel. If I was you, I'd call her bluff. Let her follow you if she's set to! I'll trail you at a distance and see if I can catch her. It shouldn't be too hard. And then I'll take her back to Sutherlands', and they can tie her to a bedpost."

Simón's frown lowered still further.

Baldy shrugged. "It's either that or let her go along," he reasoned. "I know how it is, you see. I had a kid sister that took nigh forever to grow up to the place where she'd stop taggin' after her brothers and be willin' to help her Ma in the kitchen. She was a sly one, too. Me and Ben, we'd think we'd lost her, and there she'd turn up after it was too late to go back without us missin' out on the jaunt we'd planned. It'd make us madder'n hell, but there wasn't much we could do about it. Ma would wear out a switch a-thrashin' her. But it wasn't till . . ."

"¡Señor!" objected Ruiz.

Baldy shrugged again.

"I think," Simón said slowly, "I think I ask you follow me and look for her, just as you say. But if you find her, bring her after me. I stop first in Yackson at the house of her vecino, Buenrostro. I wait there long as I dare. You don't come, I go on through Butte City. But I don't cross the river at Big

Bar. I go west to the ford. Tomorrow, I am in Mokelumne Hill and then on to the south. For I expect I find Escobar in that direction. All along, I ask for news of him. I leave you word of me in the hotels where I can. Will you do this thing I say?"

"Here's my hand on it," the cowboy agreed. "Shall I ask for news of don Simón Ruiz? Or Juan Solano?"

"I go as Juan Solano. Hasta pronto, Baldés."

"Hasta luego!" replied Hinkson. "Vaya con Dee-os."

Baldy sat his horse a moment longer in the shade and watched Ruiz ride out to intercept Ellen Sutherland's buggy which was now nearly abreast of the live oak grove but had approached on lower, more even ground. "This here's liable to be one hell of a chase," the cowboy mused aloud. "Come on, little horse. First thing we got to do is escort the boss's lady to the hangin'."

CHAPTER FORTY-THREE:

ONE OUT OF TWO

" 'Scuse me, mister."

The man standing in the open doorway of Rancheria's livery stable looked around to see a slim boy in a dark hat and a blue-checked shirt, a pair of faded dungarees, all too big for him.

"You get lost from your folks, kid?"

"Yes, sir. I think they went home without me."

"Well, now . . .! That don't seem hardly likely."

"I can't find them. And I don't care to stay here. You got a horse you'll sell me?"

"Son, I ain't the proprietor of this livery. He's somewhere in that mass of humanity yonder by the hotel. But I don't blame you for wantin' to leave Rancheria. Where do you live?"

"Near Jackson."

"What's your folks' name?"

"Smith."

"Not Ezra and Florence!"

"Nope. John and Mabel."

"Guess I don't know them."

"You got a horse yourself you'd part with for a ten dollar gold piece?" the boy asked.

"You mean in coin?"

"Yep."

"Where'd you get it?"

"Look, mister. I'm not wanting to talk. I'm wanting to leave. Have you got a horse you'll sell me? Yes or no."

"Kid, I've got a horse I'll **lend** you if you'll promise to send it back. A friend of mine, Dan'l Perrin, lives over that way, and you could . . ."

"Forget it," said the boy. "I'll ask somebody else." He moved to go.

"Now, hold on a minute! Let me see the coin."

"Show me the horse, first."

The man met briefly a pair of wary brown eyes under the drooping brim of the dark hat. He saw a small mouth, a narrowing chin and a mass of freckles. It was not otherwise a remarkable face. But there was something in it he warmed to. "All right," he said. "Come across the street."

The animal in question proved to be a long-legged black with a white forefoot and a bald face. The boy looked at it without enthusiasm. "Is this the one?"

"Kid, there aren't many horses better than this you could buy for ten dollars."

"You'll sell him to me saddled? Just like he is?"

"You drive a hard bargain."

"Yes or no."

"Let's see that gold coin."

The boy felt in the pocket of his out-sized trousers and produced a ten dollar piece. He held it out on the palm of his hand for a moment, then put it back in his pocket.

The horse's owner untied the reins from the hitching rail. "We'll call it even," he said. "And if anybody asks who sold you the horse, you can tell them it was Rob Briggs."

The boy accepted the reins and took out the coin again, put it into Briggs' open hand.

"What's your name, kid?"

"Eli."

"Well, I'll tell it around that you've gone home, Eli. Just in case your folks are still here and lookin' for you."

"Sure," said Eli. "Go ahead." He turned to the horse, eyeing it again critically while he tied the reins in a knot. Then, throwing the lines over the animal's head and catching a handful of black mane, he vaulted lightly into the saddle, disdaining the dangling stirrups, much too long for him. The horse moved sideways, mouthing the bit. "Is there a back way to Jackson?" asked Eli.

"Up the creek and over the top." Briggs pointed.

"Thanks." Urging the black to a lope, the boy rode up the street.

Nor did he allow the horse to slow until he was nearly to the top of the first draw to the right, and the noise of the town had faded to a murmur. There, he dismounted to adjust the stirrups. It proved a difficult task. The leathers were not buckled but laced with rawhide, and the boy's fingers were trembling, now. Before he was finished, he had to lean against the horse while he saw again the scene beneath the black oak tree: the three Mexicans that hung lifeless, and the tossed rope that had so narrowly missed lassoing Simón Ruiz.

But at last, he had the straps shortened and secured. And this time, when he mounted, he used both the stirrup and the saddlehorn to help himself up. Even so, his left knee cramped as he got on. Eli looped the reins across the pommel and let the black horse climb the rest of the way out of the canyon at its own pace.

But by the time he reached the hilltop and the rolling sweep of country met his eyes, the boy's breath came more normally, and his involuntary shuddering had ceased.

Noon passed before Eli gained the last low ridge above Jackson. He was tired and thirsty. The sun burned down on his dark hat and weighted his shoulders with heat. But it was not to rest that he finally dismounted again in a shady sink just below the hill's crest. Tying his horse, he continued on foot, for he wished to spy on the road from Jackson Gate without being noticed from below.

There was little traffic. Most of the people who would go to Rancheria in response to the shocking reports of what the bandits had done there had already gone. And most of those would not return home until evening.

From the top of the hill, the view of the Chapel of San Gabriel was entirely unobstructed. Eli saw that a horse stood in front of the little adobe building. Whether or not that horse's rider was gente de razón there was no way to be sure until he came out. But the boy had scarcely settled down to wait in the lee of a broken boulder when Juan Solano himself came out of the chapel below.

He paused on the step, replacing his borrowed hat and glancing about him. With deliberate casualness, he went to his borrowed horse, swung into the saddle and turned toward town. But he did not go on the road. Dropping down into the creek, he continued along its edge, splashing through its shallows. Although the footing there was heavy, Solano's passing was not visible from the street. Only from the top of the hill was his progress marked: Every step of his horse, every turn of his head, the set of his shoulders, the line of his leg, the flutter of his waist sash . . . Nothing missed the avid eyes watching him from the lee of the boulder.

Eventually, however, he passed behind the buildings of the town, reappearing only briefly between them at the gaps of the side streets. At the far corner of the block ending in the Eureka Dance Hall, he did not re-emerge at all. Eli waited while time crawled by as slowly as the beetle on a grass-stem at his elbow, afraid to blink for fear he would miss seeing Solano when he finally passed the corner, then afraid he had already missed seeing him, although he could not have.

At last, the boy saw a movement. From between the last two buildings appeared a young Mexican girl. She had a shawl over her head. Her feet and thin, brown arms were bare. She reached the boardwalk and broke into a run back toward the near end of town. But at the next corner, she turned down a side street and vanished.

Eli sat as still as the stone, his eyes fixed on the street below, waiting for something else to happen. For he was sure the girl's flight had been precipitated by the arrival of Juan Solano. Yet he saw nothing more in that quarter. There was some activity in and out of San Gabriel, and a furtive movement in its direction by several people who could only be Mexican. But that was all.

Finally, deciding to move his vantage point directly across from the scene of the hidden action, the boy crept out of the shade of the boulder and slipped back over the top of the hill to where he had left the black horse.

In the town below, it was Violeta that Eli had seen, running to her grandmother's house where she would gather together a few trinkets, most of which were worthless to anyone but herself. The girl was leaving la Magdalena and the Gold Country forever. Don Simón Ruiz had told her she should. And whatever might be commanded by the generous man of the beautiful eyes, the soft voice and the gold coins, Violeta would unquestioningly obey.

The Valley! Somewhere in the wonderful Valley stretching away to the misty hills that rose on its far horizon! That was where she would go. And there, she and her grandmother would find a new life. A better life. For people were kind in the Valley. They cared about others. It must be so. Don Simón came from there.

Of course, it meant leaving her mother's grave. And her brother's. Some tears fell for that. But Jesucristo would watch over the resting place of those two innocents, even as His angels had taken their souls to heaven.

Violeta fell on her knees before a tiny, chipped statue of the Virgin and mumbled a prayer only God's Mother might have understood. Then rising, she whisked the image into the bundle of rags she was tying together. Her grandmother would be waiting for her at the church. They would set out from there. The priest would go with them. And some of their neighbors. Don Simón had said that they should. And don Simón had been sent by the saints. Violeta's own grandmother had told her so.

He had arrived without warning, as usual, but he was not unexpected, this time. Two terrible men lay in wait for him in the house of la Magdalena, one upstairs and one downstairs. They had been there since dawn. The Rose of Jackson herself was terrified of them. But except for lustful looks, they had left her alone. It was Ruiz they were there for, and they wished to be ready for him whenever he might come.

The one called Pío Pinto had wanted to wait near the door. But the one named Mariano García told Pinto that he was a coward, (like all Chileans) and that because of something which had happened at the Grand Hotel in Mokelumne Hill, he couldn't be trusted not to run when Ruiz drew his knife.

And so Pinto was stationed upstairs. Violeta had heard him pacing around and snorting like a bull who must wait for a bear. García was quiet. He crouched in the hall behind the door and made Violeta sit at the foot of the stairs where he could watch her. Together, she and the bandit had counted the hours from dawn until noon. La Magdalena had served them. That had felt strange. But Violeta had been too frightened to fully appreciate the novelty. Every time she had moved, the cold, cruel eyes of García had glinted. García was not from the Valley. He had come from the hills in the south with a man named Gonzalves.

Hills must do bad things to men. Violeta prayed that Ruiz would not stay long enough for these hills to affect him. Even saints have their limits.

Shortly after midday, Violeta heard footsteps approaching the door from outside. She gathered herself to rise but stayed where she was at a violent gesture from García. Three knocks on the door. Then two. Then one. The bandit motioned Violeta to answer the summons. He had a knife in his hand. The blade of it glinted as cold as his eyes.

Trembling, she tripped the latch. But she threw the door back wide. And confronting don Simón for an instant alone, she cried out, "García!" Or tried to. Then she was knocked to the floor as the bandit leaped past her. But he was met by a charge as fierce as his own. Violeta crawled back to the stairs, huddled into the wall, and watched the two men wrestling in the doorway.

Ruiz had braced himself on the sill, and so forced the bandit back, for García's booted feet slipped on the wooden floor. Trying to regain the advantage of surprise, Mariano suddenly gave in and twisted to one side, hurling Ruiz against the far wall. But as quickly abandoning his intent to attack with his blade, García backed off down the corridor, drawing his gun.

Don Simón slowly pushed himself erect. "You won't do that," he said softly. "The noise will bring the gringos. They will hang you." Carefully, he drew a knife from his waist, not taking his eyes off García. "Do you not dare to fight me, cholo?" he taunted.

Then, "Ruiz!" came a voice from the top of the stairs. It was Pinto. Don Simón flinched, but he did not look around, and García aborted a sudden advance. Seizing the instant,

Ruiz struck the gun from the outlaw's hand. In his hesitation, García had not cocked it, so it did not go off as it hit the wall and then the floor, slid toward the steps. Violeta stared at it as if it were a thing alive. Then she leaned to grab it, whirled around and pointed it up the stairs.

At their top stood Pío Pinto. He held la Magdalena against him, using her to shield himself. But an awful grunting from the hallway drew Violeta's attention back to García and Ruiz. She turned to see them locked in another contest of strength. But this time, García was backed against the wall. Ruiz had pinned the outlaw's right arm over his head, holding it there with less effort than it cost Mariano to try to lower it while both men were intent upon Ruiz' blade which he was trying to advance against García's defense. The grunting issued from both sides of the struggle.

"Ruiz!" called Pinto again. "I will kill this woman!"

Don Simón gave no sign that he heard.

It was then that Pío threw la Magdalena down the stairs. Violeta heard a thumping and a breathless cry. She turned to see her mistress tumbling along the wall, tangled in the skirts of her crimson dressing gown, yet still more or less upright until the very last when she fell to one side and smashed right into Violeta who had tried to dodge out of the way but had jumped in the wrong direction. Both girl and woman were momentarily stunned by the impact. Neither was actually injured. But Pinto's purpose had been accomplished. The noise and glimpses of violent movement had broken don Simón's concentration and his hold on Mariano García. The outlaw shoved free of the wall and twisted out of Ruiz' grasp.

Don Simón lunged after him, sweeping a downcut with his knife. But Mariano threw himself backwards, falling and rolling away. Springing back to his feet, the bandit fled down the hall. Ruiz took two steps after him, then turned to see what sort of action might soon involve him from the rear.

La Magdalena had crawled free of her servant and was trying to get to her feet to run out the half open door. Pío Pinto came leaping down the stairs to stop her. Simón jumped to shove the door shut, pushed Magdalena out of the way and faced the second outlaw with his legs braced and his blade ready.

Pinto was coming too fast to be able to stop immediately. There was no railing to help check himself. But he dragged one hand along the wall and tried to reverse his motion, nearly losing his balance in the process. Ruiz saw his advantage and took it. The outlaw kicked at him as he came springing up the steps. Simón sliced Pío's leg with his knife.

With a muted howl of terror, Pinto turned to dash for the landing above. Ruiz caught him before he had taken three strides. He struck his knife deep. Pinto gave a strangled grunt. Ruiz flung off the weight of his adversary, and the chileno staggered back along the edge of the step where he stood, clutching at his breast. His knees buckled. He fell heavily, striking his head. They all heard it crack. He rolled over twice, but he had fallen at an angle so the wall stopped him. He slithered another three steps, feet first, before he lay still.

Ruiz waited where he was for several moments, his chest heaving from his exertion, his black hair falling over one eye, his grip still tight on his knife hilt. His look switched from the quiet body of Pío Pinto to where la Magdalena was pressed against the wall, her fists to her mouth, her arms folded up tightly in front of her. Violeta still sat on the floor, holding the gun that García had dropped. The outlaw himself was nowhere in sight. Beyond the closed door, the hallway was vacant.

CHAPTER FORTY-FOUR:

PURSUIT

"Are you hurt?" Ruiz asked the Rose. He had come down the stairs, pausing first to inspect Pío Pinto to be sure he was dead.

Too terrified yet to answer, Magdalena shook her head without lowering her hands from her mouth.

Simón knelt beside Violeta. "Niña. Can you get up?"

The girl nodded. "Estoy bien," she tried to say. She offered him the bandit's gun. He took it, glancing again at the vacant hallway beyond.

"I have spoken with your grandmother at the chapel," he told her. "And the priest. And others who were there. You must leave this town. There is great danger coming. You will go with your grandmother to the Valley. She is waiting for you. Tell no one what has happened here, nor even that you have seen me. Will you remember?"

"Sí, Señor."

Simón got to his feet. He would have raised Violeta to hers, but she scrambled up alone. Standing before him, she looked up worshipfully into his face. And then she went to the door, opened it and slipped outside.

Ruiz closed it quietly behind her before he turned to Magdalena. The Rose watched him, shivering.

"Are there others in this building, Señorita?"

She shook her head.

"You are certain you are not injured?"

She nodded.

"How many rooms lie down this corridor?"

"He will not be in any of them, Patrón. They are locked. The girls are there. Those who work for me. He told them to latch the doors from the inside and not to come out, or he would kill them. He will have left by another door. He would not dare to face you again alone." She looked past Ruiz at the body on the stairs. "Don Simón, you must leave here quickly."

"Yes. But I cannot go until I am sure you are mistress of yourself. Señorita, hear me! The danger to you is not over. It has scarcely begun. I am only the first breath of the storm that will soon sweep southward through the hills. They are hanging innocent people in Ranchería in retaliation for what was done there by the outlaws. Tell me, do you know where I may find Manuel?"

"Yes. I think so. García said something to Pinto about 'mi amo' in Sonora. He can only have meant Escobar. Manuel wished to be well beyond your reach, I know, if his men failed to murder you. Oh, Don Simón, I . . ."

"I do not blame you for this, Señorita." Ruiz gestured at the stairs. "What recourse had you against them? In fact, I feared I might have to face more of them. Quickly, one more question: do you know if Fidel Buenrostro has returned home?"

"Who? No. No, I don't think so. I have heard no mention made of him."

Ruiz sighed. "I had meant to visit his family, to see how they fare and to warn them, myself. But after this, I do not dare to linger. Can I leave you, now?"

"Oh, stay a moment more!" She threw both arms about his neck. "Say where I will see you again!"

Ruiz stiffened. "Magdalena, forgive me." He unhooked her hold. "A man may do many things he later regrets. But whatever your feelings may be for me, I beg you to discard them as you can."

"But why?"

"I am married."

Magdalena caught her breath. "Married!" she echoed in dismay. "You mean to the sister of . . .?"

"No. To another. Manuel shall have no claims on me."

"Oh, Señor! You are cruel, after all . . . as cruel as the rest of them."

Ruiz looked around for the judge's hat. Seeing it upside down against the opposite wall, he went to pick it up. Again, he threw a searching glance down the silent corridor.

"But you were not married before?" demanded the Rose, coming after him.

Ruiz put on the hat and straightened its brim. "No," he admitted. "Only since Saturday. To a gringa," he added.

The Rose took a step back. She looked him up and down in amazement. "To a . . . gringa!"

"I think you need not try to conceal the evidence," said Ruiz, nodding at the corpse on the stairs. "The Americans won't care who has killed him. Some one among them may even take the credit for it, himself. But you must not be here when they come. Warn the women who work for you. You must gather your things together and leave immediately. I regret that I cannot stay to aid you. Adiós, Señorita. May the saints protect you." And moving past her to the door, he went out.

Eli Smith did not see him. From where the boy had been riding slowly along the ridge above the town, he had seen instead a dark-garbed Mexican slip out a different door of the dance hall and run back along the creek to where Solano had left Jack Sutherland's horse. Eli saw the man mount and kick the animal to make it leap the stream, then gallop along the road leading to the little canyon west of town.

Determined to follow, but not too closely, Eli moved back behind the hillcrest and urged his black horse to a lope. He intended to come down near Buenrostro's adobe, where he might be able to cross into the brush beyond the trail without attracting notice. Besides, there was that in the boy's nature which reveled in the impudence of passing so close to Uncle Peter's Claim without stopping, without anyone's knowing.

Eli resisted the impulse to visit Ben Rooster's, though he was sure that Juan Solano would go there. From the rising ground behind the adobe, he could see a bay horse in the peeled pole corral. It had been there since don Simón had taken his unsuspecting bride to San Gabriel. And Ruiz would need that horse again, now. Eli wished he dared to lead the bay to town and so spare Solano the danger and delay of having to come on foot in search of the animal himself. But Eli feared it was too close to the convenient trap of Uncle Peter's. And so, he rode on.

Moving through the brush beyond the creek road, the boy came out on the trail to Butte City. Here, he sat irresolute, wondering if he ought to circle around and look for a sign of the escaping outlaw. But he expected the bandit to ride for the Mokelumne River, however clever and tortuous a route he took. And Eli could make better time himself if he kept to the road for a while. Accordingly, he turned the black southwards and kicked it into a lope, once more.

He did not ride through Butte City. His passing might be noticed and remembered, there. He circled the settlement and bore west toward the river. Only when he was within sight of the crossing place and the town of Diamond Bar, did he stop to rest and water his horse and watch for traffic over the ford.

Again, Eli's instincts proved unerring. Within an hour, a party of eight hard-riding Mexicans came thundering down the road to the river. Instead of crossing immediately, however, they milled about on the bank, looking back the way they had come and arguing among themselves.

Their presence drew the notice of the citizens of Diamond Bar, none of whom, however, dared to challenge so desperate a band. The rash and the intrepid from the settlement had gone off to witness the depredations at Rancheria and had left only their less mettlesome neighbors to defend the town.

Some preparations were made to forestall attack, but most of Diamond Bar's population prudently retreated to behind bolted doors and latched shutters, praying that the bandits would cross the river and leave them in peace.

The outlaws, far from offering violence, were impatient to be away, and only waited for the balance of their number to catch up to them before they continued on. They had been at the ford perhaps a quarter of an hour when the three they expected came galloping down to the stream.

Eli Smith had been working his way closer through the brush during the interval, and with burning indignation he saw now that one of these three wore a beautiful jacket worked with gold. Of the two men accompanying him, one was dark, almost black, and the other Eli recognized as the man he had seen coming out of the dance hall in Jackson.

He and the one with the jacket had a good deal to say. The tall man apparently wanted him to do something across the river. And it was not without a sullen display of reluctance that the other finally agreed to it. Then, at last, the outlaws forded the cold-running steam.

The boy watched the far bank a little longer before he got up and returned to his horse . . . not to follow the outlaws, but to ride into Diamond bar. Before he went on, he needed a gun.

One of the town's few defenders challenged him as he passed the first building. "Hold up, kid!" Eli checked his horse. "Who are you, and what's your business?" the man demanded.

"I'm Billy Hall from Amador City," said Eli. "And I'm

wanting to buy a rifle. You got one you'll sell me?"

"Kid, firearms are in pretty high demand just now. A band of murderin' outlaws has just rode through."

"Well, if they're gone, you won't need the guns," said Eli. "Want to sell me that one? I'll give you thirty dollars for it.

"What do you want it for?"

"I'm going after the outlaws. One of them stole my pa's horse. I mean to get it back."

"Kid, you're crazy! You can't ride after those bandits alone!"

"Not without a rifle, I can't. I'll give you forty dollars."

"If you've got that kind of money, why don't you just buy your pa another horse?"

Eli dug in his trouser pocket and produced four gold coins. He dropped them from one hand into the other, so that they jingled and clinked. The sunlight winked and sparkled on them. "I guess somebody in this town would rather have gold than a gun," he said. "If it's not you, then maybe the next man."

"Why ain't your pa with you?" the guard demanded.

"He was hurt too bad to come."

"You mean he was hurt too bad to stop you from comin'. Kid, I wouldn't ever forgive myself if I were to sell you this gun."

"Fine," said Eli, spilling the four coins from hand to hand again. "You keep it. Somebody else will sell me one." He was about to return the money to his pocket when one of the coins dropped to the ground. The man jumped forward to pick it up. The black horse moved back from the sudden motion, and Eli dropped a second coin. "Whoa!" the boy cried, slapping the black with the reins. A third coin fell in the dust.

With some further display of difficulty, Eli mastered his mount and turned back to the man in the road. "Did you find them?" he asked. "I dropped a couple of those pieces I was showing you."

"Look, kid . . . Billy . . . you'd better give up this wild idea of yours. I'd be lettin' you ride to your death."

"Mister," said Eli, "either give me the coins or the rifle."

Still, the man hesitated.

"Flapjack?" called a wary voice from across the street. "What's goin' on?"

"Nothin'!" was the quick reply. "Just a kid from Amador City! Here," the man added to Eli, handing up the long-barreled weapon. "And don't tell anybody I let you have it. Give me that other twenty dollars."

Eli lay the rifle across the pommel. "I dropped three coins, Mister," he said. "And I saw you pick up all three. Give me your cartridge belt, and I'll pay you the fourth one."

"You're too danged smart for your own good, kid," grumbled the guard. "Take it, then. I guess it wouldn't be human to send you off alone after all them outlaws with no ammunition."

Eli slung the heavy belt over one shoulder and tossed the fourth coin to the road. Then, whirling the black horse on its haunches, he galloped back to the ford.

It was only shortly afterwards that the citizens of Diamond Bar saw a twelfth Mexican come down the trail. Since he rode alone and was apparently intent only on crossing the river, he did not arouse much new alarm. Flapjack was in favor of getting together a posse to accost him, saying it would be easy, for the Mexican was having trouble getting his bay gelding to enter the water. But before the citizens could agree on a course of action, the man had succeeded in forcing his mount into the stream. They watched the animal lunge across, heave itself onto the far bank and charge on up the road. Juan Solano lay low on its neck.

CHAPTER FORTY-FIVE:

AT THE CAMP OF JUAN SOLANO

Evening drew a light mist over the Mokelumne Canyon. The river snaked silver through the timbered gorge whose walls rose in a series of steep shouldered hills, each plunging line a thinner thread of blue-violet than the one before it. High on the southern ramparts of this vastness, Juan Solano made camp near a trickle of cold water sliding out from beneath moss-clad stone.

He laid no fire. The pack behind his saddle was well stocked with acorn flour and jerked venison, but he made only a frugal supper of a few strips of the meat. The light of a campfire was too likely to be seen by others although he did not expect the outlaws to linger, much less backtrack in search of him. They would put more distance between themselves and the northern settlements, first. But they would be keeping one eye on the trail behind them, certain that he was following. And if they saw an opportunity to ambush him, they would be willing to take some risk for that purpose. García, especially, would be eager for it, now.

And where in all these miles of immensity was Sydney Simpson de Ruiz Silvestre? It was this question which dragged Solano's gaze again and again out over the darkening canyon. Baldy Hinkson had not thought it would be difficult to surprise her, but Baldy had never seen the Pecosa on a horse. He had never seen her slide over the edge of a cliff on the end of a whiplash to rescue a hat. Baldy was only watching for a girl dressed up in men's clothing.

Solano took some comfort in believing that Sydney was behind him, at least, that he himself still stood between her and the outlaws. But even to speculate on what García and Gonzalves would do to her, were they to catch her now, filled his veins with fire and ice.

Again he turned his eyes to the magnificent cleft in the earth below and beyond him, searched its deepening shadows for a sign of movement. He saw none. He heard nothing but the soft breath of evening in the pine tops towering above him. He might have been alone on the earth for all the clue to the contrary surrendered by the silent gorge. Far below, the river ran over the rocky feet of the hills as it had for the millennia before men's eyes had first looked on it.

Eventually, daylight faded into such darkness that Solano could not have seen Sydney had she been standing two trees from his camp. The moon would not rise for another hour. He lay back on the ground and closed his eyes. Almost immediately, he became aware of a strange ache in his arms and a hollowness in his chest.

"¡Ay, Pecosita!" he sighed. "Why haven't you let the cholos to kill me on the road from Ranchería and save me all this agonía?" But in trying to define the true center of his pain, he discovered that its sharpest sting no longer sprang from the horrible death of the innocent men in Rancheria, nor from his own failure to aid them. It was not his shame at being so blatantly defied by his new wife, nor even his renewed fear for her safety, though all of these contributed to his anxiety and restlessness.

At last, puzzled and weary, he fell asleep.

He was awakened in the greying hour of dawn by a stealthy noise somewhere near at hand. He stiffened but did not move, listening for the sound to come again. It was made by something dragging . . . slowly, heavily, but cautiously, over the ground. When Solano was certain that the noise was approaching him from uphill, and that its cause would momentarily invade his campsite, he rolled swiftly out of his blanket to put the huge, mossy rock between him and that cause. He heard a quick intake of breath, as quickly checked. And then silence. He waited, coiled, every nerve alive, but there was nothing more.

Slowly, noiselessly, he moved along the rock, one hand closing on the grip of the pistol he had taken from Escobar in Mokelumne Hill. Bending forward, supporting himself against the stone, he peered out at his abandoned blanket. But that was all he saw. His horse was picketed at a distance, downhill from his camp where a patch of grass grew green in a little basin below the rocky spring.

He must move back into the trees if he were to descend to it unseen. But his mind had had a chance to re-evaluate the breath of surprise and alarm he had heard. He decided to risk confrontation. "¿Quién es?" he demanded, cocking Manuel's pistol.

There was no response.

"Answer!" he commanded. "Or I shoot!"

The reply was a low moan.

Solano moved forward again, more quickly, now, his pistol ready, but every moment more confident that it was unnecessary.

"For the sake of God, have mercy!" said a broken voice in Spanish. "I am dying." It came from uphill, from behind a fallen pine, a log so long beaten by the weather it was as white as bone; the stubs of its limbs thrust up like the broken spokes of an old wheel.

Solano mounted the hillside, helping himself with one hand on the ground. He had sheathed his gun. For he knew he recognized the voice. "Fidel! Hombre, is that you?" And leaping lightly over the log, he came upon Buenrostro lying full length behind it. "¡Amigo! ¡En nombre de Dios! How do you come to be here? What has happened to you? Are you wounded?"

Buenrostro lifted his head to look at Ruiz in amazement and relief. "Don Simón . . .!"

"How badly are you hurt, Fidel?"

"You have . . . water?"

"I will bring it instantly. Lie still." Springing back over the log, Simón slid into his campsite, seized his water boot and returned with it. Kneeling beside the older man, he helped him prop himself up so that he could drink. Buenrostro groaned as his right leg dragged round. "El tobillo . . ." he explained, pointing to his ankle.

"Broken?"

"I don't know. I fell on it. There is some movement left in it. I cannot walk." Between phrases, Buenrostro gulped water. "Heaven sends you this way, Patrón. I had given up hope. Do you have anything with you to eat?"

"Surely. Your own wife has supplied me. I have just come through Jackson. I have followed Gonzalves and García back across the ford at Diamond Bar. You have not seen them?"

"No. I have seen no one since I escaped the men who brought me over the river." Buenrostro lay back against the log and closed his eyes.

"I will start a fire to make some avenate," said Simón. "It won't take long. Rest. We will talk later."

The sun had not yet risen when Fidel Buenrostro finished his second bowl of acorn gruel. The campfire glowed like a jewel in an angle of the mossy stone. Ruiz was careful not to let it smoke.

"My story is simple enough, Patrón," Buenrostro told him while Simón carefully cut the tight leather of the boot away from Fidel's swollen foot. "On my way home from town that morning, two men whose names I never learned rode up on either side of me. One was dark. The other had a dry wound in his lower ear."

"Yes. That one is now dead," said Ruiz. "He died on the back stairs of the Eureka Dance Hall."

"Ah! Who killed him?"

"A man called Juan Solano."

"Then el señor Solano has done us all a service," said Fidel.

"But why did they take you?" asked Ruiz.

"To find out what more I knew of the trick you played on García with the sorrel mare."

"But they could have questioned you in Jackson."

"Yes. But there was a fire near my house. The excitement filled the road with people. Many of them knew me. They might have come to my aid." Buenrostro chewed hungrily on a strip of dry venison. "Besides, Escobar wished to question me himself, I think. And he was in Mokelumne Hill."

"How did you escape?"

"The road passes along the edge of a steep drop, Patrón. As we neared the top of the canyon, I threw myself from my saddle. In a hail of bullets and falling stones, I slid into the trees below. The bandits could not follow me without grave risk to their own lives. No doubt they decided it was not worth the trouble to search for me. Or perhaps they thought I was killed by the fall or one of their bullets."

"But you have not come all this way on an injured foot!" Released from the restraint of the boot, Fidel's ankle was swelling still more.

"No," agreed Buenrostro. "Had I not fallen a second time, I might have returned home several days ago. But it was my fate to step down on a small stick which rolled out from under me. I landed on a slick layer of pine needles and slid with my leg doubled under me."

"And have you been all this time without food, Fidel? Yet, you must have found water . . .?"

"Yes. I spent three days near a spring. Cress grew there. And miner's lettuce. But I knew I could not stay in that place indefinitely. So I decided I would try to get down to the river and Big Bar. You see how hopeless it was. This morning, I heard a trickle of running water from this place . . . and so you have found me. I owe you my life, Patrón."

"No, Fidel. You owe me these days of pain and hunger. The bandidos would never have looked twice at you had it not been for me and the trick of the sorrel mare. And your wife, your children . . . they too were threatened. They were not hurt. But they have spent this time in fear for your life and their own. Fidel, I had no right to involve you. I do not even ask you to forgive me. For I cannot forgive myself. And now, with the Americans avenging their dead on every Mexican they can find, I do not know where to take you. But I must take you somewhere. We cannot stay here. So! I will saddle my horse."

The bay gelding greeted Ruiz with a soft whicker. Simón rubbed the animal's head and straightened its forelock between its black-tipped ears. "Why you should be happy to see me, potro . . ." he told it softly. "I have done no more for you than for Fidel. I almost drown you in the river, I ride you too far and too fast without food or rest. And for this, you thank me?"

The bay put its nose to Simón's cheek, earning another caress from Ruiz. But then it jerked away, half turning, and stared off into the trees. Suddenly, it let out a ringing neigh that echoed up and down the silent canyon.

"¡Eh! ¡No! ¡Cállate!" exclaimed Simón. Seizing the horse around the neck and forcing the bit into its mouth, he slipped the headstall over its pricking ears. Then, picking up the saddle he had put down on the grass beside him, he slung it onto the bay's back. He had not done cinching when three riders came out of the trees at the edge of the little basin. Ruiz caught his horse by the cheek strap and turned the animal broadside, shielding himself behind its shoulder and forelegs and drawing a gun from his belt.

But there was no need. "Solano!" It was Baldy Hinkson. Ruiz let out a breath and released his horse's bridle. "Baldés!" he said in relief.

"Sorry we surprised you. Did Miss Sydney find you?"

Ruiz shook his head, looking from Hinkson to his two companions as they rode up.

"Damn!" said Baldy. "She's led us a chase. Solano, this here is Rob Briggs." Hinkson tipped his head to indicate the man on his left. "Briggs accidentally sold Miss Sydney a horse in Rancheria. I mean, he thought she was a boy named Eli Smith."

Simón stared at Briggs who pulled at his hatbrim in some embarrassment.

"It seems Miss Sydney must of saw Miz Sutherland and me find that red colt of yours she'd rode from the ranch," Baldy went on. "She'd tied it up among a lot of other horses. It had been there a while because the sweat on it was mostly dry. So, the boss's wife stayed with it, expectin' Miss Sydney would have to come back after it, some time or other. And I searched the crowd for a sign of her. But she fooled the whole lot of us. By the time I'd come across Briggs and heard his story, she was long gone to Jackson."

Simón said nothing. He finished cinching his saddle. Then he looked up at the third American. This was a handsome young man with an honest eye and a square jaw. He looked to be the most uncomfortable of the entire party.

"Juan," said Baldy, following his gaze, "this other feller is acquainted with Miss Sydney, too. His name's Paul Mc-Cormick."

Simón let fall the stirrup he had thrown back over the saddle seat and stood away from his horse. "Pole . . . Ma-Cormie!" he repeated.

"Yes, sir," said Paul, also pulling at his hat and forcing

himself to meet Simón's gaze steadily. "You've probably heard about me."

"Paul was at Rancheria, too," said Baldy. "He saw what all went on. But he didn't see Miss Sydney. Nobody we talked to remembered seein' her. Except Rob Briggs. But then, nobody else was payin' much attention to such things.

"Solano," continued Hinkson, "I know you'll be relieved to learn that nobody else got hung in Rancheria. Just them three we saw ourselves. After that, the judge and Mr. Sutherland and Clark was able to talk a little reason into the crowd. Boston Williston ain't nobody's particular choice of a leader. And some of the folks was shocked at the way he manhandled the whole business. And I guess those that weren't was satisfied with the exy-cution of them three innocent fellers you tried to save. I think what all you said might have made some difference, too. Anyhow, the necktie party broke up shortly after you left.

"The Mexicans inside the rope corral was turned loose and told to get out of town. They was give four hours to get their families and their things together and leave. I reckon they didn't waste no time in doin' it, either.

"Meantime, I run into Briggs near the livery stable, and he told me how he'd sold his horse to a kid named Eli Smith. When he mentioned the freckles and the out-sized clothes, I knew what had happened: Miss Sydney had put the slip on us and had gone off lookin' for you. I got a little loud at Rob for lettin' himself be tooken in that a-way, and Paul McCormick was standin' around near there by that time, and he overheard us. So he introduced himself and offered to help us find her. And you. And the bandits. And the sheriff, if we can. God knows where Phoenix and his posse has got to by this time." Baldy stopped here in his narrative to wait for Simón's reaction before he went on, for Ruiz' brow was knotted low, and his repeated looks from one to the next of the three Americans made them all uneasy.

"Pole MaCormie," said Simón, "what has happen to the family of your neighbor in Yakson? Los Buenrostro?"

Paul shrugged. "Nothing, so far as I know," he said. "Ben Rooster himself hasn't been seen in Jackson since the day Mr. Simpson's cabin burned down. Did Sydney tell you about that?"

"The cabin of los Seensome, she is burn down by one of the bandidos," replied Simón. "Does la señora de Buenrostro tell you that?"

Paul stared. "The bandits did it? Mr. Simpson thought . . ." But McCormick changed his mind and said instead, "We stopped to talk to Mrs. Rooster on our way out of Jackson. She said you'd just been there, but not Sydney."

"The Señora was pretty leary of us," added Baldy. "It was only because you'd told her to expect me that she finally said anything at all. Jackson was buzzin' with wild rumors about the bandits' passin' through, and there wasn't a Mexican to be found in the whole damn town. They'd lit out for God knows where, hopin' to beat the panic. 'Cause I reckon there'll be one over the next couple of days."

"Have they find Pío Pinto?" asked Simón.

"No, not that we heard. Where was he?"

"In the dance hall."

"Maybe they hadn't looked there, yet. He wouldn't have left?"

"No. Mariano García has leave. But not Pío Pinto."

"Do you know where García is?"

Simón swept a hand at the canyon. "He can be anywhere, Baldés. I have fear you might be him. I have hope you might be my Saidnay.

"Desmóntense, pues." Simón gestured the three men to dismount. "There is more talk we must do before we leave here. Pole MaCormie, I have find your neighbor, Buenrostro. He is víctima of these same bandidos. But he escape. He is hurt. He cannot walk. He wish to go home. I have think to take him, even though it means I must leave the trail of the cholos and abandon my wife who is somewhere . . ." Again, Ruiz gestured at the timbered gorge. "But now you are here. I think I will ask that you take home your neighbor to his woman and children. He is safer with you than with me. Only say you will stay near his house and protect him, for I fear what the gringos of Yackson may do if he is the only mexicano they find in the town."

Paul exchanged looks with the Briggs and Hinkson. "Where is he?" asked McCormick.

CHAPTER FORTY-SIX:

THE CONFESSION OF MARIANO GARCIA

"Gonzalves? You're sure his name was Gonzalves?" Phoenix leaned one elbow on the counter to bring his eyes on a level with the bartender of the Court Room Saloon.

"I'm as sure as you're standin' there, Sheriff. 'Cause it weren't the first time I'd seen him."

"Tell me."

The bartender rubbed one hand over the bald spot on the top of his head as if to warm up his memory while he stared at the countertop for a moment. "It was last Thursday night he come here first. Let's see, we're on the eighth of August now, ain't we? So, that'd make it the second. Him and another come together. That one had been through Moke Hill before, too. Escovrar, his name is. Or somethin' like that."

"Escobar?" suggested Phoenix.

"Yeah. That was it. They come in and paid for a couple of rooms. In this here establishment, we don't ask a man for his passport before we rents him a room, you see. Whatever man is carryin' the price of our hospitality, he gets it. Don't matter what he calls himself, nor what language he does it in."

"Go on," said Phoenix. Will Sutherland leaned near him, dividing his attention between what was being said and the rest of the men in the room. George Durham stood bolt upright to the sheriff's other side. The Tax Collector's eyes were fixed on the bartender, his mouth set in a determined line.

The remainder of the posse grouped loosely behind them. Their entrance had stopped three card games and the quiet rattling of dice. None of the players were Mexican.

"Escobar and Gonzalves hadn't more'n just checked in when here comes a whole gang of Greasers after 'em," the bartender recalled.

"How many?" asked Phoenix.

"Well, hell . . . ten, anyway. Didn't all of 'em sign the register. But I think . . ."

A noise from outside the saloon interrupted the bartender, and a man pushed in through the swinging doors. "Sheriff!" he said. "You'd better come out here."

Phoenix shoved himself away from counter and moved through his posse who turned and followed him out. There they stopped while Phoenix stepped down off the boardwalk into the street and waited for the approach of five riders on four horses. Two of the men were Mexican, and both were injured. Phoenix recognized them and the three Americans with them as well. But it was one of his posse who voiced the general surprise:

"Paul! Baldy! Ben Rooster! For gosh sakes!" Cecil Simpson left the boardwalk and joined the sheriff in the road. The cowboy, Sherill, came after him. Daniel Perrin, who had joined the company with Cross and Durham at Rancheria, advanced to the edge of the boardwalk, half lifting a hand in greeting to Rob Briggs. George Durham also came forward, frowning heavily. The men of Mokelumne Hill emerged from doorways all along the street. An expectant silence gripped the town.

"Sheriff, it's damn good to see you," said Baldy Hinkson, pulling his horse to a stop in front of Phoenix.

"My pleasure," returned the lawman dryly.

"You know Rob Briggs? From Rancheria. And Paul Mc-Cormick? From Jackson Creek. He belongs to the Simpson outfit. Howdy, Boss," Hinkson added to Will Sutherland. "Sherry. Cecil. Mr. Cross."

"That man's my uncle's neighbor!" exclaimed Cecil, pointing at Buenrostro. "He's not one of the bandits, is he?"

"Nope. We're just givin' him an escort. He's been hurt fallin' down a hillside. It's this other hombre that's the outlaw. Sheriff, this here is Mariano García, one of the gang's three ringleaders."

"Where did you find him?" asked Phoenix.

"He found us. He was runnin' from somebody else. He took a bullet in the shoulder. That's what smoked him out from his cover."

"García?" said Phoenix, looking up at the glowering bandit who sat in sullen silence on his horse, his hands tied to his pommel. "You have anything to say? ¿Tien' algo pa' decir?"

García made no response.

"Get him down and bring him inside," said Phoenix. "I'll see if I can get him to talk. Señor Buenrostro," the sheriff added to the Mexican slumping in the saddle in front of Rob Briggs, "¿cómo está?"

"Como me ve," muttered Fidel.

"How bad is he hurt, Baldy?"

"Just his leg. Bad sprain, looks like. But he's weak from goin' so long without much to eat. And he's dead tired. Don Simón found him yonder in the canyon."

"You've seen Ruiz? Where's he?"

"He's ridin' on after a set of fresh tracks, Sheriff. It's a helluva story."

"I'd better hear it. A couple of you boys help Señor Buenrostro get down. Easy with him! Ike, grab that horse by the bridle, will you?"

The German Eichelburger joined the others in the dusty street. He had been with the posse since the night they had missed catching the bandits on the Lazy Q. Old Tom Quincy had turned back at the border of his property, but he had made no objection to the German's going on with them. "He ain't good for nothin' round here, anyhow," he had said. But Ike had proved himself useful. He was obliging and totally fearless, a combination which passed for folly only among those who had never seen him in action. The members of the posse now had. Ike stayed on with them and welcome.

The Court Room Saloon of the Grand Hotel in Moke-lumne Hill prepared itself with dispatch for a session at law, filling with avid witnesses. A second bartender was produced to handle the sharp increase in trade. At the sheriff's request, a cot was brought in for Buenrostro. Phoenix did not trust the mood of the townsmen and preferred to have Fidel safely under his eye. García he obliged to sit at the table where the posse converged to hear Baldy's account of the bandit's capture. Mariano listened with a lowering scowl. He knew some English. And he understood very well that his hours were numbered.

"We came across Ruiz about sunup," said Baldy, taking a long drink of beer and wiping the foam from his lip. "He'd just broke camp and was fixin' to take Buenrostro home to Jackson, even though he was some worried about what kind of reception he'd get there. Sheriff, you'll have heard by now what happened in Rancheria after you left?"

"Yes," said Phoenix. "Go on."

"Well, what you maybe didn't hear about was how the bride of don Simón has trailed her man with the cunnin' of a Redskin from the Sutherland's ranch clear to the Mokelumne Gorge. So, me and Rob Briggs and Paul McCormick was after **her**, mostly. 'Cause don Simón was feared she'd come to harm, and he couldn't catch her himself."

"Sydney's on her own out there?" cried Cecil, pushing closer to Baldy from where he had been standing with Paul McCormick.

"Well, maybe not anymore. I'm comin' to that. See, we was still discussin' what we ought to do about Old Fidel when there's a rifle shot from somewhere off in the trees behind us. And García comes staggerin' out of his hidin' place where he'd been spyin' on us. If he hadn't been alone, or if Ruiz still had been, he probably would have tried to plug him. Or us. Maybe he meant to, anyway. But he'd figured without Miss Sydney."

"She shot him!" exclaimed Cecil.

"Well, somebody did. We never seen her. But we was sure she was there. Rob and Paul and me had followed her tracks from the Diamond Bar Ford. And it wasn't no picnic. Mostly, we got on just by guessin' the general direction she was headin' in. I'd sooner try to track a coyote than your sister, Cecil Simpson.

"Anyhow, it didn't take long to get García disarmed and trussed up for safekeepin'," Baldy went on. "But almost before we had him tied to stay, Juan Solano throws himself on his horse and lights out in the direction of the rifle shot. Briggs followed him."

"That's right," said Briggs, as the attention in the Court Room Saloon shifted generally in his direction. "And I rode over some ground I'd rather have skirted in order to keep him in sight. When I caught up to him, he was off his horse and studyin' for tracks. There weren't many to find. That ground there was mostly rock.

" 'Señor,' I says to him as he looks up at me, 'I think I owe you an apology.'

" 'She was here,' he answers, pointin' at the couple of hoofprints he'd found in the only patch of soft dirt on the whole damn hillside. 'She has watch from there.' He waves at a rock overhangin' his campsite below. Then, he stands up and looks around him like he'd heard somethin'. 'Saidnay!'

he bellers, makin' the canyon ring like a bell. But there wasn't no answer.

" 'What color is the horse you have sell to my wife?' he asks me.

" 'Black,' I say, 'with a white face and a white forefoot. It's a good horse, too, long-legged and fast. I wouldn't have parted with him at all except the kid was so desperate to leave Rancheria.'

" 'I find her,' says Solano, pushin' by me. 'You take Fidel to his family. Take García to the sheriff. Or kill him, if you do not wish to waste more time with him. He is guilty. If I have find him myself, I have shoot him and leave him where he fall.' And gettin' back into his saddle, Solano rides off."

"Rob came back and told us Ruiz was gone," said Baldy, taking up the narrative again as Briggs drew a breath. "And so, we collected Bwin Roaster and García and made for Moke Hill. How do you happen to be here yourself, Sheriff?"

"We came back to Jackson from Indian Camp," replied Phoenix. "That proved a false lead." He stopped to cough.

"Yes," said Will Sutherland, hitching himself closer to the table and leaning forward in his earnestness. "And Jackson was in a terrible turmoil. One of the outlaws had been found dead in the Eureka Dance Hall. And all the women were gone. The deputy went to see what he could find at Gonzalves' house down the gulch west of town." Will paused to look at Phoenix. The sheriff had his handkerchief to his mouth, attempting to repress his coughs, but his whole body wrenched with every effort. The German Eichelburger laid a hand on the officer's shoulder in silent sympathy.

"What did he find?" asked Baldy, also glancing at the sheriff in concern but still giving most of his attention to young Sutherland.

"Not much," said Will. "The place was turned upside down as if somebody'd been through it in a hurry. But there was lots of tracks outside. Quite a group had left there and rode for the Diamond Bar Ford."

"We took up the trail," continued Phoenix hoarsely,

374

wiping his mouth. "But I told my brother Sam he'd better stay close to home. Our jail is better than some. And I mean to send Sam any bandits we catch. I don't want a lot of lynching. There'll be a proper trial held. I've sworn to uphold the law, not to head a committee of vigilantes."

"Sheriff, I hate to say it," interposed Will Sutherland, "but I doubt you can prevent the citizens of Jackson from hanging this man the moment he sets foot in the town. Or even Buenrostro."

The men in the room looked first at García and then at the old Mexican who lay on the cot beside the sheriff's chair. Fidel had drifted off into the slumber of exhaustion. His bare foot twitched occasionally in subconscious pain. It was swollen to almost twice its normal size.

Without answering Will, Phoenix turned his eyes to Mariano. "García," he said, stuffing his handkerchief back into his pocket, "your turn. Usted va 'blar."

The bandit shrugged slightly. The corners of his mouth drew down.

"¿Dónde Manuel Escobar?" demanded Phoenix.

Another shrug.

"Paulo Gonzalves?"

"I say noteen," declared the outlaw.

"You speak English? Who killed the man in the dance hall?"

Mariano's dark eyes flashed a fierce look at his questioner. "Simón Ruiz!" he hissed.

"You saw it?"

"Almos' kill me!"

"What were **you** doing in the dance hall?"

"I say noteen," replied García.

"Were you one of the men that shot up Rancheria?"

"No."

"He's lyin'," said Baldy impatiently.

"Who killed Mrs. Dynan?" asked the sheriff, ignoring Hinkson.

García shrugged.

"Was it Escobar?"

"No. Don Manuel far away. Afraid of Ruiz."

"Did Gonzalves go with him?"

"No. El brasileño stay with us. Quiso matar a Ruiz."

"Did he 'matar' Albert France?"

"No. Juan Torres do that."

"What were you doing by yourself out there in the canyon?"

"No by myself. Two more. Watch out for Ruiz."

"Was Gonzalves one of those?"

"No. Don Paulo go on. I t'ink before he no cobarde. But now, I say he is. Big coward."

"So he left you and two others to watch for don Simón while he rode on to join up with Escobar. Is that it?"

García nodded slightly. His sullen look fell to the table top.

Phoenix sat back. "Well, you've given us something to go on." He looked around at the posse. "Who volunteers to take Fidel to his house and García to jail in Jackson?"

No one answered.

"It'd better be somebody with a cool nerve," said Phoenix.

"I don't pretend it'll be easy. Sam will be in town to help stand off the lynchers. But between here and there, you'll be on your own."

"I go," said Eichelburger quietly.

"Thanks, Ike. Who else?"

"I will," said Daniel Perrin. He pushed a shoulder through the group around the table. "For Ben Rooster's sake. There's been enough ugly ideas circulated about him already. He come close to gettin' the blame for the Simpson's fire. And then, folks were sayin' he'd run off to avoid payin' his taxes to Durham. George, it seems to me you ought to be a member of his escort, yourself."

But the Tax Collector shook his head. "I have sworn not to turn back until we've caught the man or men who killed Albert France and Mrs. Dynan," he said. "I regret the rumors about Ben Rooster. I confess I did little to stop them. But they did not start with me. And regrettable though the situation may be, I will leave its remedy to others."

"I'll go," said Cecil.

Phoenix turned to him. "Son, of all the posse, you have the most right to stay on with us, if you want to. It's your sister and her husband that run the biggest risk at the moment."

"Sheriff, it seems to me you ought to go back with them yourself," said Constable Cross, putting himself forward for the first time. He was a lean man with a sparse beard and pale eyes. "You ain't feeling well. We all know it. And we're worried about you. You need to rest. Not that Jackson is going to be very peaceful for a spell, but at least, you won't be traipsing round the countryside, wearing yourself out the way you been. You're liable to get really sick if you keep on. And you're not a man the county can afford to have laid up. God knows what more is going to happen before this business is over with. We'll need you to help keep a steady grip on things."

A chorus of men's voices seconded the constable's suggestion. Phoenix was urged on all sides to give up the chase. He was told that no one else could guarantee the safe arrival of García and Buenrostro in Jackson, nor could prevent a lynching once they got there. He was assured of his followers' loyalty and respect, of their real concern for his health. Constable Cross, they said, could head the posse in his place. Or he could send his brother, Sam, to lead them.

But Phoenix was shaking his head. Finally, he held up his hands for silence. "Gentlemen," he said. "I thank you. But it would take just one man to say I was a quitter. A sheriff doesn't give up the trail of a bunch of murdering bandits just because he has a cough and a sore throat. No, I won't hear of it. And Cecil Simpson is not going back at this point, either. I know he has volunteered only because he is worried about the fate of his neighbor, Buenrostro. But he has bigger worries than that to claim him. Men, I ask you again. Who else will take these two Mexicans to Jackson?"

CHAPTER FORTY-SEVEN:

THE MASSACRE AT
MILE GULCH

In the saloon and dining hall of the Traveler's Inn at the town of Fourth Crossing, halfway between San Andreas and Angels Camp, Eli Smith sat down to supper alone. It was Saturday night. The big main room around him was beginning to fill with local miners, newly liberated from their week of hard labor after small gain. There were, besides, ten or twelve passengers from the stage line, stopping over on their way south. Among these, the most noticeable was a Mrs. Ketchum. There was a Mr. Ketchum, too, but his presence and identity were not so immediately apparent.

"The most shocking . . . the most shocking thing," the lady was saying, "anybody ever heard of!"

"Do tell, Ma'am!" urged a courteous miner, hooking his thumbs through his red suspenders and rolling his plug of tobacco into the other cheek.

"Well, everyone here already knows, of course, all about the terrible massacre at Rancheria," said Mrs. Ketchum, glancing around at her attentive audience. "We all know how poor Mrs. Dynan was murdered. And the shopkeeper. That poor, poor man! You know how they broke his legs with an axe? And how he ran out of the store afterwards, anyway? I understand it was the blow to his spine that finally killed him. He died in terrible, terrible pain."

The lady paused to press a hand to her heart and flutter her eyelids in well rehearsed horror. There were a few affirmations of her report among her listeners, and one or two expressions of sympathy for the unfortunate Albert France. But sensing that Mrs. Ketchum had scarcely warmed to her subject yet, the men waited in relative silence, eager for more.

"I'm told they caught three of the murderers' accomplices right there in town that same morning," the lady pursued. "And that their just punishment was mercifully swift. The rest of the Mexicans were expelled from the settlement. But you know that, don't you? Don't you? Yes. Well!

"That was the first day," Mrs. Ketchum confided. "On the second day, Mr. Williston, the leader of the outraged avengers . . . one can really scarcely blame him, or anyone, for the extravagance of his fury against these dreadful foreigners . . ." the lady paused and glanced around the room to find out if there were any examples of the benighted race within earshot. Seeing none, she continued:

"Anyway, Mr. Williston led a party through Rancheria,

demolishing the **miserable** huts of the Mexicans. I did hear, by the by, that one of the murderers' accomplices had been the owner of a **lucrative** claim which was afterwards bestowed on a man named Jimmy Johnson because he was the one on whose evidence the culprit was convicted.

"Well, and so, Mr. Williston and his committee were determined to discover whether or not the Mexicans had actually left the vicinity as directed. Did you **know** this? He went with his comrades across the hills toward Drytown, descending by way of a **desolate** arroyo called Mile Gulch. And there, he came upon the exiles. Can you imagine? He had never expected to find them so close by, you know.

"Of course it **is** true that they had left only the day before, and they had taken all their families and belongings **with** them, and they had only some donkeys and one or two horses, and of course, they all went **together,** so they couldn't have gotten very far. But they surely could have gone beyond Drytown, if they had tried to.

"Well, Mr. Williston and his men told them that they must move on **immediately** and take themselves completely out of the county. You hadn't heard this, had you? No. Well, in the confusion, there was a shot fired. I'm sure you can **imagine** the panic this caused. And apparently, there were several **Indians** following along after Mr. Williston, some of these hopeless aborigines that simply **refuse** to be useful in any way, even to **themselves** . . . and someone told one of them that if they wished to take revenge on the **Spaniards** who had originally deprived them of their homes and hunting grounds, this was a truly golden opportunity."

"How many Greasers did they scalp?" asked the miner of the red suspenders.

"Oh! I don't know about any **scalping,** sir! I don't think there was any. Mr. Williston was by, you know, to see that there was no actual **torture** committed. Besides, the Indians were soon distracted by the booty in the Mexican's encampment. The whole question of the Mexicans was really nothing to **them,** you know. But the truly **shocking** thing . . ."

The lady paused again to gather her resources, fluttering her lids and touching two fingers to her brow. "Oh, it's really too dreadful!" she declared.

One man jerked off his hat and fanned her with it, but Mrs. Ketchum drew back from this courtesy with an expression of distaste. And Mr. Ketchum, who seemed less interested in the drama of Mile Gulch, doubtless through increased familiarity with the story's telling, here chose to end the tale himself. "The savages killed only eight or ten of the Mexicans," he said. "And most of those were found and buried by a search party before sundown. But they do say they came across a body a couple of days later in a ditch where the poor beggar had crawled off to die of his wounds."

"Yes!" exclaimed Mrs. Ketchum. "But **tell** them, Frank, tell them how it was that they **found** him!"

"I don't believe it, myself," said Mr. Ketchum.

"Oh, but I do!" said his lady. "We heard it from an actual **eyewitness**!"

"What did they find?" asked another of the listeners.

"It was a pig. A pig! A man saw a **pig** in the ditch. The unhappy animal was actually **feeding** on the **corpse**!"

This announcement was rewarded by a moment of shocked silence, much to the satisfaction of the lady, and then a voice among the audience said, "There'll be a discount on pork this season, boys."

Laughter swept the room. Mrs. Ketchum turned first white and then pink. And amid the continued, rude amusement of her audience, she allowed her husband to lead her toward the door opening on the hotel's main corridor. "Never, in all my **life** . . .!" she was heard to say.

At the table in the corner by the window, Eli Smith had pushed back his plate, still half full, and turned to the view outside. He saw a Spaniard tying a tired, bay horse to the hitching rail beside his own bald-faced black. "Oh, m'gosh!" the boy breathed. Nobody heard him.

The entrance of Juan Solano a few moments later did not cause the mayhem that Eli expected, however. There was only a ripple of interest. "There's one the hogs missed," somebody said. A few fresh guffaws greeted this sally. And more eyes remained on the Californian than otherwise might have. But generally, the room returned to its own sundry amusements and the serious business of eating supper. Fourth Crossing was a long way from Rancheria.

Solano himself advanced slowly, his glance moving among the tables, keen on his search, oblivious to the mockery and noise. Eli watched him, heart beating fast, wishing he had left the room before, knowing it was too late to try it now, and waiting in breathless suspense for Solano's look to come inevitably around to him. Twice it slid by him. Twice Eli hid his face beneath the brim of his hat. But when he glanced up a third time, it was to meet the very eyes he had known he couldn't avoid much longer. And before he ducked under the cover of his drooping brim, again, he saw Solano coming toward him.

It seemed to take forever for don Juan to cross the room. There was an empty chair at Eli's table. From beneath his hat, the boy saw the lower half of the Spaniard's person as Solano pulled back the chair and sat down in it.

Eli's hands were on the table. He removed them to his lap where his rifle lay across his knees. He smoothed a short space on the barrel with one finger. Then he looked up.

Black eyes, bright and deep, expectant, burning, met his own. Eli tipped his head down again just far enough to shield him from Solano's gaze. But he continued to stare at the black mustache, the unshaven chin, the line of the mouth in between them. And while he watched, the mouth said softly, "I look for a boy that owns a black horse. Name is Eli Es-mitt. You know him?"

Eli nodded.

"I am call Juan Solano," the mouth under the black mustache said. "This boy, he means so much to me. I worry for him. I think he maybe goes to Seensome Bar. Is a mining camp almost as far from here as the town of Mokelumne Hill, but lies the other way. You know what are his plans?"

Eli drew an unsteady breath and braved another glimpse of
the dark eyes he could not meet for very long. "I spent some
of your money," he confessed. He touched one hand to the
hatband riding low over his brow. "There's fifty dollars of it
left. I've been trying to make it last."

"Is all of it yours, Pecosa."

Eli swallowed. "Who told you about the black horse?"
he asked.

"Rob Bricks is the friend of Baldés Hingsome."

"Oh." Eli raised a hand to rub his freckled nose. Then,
"I saw you . . . in Rancheria," he whispered.

"Yes, I know."

"I guess you must be pretty angry at me?"

Solano lay his arm down along the table top, his hand
palm up to ask for Eli's. "I am not angry," he said.

Wonderingly, Eli slipped his own right hand into Solano's, and like magic, the saloon of the Traveler's Inn vanished into thin air. It did not reappear until Solano spoke
again. "Have you spend any of these coins in your hat for a
room?"

"A room, supper, and breakfast," said Eli.

"I ask you take me to your room, then. Will be a better
place to talk. You let me talk to you?"

Eli nodded.

Solano gripped the boy's hand warmly as if terminating
a business proposition, then let go. Pushing back his chair,
he rose. "You are not finish with your supper?" he inquired
when Eli did not instantly get up as well.

"I've had enough, I guess," said Eli. The boy shoved
himself to his feet and slung his rifle over one shoulder by its
leather strap. "This way," he said, and passed the Spaniard to
walk on toward the far door of the dining room. Juan Solano
followed him.

CHAPTER FORTY-EIGHT:

THE ROOM AT THE
TRAVELER'S INN

It was a modest chamber at the end of the lower hall, just large enough for a bed and a washstand, a linen chest and a looming wardrobe which cut off most of the light from the single window, hung with a dirty curtain.

Ruiz glanced around as he closed the door behind him, tripped the latch, and threw the bolt. He took the mismatched pistols from his waist and laid them on the washstand.

Sydney stood between him and the window, her head bowed, still anticipating punishment. She had set her rifle to the wall. The evening light that filtered through the curtain outlined her hat, nose, lips and chin with a shining trace of gold.

"I'm sorry, Simón," she said reluctantly.

"Come here to me, Saidnay."

"I couldn't let you go off without me. I was afraid maybe they'd kill you. They almost did."

"Muñeca . . . come."

"I would have joined you at your camp in the canyon," she went on, "but I ran across García, and I had to watch him to see what he meant to do. And then when I saw Paul and the others, I was afraid you'd send me back with them to Jackson. To 'put me somewhere for a while,' like you said at the Sutherlands, until you were done chasing the cholos. I only wanted to help you. But you wouldn't let me."

"Saidnay, will you come?"

Slowly, she turned, and once started toward him, she could not stop herself. The space that separated them was not more than a few steps. Yet there was time for him to open his arms to her. Time for her to realize it was not punishment but amends that he was offering. And then, he was gathering her into him, pushing off the dark hat which fell on its string to hang at her back while he slid his fingers through the soft tangles of her hair and pressed her ear to his chest, laid his cheek to the top of her head.

In return, Simón felt Syndey's arms cinch tight around his ribs. Slight yet strong, alive and warm, she pushed against him, warming **him**, filling the empty hollowness still aching in his breast. He felt the swell and fall of her breathing and the rhythm of her heart beneath his own.

Turning her face into him, she kissed him, sowed his shirtfront with caresses. And every gentle touch healed a different wound his soul had taken in the last two weeks.

When she had mended every rend in the fabric of his spirit in this manner, she offered up her lips for him to kiss. He met them tenderly. But as he felt her mouth opening to his, moving with his, absorbing every shift of his, the warming oil that was already sliding through him ignited in a sweeping rush. His relief turned into ferment. This indomitable child he had married, this bundle of puzzling contradictions in his arms was suddenly the only thing he'd ever wanted, but her he absolutely had to have.

His hand swept down her back and, in passing, the wide cuff of the bandage that she wore. Its presence offended. "¡Niña! Why must you do this to yourself?" he demanded, drawing back to frown at her surprise.

"What?" she wondered, distracted still further as he jerked at her shirttail to free it from her belt. But the shirt was so long, and his patience so short, he abandoned the effort and felt for the front of the garment, began swiftly to unbutton it.

"To deny your beauty in this way," he scolded, pulling loose another length of cloth and working at its fastenings down to the buckle of her belt. "¡Es criminal!" He pushed the open shirt back off her shoulder, exposing to the half light of the room the swathing bands that bound her.

"But I have to," she explained, catching at his hand as it felt along her wrapping's lower edge for the end tucked underneath. "Without it, I'd bounce around . . . and give myself away."

"You bounce, then!" he commanded. "And yourself you give to me!"

Sydney stared at him, her face reddening more in affront than embarrassment, though she was still shy of showing herself to him and doubtful of its decency. "You want people to know I'm a girl dressed up like a man?" she asked.

"I want myself to know you are a girl when I look at you," he answered. Succeeding in freeing one end of the brown cloth bandage, he loosened its laps around her and saw her bosom push out to its normal shape. "Does it not hurt to tie the cloth so tight?" he insisted, putting back her hand as she tried to put back his.

"Some," she admitted, turning her face away. "But I have to do it or . . ." She interrupted herself with a small noise of shock and protest and involuntary pleasure at his touch. "Simón . . ."

"Mujer."

"Should you do that?"

"I will do more. These two pechos want me. ¿Sientes? They kiss at my fingers. They nest in my hand. You punish them, and so they have betray you. They tell me that you are a woman, after all. And for that I love them . . . cherish them . . . and you, just as I will." Backing her toward the bed, he undid the knot at her belt before he began to free himself from the encumbrance of his own clothes. For never had apparel seemed so useless a nuisance, strings and buttons such annoying obstacles.

And Sydney, caught in the whirl of her own emotions, could think of no way to prevent him. "Are you going to do that to me . . . again?" she asked.

"Again," he agreed, laying her down under him. "And again," he warned, as she squirmed to avoid him, "until you have learn to want it!"

This particular lesson did not take Sydney nearly as long as Ruiz expected. Between her surprising discovery that what he did to her hardly hurt at all this time, and the ever-intensifying joy of being held so tightly to him she could almost feel herself become a part of him, her reluctance rapidly diminished.

Upon sensing her attempt to participate in his passion, Simón's half anger burst in surprise and affection. He had been hungrily devouring the field of freckles on her face, but he returned now to her mouth to be met with an instantly addicting combination of hesitancy and new desire which rekindled all the liquid fire pumping through his veins.

But still he was not prepared for the power of the thing which swept them both up without warning, lifting them and binding them together as with supple coils of steel and casting them together through a nameless barrier, surrounded by a swirling force, like the eye of a hurricane.

Then as stealthily as it had come, this thing desolved around them and passed on, and they were left in a darkening, shabby room, with nothing but a lumpy bed, four blind, uncaring walls, and . . . each other.

Sydney continued to cling to Ruiz as if she were afraid to move.

"Se acabó, muñeca," he whispered, smoothing his hand over her hip. "Suéltame, pues. Relájate."

She looked up anxiously into his face. "Simón? What was that?"

He shook his head. "No sé."

"Haven't you done that before?"

"Like that, no. Let go of me, nena. I am all tangle up."

She complied hastily, suddenly conscious that their mutual position was graceless and that Simón, in particular, had some reason to complain. When she released him, he rolled to sit on the bedside and bent to sort out the puzzle of his long, linen underdrawers which were hobbling him around the knees and ankles.

Sydney used the interim of his preoccupation to shrug back into Will Sutherland's blue checked shirt, the only garment she still wore. The leather arm bands tying up its sleeves had prevented Ruiz from stripping it from her entirely, before. She had it buttoned and its long tail pulled down over her knees by the time he had straightened out his drawers and retied them round his waist.

He kicked off his boots, which he had neglected to shed earlier, and fell on his back with a sigh of satisfaction to look at her. By this time, Sydney was sitting with her legs tucked modestly beneath her and her shirt buttoned to her chin. Ruiz gazed at her a moment, then sat up to fetch her nearer. But she leaned away from his approach.

"Graciosa. ¿Qué tienes?"

"What?"

"I love you, Payasita."

"That wasn't what you said."

"You will have me loco with the funny things you do."

"I haven't done anything. Have I?"

"Payasa. ¡Payasita!"

"Are you going to tell me what that means?"

"Yes. Is what we call the one who travel with the circo, and dress in funny clothes always too big . . ." He gathered up her shirt's fullness at her waist in illustration. "The hair, he is all despeinado, going any way he wants . . ." He put back the rebellious curls from her brow. "The face, all paint to make it look like she is smiling. Yet underneath, is serious. And sad." Simón studied her quiet countenance, the red lashes of her downcast eyes. He saw a tear slide out from under them.

"You've been calling me . . . a clown," she realized aloud.

"Eh Clow? Is how you say?" he urged, interested to find out how much pain he could inflict upon himself like this, for the second tear to fall on Sydney's freckle-spattered cheek unseamed his heart and tore open all the wounds her love had sealed.

"Yep," she answered him, pulling at her shirttail as she noticed that a square inch of her knee was bared.

"But there are also other members of this circo that we call him 'Life', mi Payasita," said Simón. "One, he rides the well-train horse and wears fine, docorated clothes. Everyone they see him think he is so importante that he comes to think it, too. But then, a strange thing happens."

Syndey's gaze had started up at this, traveling the distance from the tied string of his drawers to his chin. His shirt hung open. He had not bothered to button it, again. And Ruiz could feel her look as if she'd touched him.

"Do you know what has happen to our caballero adornado?" he demanded.

She slightly turned her head from side to side.

"One day, he fall **off** this well-train horse he rides. And is a good thing that he does. Because when he looks up, he see eh clow. And this little clow, she is so beautiful, he can't believe. And she shows him how to do things he already thinks he knows . . . but doesn't. And she loves him, anyway. And our caballero learns the only thing is importante: to have his Payasita always near."

Now, Sydney's brown eyes raised to his, and though another tear or two spilled out onto her cheek, they were only those left over from her misunderstanding him. "Oh, Simón," she said.

"Mi preciosura de payasa . . ."

"I love you, Simón. I love you more than the whole, wide world is big around."

Ruiz gently stroked her tousled hair. "I cherish you," he told her.

In response, she rose onto her knees and threw both arms around his neck.

The shabby room, its ugly furniture, touched by the wand of love, was suddenly draped with cloth-of-gold and strewn with shining stars.

CHAPTER FORTY-NINE:

RECRUITING REINFORCEMENTS

"Juan Solano! Are you in there?" It was Baldy Hinkson's voice, and his fist that drummed a summons on the door. Even in his sleep, Ruiz knew who it was.

But Sydney didn't. She woke with a start against him and clutched at him in alarm. The room around them was pitch dark. They had been asleep for several hours. "Simón!" she breathed in warning.

He stirred and voiced a sigh.

"Solano!" called the cowboy outside the door.

"¡Diga, pues!" Ruiz roused himself enough to say.

"Is that you, Juan?"

"¡Sí, soy yo! ¿Qué traes, Baldés?"

"The sheriff's with me! He's wantin' to talk to you."

"Finits?"

"Phoenix. Are you comin'?"

"Sí . . . ya."

There was a pause while Baldy listened for sounds of stirring. He didn't hear any. He tried again. "Is Eli Smith in there with you?"

"Eli? ¡Ah, sí! Cómo no."

"Well, you tell Eli his brother's out here, too, and wantin' to be sure he's all right."

"Eli?" Ruiz asked loudly for Baldy's benefit. "You are all right?"

"We'd better get up, Simón," she whispered back.

"Ahora," he agreed, hunting across her face in the darkness for her mouth. Finding it, he settled down to kissing her until Hinkson knocked on the door again.

"Bueno . . . ¡bueno!" called Ruiz. Reluctantly, he rolled to the edge of the bed, pushed himself onto his feet and felt his way across the short space to the door, bumping into the washstand en route. "Carajo . . . que no veo nada," he muttered. He fumbled at the bolt and the latch and opened the door a short way, admitting enough light from the hallway for Sydney to be able to see. She sprang to the floor and snatched up Will Sutherland's dungarees, stepped into them. But her haste was not visible from the corridor.

"What time it is, Baldés?" asked Simón, first running a hand through his hair and then rubbing his whiskered cheek. "How far you have come today? How many are they with you?"

"It ain't midnight yet," replied the cowboy, looking Ruiz up and down, from his open shirt to the flared legs of his white drawers. Baldy pulled at his hatbrim and grinned beneath its cover. "The whole dang posse's here," he went on. "Except for Ike and Dan'l Perrin. They went back to Jackson with Bwin Roaster and García. We've come along from San Andreas. Where'd you find Eli?"

"Here," said Ruiz. He glanced back as Sydney came up behind him, fully dressed. She peered around him at the cowboy.

"Howdy, Eli!" Hinkson's grin widened. "You're sure one hell of a little horseman, ain't you? Has old Juan told you how we was after you? Briggs and McCormick and me?"

"I saw you myself," said Sydney.

"Yes, I bet my next wages you did! Well, Cecil's wantin' mighty bad to talk to you. Shall we send him here? Or are you comin' out to meet the posse with Juan?"

"I'm coming," said Syndey.

"Somehow I figured you would be."

But if Baldy was not surprised to see Sydney with Ruiz when Simón came back into the main saloon of the Traveler's Inn, the rest of the posse was. And they found her presence awkward, though only three of them—the cowboy Sherill, Constable Cross, and George Durham—had not already met her before.

Even Cecil did not know what to say. He rose from the table where the sheriff's men were finishing supper. Will Sutherland and Rob Briggs got up also. Paul started to but changed his mind. None of them spoke. The rest of the room watched the rendezvous with increasing interest. There were some drinkers near the bar who continued to make their jolly noise, but for a Saturday night and the size of the crowd, the atmosphere in the Traveler's Inn became almost reverent.

"Señor . . .!" said Phoenix, leaving his chair to acknowledge Simón's approach. "Solano, is it?" he added, extending his hand.

"A sus órdenes," said Ruiz, meeting the officer's firm grip.

"And you're Eli." Phoenix turned an eye of recognition on Sydney. "Or is it Billy Hall from Amador City?"

"Both," said Sydney and held out a hand for the sheriff to shake.

Cecil made a strange noise which was not quite a word and glanced at Paul McCormick. But he looked away as Paul's eyes turned toward him.

Phoenix, however, remained unruffled. "You're Solano's new partner, I gather," he said, accepting Sydney's hand and pressing it briefly.

"Yep. I am," she agreed, resisting the impulse to look up at Simón as she said it.

"Well, you'd better sit down with us, then, and listen in. Don Juan? Have a chair," the sheriff added, motioning both Ruiz and Sydney to sit down.

Will Sutherland, Rob Briggs, and Cecil resumed their seats as well. But only Constable Cross and the cowboy, Sherill, gave any more attention to their supper.

"Baldy will have told you how we sent Buenrostro and García to Jackson with an escort?" Phoenix said to Ruiz. "I think we have you to thank for the rescue of the one and the capture of the other."

"Only by coincidencia," said Simón. "Eli does more than I do. And I am still much concern about my friend Fidel."

"I can understand how you might be. I'd have liked to send more men back to Jackson with him and García, but there was fewer of us than there was of the outlaws to begin with, and I didn't want to unbalance the odds too far in their favor. Do you know anything about a Mexican found dead in the Eureka Dance Hall in Jackson?"

"Is not mexicano," replied Ruiz, leaning back in his chair. "Is chileno. Call himself Pío Pinto."

"The man who killed him acted in self defense, no doubt?"

"He did, Señor."

"Any witnesses to what happened?"

"Dos: A woman she live there. A girl who work for her."

"Where are they, now?"

"I do not know, Cheriff. I have warn them they should leave the town because I fear for what might be done to them after what is happening in Ranchería. But where they will go they must choose for themselves."

"Did you warn anybody else?"

"The padre of San Gabriel."

"Yes, I guess that would have about done the business," mused Phoenix. "García told us there were two more men with him watching for you in the Moke River Gorge," he went on. "Did you run across either of them?"

"One," said Ruiz.

"Self defense again?"

"Self defense," agreed Simón.

"No witnesses to that one, I suppose?"

"No, Señor. You have only my word."

"What happened to the other man?"

"He get away."

"Did you know the names of either of them?"

"No. But if I see the second man again, I will recognize him."

"And vice versa?"

"Viceversa," admitted Ruiz. "But these cholos, they know who I am from before."

"Where were you planning to look for them, next?"

"I go to Sonora."

"Did you intend to take Eli with you?"

Simón put a hand on the back of Sydney's chair in a gesture at once friendly and protective. "Eli goes with me from now on," he proclaimed. And he looked from Phoenix to Cecil Simpson and Paul McCormick, then on to Baldy Hinkson and Will Sutherland and Briggs. His glance settled a moment on Constable Cross before it moved to Durham. His expression contracted into disapproval as he considered the Tax Collector. But before George felt it actually necessary to object to the implied criticism of his office, Simón's attention shifted to Sherill. "Who are you, Señor?" Ruiz inquired of the second cowboy.

"My friends call me Sherry," was the reply. "I work for the Sutherlands. I went to town with Baldy and Will the night you and Eli turned up at the Dry Creek Spread."

"Ah," said Ruiz. "Cherry. Mucho gusto."

"Señor Solano," said Phoenix, bringing Simón's level look back around to him, "I have a proposition to make you. And Eli. A couple of our men have had to drop out of the chase, as you know. But the outlaws have now also lost three of their band. If you two are willing to ride with us, we'll have more than evened up the odds. There were twelve of them to start with, according to what you told Will?"

"Doce, sí."

"Is that counting Manuel Escobar?"

Again, Simón's face changed. The brightness of his dark gaze sharpened into a deep, fierce glitter. "No," he said. "Is not counting Escobar. But I have not forget him. Is that I do not think he will travel with the others. Nor dare to be associate with them. Manuel I find somewhere alone."

Phoenix felt in his pocket for his handkerchief. "Solano," he said, his voice husky with the cough he would not allow to interrupt him, "I want one thing well understood. And that goes for the rest of you men," he added, his look sweeping the group around the table. "We're not on a wolf hunt. We're not even looking to meet these bandits in a stand-off. Our mission is to capture them. And bring them back for trial. Law and Order, gentlemen, is what we represent. Not Vengeance. Not even Justice. That is the function of the court. And if any man of you tries to take the law into his own hands . . ." Phoenix looked pointedly at Durham and from him to Ruiz. "That man will find himself tied to his saddle and headed for jail. Is that clear to all of you?"

No one spoke. But a few heads nodded slightly in response.

"As for Escobar . . ." But Phoenix had postponed his cough beyond his ability to control it, and here he must pause to answer to his ailment. During his seizure, the posse exchanged looks and the spectators shifted uneasily; some of them drew closer. A few soft-voiced speculations were made in reference to the sheriff's state of health and whether he would be able to keep on in his usual tireless style. Sydney glanced up at Simón.

Ruiz had not let go of her chairback. The growing strength of his grip and the tenseness in his arm had immobilized the seat completely. Sydney sensed its new solidity. But Simón did not return her look.

Finally, Phoenix wiped his eyes and returned his handkerchief to his pocket. "Solano?" he said to Ruiz. "Are you with us?"

Simón drew a breath. "I am with you, Cheriff," he said.

"And Eli's with you?"

"And Eli," confirmed Ruiz, "is with me."

Everyone looked at Sydney. Even Simón, this time. But there was that in his eyes as she met them that gave her the courage to ignore the others. The corners of her mouth even tilted toward a smile before she looked down at her hands in her lap.

"Well, then," concluded Phoenix, "this posse had better get some rest. We're riding for Sonora in the morning. Solano, have you and Eli already had supper?"

"I did, but he didn't," Sydney informed the sheriff.

"Then, we'll get some for him," said Phoenix. And he signaled to a waiter who had been watching the scene as avidly as most of the others in the room.

"Sheriff!" said Cecil Simpson, starting up from his chair. "If the general discussion's over, I'd like a word with Eli in private. If it's all right with everybody present."

Ruiz turned a dark eye on Sydney. There was some amusement in his glance this time. "Eli? Is all right with you?"

Sydney frowned. But she shrugged her shoulders. "Sure," she said. "Fine."

Ruiz pulled back her chair with Sydney still in it. "Vete, Pecosa. I come after you, soon."

CHAPTER FIFTY:

A DISSENTING OPINION

"I hope you're satisfied, Sydney Simpson!" Cecil began, the moment the door closed behind them.

Sydney lit the candle on the washstand with the one she had brought from the dining room. "I am," she said.

"Well, you certainly should be!"

"I said I was."

"First, you trick Simón into having to marry you! Then, you force him to take you along with him after the outlaws! And now, with more brass than a door knob, you come marching out into that saloon full of men and muscle your way into the sheriff's posse!"

"I did not," said Sydney.

"Oh, no! And I suppose Simón was dead in love with you from the minute we picked him up off the road! He just couldn't help himself, could he?"

"I didn't say that."

"No, and you'd better not think it, either. While you were sitting out there with that smug look on your face, he stared us all down, but nobody was fooled. They saw that you had got your way with him, and there wasn't anything anybody could do about it. Because Sheriff Phoenix wants Ruiz along for what he knows about the bandits. And maybe to keep an eye on him so he won't take the law into his own hands any more than he already has. Maybe even for bait, in a way. The outlaws want him. They told George Durham the morning before the massacre at Rancheria that if the sheriff would just give them Ruiz, they'd leave the country. That's how much they want him! Or maybe Phoenix thinks he has to protect him. And you! Because nobody can trust either one of you to stay put and do what you're told!"

Syndey said nothing. She had been dripping wax onto the flat top of the bedpost to form a base for the second candle. She was not the first guest to have done this. But Cecil objected:

"Just what are you doing?"

"Nothing."

"Have you got anything to say for yourself?"

"Simón loves me. He told me so."

"Sure, why not? He may as well make the best of it."

Sydney forced the candle stub into the warm wax. "Have you got something more you want to talk about?"

"Why did you do it, Syd?" Cecil asked in a different voice.

She looked back at him. He stood beside the washstand, his shoulders drooping tiredly, his long, narrow face longer and narrower with his shame and defeat.

"Do what?" she said.

"All of it. Run away . . . marry Simón . . ."

"You knew why I ran away. I even told you I was going to. I guess you didn't believe me."

"Yes, I did."

"And I didn't really mean to marry Simón. I just told him I would be his vaquero, like he said before. And he asked me if I was sure it was what I wanted to do. And I said 'yes'. And then, he took me to the church and married me in Spanish and Latin. I didn't even figure out what was going on until it was too late."

"You must be stupid or something."

Sydney sat down on the bed. She smoothed a wrinkle in the blanket. Then she looked up at her brother.

Cecil stared back. His sober face suddenly flushed. "You little b . . .!" he tried to say. But he couldn't. Turning on his heel, he threw open the door and went out, slamming it behind him.

Sydney sat where she was, stroking the blanket. The minutes passed. The candle on the bedpost burned steadily, weeping tears of hot wax. Sydney boosted herself farther onto the bed and lay back on the pillow, pulled one side of the blanket around her and stared at the ugly room. She thought about leaving. There was the window. It was on the first floor, so there wasn't much of a drop below it. Her black horse still stood at the hitching rack in front of the hotel. Unless the sheriff had made someone put it in the stable. He probably had. If she had put it there herself instead of coming into the Inn for supper right away, none of this would have happened. Simón wouldn't have seen it and known she was here. Both he and the posse might have come and gone without knowing she was here. And she could have followed at a distance as before.

Too late, now. And running away was no good, this time. "Where are you running to, Sydnipper?" she could hear her father ask her. At the age of five, she had determined to leave home . . . not out of anger or unhappiness, but just to seek her fortune like the people in the stories he had told her. But she had gotten tired. And lost. And terribly lonely. She felt that way again, now. But her father couldn't come and rescue her as he had done then. Only Simón could come. And he would have to come. What else could he do?

Keeping a hold on the blanket, Sydney rolled over, wrapping herself inside its cocoon and hiding her face in the pillow. A moment later, she heard the door open. She heard Ruiz' step. She heard the door softly close. And then, it was quiet. So quiet, she wasn't sure he was still in the room. She rolled over and sat up.

He was standing just inside the door, looking at her. "¿Te dieron duro?" he asked gently.

She lay back.

He came past the washstand, pausing to blow out the candle there, and sat down on the bedside. "He is quite a man, this Cheriff Finits," he said. "You have to respect him. You see he is sick, and yet he keeps on. What he will be like when he is well?" Ruiz pried off his boots, began to unbutton his pantlegs down both sides. "But he is dreaming to think he can take all the cholos back to Yackson alive. How does he do it?"

Simón rose to fold the odd garment which now seemed to be little more than two strips of cloth, heavy on one side with buttons. The metal disks clinked as he laid the pants on the linen chest. He unfastened his shirt in a series of quick twists. "Gringos!" he mused. "With their gringo Law and Order. Their courts and their trials. Is such a parodia! Who they get to be a jury is not bias? Who will prove these men kill anyone? And who will wait for proof? Who has wait at Ranchería? Innocent or guilty, they will hang them. Why not shoot them? What difference does he make?"

Simón took off his shirt and tossed it after the pantalón. It fell on the linen chest but slid to the floor. With a quiet word of impatience, he retrieved it, draped it over the trunk. Then he came back to the bed and lay down beside Syndey, turning toward her and propping himself up on one elbow. In the light of the candle stub, the skin of his chest and arms shone like bronze. "What has my brother-law say

to my little clow to take all the smile from her heart?" he
wondered.

Sydney closed her eyes. "Was it hard for you to kill
those men, Simón?"

"Not so hard, no. Why you have ask me?"

"Because. I tried to kill García. I had him in my sights. I
knew he was after you to kill you. I knew he was a bandit,
that he had been part of all those murders in Ranchería. But
I couldn't shoot him."

"Does he see you? Does he threaten you?"

"No."

"Por eso. To kill from ambush is too hard for anyone is
not a coward," said Ruiz. "Because you know it is unfair. But
to kill a man who has attack you . . . to kill in self
defense . . . is not so hard."

"Is that how you killed Pío Pinto? And the other one?"

"Don't you hear me say so to the cheriff?"

"Yep."

"Then? You think that I have lie to him?"

"I didn't say that."

"Pecosa . . . César is very angry with you?"

"Yep."

"But surely you expect this?"

"Not exactly. See Saw knows I can ride and shoot as
well as he can. Better! So, why shouldn't I get to go with the
posse if he does?"

"You are a woman."

Sydney frowned deeply and turned her head away. "It
looks like Phoenix is taking you along to keep you out of
trouble," she said, "and you're taking me along to keep me
out of it. Why don't they just handcuff us together and lock
us up somewhere?"

"Not to let your brother to distress you, Saidnay. Is hard
for him to see you in these circunstancias. He is use to be the
one who love you most and take responsibility for you. Now,
suddenly, he sees me doing this. Is natural, his jealousy. But
he will not stay angry. Give him time."

Sydney was silent for so long that Simón finally touched
her shoulder to see if she slept. She turned her head to look
at him. "Do you really love me?" she demanded. Her face
betrayed her doubt and pain.

"¡Ay, Payasa! Not only you think I have lie to the
cheriff, but also I have lie to you?"

She turned away. "I've been a real problem for you, haven't I?"

"¡Pchss . . .! Perhaps you have take my attention away
from things less important."

"The posse doesn't want me along."

"Allá ellos."

"I wish you wouldn't do that."

"Speak Spanish? But he is my language, Saidnay. You
must learn him. I will teach you. ¡Ve! This room that we are
in is call 'la habitación'. What we lie on is the 'cama'. Light is
shining from a 'vela' is about to 'extinguirse'. But the 'luz'
that you have light up in the heart of Simón Ruiz shine on
through 'la eternidad'. Now, you repeat. What is 'the room'?"

"Lobby-something."

"Bed?"

"Camel. I don't know."

"How have I say 'candle'?"

"Payla."

"And for how long do I love you?"

She was silent.

"How long do you love me?"

She met his eyes again. And then, she threw aside the
blanket and rolled into his arms.

"¿Para siempre?" he suggested.

"That better mean 'forever'! Simón . . . . ¿otro?"

"Una multitud, Payasa," he replied.

CHAPTER FIFTY-ONE:

CHASING THE CHOLOS

The posse left Fourth Crossing early Sunday morning. They stopped in Angels Camp to eat breakfast and to ask for news of the outlaws. They learned little. There had been Mexicans riding the roads, they were told, but there had been no reports of robbery. Nor any other suspicious activity. The posse paid its bills and pushed on.

By noon, they were in Tuttletown. Here, Phoenix had more hope of gaining fresh intelligence of the fugitives, for Benjamin Tuttle knew several of the outlaws by sight, and he had his own reasons for wanting them caught. But no Mexicans had been through Tuttletown since the day they had robbed his general store.

"Like as not, they crossed the Stanislaus River between Vallecito and Columbia," said Tuttle. "That route to Sonora ain't much longer, and it'd be a helluva lot safer for them sons of bitches. 'Cause if they was to show their dirty noses here again, I'd shoot 'em off." He looked meaningly at the Californian who had entered with Phoenix and two others. One of these was a half-grown boy.

"You've heard no rumors from Sonora?" asked the sheriff.

"Nope," said Tuttle. "But Sonora's a tough town. It'd take more than a handful of chili-eaters to make a dent in it. If I was you, I'd take the road through Rawhide to Jamestown. If your band of thieves is still headed south, they'd be more apt to make some impression there."

Phoenix applied to Ruiz who stood quietly by. "Solano? What's your thought on that?"

"Is no farther to Sonora if we go first to Jame Estow. And if there is word of them there, we save ourself the longer ride. I think this advice is good."

"All right. But we'll rest here for an hour, first. Tuttle, this posse's funds are running low. I hate to have to ask it of you, but if you'll feed my men on credit, I'll send you full payment as soon as I get back to Jackson."

The storekeeper could not refuse. But his glower at Solano lowered.

"Mister," said the boy who had kept near Ruiz' elbow, "this isn't one of the bandits you're looking at."

Tuttle's glance shifted. "Some kids are always too big for their britches no matter what size they wear," he observed. "Where'd you come from, Short Stack?"

But it was Phoenix who answered. "I advise you to keep

on the boy's good side, Mr. Tuttle. He's the best shot of the posse."

The storekeeper grunted. "You're recruitin' 'em pretty young, Sheriff," he said.

"Simón?" the boy whispered as they left the building shortly afterwards. "Wasn't it Sonora you were wanting to get to?"

"I don't expect the bandidos they are there," Solano answered. "Only Manuel perhaps is there. On our way back, we find him."

Tuttle's hunch proved correct. On the outskirts of the settlement of Jamestown lived a small number of Mexicans, and Solano volunteered to find out what they knew about the bandits. Eli Smith went with him.

"Good day to you, friend," Solano greeted in Spanish the first man who would meet his eye. "I bring you an opportunity to serve the interests of your countrymen . . . all of us . . . who, like yourself, must find a way to survive among the unwelcome strangers that have taken over California."

The man regarded him suspiciously. "I am at your service, Patrón," he said.

"There may have passed this way a group of thieves fleeing the justice pursuing them from a place called Ranchería."

"Perhaps," agreed the other.

"If there is anything you are able to tell about these men, you can confide it to me without fear of becoming embroiled yourself. You see that I have not asked your name. I hold you responsible for nothing. But if these thieves are harbored by other Mexicans, our suffering as a nation of exiles will increase. Therefore, I advise you to speak."

"You are the one they call Ruiz," said the townsman.

"I am," agreed Solano.

"I wish I could trust you, Patrón."

"If you do not, it is only because the fabric of our society is so decayed, it rends at the touch of a soiled finger. Through fear, you have served base men without honor.

Through fear, you dare not serve a man who had dedicated his life to honor. I am deeply grieved by your fear, my friend. But I shall not blame you for it. I have seen the injustice of the Americans. I have seen innocent men lose their lives to unreasoning anger and hatred. Yet I cannot believe that sheltering thieves will in any way prove to our advantage. Are we to goad the Americans to further excesses for the sake of those we ourselves would not tolerate to live among us?"

The townsman was silent. But Solano did not move on. He waited for the other to reconsider.

"Who is this young gringo with you, Patrón?" the man asked.

"He is an orphan I am protecting. He knows no Spanish. You can speak freely before him."

"But do you ride with the gringos yourself in order to serve the interests of the Mexicans? Or is it only to avenge yourself on your own personal enemies?"

"The bandits I am presently helping to pursue I would not dignify by such a term, Señor. I have only one personal enemy. You may know who he is. Or even where he is. Yet I shall not ask you to tell me. Good day to you, friend." Solano lifted his horse's reins as if to ride on.

"Wait," said the townsman softly. "I would not have you think that I am an outlaw myself, or that I have any sympathy for such men. I am Carlos Ocampo, and I wish to aid you. But I must survive here, also. You may not hold me responsible, but others do. I risk my very life through what I'm going to tell you: if you ride straight on to the end of the street and turn left, in a brush corral you will see several horses that the thieves have forced some among us to accept in exchange for fresh mounts. These animals have been ridden to the point of death. We do not dare keep them, for they are stolen, and if they are seen by the gringos, we will be accused of taking them. Yet neither did we dare refuse them."

"You will not be accused," said Solano. "Tell me where your own horses are, and I will do what I can to return them to you."

"Patrón," said Ocampo, his voice sinking to little more than a whisper, "el portugués has taken the road toward Woods Crossing. He will surely go to Mexican Camp, thinking to hide among its people. Few gringos go there."

"When did he pass through here?"

"Only this morning."

"Describe the horses you have lost."

Ocampo glanced around uneasily. A few of his neighbors had come to their doors and stood openly watching. "I dare not. Only my own," he said. "It is a fine animal. A palomino with three white feet. The Portuguese took it for himself. I had raised it from a foal. Its loss is grievous to me. I would risk much to get it back."

"You need risk nothing," vowed Solano. "I shall return the animal to you personally. Until then, my friend. Adiós." And motioning his young companion to turn back with him, Solano reined his horse around and jogged off to rejoin the posse waiting for him in the Anglo heart of Jamestown.

* * *

It was nearly sunset when Phoenix and his men reached Mexican Camp. "Sheriff," said Constable Cross, pushing nearer to Phoenix as they sighted the adobes, tents and woodframe buildings of the village, "you don't think Solano is leading us into a trap here, do you?"

Phoenix looked sharply at his fellow officer. "If I thought so, would I follow him?"

Cross kept his own eyes riveted on the pair that rode ahead of them: the Californian whose elegance of bearing proclaimed him thoroughly a gentleman from sole to crown, notwithstanding the coating of road dust. And the strange girl who rode beside him, the reverse of refined, yet graceful as all wild things must be, in spite of her baggy clothes and her convincing charade of boyishness. "This is the oddest sort of chase I was ever on," said Cross. "And when we finally find ourselves face to face with the outlaws, those two are going to be more hindrance than help, I'm thinking."

"I'd rather ride into Mexican Camp with Solano than without him," countered Phoenix. "And Miss Eli Sydney Hall is his responsibility. And her brother's. Relax, Cross. You look as stiff as a gringo riding into a Mexican camp."

The constable grunted. "More than one of us may leave this place even stiffer before morning," he said.

Behind them, Baldy Hinkson rode closer to Sherill. "Is it me?" he demanded. "Or is the breeze suddenly cooler than it was?"

Sherry rolled his eyes at him. "You keep your shudders to yourself, you rat-tailed old coyote! I ain't forgot how you shivered on the steps of John Dynan's Hotel."

"You feel it, too, don't you?"

"All I feel is a shift in the wind's direction. And that ain't so surprisin' at sundown."

"Better loosen your side-iron in its holster."

"Shut up, Baldy," Sherill advised him.

The town before them was laid out in the typical Spanish square, one side of which abutted the rising slope of the hills behind it. Solano led the posse directly into the dusty plaza and reined in to the rail in front of the largest building on the square: a dance hall/cantina.

Sunday night in Mexican Camp was no less noisy than elsewhere in the Mother Lode. But there was a difference: an undercurrent of watchfulness, of discontent, which could erase the broadest smile in an instant. The arrival of the sheriff's posse drew many looks of hostility, both veiled and open.

Solano dismounted easily, apparently as oblivious to the unease of his American companions as to its cause. But he stooped under the neck of Eli's black to be near him as the boy swung down. "Pecosa," he said softly, "tonight you are my shadow. If you leave my side for one single moment, I will shoot up the town to find you. You will obey me, this time?"

Eli nodded solemnly.

"Then, come." Solano moved among the horses to where Phoenix was dismounting. Eli followed closely.

"What's your game, Solano?" Phoenix asked him, appraising the facade of the cantina and the crowd that pushed both in and out of it. Light and music spilled with the people from the open doors. The plaza itself was darkening. "You don't expect to find the outlaws inside there?"

"Señor, a dance hall is a better place to hide than many. I have even use him once like that myself. Yes, I think that we may find them here." He looked around among the animals which stood tied to the racks. Some were hitched to the saddlehorns of others. Still more were crowded round a wagon, secured to every spoke and slat available. "Do you see a palomino?" Solano asked the sheriff.

Eli plucked at the Mexican's sleeve and pointed. Under the only tree which graced the plaza, another group of mounts was tied. And between two darker rumps, a golden one was plainly visible, even in the fading light. A white tail swished as if to call attention to itself, and white hind feet moved nervously. "¡Ahí!" exclaimed Solano. "Cheriff, the chase has ended. Do you wish to go in?"

CHAPTER FIFTY-TWO:

THE CANTINA AT MEXICAN CAMP

Eli was glad of Solano's steadying hand on his shoulder as they entered the cantina. But once inside, the noise and activity, the drifting cigarillo smoke and the quick-rhythmed music so absorbed him, the boy forgot all else and stared about in fascination.

The new-arrivals did not go unnoticed. A woman of dark, exotic beauty came immediately to accost and welcome Juan Solano. Eli saw her in frank admiration. He was surprised at how coldly Solano received her warm advances. But the lady was not put off. Two other girls joined her to direct coquettish curiosity past Solano at the American men. And this drew the increasing attention of the Mexican men. Within a few moments of their entering the dance hall, the posse had become the main attraction.

They were made to sit down. Drinks were offered and accepted, for it did not seem wise to refuse. But no pertinent questions were asked by either side. The dark beauty then proposed to dance for them. And accordingly, a group of musicians came forward to accompany her. The resulting performance was the most dazzling thing Eli had ever witnessed. Several other members of the posse thought so, too. But Solano was not impressed. Nor was Phoenix. Nor Cross. Nor Durham.

The Tax Collector looked about him with such detachment he noticed what the entertainment may have been devised to disguise: three or four Mexican men were slipping out a rear exit, and a girl who stood beside it was making guarded but urgent gestures to someone else outside. George watched for a moment in growing suspicion. And then he sprang to his feet. For in spite of the girl's repeated warnings, a man he remembered only too well appeared briefly in the doorway. "Gonzalves!" Drawing his gun as he spoke the name, Durham charged across the room.

The music stopped. For the space of three heartbeats, a breathless silence was broken only by the Tax Collector's running footsteps thudding on the wooden floor. And then, the posse leaped after him, knocking over chairs and benches, spilling the table onto its side. The dancing girl screamed. Wild confusion swept the crowd.

Phoenix reached the doorway only moments after Durham. "George!" he shouted, catching the Tax Collector's arm. "We want prisoners! Not corpses!"

Durham had already fired twice. Impatiently, he locked eyes with the sheriff as from the half light of the brushy hillside a pistol spat a crimson spark in answer.

Phoenix tightened his hold on Durham's arm. He stared in stunned surprise at the Tax Collector while a scarlet splotch grew rapidly around the neat, dark hole that had just appeared in his own lapel. He tried to cough and choked. Then his grip relaxed, and he fell heavily against Will Sutherland who was pushing through the door.

"Sheriff!" exclaimed Durham. Another shot from the hillside recalled him. "You goddam Greasers!" cried George, his voice rising to a note of desperation. And he ran from the doorway, snapping bullets after a shadowy figure dodging away from bush to bush.

By the time he had reached the first cover, George had to stop to reload. "Durham!" came the voice of Will Sutherland. George did not even look back. Panting more from emotion than exertion, he peered around the bush to locate his former target. A shot from a different quarter half lifted the hat from his head, the bullet whining like a hornet through its crown. In response, a spatter of gunfire issued from the rear of the dance hall; the rest of the posse had erupted from the doorway around Will Sutherland and Phoenix.

"Is he too badly hurt?" asked Solano, dropping to his knees beside the rancher's son. Will looked up, white-faced, from where he knelt, half supporting Phoenix against him. "He's dead," he said huskily.

"¡Muerto! No!" But the light of the open doorway showed plainly enough the fixed stare of the officer's eyes, the irregular map of slick scarlet spreading downward from his breast.

A singing shell ricocheted off the doorjamb above their heads. Eli Smith sank to his heels beside Solano with a quick intake of breath. "Let's get under cover, Simón!"

"¡Cierto! Come," Solano added to Sutherland. "I help you move him."

Half carrying, half dragging Phoenix between them, the two men removed the sheriff to the shelter afforded by a cluster of large, empty barrels which stood in the shadows to one side of the door.

"Don Simón," said Will as he stood erect, "this is going to make things a whole lot worse. You know? Phoenix was . . . ah!" Sutherland was interrupted by the explosion of a pistol at close range. But Ruiz had seen the movement on the far side of the barrels, and he threw out an arm to shield the rancher's son. The bullet plunged into the muscle above Simón's right elbow, glancing off the bone and boring free.

Ruiz staggered with the impact and the pain, but he hurtled his weight against the nearest barrel, smashing it into the others. A second shot fired over their heads, and a voice began cursing in Portuguese.

Will Sutherland dodged forward among the jostling barrels, shoving them into to a still wilder dance, and sending one careening off from the rest in his search for their adversary. He came on him in another instant. The Brazilian had lost his balance as a barrel had struck him, and he was just getting to his feet. He still held a gun. Will seized the rim of a tottering cask and sent it spinning into him, felling the man a second time. Before the bandit could rise, Sutherland kicked the gun from his hand and drew his own weapon. "Freeze!" he warned. "I'll blow your head off! Ruiz!" he called without looking away from Gonzalves. "Are you all right?"

But there was no answer. Simón had regained his feet in time to see a dark man leap from the opposite side of the doorway and seize Eli by the wrist.

Ruiz caught up to them before they reached the corner of the building, for Eli did not go willingly, and his captor was not able to cuff him into either submission or unconsciousness. Had the boy's rifle been cocked, the struggle would have ended almost before it began. As it was, Eli was using the long barrel to counter the blows of his assailant while he kicked at the man's legs, impeding his stride.

Ruiz tried to draw his knife. But his right arm would not obey him. Feeling at his waist with his left hand, he took out one of his pistols, and as he came within reach of the outlaw from behind, he jammed its muzzle against his ribs. "¡Torres! ¡Suéltela!"

The outlaw cursed in surprise and let go of his hostage whose first act was to cock the rifle and level it at her captor's midriff. "Simón? Are you all right?" she asked.

"Seguro. ¿Y tú?"

"Seguro," she echoed. "Who's this?" She poked her rifle at Torres. "Is he one of them?"

"Sí. Is the man who kill Albert France in Ranchería. García tell the cheriff so. This man we give to the posse alive. They want the pleasure to hang him, I think. ¡No se mueva, Torres!" Ruiz warned as he felt the bandit stir against the muzzle of his gun. "Saidnay, if you will come behind here, I ask you take off my faja and use to tie his hands."

Sydney sidled around Torres to comply. But she gasped as she saw Ruiz' dangling arm and blood-soaked sleeve. "Simón! You're hurt!"

Counting on the unguessed injury to be enough to delay Ruiz' reaction, Juan Torres acted in the instant of what he hoped was his advantage. But he was mistaken. As he threw himself forward, Simón fired. And Torres fell, shot through the side. Still, the outlaw lived, and in a desperate attempt to take Ruiz with him into death, he rolled over and fired back at the figure he could see silhouetted above him against the evening sky.

Then Sydney's rifle spoke, and Torres did not shoot again.

"Simón!"

"He miss me, Saidnay. Sutterlan!"

"Ruiz!" returned the rancher's son from the far side of the doorway.

"Simón, your arm . . .!" said Sydney.

"Bandage him for me?"

"I need more light to see to do it. Come to the corner."

Will Sutherland soon joined them there, bringing Gonzalves with him. "Who was that on the ground?" he asked, stopping his prisoner before him. He kept a grip on the Brazilian's collar and a gun point to his back.

"Juan Torres," replied Ruiz, eyeing Gonzalves.

Sydney was using part of Simón's waist sash to bind his arm. She looked past him at the outlaw.

Gonzalves returned their stares until repeated gunfire from the town beyond claimed all their attention.

Wounded but still mobile, another of the bandits had turned at bay in a doorway to the side of the adjacent building, a two story frame house. Every few moments, he knocked at the door for admittance, but it remained closed against him. And meanwhile, three possemen were working their way through the brush on the hillside, trying to gain a clear shot at him without exposing themselves to his return fire. One of these was Cecil Simpson. Another was the cowboy, Sherill. And the third was George Durham.

The Tax Collector had used up his ammunition. He was armed with only a hatchet that he had taken from the belt of one of the two Mexicans who lay dead in the brush behind him. George crouched like a wolf beside a clump of greasewood, his eyes fixed on his quarry, waiting for the moment in which the bandit would fire his last bullet and have to reload.

That moment came as the cowboy Sherry risked a short run to the next cover. The outlaw in the doorway had one shell left. He made it count. Sherill stumbled and fell, rolled downslope.

As if possessed by demons, Durham charged. The wounded outlaw did not see him coming until the very last. He turned in an attempt to parry the blow of Durham's hatchet, but George fell on him with a reckless fury that brooked no opposition.

Those watching from the corner of the cantina saw the Tax Collector swing his avenging blade again and again, though its first blow had split the man's skull and killed him.

"Durham!" shouted Sutherland; then, "Cross!" as he saw the Constable making for the hillside. "Damn it, Ruiz, I know you're hurt. But can you and Eli hold this prisoner between you? Cross! Over here!" And surrendering Gonzalves to Simón and Sydney, Sutherland ran to intercept the constable.

It took Cross and Will both to stop the Tax Collector. Durham's blood was up, and he had seen Albert France in Rancheria after the bandits' attack. The shopkeeper had been one of the few men George had counted as a friend.

He resisted Cross when the constable tried to take away

his hatchet. Will Sutherland shoved him back against the door. "Durham! Are you gone crazy?"

George looked from one of them to the other, slowly relinquished his hatchet to the constable. "This one killed Phoenix," he explained hoarsely.

"The sheriff wanted prisoners," Sutherland reminded him. "I heard him tell you so. Come to your senses, man! Don't you remember what he said before? Law and Order! Not Vengeance! Not even Justice . . .! Do you think the rest of us aren't shocked and grieved?"

The door that had held against the bandit here opened wide, and Rob Briggs was with them in a flood of light across the sill. "Cross! Sutherland! My God! What's happened here? Mr. Durham? Are you bad hurt?"

"He's all right, Briggs. The blood's not his. He just needs a minute to steady down. How're things with you?"

"We've taken quite a number prisoner, Constable. Some of the townspeople have helped us. But we're damned if we can tell the innocent from the guilty. McCormick and Hinkson are holding them all in the plaza while I came looking for you and Ruiz. I mean Solano. Likely he can sort things out for us. Where is he? Have you seen him?"

"He and his . . . boy are there by the corner," said Sutherland, gesturing. "Or they were. Suppose you walk Mr. Durham to the plaza. The Constable and I will bring Ruiz as soon as we find him. Sherry's down. We saw him fall. Cecil's probably with him by now, but we don't know how bad he was hit."

Will found Simón and Sydney where he'd left them. But not quite as he'd left them. Gonzalves lay unconscious on the ground, his hands tied behind him with the rest of Simón's waist sash. Ruiz leaned against the wall, holding his right elbow. Fresh blood ran through his fingers. Sydney was just rising from securing the Brazilian's feet. "Ruiz?" said Sutherland. "What's he done to you?"

"Is only for sake of Cheriff Finits I have not kill him," replied Ruiz. "But the posse still have this prisoner at least to take to Yackson. No, I am all right. Only my arm. Gonzalves strike my wound to try to get away. Saidnay trip him with her gun, and he has hit his head, must be, in falling. Is soon awake again, I think. How many get away?"

"We don't know, yet. Watch him a little longer, will you? I want to see about Sherry. Baldy and the others are holding some prisoners. Will you be able to help us with the questioning?"

"Sí, cómo no. Any way I can serve you . . ."

Sherill was alive. But he was unable to rise, having taken the bullet high in the groin. Cecil was with him. "Boss . . .?" the cowboy greeted Sutherland softly as Will dropped to one knee beside him. "Where's Baldy?"

"Around front. He's fine, Sherry. Worried about you, is all."

"Where's Sydney?" was Cecil's question.

"With Ruiz. There by the corner. Go see how she is if you want. Constable, I think we'll need a blanket to move Sherry. Do you want to stay here with him while I go find one?"

"Boss?" whispered Sherill again, licking his dry lips with a dry tongue.

"You stay, Will," said Cross. "I'll go." And the constable turned away.

"Take it easy, Sherry," Sutherland advised, catching the hand that the cowboy reached out to him. "You'll be all right."

"Is Phoenix dead?"

"Yes. But no one else with the posse got hurt except you and Ruiz. And both of you are going to make it fine."

"Solano was hit?"

"In the arm. And a good thing for me. Or I might not be talking to you, now."

"Is there . . . any water, Boss?"

"I'll get you some, Sherry. As soon as they come with the blanket. Don't try to talk any more."

"It burns," said the cowboy. "God, how it burns!"

CHAPTER FIFTY-THREE:

TRIAL BY FIRE

In the plaza, a bonfire had been built to afford some light as the darkness grew. And to its heat and brilliance, the men of Mexican Camp were drawn like moths. In silent groups they stood about, looking at the prisoners who were roped together near the blaze. They saw Juan Solano come from behind the dance hall, holding his right arm above the elbow. Behind him came Eli Smith and Cecil Simpson with Gonzalves.

At the sight of the Brazilian, two of the outlaws identified themselves for their captors with calls and struggles. They were promptly separated from the rest.

"¡Desgraciados!" called Solano to the others. "¡Confiesen! Who else among you knows this man? Three more must answer to that question for all to be accounted for. If not, then more than that may die. And how many innocent of any crime have died for you already? Cowards! Will you hide among your betters and condemn them?"

"Don't answer him!" advised Gonzalves in thick Spanish from where he stood apart under the guard of the Simpsons. "You are safe enough! Ruiz won't let them kill so many. His heart is too soft. See, he takes everywhere with him a homeless harlot who passes for a boy. And only because . . ."

But this was more than Simón would tolerate. He sprang at the Brazilian and delivered a backhanded blow to his mouth with such force it knocked the man off his feet. Cross interfered, catching Ruiz by his good arm as Simón felt for his knife.

"Solano! What's going on?"

"You will gag him," Ruiz advised in English. "Or I kill him after all!"

"Simón!" cried Sydney, pointing. "Look! It's Torres!"

Every man in the plaza turned. But they saw only Baldy and Will Sutherland, bringing Sherry in a blanket litter along the wall of the cantina.

"Where, Saidnay?" asked Ruiz.

"I saw Torres crawling from the corner! Into that tent."

Between the dance hall and the wood frame house was a cloth shanty, its soiled canvas tingeing with orange and gold from the light of the bonfire.

George Durham, who had retreated into brooding docility under the watchful eye of Rob Briggs, now came back to violent life. Seizing a burning brand from the fire, he ran to investigate. Briggs followed. Then Cross. A quick search of the ground resolved the question. Smears of blood, glistening wet in the torchlight, stained the dirt and the flattened grass between the dance hall and the tent. "Torres!" called Durham in a voice so unlike his own that the two men with him started and exchanged a look. "Torres, I know you're in there! Come out!"

There was no answer.

"Come out, or I'll burn you out!"

"George . . ."

The Tax Collector turned fierce eyes on Cross. "Torres killed Albert France," he said. "I mean to have him. Or were you going to volunteer to go inside there after him yourself?"

The constable shook his head.

Durham shoved his fire-brand against the wall of the tent. A brown aura grew in a widening circle through the canvas. Short tresses of smoke curled up. And the cloth burst into flame. The Tax Collector ran around behind the shanty and touched a second side, and then a third. He threw the stick in through the door flap in front before he came away.

The heavy tent was dry and weathered. It burned well. Flickering light licked up the dark walls of the buildings to either side. From within there was no sound, no movement. But when it must finally be concluded that Torres was already dead, there suddenly came a terrible scream, and a sluggish, blazing form floundered from under the loose edge near the shanty's flame-ringed doorway. Yet before it had more than half freed itself, the tent collapsed on top of it, burying it again in a shower of sparks and burning cloth.

In the plaza, men stirred in horror. No one spoke. Until, "Ruiz!" cried a striken voice from the group of prisoners there. "¡Confieso! Have them to shoot me! Or hang me, Patrón! But not to let them burn me alive!"

Simón turned heavily from the sight of the burning shanty. "Sáquenlo," he said to one of the townsmen who stood guard on the prisoners. He passed a hand across his eyes.

When he looked again, Sydney stood close before him, her face chalk-white beneath its freckles. "I thought I'd killed him, Simón!"

"I have thought so, too," he said. "But it was too dark to know. Bueno . . . ya no más. Is over, now. Almost."

The bandit who had called out to Ruiz continued to confess what he knew while they extracted him from the group of prisoners. Speaking partly in Spanish and partly in English, he swore that the other two outlaws who had ridden with Gonzalves had left the cantina before the posse entered and were no longer in Mexican Camp. He thought they had returned to Sonora to look for Escobar. Since don Manuel had found ways to protect them from the gringos in the past, they might well hope for aid from him.

"Do you know him still to be in Sonora, then?" asked Ruiz.

The outlaw swore that he did.

"And the names of these two men who may have gone to look for him?"

"Antonio Méndez and Octavio Guzmán."

"Señor Cross," said Simón, turning to the constable. "The rest of these will be innocent. They do nothing worse than come here to drink and dance and look at women. I ask you release them."

This was eventually done, though not without a certain reluctance on the one side and mixed relief and resentment on the other. Then, the town turned its attention to locating and burying the dead . . . all but Torres, whose smoking pyre was still too hot to approach.

But the posse would not leave Phoenix behind. The sheriff's body was wrapped in a blanket and put in the back of the wagon standing in the plaza. The vehicle was instantly surrendered when the posse made it understood they would leave Mexican Camp and return to Jamestown yet that night. Except for Baldy Hinkson.

"Boss, Sherry's too bad to move," the cowboy told Will Sutherland. "He'll die on us before morning if we cart him all the way to Jamestown."

"I'm afraid we're going to lose him, anyway," was Will's quiet reply. "And we can't very well leave him alone in this town full of Mexicans after what's happened here tonight."

"I'll stay with him."

"Without Ruiz to run interference for you? By morning, there'd be two of you for them to bury."

"Ruiz would stay with me if I asked him," argued Hinkson. "I know he would."

"Don't ask him," advised Will. "He's wounded, himself. And he's got his wife to worry about."

"Boss, I can't believe you're turnin' your back on Sherry."

"I'm not, Baldy. And I'm sorry you think of it that way.

Listen to me. If we can get him to Jamestown, there may be a decent doctor there who can do something for him."

"You could send the doctor here."

"What if he wouldn't come?"

But Ruiz himself put an end to their discussion by his approach. Still holding his wounded arm, and with Sydney behind him, Simón strode toward them, stopped beside them, close to the front wall of the cantina. Sherill lay unconsious on the ground at their feet. "Baldés? How is Cherry?"

Hinkson looked at Will. Sutherland frowned. Ruiz knelt quickly beside the cowboy. "He is not dead!" he demanded.

Baldy dropped to his heels next to him. "Not yet," he said. "But he will be! If we go haulin' him around the country in the back of that damned wagon."

"You don't know that for certain, Baldy." Sutherland stood where he was, looking down at them.

"He took a ball in the gut!" Hinkson's voice shook. "And I ain't about to let him be jounced over that raw trail they got the nerve to call a road between here and Jamestown!"

"There is no necesidad," said Ruiz. "We find him someplace here that he can stay, and they take care of him."

"I won't leave him!" maintained Hinkson. "If he stays, I stay."

"Of course, if you wish."

"Don Simón . . ." Sutherland demurred.

"There is something wrong you have not told me?"

"How welcome do you really think these two will be here?"

"Ah. Por eso. Then, you wish that I stay, also?"

Will did not answer. Hinkson bowed his head.

"Why you are worry to ask me?" wondered Ruiz.

"What about Escobar?" said Sutherland.

Simón sighed and rose to his feet. "You do not need me

to find him," he said. "El colector will know him by sight. And as for me . . . amigos, I do confess to you that all this time I keep my thought to find him first, to kill him if I can. I have not give up that plan until tonight. But now . . . ." He indicated his wounded arm. "What I can do like this? Nada. Manuel is safe from me. Take him. Hang him if you will. I have not want for him to die that way, before. But those things so important then are less important now. What is Manuel to me? I have more feeling for the death of Cheriff Finits. And for the pain of Baldés with his amigo, Cherry. I am tire. Me rindo ya. Come, Saidnay, we find a place to stay here for ourself and for these friends."

Cecil Simpson objected the moment he was told. "I'm not going to leave my sister in this Greaser Camp!" he cried, jumping down from the wagon he had volunteered to drive.

"Don't shout insults, son," the constable advised. "Remember, she's married to one. And it's for him to say whether she goes or stays.

"Maybe I'll find a few things to say to **him**, then!"

But Cecil was talked out of this, as well. And though he eventually remounted the wagon's box and took up the lines, he continued to protest against the whole situation and to blame himself for ever signing any contract with Matthew Hindshaw in Drytown. He even was heard to regret not having pushed don Simón Ruiz Silvestre over a certain cliff after his hat instead of rescuing him from death.

But none that heard him were offended. Simón had disappeared with Sydney into the house of the town's most prominent citizen, and four other Mexicans had promptly gone to fetch Sherry and Baldy after him.

Hinkson followed the litter bearers warily, glancing back at the posse's final preparations for departure. "Good luck to them," he muttered to himself. "They've got a ways to go before they're back in Jackson. And that ride won't be much fun, especially with Phoenix gone. I reckon I'm not so sorry to be stayin' here with Sherry, after all."

CHAPTER FIFTY-FOUR:

THE UPRISING

On the afternoon of August fifteenth, Carlos Ocampo left the Mexican quarter of Jamestown on a stolen horse. He knew it meant he would hang if they caught him, but since he expected to be hanged or shot anyway, that certainty did not deter him. He rode as fast as the animal could carry him over the rugged land between Jamestown and Mexican Camp. He did not go by the road.

But when he came over the top of the hill behind the cantina/dance hall, he pulled to a halt. For he saw most of the townspeople assembled on the slope below him at the end of a fresh row of graves. Two of the mourners were American. One of these was a woman, dressed in a neat white waist and a long, split skirt of dark leather. Her short, curly hair looked even redder than it was among so many black, bared heads. The cowboy who stood beside her put a hat on his own brown mop of curls as he caught sight of Ocampo. And the Californian facing him across the last grave turned round. This was the man Ocampo sought. "¡Ruiz!" he called and spurred his horse.

Don Simón's right arm was in a sling. But he was now clothed more in keeping with his proper station than when Carlos Ocampo had seen him before; the first family of Mexican Camp had not neglected their distinguished guest and his American wife. Nor his American cowboy friends. But they had not been able to save the life of the one called Sherill who had died quietly that morning amid such comforts as could be afforded him and with his range-riding partner watching anxiously over him.

"¡Señor Ruiz!" cried Carlos again as he reached the graveside. The people had parted to make way for him. Ocampo threw himself from the saddle. "¡Patrón! The Americans! They will be here soon! I have ridden to warn you. You must leave at once. All of you!" he added, sweeping an arm at the rest as if to clear them off the hillside.

"What's he sayin', Solano?" the cowboy Hinkson demanded, for Carlos had spoken only in Spanish.

Ruiz stayed Baldy with a gesture. "What Americans, Señor?" he asked Ocampo. The people moved restlessly, ready to run if they had to but wanting to know the full reason, first. "Why are they coming here?"

"There is a false rumor of a Mexican uprising in the Motherlode, Patrón. The bad conscience of the gringos has invented it. For if they were themselves treated so badly as they have treated us, they would revolt. And so they have assumed it of us. And to prevent our taking their towns by force and avenging our sorrows with blood, they are disarming and despoiling every Mexican community, herding our people out of the country, killing those who dare resist. I have myself barely escaped them. I have stolen this horse to save my life and yours. And I will beg from you another horse that I may ride on to the Valley and so get beyond their reach before they discover their loss. Fly! We must fly! All of us!"

There was a flurry downslope toward the deserted town.

"Wait!" shouted Ruiz, bounding a few steps up the hill to a more commanding position. "We must not panic, friends! In panic, we are lost! The retreat must be orderly! And calm! We must keep our heads to save our lives! Ocampo! There in the plaza stands your own palomino. Take him and go. This horse you have ridden we will unsaddle and turn loose." Ruiz then called on the head of the first family of Mexican Camp to organize his people and prepare both for flight and defense.

In a sliding wave, the town moved down the hillside to repool in the plaza. But Carlos Ocampo lingered nervously beside Ruiz. "Patrón," he said, "forgive my cowardice. Yet I dare not take my own horse back. He is too well known and too easily recognized. I give him to you to use for your own or to dispose of as you see fit. I will beg a less conspicuous mount for myself."

"As you wish," said Ruiz. He held out his good arm to Sydney and received her close to his side. "What news of the posse, Ocampo?" he asked. "Did they spend the night in Jamestown?"

"No, Señor. They went on to Sonora."

"And what happened there?"

"Don Simón, it is said that the gringos gathered more than forty Mexicans from the vicinity and were holding them for the posse."

"Forty! There is still some safety in numbers. Manuel may yet get away. But not if Durham sees him," Ruiz added. "Bueno. I will delay you no longer. Go. And God go with you, Ocampo."

Carlos turned and ran down the slope, leaving his stolen horse where it stood. Simón took his arm from around Sydney and went to uncinch the saddle himself, but Baldy stepped into his way. "Are you goin' tell us what's happened?" he asked.

"This man Ocampo," replied Ruiz, "he thinks the americanos from Jame Estow, perhaps Sonora, will attack the people here."

"But why, in God's name? They helped us catch the outlaws!"

Ruiz frowned into Baldy's blue eyes. "They are mexicanos," he replied. "Is reason enough! The storm has spread swiftly. We have not much feel its effects before because we have ride always ahead of it. But now, it catch up." Simón pushed past Hinkson to pull at the horse's cinch strap with his left hand.

"Let me do that," said Sydney, deftly ducking in front of him.

"Baldés," said Ruiz, facing the cowboy again, "you must decide quickly that which you will do."

"How do you mean? Are you and Miss Sydney going to join up with these people from here on?"

"No. Not unless they ask that I go with them. For I wish to return to Yackson."

"Jackson! What for?"

"My friend Fidel . . . I fear what has happen to him. I wish to know. And to help him if I can. As you have grieve for your friend, Cherry, so I think with fear for Fidel. And was for my sake he is hurt."

"Not only that," the cowboy said, "but you can't rest till you find out just what the hell's become of Escobar. Ain't that right? Not that I blame you," he went on as Simón's expression changed. "I'm some curious myself. But it'll mean riskin' your own neck, again, won't it? And I have a feelin' Miss Sydney would rather you wouldn't. Shall we ask her?"

Sydney was hauling the saddle from the horse's sweaty back. She dumped it onto the dry grass before she looked around. "Whatever Simón wants to do is fine with me," she said. "And I'd just as soon find out about Ben Rooster and Escobar, too. So don't use me for the excuse to try to talk him out of it, Baldy Hinkson."

The cowboy smiled wryly. "I don't know whether you two are more brave or just plain loco," he said. "Whatever it is, it's catchin'. If you'll have me along, I'll go with you. And I'll say this minute how much it's meant to me the way you've stood by me and Sherry." His glance strayed back to the last grave on the hillside. "I'm goin' to miss him, damn it. I hope he rests peaceful, here. I reckon the Spanish angels will be some surprised when he shows up yonder with all the rest. But I s'pose they'll get things sorted out." Baldy pulled at his hatbrim and scuffed the toe of his boot in the dirt.

Sydney pulled the bridle off the horse's head and threw it over the abandoned saddle. "As I understand it," she said, "what counts where Sherry is now has nothing to do with where he's buried." She went to touch the cowboy's arm. "He was a good man, Baldy," she told him.

Hinkson dropped his gaze again to the ground. "Solano," he said huskily, " 'according to my judgementals' ", as Sherry used to say, you're one hell of a lucky hombre. Let's rustle some ponies and make tracks for Jackson, shall we?"

Leaving the stolen horse free to roll and snort in the grass of the slope, the three friends went down to the plaza together.

The people of the town had already dispersed to gather up such things as could be easily transported. With a haste spurred by fear, and a reluctance sustained by their sense of belonging, they packed trunks and loaded wagons and burdened donkeys. Men looked grim. Women wiped away silent tears. Small children stood in the way of the work and cried openly.

Amid this determined confusion, Simón and Sydney and Baldy Hinkson replenished their saddle packs and chose new mounts from those offered them. For when it was made known that don Simón intended to ride to Jackson, he was urged to take for his party any horses he wished from the town.

The animals for which the outlaws had forced trade in the Spanish sector of Jamestown were to go with the people of Mexican Camp since it was uncertain whether their owners would be able to receive them, even if it were possible to return them. They were good horses. Gonzalves had taken the best. And they were fresh, having come only one way from Jamestown two mornings before.

Sydney chose from among them a short-coupled dun with a wild eye and a Roman nose. The animal looked tough enough to run all the way to Jackson and back in a day. Simón tried to convince her to ride the palomino, instead, but Sydney refused. What she did not explain was that she preferred to admire the figure he cut on the gold horse, himself. Hinkson put his saddle on a blue roan.

"I'm sort of sorry to leave old Blacky," Sydney confided, looking back at the horse she had bought from Rob Briggs in Rancheria. But though he was not wholly spent, the black's flanks were gaunt, now, and his neck thin; he could not have matched the pace set by the palomino. "I hope these folks here get away all right. Do you think they will, Simón?"

"They have the warning in time," said Ruiz. "So, at least, they are prepare. Is better than for others between here and Yackson. I have try to warn them as we come south, but not many believe me. It seems too far away from what has happen in Ranchería. But that incident is no longer the reason. Is only the excuse. Baldés? You are ready? Bueno. ¡Nos fuiinos!"

CHAPTER FIFTY-FIVE:

NIGHT RIDERS

They did not return through Jamestown, but crossed the river at Byrnes Ferry and pushed on till they reached the Stockton-Murphys Road. By sundown, they were within sight of the Inn at Fourth Crossing.

Baldy suggested that Ruiz and Sydney make camp in the cover of a narrow draw two hills over while he went to the hotel to learn what he could of the posse. Simón preferred to go with him. But Baldy won this argument:

"If all the Gold Country is as up-in-arms against the Mexicans as that Ocampo hombre seemed to think, you'd better be savin' your nerve for Jackson. You'll likely need all of it there. Why, just Miss Sydney's walkin' into the saloon of the Traveler's Inn would stop the whole show. 'Cause the way she's dressed now, there ain't nothin' to keep men from seein' for theirselves that she's a mighty handsome woman. And by the time you'd got done explainin' whose woman she was, you'd be talkin' with both guns. Anyhow, what's the point of havin' a gringo like me along if you won't let me ride scout for you in places like this?"

Simón looked at Sydney and frowned. Mistaking that frown for criticism, Sydney turned away. She had been secretly pleased with her appearance this day. The clothes given to her by the first family of Mexican Camp were exactly to her own liking. The white linen shirtwaist fastened modestly up to her throat and buttoned at the wrists. And the split riding skirt was a good compromise between practicality and femininity. It fell in a smooth line from waist to ankle and was heavy enough not to fly in the wind but not so heavy it weighed her down. Her feet were encased in a pair of fine riding boots. Her face was shaded by a rakish flat-brimmed hat that fit—Simón now wore his own—and Sydney thought she had read full approval in his eyes whenever he looked at her. But now, she felt betrayed. And she wished she had brought Will Sutherland's dungarees and blue checked shirt in her saddlepack after all.

"We wait for you here," Simón told Hinkson. "But we don't make camp. I wish to catch up to the posse if is possible before they reach Yackson. You will learn what you can as fast as you can, eh?"

"You can count on it," Baldy agreed. And remounting his roan, he made for the road and the Traveler's Inn.

Ruiz was not fond of waiting. His patience with Fate did not extend to enforced idleness. And he moved restlessly around the little clearing.

Sydney watched him, blaming herself for his predicament. She loosened the cinches of both saddles to give their horses some relief and helped herself to a drink from the waterskin. When Simón looked at her, she offered the boot to him, but he shook his head.

Finally, he seated himself on a stone as if it were to be the last act of his life. Sydney longed to join him there, but doubting her welcome, she remained where she was near the horses. The silence had become almost unbearable to her by the time they heard Hinkson returning.

Simón started quickly to his feet and came to tighten his cinch, nodded for Sydney to do the same. "Móntate," he advised softly, motioning her with a jerk of his head to get on even as he struggled one-handed with the cinch knot. ". . . In case is not Baldés!"

Sydney leaped lightly astride, checking the dun, for the little horse offered to run the moment he was mounted. The palomino, too, whirled nervously around the axis of his rider. The horse's white tail flashed like a light in the deepening dusk. Sydney watched, her heart in her throat as she realized fully for the first time how much Ruiz' injured arm was hampering him. He could not have both controlled his horse and drawn his gun, if he'd had to. Forgetting her own moodiness, she unslung her rifle.

But it was only Baldy, after all. He reined his roan to a stop between them. "The posse came through Fourth Crossing this morning," he said. "They was travelin' fast and light. They buried Phoenix yesterday afternoon in Sonora, and there was some trouble with the prisoners. I gather one of them tried to take advantage of the business of the funeral to escape. He was shot. And two others. But the posse's supposed to have four Mexicans along, mounted and tied to their saddles. And by my reckoning, that must mean they picked up Escobar. I'd have tried to learn more particulars, but if we're goin' to overtake them, we've got to ride hard enough as it is."

That ride was still harder because they must keep to the

hills until they passed San Andreas. But by that time, night had fallen fully, and they dared to ride on the road.

It was ominously quiet. At the Calaveras River crossing, they half expected to be challenged. But they met no one. The river ran noisily over its bed at the ford, masking their hoofbeats which had broken a jumbled rhythm like tumbling wood blocks on the hard-packed trail. The starlight shone dimly on the wet rocks and twinkled in the deeper pools where the glossy water carried their reflection like bits of silver sewn to silk. The three friends let their horses drink and then pushed on.

Halfway between San Andreas and Mokelumne Hill was Chile Gulch. Since it was inhabited primarily by South Americans, Ruiz did not feel it necessary to ride around the camp. They jogged straight on between its silent buildings without seeing anyone. Nor even a light. Only a dog barked once.

Determined to learn if the posse were indeed still ahead of them, Simón dismounted at the door of the last adobe on the road. His knocking raised nothing but echoes. "¡Oigan! ¡Que soy californiano!" he called. "¿No hay nadie vivo en este pueblo?" But there was no response.

"You reckon they're hidin' in the hills?" asked Baldy, turning in his saddle to survey the humping country round the town.

"They will be hiding in their beds," judged Ruiz, a note of scorn in his voice. His spurs clashed loudly as he returned to his horse. "These chilenos, they pretend to be a different race so they are left alone. They pretend not to be concern in what goes on around them. ¡Cállense, pues!" Simón called back down the quiet street. "¡Ya les tocará gritar!"

The next town was Mokelumne Hill. And Ruiz wished to approach that settlement closely to find out if the posse were spending the night there.

"I don't think it's too likely," Hinkson said. "Their jail ain't the best. And Moke Hill sure ain't a town to go to sleep in. The card houses and saloons are hummin' all night long.

Hardly a night goes by without a fight. Besides, it's only ten or twelve miles more to Jackson. And once the posse come this close, my guess is they'd keep on."

"Simón," said Sydney, reining her dun nearer to his palomino, "let's leave the road, again, maybe make camp in the gorge. You don't want to ride clear to Jackson yet tonight, do you?"

"You are tire, Pecosa?"

"Me! You're the one with the wounded arm! Isn't it bothering you an awful lot?"

"Un poco," he admitted. "But I bear it."

"But when we do get to Jackson, we're not going to be able to rest much, are we?"

"She's right, Solano," Baldy said. "It ain't as though we can just put our horses in the livery and rent a couple of rooms at the National for the rest of the night. We'd better turn off and look for a safe spot to close our eyes this side of the river."

"Listen!" hissed Sydney. "Horses!"

Quickly, they left the road. But before they could gain cover, a group of riders came over a rise. They were talking and laughing among themselves, their good humor evidently fortified by a certain amount of alcohol.

"I still say we should be ridin' the other way," maintained one. "The place to be tomorrow is Main Street in Jackson."

"Don't fret, Bill. They won't hang nobody afore noon. They have to give folks a chance to gather for the spectacle. We got time to trot home, sleep late, and trot back without missing out on any part of that performance."

"Looky there!" said another, catching sight of Hinkson, Simón and Sydney. "Hey!" he shouted at them. "Hold up!"

"Get into the trees," Baldy advised, waving Ruiz and Sydney on before him. "I'll do the talkin'." And he lagged back to respond to the challenge. "Keep your distance!" he called out. "Say who you are and what's your business!"

The group of horsemen slowed to a walk. "Mister," one of them replied, "we aimed to ask **you** that question."

"Stop right there!" warned Hinkson. "I'm not wantin' much company tonight." He backed the blue roan a few steps and felt for the pistol at his hip.

The riders drew rein and sat their mounts in the tall grass just off the road. "Who are you?" demanded another of them.

Baldy could distinguish five separate shapes against the starry skyline. "Nobody you ever heard of!" he retorted. "Some folks call me One Shot. But my name means trouble, no matter what. You boys better mosey on home to bed and forget you ever saw me."

"Who are your sidekicks, One Shot?" the first speaker demanded.

"That's Old Hair Trigger and his partner, Quick Draw. They're even less sociable than I am."

"Yeah? One of them looks kind of pint-sized." The man who spoke peered through the darkness at the white patch that was Sydney's shirtwaist hovering among the black stems of the trees. "Which one's that?"

"Quick Draw," said Baldy. "And his size has got nothin' to do with it. He's mean as a rattlesnake. Better not mess with him."

"Is that so? And where might all you terrible gunslingers be a-ridin' to this time of night?" the man asked amicably.

"Over the river," said Baldy.

"To Jackson, you mean?"

"That's what I mean."

"Well, we'll see you there tomorrow at the hangin', then, I reckon."

"You might," said Baldy. "But you won't know who we are. Now, you fellers ride on and leave us alone. Unless you're keen for a fight."

Still curious, but amused and disarmed by Baldy's extravagant bluff, the five riders slowly returned to the road. Hinkson stayed where he was until they were well on their way, and then he rode for the trees.

"That was good lying, Baldy," Sydney greeted him

softly. There was true admiration in her voice.

Hinkson was surprised at how much her praise warmed him. "Yeah, but they liked that game almost too well," he said. "I was half afraid they wouldn't let it pass. Solano? Where to from here?"

"No, you have convince me we find a place to make camp," replied Ruiz. "But is so dark, will not be easy. The moon, she does not rise for another hour and more. And the gorge is steeper pronto."

"I'll go ahead on foot," Baldy suggested.

It proved a wise precaution. Within ten or fifteen minutes, they had come to the crumbly brink of a precipice which in the starlight looked like a clearing ahead. Baldy's blue roan snorted and pulled him back from the edge on the end of the reins just as Hinkson's feet started to slide out from under him.

Carefully, the cowboy felt his way along the brink, trying to find a safe way down. There was none. He settled for a small pocket basin with a patch of oozy moss in its far corner. "I doubt we do better than this before mornin'," he said. "Get down and come in. Just don't be sleepwalkin' over the cliff later tonight."

"Do we dare make a fire, Simón?" asked Sydney, swinging from her saddle and leading the dun forward. "We've got some provisions in our packs. Aren't you men hungry? I am. We could make a little cookfire easy enough."

This proposal was also agreed to. And by the time the waning moon rose into the notch of the Mokelumne canyon, the three friends had devoured a full, smoking panful of supper.

"Is better you put out the fire, Saidnay," said Simón, though all three of them found cheer and comfort in its glowing heart. "I doubt anybody see it from this side of the river, but we take precaution, anyway."

"Shall we set a watch?" asked Baldy.

"Pues," sighed Ruiz, "I don't wish to ask from you what I cannot do myself, Baldés. For I feel I will sleep the moment that I close my eyes. I do not realize before how tire this wound has make me. Besides, I think we all do better to rest as much as we can before dawn. Tomorrow, perhaps, is a long day, too."

"I wouldn't be surprised," said Hinkson.

But Baldy did not go to sleep for some time. He made a great show of spreading out the blanket from his roll and casting himself down on it, pillowing his head on his saddle and closing his eyes. But from under lowered lids, the cowboy watched while Sydney moved quietly around the little campsite, reorganizing her pack before putting out the fire. The unconscious grace of her movements thrilled him to the soul as the warm light of the campfire gilded first one part of her and then another.

Baldy turned his head slightly to see if Ruiz was watching her, too. But Simón lay on the ground like one dead.

Sydney took care to separate the flaming sticks and smother them with earth and damp moss. Yet by the wan moonlight Baldy could still see her sit down close to Simón. He could see her lean over him and hear her murmur something.

Ruiz raised his head to let her untie the sling at the back of his neck. He groaned in mixed pain and relief as she gently guided his injured arm to rest beside him. She bent still lower, then, and kissed him.

Baldy felt a strange burning in his breast. He wished ardently he might trade places with Ruiz and wondered that the man could lie there so without responding. Surely no wound could hurt so much that the ecstasy of Sydney's touch would not by far outweigh the pain. Baldy would have gladly taken bullets in both arms just to try it.

Sydney snuggled down beside her man, resting her head on his good shoulder. And then at last, Hinkson saw Simón's hand lift to her waist and slide around it. Baldy's longing grew so painful he considered throwing himself over the edge to put an end to it. Next, he tormented himself by remembering every callous word he'd said about Sydney at Rancheria. He wondered that Solano had not shot him off his horse. He thought about how Sydney had run after Simón at the Sutherlands' to beg him to take her along. He wondered how Ruiz could have refused her.

"Lord have mercy on me," the cowboy breathed, looking up at the stars above the lip of the basin. "I know she'd never care for me. But that don't keep me from wantin' her. How am I goin' to live with this? I'm doomed to a lifetime of loneliness. But I'll live it on the chance of just her smilin' at me, someday. That ain't so much to ask of heaven. That the wife of don Simón Ruiz should smile at Baldy Hinkson . . .?"

CHAPTER FIFTY-SIX:

THE TREE ON MAIN STREET

As the morning sun climbed toward midday on Thursday, August 16, the town of Jackson filled to repletion with people come to witness the grisly pageant of execution. They had been arriving since the preceding afternoon. For news of the outlaws' capture and of the posse's return had swept through the Mother Lode like wildfire.

Normal business was suspended. Claims were deserted in midweek. Sunday suits and gowns were donned. Hair was combed. Men shaved. Women flirted. Children with new-scrubbed faces chased each other through the crowds.

In the sheriff's office and jailhouse, Sam Phoenix sat at his brother's desk, now officially his own, and played solitaire to keep his grief at bay and his mind well ordered. Most of the posse had stayed with him through the night to insure the safekeeping of the prisoners and to take turns sleeping on two empty cots in the unused cell.

At ten o'clock that morning, Judge Curtis had arrived from Drytown with William Clark and a conspicuously small delegation advocating fairness and moderation. Both the magistrate and the orator offered the new sheriff their sympathy for his loss and their approval of his appointment to his brother's vacant office.

"The name Phoenix," Clark declared, "has come to be synonymous with fair play and dedication in this county. We have full confidence in you. And we are superlatively grateful that you have had the courage to accept this enormous burden of duty in spite of your bereavement. You shall have our full support."

"I thank you, gentlemen," said Sam.

"Where is don Simón Ruiz?" inquired Curtis. "Does anyone know?"

"At last report, he was still in Mexican Camp," said Phoenix.

"But the town was attacked, I hear."

"Deserted, first, I think. Constable Cross expects that Ruiz took charge of getting the people away."

"That would be like him," agreed Curtis. "But what about the others . . . Mr. Hinkson and Mr. Sherill?"

"There's been no word," said Phoenix.

Noon came. The sun beat down on the roofs of the town, and on the heads of the people. Ladies sought the covered boardwalks and protected doorways. But there was one patch of shade in town which remained untenanted. No one wished to stand for long beneath the Hangman's Tree. Only an occasional braggart swaggered under it. And a boy or two. On his brother's dare, Timothy Simpson dashed twice across that no man's land. Also, he was privileged to point out to anyone he chose that his cousin, Cecil Simpson, was a member of the posse. (There was a titillating rumor in circulation that **both** of Timothy's cousins had been with the posse for a time, but the boy's parents had forbidden him to repeat this.)

Uncle Peter stood with Aunt Aggie on the edge of the boardwalk across from the jail house, his face unreadable, his mouth firmly closed. But his eyes followed every movement of his nephew as Cecil came out of the sheriff's office to take his turn on guard at the door.

Aunt Aggie's pride was completely undisguised. She told as many of the bystanders as would listen how the tall, curly-haired boy with the serious look was related to herself and to her husband and how bravely he had borne the loss of his beloved father, how he had volunteered to go with the posse out of a sense of duty to the community. She claimed that Cecil's exceptional character owed much to the examples set for him by his father and uncle, and she added that all the Simpson men were noted for their valor and persistence, exceeded only by their responsibility and loyalty to family.

She might have said still more, but the tolling of the twelfth hour resounded from the belfry on Church Hill. The people jostled eagerly, then silence fell. The door of the jail house opened. Sam Phoenix appeared. He carried a coiled rope. There was a hangman's noose in one end of it.

The new sheriff looked around him with less expression than Uncle Peter. He gave the rope to Cecil who still stood by the door. "Shinny up the Tree with that, Simpson," he said quietly. "Briggs," he added to the man just visible in the doorway behind him, "you can bring the wagon from the livery, now."

With baited breath, the people watched Cecil and Rob Briggs move across the keyhole shape of open space leading from the jailhouse to the live oak tree. There, they parted, Briggs to penetrate the crowd and Cecil to climb the Tree.

The boy put the coil of rope over his shoulder and laid hands on the grey bark of the branching trunk that arched over the street three times his height above him. Its lowest bough sprouted ten feet from the ground. But he stepped confidently onto the saddle of the Tree's low forking to scale the slender trunk. The rough bark rasped through his sleeves and pantlegs and scraped the skin of his hands before he gained the first sharp angle. But from there, it was much easier to scramble higher.

As he passed the second angle, thick clusters of dark,

waxy leaves on a long branch springing from the second trunk brushed his back and scratched his cheek. His hands burned with the bits of bark embedded in his palms. The coil of rope dragged at his shoulder and pressed grooves into his chest.

At the apex of the arch, the heavy limb divided into a pair of smaller branches of almost equal size, both of which thereafter forked again into a spreading, drooping tangle of slender twigs and crowding leaves. Here, Cecil squirmed to lie out fully on the soaring arch, braced himself with one foot on the stirrup of the branch below, and unslung the rope he carried, fed the looped end through the splayed knotch in the limb.

When he looked down, he saw Sam Phoenix looking up. The sheriff stood alone beneath the Tree. "Another few feet of line," he said. He spoke in a normal tone, as if he were completely unaffected by the sight of the open noose that Cecil lowered toward his face. "That's probably far enough," he judged when the rope hung even with the second angle of the trunk. "Throw me the other end."

Cecil complied.

Phoenix caught the falling coils, took them to tie the line to a waist-like indentation in the live oak's lower trunk. Then, he turned to greet the wagon Rob Briggs had driven from the stable. Its progress was slow, for the spectators must make way for the bulky vehicle with its scant load of four pine coffins. Three youngsters, one of whom was Jacob Simpson, were hanging on the open tailgate. But they dropped off as the wagon entered the shade. And sensing they had dared as much as their elders would tolerate from them, they scurried to take their places by their respective relatives.

Uncle Peter dropped a heavy hand on Jacob's shoulder and steered the boy to stand in front of him. Aunt Agnes already had Timothy in custody.

Briggs drove his team in a tight circle to head them back downslope. He stopped them when the wagon's open end was directly under the noose.

Sam Phoenix came to lean a forearm on the wagon's boards and look up once more. He saw Cecil move as if to descend. "Stay up there, Simpson," he directed. "We'll be needing your services some more." Then he signaled to the constable who was watching from the jail house door.

Cross stepped aside. And another man came out: a Californian. He was well-built, and he carried himself with pride although his hands were tied behind him. His hatless head he had thrown back even with his shoulders, and his dark eyes swept the crowd with scorn. His face, though half obscured by two days' growth of beard, was handsome, its features finely chiseled. At the sight of him, a whisper passed among the spectators. For many recognized him. And the rest guessed who he was even before their neighbors told them: "It's Manuel Escobar!"

Behind him came three other prisoners. Two of them were Mexican. The third was not: Paulo Gonzalves bore himself with less defiance than Escobar. His tawny eyes flashed shrinking glances at the Hangman's Tree, nor did he openly survey the crowd. And yet, his look was not so much of fear as calculation. He was watching for an opportunity where it seemed that there could be none.

After the prisoners came the rest of the possemen: George Durham, the Foreign Tax Collector; Will Sutherland, the rancher's son; Paul McCormick, the apprentice; Daniel Perrin, local miner; and Eichelburgher, immigrant. The latter two had rejoined their former companions to spend much of the night exchanging opinions and reports.

The last of the company to emerge from the sheriff's office was the magistrate from Drytown. Sam Phoenix had requested him to preside over the proceedings to afford them some semblance of legality. For under such extraordinary circumstances, a proper trial could not be held. Only Mr. William Clark still thought that was possible.

"My friends and fellow citizens!" Judge Curtis called when the company had halted near the Tree. "Decency demands of us adherence to certain guidelines. We do not want today's event to be thought of as a lynching, but as a legal execution. That twelve unbiased jurors be found among us is, no doubt, impossible. But let us choose, at least, a committee of responsible and sober men to review the evidence against these prisoners. Let history show that what we mean to do is a warranted and proper action."

"Judge, we ain't come to confab!" was the insolent reply. Boston Williston shoved through the crowd. Close on his heels came his accomplice, Jimmy Johnson.

But Sam Phoenix stepped away from the wagon to confront the freight driver. "Williston," he said, "you've got no influence here. This isn't Rancheria. Stand aside."

Boston gave way. For the moment, he was satisfied with having made his presence known. But he kept to the forefront of the observers' inner ring.

Judge Curtis asked again that several sober citizens be selected to serve Justice. But response was sluggish. People had come to witness, not to participate in the drama of the hour. As it became apparent that nothing else would happen until the magistrate's request was met, however, the crowd produced five of its number answering to the qualifications he had mentioned. William Clark, the obvious choice, was overlooked. But so was Boston Williston. Among those who **were** singled out was Peter Simpson.

Uncle Peter had not anticipated such an honor. Had it been possible, he would have refused it. A variety of reasonable objections occurred to him. He was too personally involved to be objective. His apprentice and his nephew both were possemen. (His niece he would not even mention.) His cabin had been burned down by the bandits. Members of his family had been threatened. But he had not been asked to be objective; there was not a man on Main Street without bias. By stepping forward, he acknowleged himself only to be sober and responsible. And these things Peter Simpson had always thought himself to be. So, after a moment's hesitation, he complied. Aunt Agnes caught Jacob by the arm.

"Gentlemen," Judge Curtis said when the five men chosen came to stand before him, "you represent the best judgment of this gathering and the best hope of these prisoners. I charge you to be as fair-minded and as patient as you can. Sheriff, will you review the case against the captives?"

CHAPTER FIFTY-SEVEN:

ESCAPE

Sam Phoenix thought a moment. He looked at Manuel Escobar who returned his gaze defiantly. Paulo Gonzalves would not meet his eyes at all. Of the others, the first stared at him blankly and the second looked away.

"On August sixth," said Sam, rolling the words slowly off his tongue, "about ten o'clock at night, twelve Mexicans attacked the town of Rancheria. They killed six men, one woman and one Indian. They stole twenty thousand dollars from the safe of the general store. The sheriff and his posse were already on their trail, but the outlaws had lost them twice. So, the posse didn't get to Rancheria until after dawn of the following morning. From there, they took up a new trail toward Indian Camp. But that turned out to be a false lead, too. They arrived in Jackson on the ninth and found one Mexican dead in the Eureka Dance Hall. All the others had fled the town.

"Next, the posse went to Diamond Bar where folks said a dozen outlaws had crossed the ford. The sheriff kept on to Mokelumne Hill where he was met by Mr. Hinkson who had been with the posse earlier but had gone to the Dry Creek Ranch on the morning of the seventh with a message from Mr. William Sutherland. Then, Mr. Hinkson had returned to follow after the outlaws again. Mr. Briggs and Mr. McCormick came with him.

"When these three gentlemen met the sheriff in Mokelumne Hill, they had two prisoners with them. One, a man named García, identified several of the outlaws by name, including a Manuel Escobar.

"It was determined that the other man Hinkson's company had brought was innocent. Two of the posse escorted both men here to Jackson. The one called García was hanged without a trial, though the sheriff had asked that he only be jailed until the rest were captured." Sam Phoenix paused to stare at the ground. But he went on again almost immediately.

"The posse continued south and came across the remainder of the bandits in a place called Mexican Camp. The outlaws put up a fight. My brother . . . The sheriff was killed. Another of the posse was severely wounded. Four Mexicans were killed. Three were taken prisoner. One of those was this man, here." Sam gestured at Gonzalves.

"Hang him!" called Boston Williston.

"You keep quiet, damn you!" cried Phoenix, straightening with a sudden motion and glaring at the freight driver. "I'm not done, yet!"

There was a stir of surprise at this. Sam Phoenix was as well known for his steady nerve as ever his brother had been.

"On their way back to Jackson from Mexican Camp," the new sheriff resumed in his former careful tone, "two of the prisoners tried to escape. They were shot. But three more were taken in Sonora: these three," he added, nodding at Manuel Escobar and the others who stood beside him.

"Are you done now, Sheriff?" called Williston.

"Yes! But I mean to give the prisoners a chance to talk if they want it. And then I'll ask this committee of responsible citizens to give us their opinion on the business. And afterwards, Judge Curtis will pronounce sentence as he sees fit. And if you can't hold still for that, Williston, I'll ask one of my deputies to escort you to a jail cell until it's over!"

"It's all just a goddam waste of time," said Boston. "But go ahead! We can wait a little longer. I guess the rope won't rot before we get to see it used."

Jimmy Johnson snickered through his nose.

Phoenix swung round to face the prisoners. "Manuel Escobar," he said, "were you the leader of the outlaws that shot up Rancheria?"

"No hablo inglés," retorted the Californian.

"Don't try that," said Sam. "I've heard you speak English, myself. And folks from Drytown know you can, too. You lived there for a while. Didn't you?"

Manuel shrugged. "Tal vez."

"Where were you on the sixth of August?"

"Does he matter?" Manuel inquired acidly. "If I say the truth, you tell me that I lie. But the truth is, I was not in Ranchería, Señor Cheriff. I was in Yackson. I visit someone here. A lady. Several of these people see me, I am sure. But they don't confess it. Because they want me to be guilty. Why should I say more?"

"Do you know these others?" asked Phoenix, nodding at Gonzalves and the rest.

"Two of them," said Escobar. "But that man, I never see before the posse catch him in Sonora." He jerked his chin at one of the two Mexicans who were as yet unidentified.

"What are the names of the two you know?" demanded Sam.

"Ask them," said Escobar.

The sheriff looked at the Brazilian. "Are you Pablo Gonzales?"

Gonzalves' face reddened in sudden wrath. "No!" he said and snarled a phrase in Portuguese.

Phoenix sighed. He turned to the other two prisoners. "Señors? Who are you? Er . . . Como see yamma?"

One man continued to stare at Sam blankly. The other burst out in Spanish and talked on until Will Sutherland stepped forward to catch his arm, thus cutting off his flow of words.

"Judge," said Phoenix, "my Spanish is too limited. We need a real interpreter to do this right."

Before Curtis could answer, a ripple of noise and confusion spread through the crowd from the direction of the livery stable. Its cause was not immediately apparent to the group near the Tree. But Briggs, who sat in the wagon, had a clear view of the sloping street. He turned around and called back, "Sheriff! Judge! It's Simón Ruiz!"

"Ruiz! It's Ruiz! It's Simón Ruiz!" The name was repeated randomly throughout the craning crowd.

Paulo Gonzalves chose this moment of distraction to attempt an escape. The posseman who stood nearest him was Paul McCormick. He saw what was happening too late.

Gonzalves' wrists had not been tied, but manacled. And one of the cuffs was defective. Gonzalves only knew it had not been closed as tightly as the other. Testing it to see if he had space enough to free his hand, the outlaw felt the bracelet loosen yet another notch. After that, he had maintained a careful tension to keep the cuff from slipping. Now, he tore it loose, and with the hand still shackled, he lashed the free end of the manacle across McCormick's face.

Paul staggered back. Diving after him, Gonzalves jerked the pistol from his belt and pushed the apprentice off his feet. Then, Gonzalves hurled himself toward the boardwalk. The people there, including Aunt Aggie and her boys, hastily gave way before him. No one tried to stop him. Few were armed. And those that were did not dare shoot for fear of hitting bystanders by accident.

The Brazilian plunged through the nearest open door: a harness shop's. He sacrificed one bullet to send those that were inside crouching under cover so that he could charge on to the rear of the building and out into the alleyway behind it just as George Durham and Constable Cross dashed into the front of the store, their pistols drawn.

In the street, Uncle Peter helped McCormick rise. Paul's cheek was torn open, and his mouth was full of blood. His head rolled on his shoulders. "Get this boy a doctor!" Uncle Peter shouted.

The rest of the Responsible Committee laid rough hands on the prisoners and bore them stumbling to the wagon. Sam Phoenix rallied his three remaining possemen and followed. Judge Curtis looked about him, trying to decide which quarter most required his assistance. He put himself in Boston's way as Williston pushed forward with other members of the crowd. "Keep back!" he said. "You heard the sheriff. This is not to be another Rancheria!"

But Jimmy Johnson ran past him to join the struggle near the wagon.

By this time, Hinkson, Sydney and Ruiz had forced their way on horseback as far as the vehicle's front wheel. Their animals were frightened by the agitated, closing mass of people all around them. The palomino danced in place and tossed its head against the lines. Baldy's blue roan shied against the wagon. And Sydney's dun backed rapidly into the crowd, colliding with more than one man, and threatening to kick.

Strong hands caught at the horse from both sides to restrain it. Sydney looked down at a swarm of men who seemed bent on forcing the dun to its knees. And then she was swept from the saddle and carried to the wagon by one of the possemen: Daniel Perrin.

"You let go of me," she said.

Perrin paid no attention. "Briggs!" he called. "We're comin' up! Lend us a hand!" He boosted Sydney over the wheel. Rob Briggs leaned down to catch her arm and hoist her higher. Daniel climbed quickly after.

Simón and Baldy had mastered their mounts and passed into the tightening circle of space beneath the Tree. But in the meantime, the Responsible Committee had worried one of the prisoners up into the back of the wagon. They would have hanged him instantly, but Cecil had pulled the noose out of reach, preferring to wait for the sheriff's orders.

"Let down the rope!" someone shouted.

"The rope! God damn it, kid! The rope!"

A gunshot settled the question. The prisoner jerked in the arms of his captors and slumped to the wagon bed, his sudden deadweight bowing them down. Just inside the shade of the Tree stood Jimmy Johnson, a smoking pistol in his hand. He pointed it next at Ruiz.

But the shot had startled Simón's already nervous horse, and the animal reared, delaying Jimmy long enough for Will Sutherland to spring in front of him and knock his aim higher; Johnson's second bullet narrowly missed Cecil Simpson in the Tree overhead. Dark leaves fluttered down. "Hey!" yelled Cecil, flattening against the branch.

"Solano!" cried Baldy, pushing his roan into the palomino and leaning to catch at Ruiz' reins. "You're too easy a shot! You make a clear target! Get off!"

"Where is Saidnay?" demanded Ruiz, looking about him anxiously.

"There in the wagon with two of the posse! She's all right! Get off!"

"Simón!" Sydney shouted as he saw her. She would have leaped down among the coffins in the wagon bed, but Perrin grabbed her from one side and Rob Briggs from the other.

"Steady, Eli," said Briggs. "We want you to stay right here and keep us company."

She turned from his cool, ironic eye to Perrin's ardent look. "You ain't goin' nowhere," Daniel said.

"Let go!" Sydney tugged against their combined grip. "Simón needs me!"

"No, he don't," said Briggs. "All he needs is for you to stay out of harm's way for once."

"Hold still, girl!" warned Perrin. "I'll turn you over my knee and give you that lickin' you been wantin' since you was ten."

"You lay a finger on me, Dan'l Perrin, and Simón will kill you!"

"Let him try it," said Daniel. "I'll marry his widow."

"You'll do what?"

"Even though it'd mean leavin' the pastor's daughter standin' at the door of her daddy's church."

"What are you talking about?"

"Amy Thomson promised me."

"She did?"

"The minute I asked her. But I'd trade her for you even yet." Perrin shifted his grip on Sydney's arm, working his fingers higher. 'Ridin' posse seems to have agreed with you, girl. You're lookin' mighty handsome. Ain't she, Rob?"

"Don't play with fire, Dan'l," Briggs advised.

"Maybe it ain't so much the ridin' as bein' rode has done it for you," mused Perrin. "I hear these Spaniards are regular devils with women."

Sydney stared at him. Then, without warning, she spat in his face. She went on spitting until her mouth was dry. Briggs threw an arm around her as Daniel would have slapped her. "Lay off, Perrin!" he said.

"I wanted to marry her!" Perrin explained, wiping his face savagely with his sleeve. "Her folks even wanted me to!"

"Well, she ain't yours for the askin' anymore. And if you can't keep that thought straight in your head, you'd better leave the takin' care of her to me. You've already got the only single girl in Jackson engaged to you. Ain't that enough?"

"But it's this one that I really wanted!"

"Too bad. She ain't available."

"Somethin' maybe can be done about that," said Perrin. And he jumped down out of the wagon.

"Don't be a damn fool, Dan'l!" Briggs called after him.

CHAPTER FIFTY-EIGHT:

REQUEST AND DENIAL

Will Sutherland had Jimmy Johnson disarmed before Simón dismounted. And Baldy Hinkson made it his business to watch the crowd from horseback to make sure there was no more outside interference.

"Sheriff," said Will, thrusting Johnson's gun through his own belt and turning to Sam Phoenix, "here's that interpreter you wanted. Have you met don Simón Ruiz?"

"No. But I've heard a lot about him," said Phoenix. "Señor, do you recognize these prisoners?" The sheriff had a firm grip on Manuel Escobar to prevent his surprising his captors as Gonzalves had. The remaining prisoner was held by Eichelburger. The Responsible Committee had dumped the dead Mexican into one of the coffins in the wagon. But uncertain of what they ought to do next, they only waited, for the moment, and watched Ruiz suspiciously.

"Yes, I do know who they are," Simón answered Phoenix. "One is the man who likes to think himself as leader of the outlaws. Other man escape me in the Canyon of Mokelumne when I have help to chase them. ¿Quién es usted, desdichado?" Ruiz asked Eichelburger's prisoner.

"I am a true Mexican," the outlaw replied in Spanish. "Not a bastard brother of the gringos who will slay his own kind for the sake of his enemies! My name is Guzmán."

"Octavio Guzmán?"

The man hissed an affirmative.

"And who was that they have killed moments since?"

"One of your countrymen, Don Simón Traicionero. He had the misfortune to be staying in Sonora when the gringos seized the Mexicans there. When they asked him his name, he unwisely confessed it to be Méndez. Not Antonio. Antonio was released because he said his last name was Moreno. And I would not betray him."

"This man they have shot was not an outlaw? He did not ride with your company?"

"I had never seen him before he was taken in Sonora."

"Did you tell the posse this?"

"I speak no English. But if I did, it would not matter. They would not have released him on my word."

Here, Sam Phoenix interrupted. "What's he said, Ruiz? He claims he's innocent, of course? And what else? What name is he calling you by?"

"He does not say he is innocent, Señor. He say this man now dead is innocent. I cannot tell myself if it is true. I do not know all the outlaws, who they are. I wish I have come sooner to help you with the questioning, but I was delay this morning near Mokelumne Hill. But at least, I tell you with certainty that both these other men you hold are thieves and murderers. They are guilty of many crimes."

"He called you 'Try-sun-arrow'. Why? Is that your real name?"

"No, Señor. Is only an insult."

"What's it mean?"

"Traitor," said Ruiz.

The sheriff grunted, then turned to the Committee in the wagon. "Gentlemen? Is there anything you'd like to ask this prisoner?"

"Does he confess to taking part in the massacre at Rancheria?" one of them demanded.

Simón relayed this in Spanish to the prisoner.

"They will kill me no matter how I answer," Guzmán replied. "So let them wonder. I will not confess only to ease their consciences."

"What of your own conscience?" asked Ruiz.

"What I have done, I would do again. I kill gringos as I kill cockroaches. Both are vermin."

"How many gringos have you killed?"

The bandit shrugged. "I have not kept a count. How many cockroaches have you ever killed, Don Traicionero?"

Ruiz turned back to the sheriff. "He does not answer directly, Señor. But he imply that he has murder more than one americano."

"Hang him!" called one of the Committee from the wagon.

"Judge?" Phoenix turned to Curtis. Both the magistrate and Williston had approached during the interval; Boston to defend Jimmy Johnson, Curtis to defend Ruiz.

"Don Simón," urged Curtis, "is there anything to be said in defense of this man, Guzmán?"

"No, Señor. Only that his hate has blind him until it is all he sees. But through such eyes do many gringos also view the world. One may say, therefore, that he is no more guilty than is, for instance, Yeemy Yohnson." Ruiz glanced at the human cockroach that was Boston Williston's partner. "But he is no less guilty, either. So, you may hang him in good faith. If your heart trouble you afterward, will only be because you have let this Yeemy Yohnson live."

At this, Williston started for Ruiz. But Curtis stopped him with an elbow to his chest. The freight driver would have liked to push on by, but he did not quite dare defy the judge so much. "Señor Ruiz," said Curtis, "in order to prevent further loss of innocent life, I beg you limit your role to that of interpreter. Tell the prisoner we are convinced of his guilt and that he shall hang for it."

At these words, the restless crowd on Main Street quieted, again. They plainly heard Ruiz' voice though they did not understand his words: "Octavio Guzmán, le declaran culpable. Que lo van a ahorcar."

The prisoner also spoke in Spanish: "Don Traicionero, may they hang you afterwards. Don Manuel!" he cried to Escobar, struggling violently as Eichelberger pushed him toward the wagon. "Let him die as I do! Make him seem guilty if you can!"

"I will, my friend," responded Manuel, breaking silence for the first time since Ruiz had ridden onto Main Street. And he looked from the anguish of Guzmán into the level eyes of Simón. Nor did he look away again while the possemen wrestled their prisoner into the wagon. Yet both Ruiz and Escobar saw Phoenix beckon down the hangman's noose. They saw one of the Committee put the loop over the outlaw's head and draw it up around his neck behind his right ear.

"Briggs!" called Phoenix. "Drive on!"

Briggs let go of Sydney and picked up the lines. But it was not necessary. Two men from the crowd around the front of the wagon seized the team by the bits while still others slapped the horses' flanks. The wagon jerked ahead. Deprived of his footing, Guzmán fell. But the drop didn't break his neck; he swung out heavily beneath the limb where Cecil Simpson lay looking down, numb with horror at the man's helpless writhing as he gagged and strangled while his executioners debated cutting him down to try again.

"San Simón," said Manuel Escobar under cover of the noise, "I beg of you a boon. Not for my own sake. I know you have long hated me. But for the sake of my father I know you have long respected. For the sake of my sister I know you have come to love. For the sake of the Old Days and the Old Ways I know you still revere . . . Simón! In the name of All That Is Lost . . . I beg you draw your gun and shoot me through the heart."

Ruiz' black eyes flickered. The muscles of his jaw tightened. He said nothing.

Manuel watched him carefully, then tried again: "If you refuse me, Simón, what will you say to Amanda? Will you tell her that you denied me this simple act of mercy? Or will you lie to her and say that there was nothing you could do? That the gringos held you to prevent your trying to aid me in this way? Will you tell her how you stood by and watched me gasp for breath? Look at Guzmán! His face is purple. It will soon be black. But still, he lives. He lives, Simón! They have let him die by inches! The wretch that went before him, the innocent man named Méndez, how lucky was he! The gringo's bullet killed him quickly. He died in a single instant. But Guzmán . . .! He is not dead yet! He is twisting, still. His eyes! Look at his eyes, Simón! If my hands were free, I would take your gun and shoot him, myself, though it spared him only the final moment of his mortal agony."

"What's he saying, Ruiz?" demanded Phoenix, suddenly aware of Manuel's pleading.

"He begs me to shoot him," said Simón, 'so he does not have to hang like the man who has serve him."

Manuel's eyes widened in surprise, then narrowed.

"He thinks I will risk my life to afford him a merciful death," continued Ruiz. "But he is wrong. His death will not be on my hands. And the manner of it will not be on my conscience. Manuel, I abandon you to the mercy of the gringos. Is they who punish you. Not I. Beg **them** to shoot you." And Simón turned his back on Escobar. "Señor Cortés," Ruiz added to Curtis, "do you know what has happen to the brasileño? I have go to some trouble not to kill him so that he can be here alive, today." Simón indicated his wounded arm.

"Don Paulo escape!" Manuel answered in English from behind Ruiz, raising his voice as if Simón were deaf. "But you will not be so fortunate, my friend. Cheriff! I have a confession to make! Call your committee to hear me! Señor Magistrado, listen to what I will tell you of this man call Simón Ruiz!"

"Sheriff," said Curtis, "I suggest you gag the prisoner."

"Why, Judge!" called Daniel Perrin from where he had stationed himself near the base of the Tree to be able to watch and listen more closely to what went on around Ruiz. "Judge, I'm surprised! Are you askin' the sheriff to help supress some sort of evidence?"

Thereafter, the body of Octavio Guzmán might jerk and twitch as it would. The attention of Main Street was riveted on the men who confronted each other inside the pool of shade.

"Mr. Perrin!" responded Curtis, surprised at the unsavory insinuation. "Do you have something to add that bears upon this case?"

"I might," said Daniel, sauntering forward. "But first, I'm curious to hear what Señor Escobar has to say."

A ghastly smile passed over Manuel's face. He knew he had found an ally in vengeance, though he could not even guess at Perrin's motive. "Señor Cheriff!" he said eagerly. "I do not deny I have associate with the outlaws who commit the crimes at Ranchería. But I am guilty only of hiding them in my house in Drytown. I have never steal. I have kill no one. No man can say with truth I do. And if it is not for Simón Ruiz, I would never have help the bandidos. For when they come to me, they tell me he send them and say I must hide them or he will kill my father! I do what he command me. But later, I discover he has sacrifice my father anyway! By that time, is too late. He has trick me to buy his horse so that people think I have steal it. I give it back only to learn that he accuse me of taking six thousand dollar he is robbing from his uncle! And when I protest to him, he threaten me through my sister!"

Ruiz listened to this harangue without deigning to contradict it. Baldy Hinkson answered for him. "That man's a damn lair!" he shouted, riding closer and dropping his hand to the butt of his pistol. "If you let him go on talkin', you'll have to hang him up dead!"

Will Sutherland gestured Baldy to wait. "Sheriff," he said, "no man that knows Simón Ruiz could believe a word of what Escobar is saying. And I know Judge Curtis will back me up. Why, Ruiz saved my life in Mexican Camp! And he volunteered to stay there with Baldy and Sherry to ease the way for them when Sherry was so badly hurt."

"Damn right!" said Baldy, reining his roan around to make Williston back off. "And thanks to him, Sherry was eased out of this world as comfortable as ever a wounded man could be! Both Solano and Miss Sydney did everythin' they could for him. And I ain't about to forget it! So, Dan'l Perrin, if you got anythin' to say against don Juan . . . I mean Simón Ruiz . . . you up and say it here and now! But I'm warnin' you . . . if you can't substancy-ate it, both Will and me are goin' to take it mighty personal!" Nor did Hinkson's hand leave his gun.

Perrin looked from one to the other of his opponents, seeing the wisdom of Briggs' advice too late. But he could not back down in front of all the audience on Main Street. "I got a couple of questions I'd like to hear the answers to, is all," he said.

"Go ahead, Mr. Perrin," conceded Curtis. "You have that right."

Daniel shifted his weight. "Well, while the sheriff was givin' the facts of the case a while ago, I notice he left out a few details."

"Surely some abbreviation was warranted," said the judge.

"Yes, sir. I reckon it was. But he left Ruiz out of his account entirely. And I wondered why, you see. What ever happened to that story about Ruiz abducting Peter Simpson's niece? As I heard it, that was the main reason Sheriff Phoenix left Jackson in the first place! And there was a rumor even then that Ruiz might be one of the outlaws. Afterwards, we heard how the bandits was wantin' him bad . . . as if he'd maybe pulled a fast one and they meant to make him answer for it.

"And now, Escobar has made these other accusations. Can Ruiz prove that he **didn't** mean to steal that money from his uncle? After all, he used it to pay his debts to Albert France, although a man might think it wasn't his to spend. And this bit about the prisoner's father strikes me as somethin' we might want to dig a little farther into, too. Can Ruiz or anybody else produce some proof these things ain't so?"

"I can!" said Baldy. "I first met Ruiz when he was comin' back from the Valley after takin' that very money to his uncle. And he told me then how don Fernando Escobar had been murdered by Americans and how his own uncle had taken a couple of the culprits to Sacramento in search of justice! So diggin' farther into that particular subject ain't apt to leave much room for argument.

"As for the outlaws wantin' him . . . hell yes, of course they did! 'Cause they knew damn well he wouldn't quit till every last one of 'em was either jailed or dead! And you can bet Manuel Escobar knew that best of all.

"One more word!" Hinkson added loudly as the sheriff would have intervened. "About Miss Sydney Simpson! That's Miz Ruiz to you, Dan Perrin! Solano didn't abduct her. He rescued her! And married her! And I ain't never seen no gal happier with her man. Briggs!" he called. "Escort Miss Sydney over here! I'd like to hear what she has to say about all this!"

CHAPTER FIFTY-NINE:

BY A SHORT ROPE

All Main Street watched Briggs vault the back of the driver's box to land among the three empty coffins. All saw him turn back to lift down after him Sydney Simpson de Ruiz Silvestre. And all saw her refuse his assistance. She sprang down lightly alone. Nor did she take his arm to walk the length of the wagon though she must pass the open coffin of the murdered Mexican. She did not look at the Committee responsible who courteously removed their hats and stepped back to let her by. She dropped from the tailgate without so much as glancing at the strangled outlaw hanging now so quietly above the street.

She moved smoothly, with unknowing grace, leaving a straight row of small footprints in the dust across the no-man's-land beneath the Tree. She did not pause nor turn until she had gained Ruiz' side. From there, she looked first at Hinkson. "Thanks, Baldy," she said in a clear voice. Then, she looked at Curtis. "Hello, Judge," she greeted him.

Curtis inclined himself slightly in acknowledgment. "Mrs. Ruiz, you have been asked for your appraisal of what has been said by and concerning the prisoner and these several doubts expressed by Mr. Perrin."

Sydney looked at Escobar. "The prisoner," she said, "is a rotten liar. But I feel sorry for him. Because he knows he's rotten. And underneath, he's ashamed of it. Dan'l Perrin," Sydney went on, "is rotten, too. Only he doesn't know it. So I don't feel sorry for him." She paused, then added, "I feel some sorry for Amy Thomson."

The reaction to this blunt evaluation was mixed. Surprise was universal. There was a smattering of disapproval. But amusement won out. A storm of laughter broke over Daniel Perrin's head. The man himself stood aghast, outraged; but his indignation rapidly degenerated into painful chagrin. And Perrin suffered several moments of excrutiating humiliation before he sought relief in flight.

Surprised herself at the response to her words, Sydney looked to Simón for explanation.

Ruiz lay his free arm about her shoulders. "Payasita," he said softly, "still you are the best shot with the posse."

With little change in its jovial mood, the crowd called out for the immediate execution of Manuel Escobar. Sam Phoenix looked to the judge. Curtis frowned but nodded. And the son of don Fernando was marched to the back of the

wagon amid shouts of brutal derision. Sydney's evaluation of
the man was echoed and embellished. She heard it in con-
sternation, glancing up often at Ruiz. She saw his face was
serious, but the arm he had draped around her shoulders
sustained a light and steady weight.

There was a short struggle to get Manuel into the
wagon. He was cursing a mixture of Spanish and English,
his resentment fueled by fear and shame. The stream of foul
language flowing off his tongue did not cease until, at the
sheriff's command, Cecil Simpson cut the rope which suspended Octavio Guzmán.

The Tree lifted its arching arm a little at its loss. The
rope snapped up at Cecil, striking like a headless snake, falling back to dangle its short length, its loose end frayed and
empty. The body of the outlaw dropped directly to the dirt
and lay as limp and crumpled as an effigy. Manuel regarded
it in awful horror, suddenly struck dumb.

"Simpson!" called the sheriff. "Put a new knot in that
rope!" And Sam Phoenix strode to the base of the Tree and
retied the line at its very end to afford enough slack to use it
again.

Meanwhile, three of the Committee dragged an empty
coffin off the wagon and carried it to the corpse, set it down
in the dust, and lifted the outlaw into it, rope and all. Eichelburger brought the lid. Will Sutherland tossed them a mallet
he found in the wagon. Everyone watched while the lid was
hammered on.

. . . Except for Cecil who, in the top of the Tree, was
fashioning a second hangman's noose. He was hampered by
an annoying feebleness in his fingers and a quaking in his
arms. He was aware of a growing heat and airlessness
around him. He longed for a breeze. The trembling of the
waxy leaves was only an extension of his own unsteady motions.

Before he had finished with his task, there was a new
distraction: From the doorway of the harness shop across the
street came Durham, the Tax Collector, and Drytown's Constable Cross.

The officers were in no hurry, now. Their guns were sheathed. The constable carried a dirty jacket by its collar. The garment had been resplendent once. It was elaborately embroidered with gold braid. All Main Street recognized it. Gonzalves had been wearing it.

The Committee straightened up from closing the coffin of Guzmán. Those in the wagon turned their attention from Escobar, then redoubled their hold on him as he cried out in dismay and struggled anew.

"Dead?" Phoenix asked the constable.

"Dead," agreed Cross. "As soon as we had him cornered, Gonzales shot himself. He's yonder up the creek a ways. When you're finished here, you can drive the wagon over there and pick him up."

"Good. I'm glad. This business has lasted long enough. All right, men!" Phoenix called. "Go ahead and hang him!"

"Can I see that coat?" Sydney asked the constable as the general attention shifted back to Escobar.

Cross turned. Sydney was holding out a hand. The constable looked down at the bedraggled garment he carried and with a shrug, surrendered it. Sydney took the jacket by the shoulders and held it up, turned it from side to side.

It was heavily soiled with dirt. A wide smear of fresh soot blackened the rich braid on one sleeve. Blood stained the collar in several places and had soaked partway down the back. Sydney looked up again at Simón. But Ruiz only glanced at his former jacket before he returned all his thoughts to Escobar.

"Simón . . .!" said Sydney softly.

"¿Amor . . .?"

"Don't look!"

Surprised, Ruiz met Sydney's eyes.

"Did you know Escobar's father from before? I mean, when things were different?"

"Yes."

"And his sister?"

"Also."

"What's her name?"

"Amanda." Ruiz' look dragged back toward the Tree. The hangman's rope had proved too short by more than a foot, and one of the Committee was wrestling another empty coffin from the front of the wagon to the back. There, it was turned upside down, and Escobar was made to mount it. Two of his executioners climbed onto it with him, half supporting him from either side. For Manuel was deathly pale. His legs would scarcely hold him up.

"Simón . . .?" said Syndey. "Do we have to stay here? Can't we go, now?"

Ruiz glanced down at her again. Sydney had draped his jacket over one arm. She reached the other around his waist. "Manuel wasn't always so bad, was he?" she asked.

"No. But I have never estimate him."

"Don't look, Simón."

He frowned in irritation. "Why you would protect me from this sight? Manuel means to me nothing."

"Then you don't need to watch him hang. Let's go."

"We can't go, Saidnay, with so many people in the way. Be patient. Soon is ended . . . all of it. I need to know is ended. Be silent, now."

She said nothing more. But she continued to watch his face. And watching him, she did not need to see Manuel's neck fitted with the noose to know the moment it was done. She did not have to see them push him off the coffin and pull it back out of reach, nor see the Tree arch lower so that Manuel's booted feet were not eight inches from the wagon's boards. Her ears were deafened to the jubilant cheering of the crowd as the last of the outlaws trod the air. The pain, the sorrow, and defeat in the dark eyes of the man she loved were by far more terrible to her than the spectacle of one more prisoner put to death by such a means. And abuptly, Sydney hid her face in Simón's shoulder.

In response, his arm drew tighter round her. She felt his chest and side expand with a long, deep breath. "Bueno, niña. We see if they will let us leave. ¡Señor Cortés!" he added more loudly to the judge who still stood near them. "My service is require longer here?"

"I think indeed, you would do well to withdraw now, Don Simón," said Curtis, moving closer. "Before the mood of the crowd changes for the worse. Mrs. Ruiz? You are not ill?"

Sydney left the sanctuary of Ruiz' shoulder with reluctance. Without having known her own need for relief, she had found some, nonetheless, in that sightless moment close against Simón. "I'm tired," she said. "I want to go home. Anywhere. Away from here."

"Take her into the sheriff's office, first," Curtis told Ruiz. "It will look less as though you were trying to escape. I will have Mr. Hinkson take your horses around back. You can leave from there."

"Gracias, Señor. Hasta la vista."

"Oh!" said Sydney, blinking at the magistrate. "We won't be seeing you for a while now, will we, Judge? But you'll come to the Sutherlands soon? Oh, heck. Judge . . .? I've never even thanked you . . .!"

"It is quite unnecessary, Mrs. Ruiz. My pleasure entirely." And Judge Curtis moved away in the direction of Baldy Hinkson while Ruiz steered Sydney toward the sheriff's office. No one objected. Boston Williston would have, had he noticed them. But he and Jimmy Johnson were still watching avidly the final, futile dance of Manuel Escobar.

CHAPTER SIXTY:

TYING LOOSE ENDS

On that same Thursday, August 16, supper at the Sutherland's was served three times. It was nearly midnight when Ellen put the dishes on the table for the third time. But she did it gladly. For her son Will was one of the three men who arrived hungry from Jackson at that hour.

"Mother . . . these are two of the boys that rode with us on the posse," he explained.

"Oh, I see. You must be Sydney's brother?" Ellen inquired of the tall young man with the long, freckled face and curly red hair who had come in on Will's heels and now stood looking round him uncomfortably.

"Yes, Ma'am. My name's Cecil. Mr. Sutherland said my sister and her uh . . . Did she get here all right?"

"Yes. Several hours ago." Ellen nodded at the closed door of the guest room. "It's been a long and terrible day for all of you, I'm sure. Who is this other man, Will?"

"Oh. Sorry. This is Ike. Lately from the Lazy Q. But he doesn't want to go back there. I told him he could work for us. And Cecil is thinking of signing on, besides."

"Frau Suderland," said the German politey, "forgive for disturbing you."

Ellen smoothed her apron over the skirt of her dressing gown. "Of course. Can I give you men something to eat?"

"If it's not too much trouble," said Will. "I told Dad we would wait for breakfast, but he sent us on inside. He'll be along in a minute. He's looking after the horses."

When Jack Sutherland came in, Baldy Hinkson was with him. The cowboy had been asleep in the bunkhouse when the arrival of the others had awakened him. And the opportunity to rehash the events of the day was too compelling to ignore. Pulling his dusty breeches back on and running his fingers through his mop of hair, Baldy presented himself for supper a second time. Through the meal, he looked at the closed door of the guest room even more often than Cecil.

"So, it's over," Will began by concluding. "It cost Amador County the best sheriff it'll ever have. It cost the Sutherlands a darn good man. It cost Baldy here a close friend. It cost a lot of innocent Mexicans their lives, and still more of them, their homes and property. Justice can be uglier than Crime."

"It's not Justice you're talking about, Will," said Jack.

"Yes, it is."

"See Saw Simpson knows somethin' about Justice, now," Baldy prompted. "Tell us how it felt to ride that damn Tree all afternoon."

"Terrible," said Cecil. "I wish I could have left when you did."

"How much longer were you up there?"

"I don't know. It felt like a week. But . . . maybe an hour."

"That long! What for?"

"They took photographs," said Will.

"Foty-graphs! You mean of Escobar? And all?"

"That's right," said Will. "They got Clancy the Cameraman to bring out his paraphernalia. He set up his tripod and crawled under his black cloth and recorded the moment for history. Boston Williston hung his hat and coat in the Tree and posed with Jimmy Johnson at the foot of it. Then somebody else wanted to do it. They made Cecil pretend to cut the rope three times. The way that crowd behaved, you'd think they were on a picnic. I couldn't believe it. From the moment Miss Sydney put the laugh on Daniel Perrin . . ."

"By God, she nailed him, didn't she?" said Baldy. "The poor cuss lost the argument and his girl and his self-respect in a single blow! Do you know why was she so rough on him, See Saw?"

"Well, Daniel was talking to her in the wagon. Whatever he said made her pretty angry, I guess."

"I guess!" agreed Will. "I saw her spit in his face."

"Spit in it!" exclaimed Baldy. "By damn, I'm sorry I missed that! Anyhow, Dan'l Perrin's posse-in' days are over. He won't dare show his handsome face anywhere around for quite a spell, unless he wants folks to laugh in it, again. See Saw? Do you know anythin' about the girl Miss Sydney called him on? That Emily Thomson?"

"Amy Thomson," Cecil corrected and blushed from collar to hairline. "Yes, I know her. But I don't know where Sydney got the idea Daniel was paying court to her. Paul McCormick told me when he and Rob Briggs and you joined the posse in Mokelumne Hill that **he'd** proposed to Amy, and that she'd accepted **him**."

"Yes," agreed Will Sutherland. "It certainly looked that way in the jailhouse. Cecil and Ike and I went in there after the hanging was finally over. Peter Simpson had taken McCormick inside after Gonzalves laid open the side of his face with the handcuffs, and . . ."

"Hold on!" Hinkson interrupted. "I missed that, too."

Will recounted briefly what had happened and continued: "The whole Simpson family was in the sheriff's office by the time we got in there. Old Doc Shields and the local parson were there besides, and the parson's wife and both his daughters. The older one is married to George Durham. The younger one is this girl, Amy. And the way she was hovering over McCormick, you'd think instead of letting an outlaw get away, he'd just saved the town from dragons."

"Amy's kindhearted," muttered Cecil.

Will threw him an incredulous glance, but seeing the embarrassment in Cecil's face, did not go on to say what he might have.

Baldy said it for him. "Fickle-hearted, more'n likely," the cowboy surmised. "Is she good-lookin'?"

"Yes," said Cecil.

"Very pretty," said Will.

"Ja!" agreed Eichelburger, breaking his courteous silence. "Nice blue eyes!"

"Eyes!" exclaimed Will, much surprised. "I wasn't looking at her eyes!"

"Aw, neither was Ike," teased Baldy.

Jack Sutherland chuckled. "It sounds to me like Dan'l Perrin is well out of it. Little Miss Amy must be fairly hard to keep track of."

"Well, I reckon!" agreed Hinkson. "See Saw, don't look so glum. At the rate that gal is goin', she's as liable to marry you as anybody."

"Don't rib him, Baldy," said Will. "You're not so immune to feminine charms, yourself."

Young Sutherland was never to know how near to Hinkson's heart this shaft struck. "Well, hell," the cowboy said, "Cecil can do better than a parson's daughter, anyway. I got me a sister that would swoon with love at the sight of him. See Saw, afore we go back to work punchin' cows for the boss, you'll have to ride on over to Pokerville with me and meet her. I wouldn't much mind bein' related to you."

"Did you and Sydney and Simón run into any trouble on your way here from Jackson?" Will asked Baldy.

"Not exactly. Only Solano thought he had to circumnavvy-gate the town to check on his friend Bwin Roaster. And I got to admit I was some worried over that old Mexican, myself. But he was all right. And set on stayin' where he was, though Solano offered to bring him along with us. I noticed Miss Sydney and Bwin Roaster's wife was happy to see each other and sad at partin', though neither one of them said much."

"Yes," agreed Cecil. "Mrs. Rooster has been good to my sister. So, Old Ben is the only Mexican left in Jackson? He's brave to stay."

"Oh, he'll be all right. He told Cross and Durham where Gonzales was hidin' so they could smoke him out. The town owes him that."

"What happened?"

"Well," said Baldy, "accordin' to Bwin Roaster, Gonzales come dashin' to his place wavin' a gun and threatenin' to shoot him and his family if he didn't help him hide. And it seems the old man has a good-sized glory hole dug in the hillside behind his house. He put the bandit down it and dragged some brush across it. He told his wife and kids to watch it, then he went limpin' off to get help."

"He took an awful chance," Cecil interposed. "If he had made it into town . . ."

"Well, he didn't have to go so far. Because Cross and Durham were right on the outlaw's tail. And Bwin Roaster led them back to his place. But they couldn't get Gonzales to come out. First, they shot at him, tryin' to make him use up his shells. He wouldn't shoot back. They hollered at him. He wouldn't answer. They thought maybe they had killed him. But they didn't dare count on it. So, Durham dragged the brush back across the hole and set fire to it."

"He would," said Cecil.

"Well, anyway, Gonzales was still alive because to keep them from takin' him, he shot himself in the head. Sorry, Miz Sutherland," Baldy added, seeing Ellen wince.

"Speaking of getting away," said Will, "what happened to you in Moke Hill? Don Simón said something about being delayed there . . .?"

"Yep. The three of us had camped near a cliff in the gorge," said Baldy. "We come close to walkin' right over it in the dark, but we managed to stop short of the brink. It was

late. We'd rode all afternoon and most of the night, 'cause
Solano wanted to catch up to the posse if he could. We'd
buried Sherry that mornin'." Hinkson's eyes clouded.

"We're all sorry, Baldy."

"I know." The cowboy sighed. "Miss Sydney was so
good to him, Boss. She and Solano and I took turns watchin'
over him. But she did it best. I know 'cause I came to spell
her early a couple of times. She sat by him quiet and wiped
his face when the fever was burnin' him, and talked a little to
soothe him, her voice all calm and low. I tell you, if I thought
there was some gal nearby to take care of me that-a-way, I'd
go lookin' for a gunfight tomorrow. Anyhow, Sherry didn't
make it. Nobody really thought he would. A ball in the gut
like that . . ." Baldy stopped and shook his head. No one
interrupted his silence.

"So this mornin'," he went on again, "the three of us
was pretty wore out. Solano was wounded, besides, and he'd
near overdone it with pushin' himself. So we all slept later
than we might have. And that was almost a fatal mistake.

"The night before, you see, we'd met five fellers on the
road from Moke Hill. They was some liquored up, but they
remembered us and wondered. And the next mornin', they
tracked us to the cliff. I don't really think they was anything
worse than curious about us. But when they saw a Mexican
man with a 'Merican gal, they began puttin' ideas together
all inside out and backwards. They was determined to hang
Ruiz and rescue Miss Sydney. Or at least have her for theirselves. And before we knew it, we was fightin' for our lives."

"Did you manage to kill all five?" asked Will.

"Yep. One way or another. We didn't know who they
was nor anythin' about them. But we was sure if they got
away and went back to Moke Hill for reinforcements, it
wouldn't be so funny. One man almost made it. He threw
hisself on his pony and headed for town. But I was disentan-
gled by that time, and I went after him. He was in sight of
the road when I caught up with him."

"What did you do with the bodies?"

"Well . . . the cliff was right there, handy. And so far as I know, there ain't no trail at the bottom of it."

"Don Simón must have had a hard time with his right arm in a sling," mused Will. "You and Miss Sydney must have about split that business between you."

"No . . . Solano did his share," said Baldy.

"Come on, Hinkson!" put in Cecil. "Let's have it. How many men did Sydney shoot?"

"Only one. She hit the other one with her rifle butt, and Solano steered him on over the edge . . . almost went with him. I was too busy to do much about it."

"Was all this before or after breakfast?" Jack asked dryly.

"After. It was the smoke of our fire that gave us away, I think. And then, we had to get down to the river without attractin' more notice. And across it. And to Jackson without ridin' on the road."

"Mein Gott!" said Eichelburger, reminding the group again of his quiet presence. "Not so surprise that delayed you were coming! That you come at all the surprise is!"

"We were some surprised ourselves," admitted Baldy.

Then Jack asked the German to describe his impressions of the Main Event, saying he trusted Ike to recount the facts with less emotion and fewer digressions than any of the other narrators available.

Ike did his best to accommodate his host, but he was given considerable aid at the task. And the talk continued far into the night.

CHAPTER SIXTY-ONE:

FRIENDS AND FAMILY

Sydney woke several times Friday morning before she felt it was actually necessary to get up. She knew it was late. But Simón was still asleep. And she was reluctant to disturb him. He had slept like a stone through the night, having surrendered completely to his relief and exhaustion.

Sydney rose carefully and put her pillow next to him, in case her absence might rouse him. Noiselessly, she dressed herself in the green gingham Ellen Sutherland had again provided, together with the ruffled, white apron. Sydney did not feel completely comfortable in such attire, but it did not occur to her to complain. The clothes she had worn from Mexican Camp must be washed before she could put them on again. And in the meantime, anything else would do.

But she did pause at the mirror to brush her hair before she gathered up the things that needed cleaning and carried them to the door. From there, she looked back at Simón.

He lay on his back, his eyes closed, his breathing quiet. His injured arm lay beside him, wrapped in the fresh bandage she had applied for him the night before. As she looked at him, Sydney wanted to drop the soiled clothing in a heap and return to the bed. But she knew that if she did, she would not be able to keep from touching him. And if she touched him, she might wake him. So, instead, she opened the guest room door and let herself out, closing it softly behind her.

She turned to look around, expecting to see Ellen, at the very least. But Ellen was not there. The big room was pleasant and comfortable as always, but at the moment it was uninhabited. Sydney went to the kitchen. It was also a pleasant place. Good smells of baking lingered in it. Sydney looked around it with a new awareness.

Still holding her armload of clothes, she returned toward the table and looked again at the long, main room that stretched the width of the house. She looked at the windows opening onto the front porch. Red and white checked curtains hung to either side of every one. A colorful rag rug described an inviting oval in front of the leather sofa. On the wall behind the sofa hung a picture. Sydney did not remember any of these things, though they all had been there before.

She carried the clothes across the room and stood on the rag rug to stare at the picture. It was a watercolor, done with a delicate touch. It gave the observer a fairly accurate impression of a ruined garden pump overgrown with honeysuckle. A wooden bucket sat on the ground beside it. Three yellow butterflies were fluttering near it. A fourth had apparently just landed on the bucket's weathered rim. In Sydney's eyes, this modest painting was a glorious masterpiece. She could not imagine any scene more beautiful. The butterflies looked so lifelike, she would have hardly been surprised to see them move. She was lifting an experimental finger to the paper when she heard the back door open.

Hastily, she drew away and returned to the kitchen. Ellen was just coming in from outside, bringing water in a bucket very like the one in the picture. "Good morning, Sydney!" she said.

"Morning," said Sydney. She looked down at the clothes she held. "I want to wash these."

"Don't you want some breakfast, first?"

Sydney shook her head. "Simón's not up, yet. I'll wait for him."

"Your brother is here. He came with Will and another man, last night."

"I know. I heard them." Sydney hesitated. "Where is he?" she asked.

"In the bunkhouse with the others. They're up . . . after a fashion. They've had breakfast, and they're giving themselves the day off. The last I knew, they were still sitting around, drinking coffee. Jack's out on the range. But he should be back for lunch. Why don't you let me wash those few things? Cecil would like a chance to talk to you."

Sydney frowned. "Did he say so?"

"Not in so many words. But I know he would. He thinks you have deserted him."

"What?"

Ellen put down her bucket. "You and he have been close, growing up, haven't you? You must be nearly of an age? How old is Cecil?"

"Eighteen. The same as me. We're twins."

"Oh. Yes. Well, he thinks the world of you, Sydney."

Sydney's frown deepened. She looked down at the clothes in her arms.

"And when you married Simón," said Ellen, "Cecil thought it was because you didn't trust him anymore. Because you didn't love him as you used to."

"That's stupid. Did he say that?"

"No. But I know it's true. And if you were to go now and tell him you wanted to talk about things, I'm sure it would help."

"But Simón will wake up pretty soon."

"That's all right. He'll understand. He's a pretty special man, your don Simón. You're very lucky, Sydney."

Sydney's face softened toward a smile. "I am, aren't I?" she said.

"But your brother's not so fortunate. He hasn't started a new family for himself, yet. You're all he has. And he feels that he's losing you."

"Oh." Sydney's face grew solemn, again. "I see what you mean, Miz Sutherland. I hadn't looked at it like that. I thought last night that he'd come here to try to get me to go back to Jackson with him. To Aunt Aggie and Uncle Peter. But then, I heard Will say that See Saw was going to work for you folks. So, he must have left Jackson Creek for good. I wonder why?"

"Go and ask him," said Ellen, holding out her arms to take the soiled clothes.

Sydney surrendered them reluctantly. "It must have been awful for him to have to be up there in the Tree all that time."

"Go and ask him," said Ellen.

"And then he had to see Amy Thomson making such a fuss over Paul McCormick . . ."

"Don't mention that," advised Ellen.

"If Simón wants me for anything, you'll call me, won't you?"

"I certainly will."

"But if he just asks where I am, tell him I won't be long."

"I'll do that, Sydney."

* * * *

Ruiz woke gradually. His first sensation was one of comfort. He seemed to be lying on a cloud. There was no pain in his right arm, and a large weight seemed to have been lifted from his chest. Then, he moved. And the illusion was instantly replaced by a much less pleasant reality. He groaned aloud and felt for Sydney. His groping hand found nothing but a pillow.

Surprised, he started to sit up. But the twinge in his right arm stopped him. He rallied his will against the discomfort and slowly pushed himself to a sitting position. The wounded muscle felt as if it were sewn through with rusty wire. And the back of his neck ached from the pull of the sling he had worn for three days. Griping pain spread across his shoulders and down his back.

Taking his wounded arm by the wrist, he laid it around his waist and pushed his legs over the edge of the bed, sat looking at the silent room while he waited for new endurance. He wanted to shout for Sydney, but he would not let himself.

Drawing a breath, he leaned after the clean shirt he saw draped across a chair near the bed. Getting his right arm into its sleeve was exquisitely painful. But once he had the garment on and buttoned, he could loop a belt over his head for a sling. And in spite of the increased ache in his neck, this made things easier. For his arm hurt less if he did not let it dangle.

He had struggled into a pair of Will Sutherland's dungarees and was trying to tuck in his shirttail when the door to the guest room opened, and Sydney came in. "Simón!"

"My nurse, she has leave me," he explained.

"Why didn't you yell? Here, let me help. Simón, your

uncle's here."

"¡Qué!"

"He met Mr. Jack on the range this morning. He's just come from a town south of here called Jenny Lind. Lots of the Mexicans that left Rancheria and Jackson and other places went there. And they told him what all you'd done, and so on, but they didn't know for sure where you were. So, your uncle came on toward Drytown to see if he could find somebody that did, and he ran into Mr. Jack. And of course, Mr. Jack brought him here."

Ruiz listened to this in amazement, glancing frequently at the closed door. "Mi tío . . . ¡aquí!" he exclaimed. "He is in this house? Now?"

"Nope. He's still at the corrals. Everybody was talking to him. Except me. I came in to wake you up. There's another man with him: your cousin, I guess."

"Francisco?"

"Yep. Wait, Simón. Your boots . . ." Sydney went quickly to fetch them from the bedside.

Ruiz stood watching her, rubbing his unshaven chin. She came back to set his boots down in front of him, offered him a hand to help steady himself while he stepped into them. Then she knelt and rolled a cuff into the long legs of his borrowed trousers. Simón caught her by the arm as she rose. "Mista Yak has told my uncle about you?" he asked.

"I don't know. Maybe, by now." She sighed and looked down at herself. "I wish I didn't have to meet your relatives this way. I look like Christmas dolly in this get-up. I'd almost rather be a clown."

"Saidnay. You are beautiful. Always."

She ducked her head to hide her quaint smile, but he let go of her arm to catch her chin. "In this dress you are a spring morning," he said. "With white clouds in your sky. And if I have my both arms free, I show you better what I think of this get-up, you call him. Even so, I kiss you. Come close to me."

Sydney received the homage gladly and inspired him to

prolong it by feeling her way around his waist and up his back with both hands. "Well," she sighed, when he lifted back at last, "I guess I don't look any funnier than you do, anyway."

Don Diego Silvestre Cisneros came into the ranch house of the Dry Creek Spread just as his nephew came out of the guest room. And it was apparent that Ruiz' appearance was something of a shock to his uncle. "¡Simón! ¡Por Dios . . .!"

"Tío . . ." Ruiz took a few steps forward and stopped. Behind the Spanish rancher came his son, Francisco, and then Jack Sutherland and Will. Simón collected himself. "Tío," he said again, "I am honor you have look for me. And much please you have find me."

"Pero, ¿estás herido?" Don Diego had come on toward his nephew quickly, lifting a hand as if to take him by the shoulder. But he stopped as Ruiz half turned and drew Sydney up beside him. For she had lingered uncertainly in the guest room doorway.

"Tío, I present your niece: Saidnay. My wife. Amor, I introduce to you don Diego, my uncle. Your uncle. And your cousin, Francisco. As they have been always to me like the father and the brother, so do they greet you as their daughter and sister. Señor," Simón went on as don Diego drew a breath, "I know you have not expect this. You will forgive us to surprise you. Primo," he said to Francisco who stood thunderstruck, "I do assure you that this is the woman who means to me the most in the world."

Don Diego had almost recovered his equilibrium. He again came forward. "Doña Said-nay," he repeated. "Tanto gusto." He glanced at Simón. "¿No habla nada de español?" he demanded incredulously.

"No. Nada," agreed Ruiz.

"Pero . . . ¡m'hijo!"

Simón's expression changed, hardened. He said nothing.

But Sydney had been studying don Diego's face, and she liked what she saw there. It reminded her somewhat of

Buenrostro's. It was more refined and more reserved, but the eyes were kind and the general impression benevolent. She could also trace a certain resemblance to Ruiz. She put out her hand. "Tanto gusto," she repeated.

Don Diego took her hand politely and bowed over it. Sydney's firm grip dissolved instantly at the touch of his white mustache.

Francisco had rallied also, by this time, and he came closer as well, though there was more of curiosity and incredulity still in his look than in his father's. "Primita," he said, "I am eh sharm."

"What? Oh. Likewise." And Sydney gave her hand again . . . a little awkwardly. She didn't like the hint of mockery she saw in his eyes.

Simón didn't, either. "Who protects my aunt and her unfortunate young neighbor while you are absent, Francisco?" he said. "I fear my uncle has not consult the wishes of everyone concern when he ask that you accompany him to search for me."

Francisco's face darkened. "I assure you, primo, that he has."

"Simón," said don Diego, "we have much to say to you. And much to ask. What they tell us in Yenny Leen and other towns has fill us with admiration and pride. But we have fear for your death at the hands of the americanos. And to find you here among them as your friends . . . and married! We are astound! But glad. Relieve! Sobrino, will you wish to go back with us?"

"If you are so kind to invite me," replied Simón. "For I have make a promise to a lady. I owe that lady to tell her in person how I have keep my promise and what has happen to her brother. And why. Yes, I will go back with you, Señor."

CHAPTER SIXTY-TWO:

LA CASA GRANDE

In spite of various advice to the contrary, Simón declared himself prepared to ride for the Valley immediately after lunch. And this new urgency completely changed the tenor of the day.

There was no packing to do. Syndey and Simón had only the clothes they had worn from Mexican Camp. Ellen had washed them, and hanging in the midday sun, they were soon dry and could be put back on. Meanwhile, Ruiz asked his cousin to shave him, since he was unable to manage it alone, left-handed. Sydney watched the operation jealously but from a distance. She did not presume to interfere.

She couldn't turn around herself without running into either Cecil or Baldy Hinkson. And she kept finding things she had to say to Ellen Sutherland, though when she said them, they sounded unimportant or unclear. She never did manage to tell her hostess how beautiful the picture was that hung above the sofa, though every time she passed it, she would pause to look at it, again. And then, suddenly, they were saying goodbye.

484

"Here, Sydney." Ellen put a cloth-wrapped parcel in her hands. "This is something you will want to take with you. It's your wedding dress."

Sydney received the padded square and hugged it to her, gazing at Ellen with such wistfulness that the rancher's wife could not keep from hugging **her**. "Goodbye, Sydney. And come back. Won't you?"

"I want to," Sydney agreed.

"Bring the baby," whispered Ellen, kissing Sydney's cheek.

"What baby?"

"Yours. Unless you can come back before you have one. Whenever you can . . . We'll always be thinking of you and hoping to see you."

"Thanks, Miz Sutherland. For everything."

"You're welcome. Take care of Simón. He truly needs you, now. Even more than he knows."

Sydney met her brother on the porch. He had gone to saddle a horse for her. Not the dun. Simón had traded it and the palomino to Jack Sutherland for fresh mounts. The rancher had much admired both horses and offered to pay extra for them, though they were tired and would need rest before they could be put to use.

"Syd . . ." said Cecil. And stopped. Sydney handed her wedding dress to Baldy Hinkson so she could throw both arms around her brother.

" 'Bye, See Saw," she said. "I'll be back."

"Well, you'd better be!" said Cecil, hugging her awkwardly at first, then tightly.

She looked up his chest at him. "Good luck with Baldy's sister."

Cecil blushed. "You mind your manners in the Valley, Syd. That's high society you're going to."

"Don't **you** forget about the clock you promised to buy Aunt Aggie."

"I won't. I might even take it to her in person."

"If I get back in time, I might go with you," Sydney said.

"Good. I'll wait for you, then." He gave her a parting squeeze and turned to Simón who had come to say his own goodbyes to his brother-in-law and the German Eichelburger and the Sutherlands. Don Diego and Francisco were close behind him. Sydney turned away and started down the porch steps.

The cowboy Hinkson moved hastily after her. "Hey, Eli! Ain't you forgettin' somethin'?" He proffered the cloth-wrapped package.

Sydney stopped halfway down the steps. "Oh. Thanks, Baldy." She reached for the parcel.

But he did not give it to her until he stood on the stair below her, so that their eyes were nearly on a level. And as he let her take the dress, he leaned in to touch a light kiss to her lips. Startled, she drew back to stare at him.

"I won't never forget you, Sydney," he confided, his eyes anxious.

"Well, I didn't expect that you would!" she returned. And she gave him her quaint and piquant smile.

Baldy was still standing at the bottom of the steps alone when the rest of the company came down off the porch. He felt Ruiz' friendly grip on his shoulder. "Adiós, Baldés," Hinkson heard him say. "Nos veremos."

"I reckon so," he muttered. "Meantime, take care of her, Solano."

Together, the two of them watched Sydney swing smoothly into her saddle and adjust the tilt of her Spanish hat to better shade her face. "Damned lucky . . ." muttered Hinkson, more to himself than to Ruiz.

"I know it, amigo," Simón assured him. "But there is something more than luck to it. And any man who tries to take her from me will find out what I mean. ¿Sabes?"

This brought the cowboy's blue eyes back round to Simón's black ones. "Sure," he said. "I savvy. Adiós, Don Juan." Baldy pressed Simón's good arm in return before Ruiz strode on to his horse which stood beside Sydney's. His uncle and cousin followed him.

Jack Sutherland went, too. As a courtesy, the rancher

intended to ride with them for a ways. "I'll be back in time for supper!" he called to Ellen.

"I'll keep it hot!" she answered.

Amid a chorus of friendly farewells, the riders turned away in the sunshine, leaving behind in the shade of the porch still braver hearts who must watch them go.

*　*　*　*

Through the long afternoon, Sydney rode contentedly beside Simón while the foothills rolled lower and lower around her. That she was traveling toward the unfamiliar did not bother her. It was something she had done since she had left Indiana. She enjoyed watching the country change and took pleasure in the steady, shifting movements of her horse; the languid circling of the buzzards in the cloudless sky; the round, dark heads of the scattered oaks; and the hot breath of the summer wind across the sun-cured grass.

Their company traveled silently, for the most part. Now and then, don Diego said something to Simón, usually in Spanish, but often in English, since Ruiz now refused to speak anything else, himself, in deference to Sydney. Not that she would have minded. As long as he did not expect her to understand what was said without explanation, she had no objection to his occasionally excluding her from the conversation.

"The padre of San Gabriel seem much worry for you, hijo," don Diego ventured.

"He is at Yenny Leen?"

"Sí. With most of his people from Yackson. He say they have save their lives because of you."

"He is generous."

"But he fear you have make the big mistake."

"What mistake?"

"He does not say."

"He is kind," said Simón. "Tell me, when you are in Yenny Leen do you notice a young girl with the lip split? She would be with her grandmother: an old woman, half blind, a long nose."

"Sí. The old woman you say, I talk with her."

"And she is taken care of? She and her granddaughter do not go hungry? They have a place to sleep? People are good to them?"

"She does not complain."

"No. But what do your own eyes tell you?"

"That she is poor. She has great sorrow. But she is not afraid. She seems content."

"Content? Or resign?"

"No, m'hijo. I think she is happy enough. She speaks to me of you with much gratitude and many prayers for your safety and success. But if you wish, more can be done for her. I am sending cattle and grain to that town as soon as possible. I make sure then she is well cared for. What more you would have me do?"

"Nothing more, Señor. But if she ask for something in the name of her granddaughter, I hope it may be given."

"Then, it will be."

"Are there any others who escape from Yackson who speak to you as if they know me?" asked Simón.

"No. Though all have learn the name 'Ruiz'. I hear it everywhere."

"**She** is not there, then, certainly."

"She? Another desafortunada?"

"A young widow. Her name is Magdalena Obregón." Ruiz glanced at his uncle.

But don Diego's calm expression did not change. "No, I do not hear that name."

Ruiz drew a quiet breath of relief. "This must be the reason the old woman is content," he said. "And may heaven better guide la Magdalena, wherever she may be. I am glad I do not know. And yet, her sorrow is as real as that of the old grandmother. And I did nothing to relieve it. Enough! Tell me of your luck in Sacramento. What has happen to the gringos that you took there?"

"They pay a multa to the government. They are in the

cárcel thirty days. Is more than I expect."

"And when they are let out? What is to keep them from seeking revenge against you?"

"My vaqueros carry arms. I have cause an iron gate to be put across the entrance of the house. I will have a wall construct around it. What more I can do?"

"Nothing, Uncle. Nothing."

The landscape flattened further as they moved on steadily westward until the Valley sprawled its vastness wide before them. The sun rode lower, first glaring a fierce gold, but bronzing as it sank, then reddening. The day's heat lost its strength; the evening wind fanned lazily first one direction, then another.

Sydney now looked often at Simón. She saw that he was tiring. Pain wrote harshly on his face. But when he met her eyes, he smiled reassuringly before he turned his gaze back to the sun's vermilion ball swimming in the haze of the horizon. "Is not too far from here," he told her twice even though she had not asked.

Then, from the lip of a gradual rise they had scarcely felt their horses climbing, a long, wide swale sank unexpectedly before them. Ruiz exclaimed, pointing at the house and stables, the barracks and corrals of the Rancho Silvestre, clustered loosely in the bottom of the land's gentle troughing. "¡Ahí, Saidnay! There it is!"

"Golly!" she responded. Even from a distance, the grand dimensions of the house, the number of corrals, the majestic willows, were impressive. To say nothing of the garden-patio whose palms and flowering trees were visible within the mansion's walls, and the deep green of the fruit grove filling the swale to the south.

Francisco, who had ridden most of the afternoon without opening his mouth, hallooed to several riders who were gathered near the corrals. They looked up, waved, and shouted back. Three jerked their mounts around and spurred to meet the new arrivals. A fourth decided he would come, as well. And then, a fifth.

"These that you see are more of your cousins, Amor," Simón explained to Sydney.

At this, Francisco could keep back no longer. He kicked his horse to a gallop and plunged downslope to intercept his brothers even though his father called out to him to wait.

"¡Impetuoso!" complained don Diego. "He will tell them everything he knows. You will bring no news, Simón."

"I have no especial wish to surprise your household, Uncle. Francisco does me a service. Déjelo."

That don Diego's other sons were surprised by what Francisco told them was apparent. Their horses crowded close to his; they looked back at Ruiz and Sydney, pointed and gesticulated. Their voices, questioning, exclaiming, floated up the slope. Two of them turned with him as Francisco pushed on through and galloped toward the house. The other three sat where they were a moment, making up their minds. Then, they came on to meet their father, their cousin, and his bride.

CHAPTER SIXTY-THREE:

AMANDA

"¡Mi madre! ¿Dónde está mi madre?" Francisco ran into the house and stopped abruptly, causing one of his two younger brothers to collide with him from the rear. "Watch where you are going, Teodoro," he admonished. "Mother!" he greeted doña Graciela as she appeared with Cristina in one of the doorways opening on the lower gallery and garden. "Simón is here! With my father! Back from the hills!"

"I am glad," his mother said. "But what is wrong, Francisco? No one is hurt? Are you all right?"

"Yes. No! Mother, Simón is married! He has brought along his bride! She is American!"

Francisco had scarcely time to see his mother's astonishment when he heard a breathless cry from the staircase. He whirled as Amanda Escobar caught herself against the railing.

"Oh, Francisco!" exclaimed doña Graciela in dismay. But the damage was already done. Amanda turned back up the stairs. Yet Francisco followed, for though her cry had lanced him through, his hope rode higher now than it had since spring, and he sprang up the steps with an alacrity inspired more by ardor than by sympathy.

She fled before him, hoisting her black, silken skirts, half stumbling in her haste. He caught her easily before she gained the top. "Amanda! Amanda, forgive me! I did not know you would hear."

She clutched the banister rail again and tried to ward him back. "Please don't speak to me!" she said.

Francisco seized her hand to his heart and watched her face, no less lovely in her agitation than a flower in the wind. "Amanda! I would murder my cousin for his inconstancy, did I think it would appease you. But how shall I pretend I am not glad he's proven false?"

"False! Simón . . . false? No. Never! How can you say it? He has made me no promise of constancy. Nor asked me for mine. It is only my own vanity which has taught me to rely on his regard. I thought he loved me! Shameful error! Why should he love me? Only because I wished it? Because I thought I could not live unless he did? How foolish! How immodest! How childishly I've acted! Please. Let me go. Let me compose myself before I see him. I cannot bear for him to know how much I feel. Be merciful, Francisco! Let me go! I will be grateful to you. Please!"

And Francisco, his heart as full as hers, could do nothing but comply. He stood and watched her mount the stairs, hurry down the hallway to her room, the black silk of her mourning rustling around her. And she had yet to hear the news about her brother.

Francisco leaned against the rail, struggling with the conflict of his own emotions. He bled to see her weep. But he was deeply, savagely triumphant that Ruiz should be the cause.

"Francisco. Hijo." His mother's voice recalled him. He glanced down. Doña Graciela had come to the foot of the staircase. "Do you know what has happened?" Voicelessly, she added, " . . . To Manuel?"

Francisco nodded curtly, drew his finger across his throat in illustration.

His mother closed her eyes a moment, breathing in. But she opened them again to ask silently, " . . . Simón?"

"No." Francisco spoke aloud. More calmly, he came back down the stairs. "The Americans," he said.

"They caught him, then?" she asked.

"You knew about this!"

"Simón told me. Before he returned to the Gold Country."

"Why did you not tell us!" Francisco wondered.

"I told your father."

"Truly? But he . . ." The sound of footsteps and mingled voices from the entrance interrupted him. Before he could say more, Simón himself came in.

Doña Graciela turned. And from the moment that she met her nephew's eyes, she knew that all her questions would be answered reasonably and well. Relieved, she went to greet him, repressing the desire to exclaim over the sling that carried his right arm, and putting on a face of welcome to receive the strange girl at his side. "¡Simón! Bien venido, m'hijo. Nos han informado de todo."

"Tía," Ruiz said, leaning to kiss her cheek, "this is Saidnay. She knows three words in Spanish. Maybe four. But the mind and heart of Simón Ruiz she knows better than I know myself. And I am proud that I present her to you as my wife. Amorcito," he added to his bride, "this is your aunt. You call her 'Tía', if you like."

"Tía," said Sydney, looking at doña Graciela. "Tanto gusto," she added and held out a trusting hand.

Already so surprised by the girl's mere appearance that she could scarcely feel any more, doña Graciela took that small, strong, callused hand into her own small, soft one, hoping her astonishment would not offend. "Said . . dee . . nay," she repeated. "So good to meet. We were not expecting . . . . but you are very welcome."

"It's good to get here," Sydney said. "Simón's tired. His arm's hurting him."

By this time, the rest of the Familia Silvestre had come in. The entire party moved into the garden. The afterglow of the sunset blushed on the slender trunks of the several palms whose airy heads stirred drowsily above the tiles on the roof. From the great, blossoming beard of bougainvillaea which draped the stairwell to the upper gallery, a tree toad sang.

Sydney gazed in open awe. "Golly!" she whispered.

"What is the matter, Saidnay?" Simón asked, stooping to receive her answer confidentially.

"Have you always lived in places like this?"

"You admire it?"

"I can't believe it! It's like a palace or something."

"They are only bricks and flowers."

"Well, they're a lot more bricks and flowers than I ever saw together before."

"Is a beautiful house," he conceded.

Doña Graciela was expressing concern that Sydney must be right about her nephew's needing rest and recommended they retire immediately after supper which would soon be served. She and Cristina had been overseeing its preparation when they arrived.

"Will Amanda join us?" Simón inquired coolly.

Francisco started but said nothing.

"I am not certain," said doña Graciela. "Cristina, hija, go and ask."

"I will go, myself," announced Simón. "Cristina will prefer to get acquaint with her new cousin. Saidnay, you excuse me for a moment? Primita," he added to Cristina, "¿me la cuidas mientras tanto?"

"Pero, Simón . . . ¡no hablo nada de inglés!"

"Aprende," suggested Ruiz. "Saidnay, if you can teach your little cousin four words in English before I return, I am made happy."

"Only four?" asked Sydney.

"Five, then. Well learned. So she know them at supper."
And Ruiz turned away toward the stairs.

Francisco would have followed instantly, but don Diego
caught him by the elbow and asked him to describe for his
brothers the situation as he'd found it in the town of Jenny
Lind. Francisco complied with a poor grace, but he complied.

Simón scaled the staircase lightly, almost eagerly. He
wished to have the business of Amanda finally ended and
behind him, though his dread of it had grown until it
weighed on him as heavily as his wounded arm.

He rehearsed the several things he meant to say and
braced himself against the impact of their meeting. For while
he was certain that his love for Sydney was unalterable, still
the image of Amanda in the peach grove had not completely
dissipated from his mind. And he wished to test himself.

The door of the upstairs parlor was half open. No candle had been lit within. From behind the mask of growing
darkness Amanda might have witnessed his arrival without
being seen herself. Certain that she had, he pushed the door
wider, knocking a brief warning as he entered.

The room was empty. Shadows lay heavy in its corners
and greyed its furniture. But the door opening opposite onto
the outer balcony also stood ajar. Ruiz strode across to it and
knocked again upon this second door before he pulled it
wide.

He saw Amanda instantly. She stood looking down on
the corrals, watching the horses feeding there. Her hands
rested lightly on the railing. "Amanda . . . ." said Simón.

She turned, apparently as resolute as he, her face a perfect cameo of calmness, delicately revealed by the last light of
the day. But as he saw her, Ruiz was reminded rudely not of
spring and flowers but of Manuel's last appeal. He had never
thought to trace Amanda's resemblance to her brother. That
they were related had been bad enough; there had been no
need to look for proof. But proof looked back at him unasked from her dark eyes. And both Manuel's smooth supplication and his frantic, final lies resounded in Ruiz' ears.

"Don Simón," Amanda said. (Her voice was also like Manuel's. Only lighter, softer, feminine.) "I am grieved to see you're hurt. Is your arm broken?"

Ruiz let out a breath of pure surprise. He found he felt no love, no longing, no desire for her at all. He felt pity. But it was a cool emotion, not one from which new warmth might grow. He came forward, letting his eyes pass over her, expecting still to feel the heat her presence caused him formerly. Instead, he felt critical of her person. She looked too soft. Six hours on horseback in the sun would surely kill her. And her movements were too languid. They were graceful, but they lacked the certainty and suppleness he had come to admire.

Still, he must admit, Amanda wore black well. The rich cream of her complexion, tinged with peach; the lustrous darkness of her eyes, so thickly lashed; the ripe redness of her mouth, so sweetly shaped; the smooth ebony of her hair, wound back into a heavy knot . . . none suffered from the sable foil of mourning. And yet, Ruiz discovered that her face lacked character. And interest. There was not a blemish, not a freckle on it. And it was freckles that his eyes had learned to want! Vastly relieved, amused at his own reaction, Simón relaxed.

Not so, Amanda. She could not even meet his look for the length of time it took him to answer her concern: "My arm is not broken," he said. "But its wound is bothersome. And I will be glad to have back the use of my hand when it heals. Amanda, I have sought you boldly in this way with the excuse of requesting your presence at supper. But what I have actually come to tell you may preclude it. And I beg you to pardon me for giving you no warning."

"Are you talking of . . . your marriage?" she asked bravely, returning her gaze to the corrals.

"No. Truly, I wish it were no more than that. Amanda, I have been cowardly and selfish. What I must now relate to you would be much easier for me to say if I had told you earlier what was known to everyone acquainted with your brother and his dealings."

"Manuel?" Her hands tightened on the railing.

"Yes. And I fear all this may be incomprehensible to you. I hope you have the strength to hear it."

"Strength? Your news is tragic, then." She voiced the words without emotion. "Manuel is dead."

"Yes," agreed Simón.

"Yes! Yes? He is dead? Manuel is dead?" she cried in horror.

"He has been executed."

"Executed!"

"By the Americans."

Amanda held to the balcony rail to keep from falling. But she lifted a hand to check Simón as he stepped closer. "Why?" she demanded. "Tell me why!"

"He had become an outlaw. He harbored thieves and murderers. He used his birthright of respectability to shield them. But eventually, they were found out. And they betrayed him. The Americans took him. They hanged him in Jackson."

"Hanged him! And you . . .?" Amanda whispered, clinging to the rail with all her strength. "What did you do?"

"Nothing."

"Nothing! You did nothing!"

"No. Amanda, when I left you here, I knew what your brother had become. But I could not force myself to tell you."

"You wished to spare me?"

"Yes, of course. But I wished still more to spare myself. I knew that if you heard the truth, you must disavow Manuel . . . or me. Yet I saw it as my duty to seek him out and kill him. And I knew that if he died by my hand, you could never learn to love me."

"Learn . . . to love you!" gasped Amanda.

"Or that if you had already, you would hate me more because of it."

"Hate you! Oh, Simón!"

"But it was not my fate to kill him, after all. Although I swear to you if I had not been wounded, I would have tried to reach him still before it was too late. And not to save his life."

"Yes," she said. "I understand. Oh, yes! How well I understand! You knew his guilt! You knew that they would hang him. You wished to spare him that disgrace. Noble. Always noble, Simón Ruiz! No, no! I do not mock you!" she professed, eyes brimming with her earnestness. "And you were much too noble to guess how much I loved you. You would not have believed it, had I told you. And so, you married a stranger, a girl that you could not love, in order to be free to kill Manuel. Because you thought I'd hate you if you killed him! Because you couldn't kill him while I loved you! But Simón . . .! Oh, why should I say it? It is so useless, now. Yet I cannot help myself. Simón, I would not have loved you any less."

He stirred in surprise at this. "Amanda!"

"Manuel was my brother. Do you think I did not know him, all his weaknessnes? His pride? His anger and resentment toward the gringos? Your terrible news does not surprise me. I have long feared . . . expected it!" She brushed away the tears that spilled onto her cheeks. "Your noble sacrifice, Simón, was all for nothing."

"But Amanda! If I had killed Manuel, you could not have married me!"

"You did not kill him," she replied and turned away.

"But I would have!"

Amanda looked again at the corrals, swallowing her tears, trying to contain her sighs. "And are you happy with her, Don Simón?"

"With Saidnay? Yes."

"**What** is her name?"

"Saidnay. Seensome. De Ruiz Silvestre."

At the addition of his surname to his bride's, Amanda winced as if a pin had pricked her. "And do you love her?" she demanded. "In so short a time as this, have you learned to love a stranger? A gringa? Perhaps you knew her from before?"

"No. I first met her on the road near Ranchería."

"You met her on the road!"

"Under memorable circumstances. She saved my life."

"Indeed! And is she beautiful?"

"Infinitely."

"Oh!" She whirled on him, her face sweeping with new color. "I no longer wonder, then, how you have managed to forget all that we shared last spring! It seems that it remains for me only to dismiss your ardent attentions then as merely a pleasant pastime! And to dismiss my former feelings as unworthy of my father's name! Perhaps I would do well to listen to Francisco!"

Simón said nothing. But Amanda plainly saw that she could not touch his heart either through regret or jealousy. She turned back to the balcony.

"Amanda . . ." he said softly. "I do not wish to leave you here alone. Let me call my aunt, Cristina, or a servant. Or Francisco, if you will take some pity on him. My cousin loved you long before I came between you. He will love you after you have long forgotten me."

"Simón Ruiz," she answered, "do you so little know me? Do you think so meanly of me? Forget you! Shall I forget Manuel? My father? My former happiness? My dearest dreams? ¡Adiós, Señor! May heaven bless you. Seek the infinite charms of your American bride and leave me to my solitude!" And pushing away from the rail, Amanda ran to the next door which opened on the gallery and her own room.

But she paused before she entered it. To look back at him. To see him standing on the balcony, the pearly light of evening deepening to dusk behind him. "¡Adiós, Simón!" she said again. And left him.

CHAPTER SIXTY-FOUR:

REVELATION

"This is a tree," said Sydney, patting the bole of the nearest palmera and looking expectantly at Cristina.

"¿Cómo?"

"A tree," Sydney repeated.

"Eh teh-ree," essayed Cristina and burst into a musical laugh. It was contagious. Sydney smiled and nodded. Cristina plucked at a flowering shrub. "Y esto, ¿qué es?"

"That's a rose bush."

"Eh rossy butch! ¡Ay, qué difícil decirlo! ¿Y esto?" she

demanded, bending to sweep her touch across a garden seat.

"Bench," said Sydney.

"Pinch . . .?"

"Yep."

"Eee-yap?"

"Sí . . . Yes!" Sydney considered Cristina's pretty face, her dancing eyes, the dimple that appeared and disappeared in her left cheek. And she thought of Cecil and wondered what Baldy Hinkson's sister was like.

As the company in the garden talked, lamps were lit in the dining room and open corridor, for darkness had gently invaded both house and garden. The upper story stayed lighter longer. Sydney was looking up at the gallery in search of another useful noun to teach Cristina when she saw Simón come quickly from the half-open doorway he had entered earlier. "¡Tía!" he called to his aunt. The urgency of his voice commanded instant attention from every quarter.

Doña Graciela ran for the staircase. But Francisco reached it first. Simón came down a few steps to block his way as he bounded up. "No, Francisco," he advised. "No todavía."

Simón's cousin stopped before him, bristling, every inch of him a challenge. But Ruiz only stood in his way until doña Graciela hurried past them. Then leaving his cousin to do as he chose, Simón descended slowly.

Sydney went to meet him. "What's going on?" she asked, coupling herself to his side with an arm about his waist. "Is somebody sick?"

"Somebody is sad," he replied, laying his embrace lightly round her shoulders. "The sister of Manuel."

"Oh. You told her? I guess she won't be down to supper, then, will she?"

But at an exclamation from Francisco, they turned to see that doña Graciela had not even gained her guest's room before Amanda herself came out of it. Perfectly composed, her bearing gentle, the sister of Manuel Escobar moved along the railing to the stairs. Francisco mounted swiftly to the top to offer his assistance. She thanked him with a inclination of her head, yet she declined his aid. His mother claimed Francisco's arm, instead, obliging him to lag behind.

Amanda came on down the stairs alone, wearing her pride and pathos as beautifully as she wore her silks of mourning. When she allowed herself to notice that Simón stood at the bottom, and with whom, she almost missed a step but caught herself and continued to descend as serenely as before.

Sydney felt the muscles in Simón's arm hardening. But otherwise, he gave no sign he was affected by Amanda's little drama. He greeted her in Spanish: "We are honored by your presence, Señorita."

Another inclination of her head acknowledged this. She did not look again at either of them until she had come quite close. Then, she stopped and put a hand out to the banister. "Introduce her to me, Don Simón," she said.

"With pleasure. Amanda, this is the woman I most cherish, and most honor, most adore: my wife, Saidnay."

Amanda stared at Sydney; at her freckled face with its snub nose and small, unsmiling mouth; at her short, curly, wind-blown hair; her plain, neat clothes; her narrow waist; her arm around Simón. And then, not uttering another sound, Amanda fainted dead away.

Sydney and Simón both jumped to catch her. But Ruiz could do little with his right arm in a sling and Sydney in his way. Amanda had fallen slightly forward as she crumpled, and Sydney kept her from tumbling on, supporting her until Francisco arrived, his brow thunderous, to sweep Amanda into his arms and glare accusingly first at Sydney, then Simón.

"Cousin," said Sydney evenly, breaking the tense silence, "you'd better take her back to her room. I don't think she's going to be having any supper."

Francisco's indignant look passed over Sydney once again. He turned and bore Amanda up the stairs. Doña Graciela joined him as he passed her. Cristina hurried after them.

Supper was to be delayed another half an hour and

more while Amanda absorbed all the attention of the household. Simón led Sydney to a circular bench in the center of the darkened garden and sat down there, settled her beside him.

"Payasita," he said quietly, "I ask that you forgive my family. Such an alboroto! You think they never see an American before. And yet, two years ago this very month, they are rejoicing at the wedding of Joaquín Murieta who is marry in this house. And his wife is a gringa."

"Walking Murray Etta? That same man you told about before? The one the gringos thought they'd killed?"

"Sí. El mismo."

"He married an American?"

"If you like, I take you to meet them. They stay sometime in Santa Bárbara, sometime in San Luis Obispo. Sometime, in the house of my father. You want to meet my father, Saidnay? And my mother? My brothers and my sisters?"

"Sure. Simón . . .? Will Amanda be all right? I never saw anybody just keel over like that. Like she was shot. Was it because you'd told her about Manuel?"

"Seguro."

"I feel pretty sorry for her. Don't you?"

"Yes. But she has many friends to be concern for her."

"Like Francisco? He's really gone on her, isn't he?"

"Gone. Ido, perdido," agreed Ruiz.

Sydney sighed and cuddled against him. "I can see why," she said. "Amanda's like this house: so beautiful you can't believe your eyes. Why doesn't she love him back?"

"Perhaps she learn to, someday."

"He's not like Dan'l Perrin, is he? Dan'l wasn't completely rotten, you know. He did good things for folks, sometimes. But I couldn't stand him. Just being near him gave me the shudders. He was always trying to touch me. And I didn't want him to. And then, Aunt Aggie was so keen to have me marry him. Maybe if Francisco would lay off for a while, Amanda would like him better."

"May be."

"Why don't you tell him?"

"This is not advice that he would take from me, Muñeca."

"Oh." She was quiet a moment. "How's your arm feeling, now?"

"It wish to be well. Is tire of hanging from my neck. Saidnay, I confess to you I am annoy. Resent. This garden should be full of lights and people. Music and dancing. To celebrate that we are marry. To congratulate. Fandango. All night long. Instead, we sit here in the darkness, wait to eat a supper with my uncle family as if nothing, he has happen. My aunt says you are welcome. But is Amanda she takes care of."

"Well, Amanda is the one that needs it. I don't mind. I'd rather be with you like this. Except I wish your arm was well. Want me to rub it again tonight? It helped last night at the Sutherlands', didn't it? Want me to rub it right now? You can get some rest from that sling, anyway. Here." Sydney squirmed out of his half embrace and rose to her knees on the bench so that she could reach around his neck and untie the knot in the strip of cloth.

But as his arm slipped from its cramped position, his fingers caught in her belt. And though pain shot through his wounded muscle, he held to her waist while with his good arm, he drew her close against him and buried his face in her breast. "Infinitamente bella," he sighed. "My little clow."

Sydney closed her arms about his head, cradling him to her. "Are we going to have our own place somewhere, Simón?" she asked. "Now that the outlaws are out of the way, and Manuel is dead and so on . . . Had you thought about it, yet?"

"Mmmmm," he demurred, nuzzling her. Through the cloth of her shirt, she could feel the soft prickle of his mustache. The warmth of his breath. The changing shape of his mouth as it moved from kiss to kiss.

"Some place for just the two of us," she said, "like Mr. Jack and Ellen have. Some place where we can stay. And live.

And work together."

"Por dios. My gringa wife, she wants to work."

"It won't seem like work," Sydney assured him, "if I'm with you." She felt at her waist for his hand. A tremor in it told her it was about to lose its hold. She unhooked it gently, lowered it carefully as she sat back down beside him without leaving the circle of his other arm. But when she laid his right hand in her lap, its fingers molded themselves to the shape of her thigh. "Simón . . .!" she admonished him in a whisper. "We still have to eat supper!"

"I eat you, instead," he proposed. Cautious with pain, his fingers moved higher.

"But you can't do . . . **that** . . . with your arm like this, can you? Won't it hurt you?"

"It hurt me not to. Six day, five nights I am deny since you give yourself to me in the hotel of Fourth Crossing. You think I have forget that? Saidnay, I am gone for you. Each time I look at you, I want you. I hold you close, I lose myself. I wish my arm is heal; I show you better what I mean."

"You're getting the idea across all right as it is," she said, her eyes closing of their own accord as the silky fringe of his mustache wiggled its way across her cheek. And surrendering all propriety to the moment, she cast both arms about his neck and met his kiss with frank desire.

The tree toad in the bougainvillaea rasped out his little song. The palmeras stirred and sighed.

For the two that sat beneath them, lost completely in each other, a new future opened wide . . . wider than the Valley, higher than the Hills . . . and beckoned irresistibly. What Had Been made no difference, now. What mattered was: What Was To Come. And eagerly, they welcomed it, together.

The End